A HINT OF SCANDAL

The Mismatched Lovers
Book Two

Fil Reid

Dearest Reader;

Thank you for your support of a small press. At Dragonblade Publishing, we strive to bring you the highest quality Historical Romance from some of the best authors in the business. Without your support, there is no 'us', so we sincerely hope you adore these stories and find some new favorite authors along the way.

Happy Reading!

CEO, Dragonblade Publishing

Additional Dragonblade books by Author Fil Reid

The Mismatched Lovers Series
A Sham Engagement (Book 1)
A Hint of Scandal (Book 2)

The Cornish Ladies Series
The Cornish Mermaid (Book 1)
The Cornish Bride (Book 2)
The Cornish Inheritance (Book 3)
The Cornish Widow (Book 4)

Guinevere Series
The Dragon Ring (Book 1)
The Bear's Heart (Book 2)
The Sword (Book 3)
Warrior Queen (Book 4)
The Quest for Excalibur (Book 5)
The Road to Avalon (Book 6)

Dedication

To my friend Jeannette.

CHAPTER ONE

THE TWO GENTLY bred ladies sitting opposite Captain Max Aubrey were both staring at him with expectant expressions on their faces. This, not unnaturally, was making him feel most uncomfortable. In fact, the close scrutiny of anyone was likely to do that to him nowadays, ever since he'd been invalided out of the 20th Light Dragoons, the cavalry regiment that had been his life for almost ten years, and sent back to England to recuperate. Not that recuperation was ever going to do him any good. His regiment would never have him back now he was in this state.

That one of the aforementioned ladies was his mother made no difference to Max's discomfort. Georgiana, Dowager Countess of Westbury, was a formidable lady in her sixties who'd never been inclined to shower affection or compassion on either of her two sons. Not even when one of them, Max himself, had fallen off his pony at their home of Bratton Park and broken his arm in not one but two places. Her reaction then had been to sternly advise him to get straight back on again and not be a baby. The fact that he'd returned badly wounded from Portugal had not brought about any change in her attitude.

Max's sister-in-law, the dainty Maria, current Countess of Westbury and wife of Max's older brother, was an altogether gentler creature than his mother. Nevertheless, she was equally determined in what she was demanding of him. Against the joint onslaught of the two chatelaines of Bratton Park, Max was feeling decidedly besieged. As well he might do.

"You understand, don't you, that it would be too much for Julian's fragile health if he were to have to come up to Town with us," Maria said, at her most persuasive. At fifty-one, she could still be classed as a pretty woman, although nowadays with a somewhat faded air about her that wasn't unattractive. Her wide hazel eyes beseeched her much younger brother-in-law as only a spaniel's eyes should have the right to do.

That her words were probably true was inarguable. Max's older brother, the present earl, hadn't enjoyed good health for the last ten years. Since just after Max had taken up his commission, he'd put on a lot of weight in pouchy flesh, and old Dr. Ellison had pronounced some time ago that he was suffering from a congested heart and required a quiet life. Which was why, instead of being a part of this conversation, he was hiding in his first-floor study, taking one of his increasingly more regular naps. In fact, all of the rooms Julian used were on that level, as he could no longer manage the stairs alone.

As Max had always been very fond of his older brother, he was inclined to agree with Dr. Ellison and also with Lady Maria. Or he would have done, had it not been for what the two ladies had just asked him to do.

"If you escort us instead of Julian," Maria said, in what she must have considered her most appealing tones, "then he will be able to remain here at Bratton under Dr. Ellison's care. I would rather that than he should suffer the long journey up to Westbury House in Town and have the upheaval of us having to find him another doctor to attend him. You know he's used to Dr. Ellison and doesn't like change and that he needs to see him every day. Besides which, the upset of traveling would set him back in his recovery."

Which also was true. Dr. Ellison had been caring for the Aubreys for as long as Max could remember, including having dealt with his own broken arm as a boy. The whiskery-chopped old fellow walked with a stick and a decided stoop nowadays, and if he hadn't still been clinging to the old-fashioned habit of wearing a horsehair wig, no doubt whatever hair that remained on his head would be white as snow. When Max had still been a boisterous youngster, he'd made it his goal to dislodge that wig and take a peek underneath it. As indeed he'd once done to his father's man of business, who most satisfactorily had proved to possess a scalp as hairless as an egg, save for a wart right on the top.

"Have you not thought," Max said, in the vain hopes of appealing to their common sense, "that if you were to bring Julian up to Town and find him a different physician, you might happen upon one with some newer, more up-to-date methods of treatment for his heart? Someone who might be able to effect some actual good?"

The dowager tutted her tongue, as she'd been wont to do when either of her sons had been brought before her for some misdemeanor when they were small. Such as the dislodging of the man of business's wig with a fishing line and hook. "It is most unlikely that any of the jumped up nincompoops in London who call themselves physicians will know more than Dr. Ellison with his extensive experience gained through years of treating this family." As though treating one particular family made you an expert in heart care. Max frowned at her logic, uncomfortably aware that it matched Maria's foolish belief that Julian was going to get better.

His mother's grip on the teacup in her hand tightened. "He was your father's physician and now he is your brother's. And yours if you would only allow him to look at your arm."

She fixed a hard stare on Max's right arm, which hung useless in a sling, and had done ever since the aftermath of the Battle of Vimeiro, back in August. A cavalry officer needed both arms working.

Max heaved a sigh. "I've been poked about more than enough, Mama, and I refuse to believe that a country quack can know more than the best doctors in the army, who are used to dealing with wounds like this."

"Intractable," his mother snapped, to no one in particular. "Just like his father."

Lady Maria, ever the appeaser, hurriedly interceded. Perhaps she'd noticed the heavy frown settling on Max's forehead as he glared at his mother. "You would be doing me the most enormous favor, Max, my dear. I really think that without a man to escort us to London for the Season, we won't be able to go. I would not be confident enough to go alone. And Arabella has been so looking forward to her coming out." Those spaniel eyes sent him a fresh appeal.

Max had never been able to resist his sister-in-law, a woman he'd known since he was a boy of ten, and who'd been more of a mother to him than his own had ever been. He heaved a second sigh. "Would you expect me to attend balls and routs and soirées?"

Maria appeared to be fighting with herself about whether to be honest or not. Compromise won. "Well... a few, I should think. I really don't think I could take Arabella out on my own, after all. You know how headstrong she can be. If I have to go alone then who knows what sort of a fortune hunter she might end up with. Preventing that is the whole point of you accompanying us."

What she really meant was that she, personally, didn't want to go alone. Women had been known to present their daughters in society without a husband or male relative as an escort. But not Maria. She was a woman for whom the presence of a man was essential, or she felt incomplete. Or that was the impression she liked to maintain.

His mother interrupted his thoughts. "And of course, it will be the ideal opportunity for you to secure yourself a bride. What better way than to attend the social gatherings of London where all the most eligible young women will be on parade. Perfect."

Max's frown returned. So that was really what all this was about. Might Julian himself be behind their subterfuge? Max cringed inside at the thought of having to go out in public and make himself be polite to people he didn't know and didn't want to know. He tapped his useless arm. "Like this? How much good do you envisage me being if I can't dance with anyone?"

He used to like dancing. Prided himself on being good at it, in fact. Not any more though. Those days were long gone.

"Oh, you won't need to dance," Maria said, clearly a little flustered. "Just your presence is required. In lieu of Julian's. In the way of moral support, so to speak. You would be most welcome to spend the evenings in the card room if you prefer."

Max forbore from telling her how much he abhorred the card room and the sort of false male camaraderie to be found in there. It paled into insignificance compared with the bond between officers in the mess room, and between each of those officers and their men. Something he was never going to get back again. You couldn't be a cavalry officer if you only had one working arm, and neither could you be an infantry officer, nor even just an ordinary soldier. Two hands were essential for carbines. Well, for almost everything, as he was rapidly discovering. Even such mundanities as eating and dressing.

"This is quite ridiculous," his mother snapped, sounding as though she was allowing her temper to take control. "If you don't agree to go with Maria, then Julian will feel he has to drag himself up to Town and do his duty by Arabella. And we don't want that, do we? Who knows what it might do to him."

Maria bridled, perhaps because she believed Julian was not so ill as they were making out. "And of course, as you are now nearing your thirtieth birthday, it is quite essential that you find yourself a bride." She paused. "Or you will not receive your inheritance."

Max sighed. The nub of the matter. His father had died when Max had been at Harrow. Julian, already married and with two children and another on the way, had inherited the earldom and everything that went with it. But the old earl had decided, in his wisdom, that his much more wayward younger son had needed an incentive to settle down. He'd left him the property his own mother had brought into the Aubrey family, everything else having been entailed to the heir, but only as long as Max married before the age of thirty. Otherwise it would revert to his brother.

Max had kicked over the traces when he left school and, to spite his dead father, had persuaded Julian to purchase a commission for him with the 20ᵗʰ Light Dragoons, thinking he could forge himself a career as a soldier. Until a French musket ball had put a stop to that. And now he was back, living on his brother's charity rather than at the house he would only inherit if he chose to marry. In the next four months.

As if any girl in their right mind would have him with this arm—or rather, without it. Not that he imagined he possessed any propensity for love, for it was something he'd never experienced so far, despite his fair share of encounters with women.

However, the last thing Max wanted was for his beloved older brother to do something that might be detrimental to his fragile health. But still... why couldn't bloody Maria just take the bull by the horns and go by herself with Arabella? Plenty of society mamas did just that, if they'd been widowed, for example. But no. This was all a plan to marry him off.

Damn Julian and his generosity. Any other brother might be all too happy to add Max's inheritance to his own wealth and actively encourage the potential recipient not to marry. Not Julian. It was a subject he brought up every time he and Max met. Which was several times a day here at Bratton Park. So it might be a relief to get away from his nagging.

"And poor Arabella has so set her heart on coming out this year," Maria put in, still following the line of her original excuse to persuade him to come. "She's talked of nothing else for the past month. No, longer than that. You know what girls are like, Max."

Did he? Not really. His exploits with the gentler sex had been more along the lines of encounters with camp followers, but

Maria didn't need to know that.

Under this onslaught, what was he supposed to do? Give in, of course. Let the two most important women in his life have their way. "Very well. But as soon as she finds herself a husband, I mean, gets herself engaged, then I want to be absolved of any further escort duties. The whole point of her having a Season is for her to make a match, and I can see the point in that, I suppose. But once that's done, I'd appreciate it if we could regroup and change the plan."

His mother shot him a narrow-eyed look. Clearly she saw this journey to London as the opportunity to marry her younger son off and see him "settled" into his inheritance, rather than to do the same for her granddaughter. In fact, Arabella seemed to be just an excuse.

Maria, however, smiled at him in obvious relief. "Oh, thank you, Max. I shall go and tell Arabella straightaway. She was so upset when I told her that her papa wouldn't be able to present her, and that I couldn't see myself doing it alone." She dimpled at him, as charming as she'd been as Julian's bride, nineteen years ago, but Max knew her sweet exterior housed a core of inner steel. "And we'll be able to see Grey and Louis as well. They're sharing rooms in London for the Season. I daresay a few mamas will be setting their caps at my boys in the hopes of snaring them for their daughters." She giggled. If Max hadn't known better he could have been forgiven for thinking her a simpleton. Which she was not.

He'd almost forgotten about Maria's two sons from her first marriage. Henry, Lord Grey, and his younger brother, Louis, had been seven and five when their widowed mother had married Julian, and the age gap had been just a little too big for Max to have ever been able to make lasting friendships with them. And then, of course, he'd gone off to Harrow at thirteen, something Maria had refused for her two boys, keeping them at home with a tutor instead, much as she was doing for her two sons by Julian. Still, they were in their early twenties now, and although he'd never seen much of them, having gone up to Oxford straight after Harrow, and from there to take up his commission, Max had always tolerated them, much as one would tolerate a pair of boisterous puppies.

"That'll be nice," he said, for want of any other remark to make. A spell in the army would have done those two would-be rakes the world of good.

Maria got to her feet. "This will be such fun. You'll see. I promise that you won't regret your decision for a minute." And with that she bustled out of the room with a light and airy tread, as though she were the same age as her oldest daughter.

When she'd gone, Max turned back to his mother. "Is Julian really so bad he can't go up to Town?"

Since he'd been back from Portugal, via London and several well thought of and very expensive doctors, he'd only fleetingly seen his brother each day—just long enough to be reminded of what Julian saw as his obligation to wed. The earl tended to rise late and spend most of his time either in his study, where no one was permitted to disturb him as he was writing a book on Egyptian antiquities, or resting in his room.

His mother's eyes took on a troubled expression, her brow furrowing. "When I spoke to Dr. Ellison after his last visit, he seemed hopeful that there'd been an improvement since your brother went onto the new medicine." Her tone was doubtful. "But I don't know. He seems to me to be just as your father was… toward the end. I see the parallels all too clearly."

John, the fifth Earl of Westbury, father of Julian and Max, had died of the same thing Julian was suffering from. There was no denying that. Despite having been sixteen when it happened, though, Max had little recollection of his father's illness due to having been away at school throughout most of it. He eyed his mother in speculation. "And how near the end was Father the way Julian is now?"

She pressed her lips together in a hard line and gave an eloquent shrug of her shoulders. "I wouldn't like to say." Her brown eyes, normally so calm and emotionless, clouded. "A mother should not outlive her children."

What was there to say to that? They both knew Julian couldn't go on forever the way he was. Neither of them wanted to put it into words, but it seemed likely the dowager would outlive her oldest son by some years. And then, of course, there'd been the children born between Julian and Max who hadn't lived. Children who were never mentioned, but whose names were written in the front of the large family Bible, along with their birth and death dates. As a small boy, Max had been fascinated by their phantom, almost denied, presence and had memorized their names. Rose and Emily who'd died on the same day in 1769, but what of, he had no idea. And Richard, who would have been six years his senior had he not succumbed and died as a three-year-old. Their documented presence accounted for the nearly eighteen year age gap between Julian and Max.

"Your brother has a strong sense of what is right," the dowager said. "And what is right is that you should inherit your grandmother's property." She tutted her tongue. "It has always irked me that your father put such a caveat on the inheritance, although as you've grown older it has become evident to me that he knew you better than I do." The ghost of a smile touched her lips. "Julian wishes to see you married before he dies. He wishes to pass on the property you should have inherited when you came of age, had I had my way. It is yours by right, in my eyes. Unfortunately for both of us, your papa's opinion differed. All you have to do is marry, Max. No one is asking you to love. That is altogether a far too modern idea. Just choose yourself the sort of woman you feel you could rub along with. One who could run your house for you and perhaps give you an heir. That's all I ask of you. And do it before you turn thirty or you won't have a house for anyone to run."

Did she think Julian would be dead by April then? Perhaps Max himself should speak with Dr. Ellison. Julian hadn't seemed all that bad when Max had seen him yesterday. Well enough to chide Max about his still being unattached, at least. Although he mentioned that every time they met, so what was different? But who was he to know? And his mother was right, his marriage was further to the front of his brother's mind than Arabella's was.

"I shall propose to the first girl who crosses my path," he said, with a disgruntled huff. "For, like you, I don't believe in love. If she has a brain in her head and isn't too ugly, then I shall marry her. And retire to my new estate."

His mother rose to her feet, spine stiffening. She wasn't the sort of woman to allow grieving to be obvious. He could have taken her hand in reassurance, only he didn't. She would have frowned on any show of weakness or acknowledgement of her sorrow. "You will do as you should, I'm sure. Now, I shall go and speak with Mrs. Howard about tomorrow's menu. Good afternoon, Maxim." And she was gone.

CHAPTER TWO

MAX DIDN'T BOTHER to knock on Julian's study door, but opened it quietly and slipped inside. He needn't have worried about being quiet, though, as Julian, wearing a deep red banyan and a turban covering his thinning hair, was seated at his desk, his back to the roaring fire. Not asleep after all.

He looked up as his younger brother entered the room, and his face, where illness had blurred the planes of youth and made his skin hang in pouches beneath his eyes and chin, suffused in a genuine smile that lit eyes as dark as Max's own. But apart from the similarity of their eyes, it would have been difficult for a stranger to recognize the two as siblings. Julian, although not yet fifty, had the appearance of a man twenty years his senior, with a body grown bloated with the dropsy caused by his inefficient heart. Whereas Max, despite having been invalided out of the army after a serious wound, still had the military bearing of a soldier and the physique of an athlete. As well as all his own hair. The eighteen year gap between them had never been wider.

Outside, the December rain rattled against the windowpanes. Inside, the study was warm and cozy to the point of being stuffy.

"I thought I'd find you here," Max said, dropping into the empty chair on this side of the desk.

Julian coughed discreetly into his handkerchief. "Always good to see you, Max. I feel I haven't seen enough of you since you returned from Portugal. If I had a little more energy, it would be different, I swear."

Max leaned back in his seat, stretching out his long, boot-clad legs. "You're looking tired, brother, so I'll get to the point. Mama and Maria ambushed me in the parlor just now. I'm sure you know what about."

Julian showed no contrition and nor did he object to Max's assessment of him. "You're right. It's late in the day, and I am tired, and I do indeed know what you're referring to. It was my idea."

"I suspected as much. You've been plotting with Mama again."

Another cough into the handkerchief and a clearing of his throat. "Not so much plotting, Maxim. Merely acting in your best interests. As I've always done."

Max frowned. "I don't know why everyone thinks they know what my best interests are. I find it a little amusing that you all profess to be able to organize my life better than I can myself." But he wasn't angry.

Julian smiled again, also not angry, an act which served to make him appear altogether younger and more approachable. All four of Max's nieces and nephews stood in awe of their father due to his inability to have much to do with them and his somewhat frightening appearance. He usually resembled their forbidding grandfather, not their father, but right now he was suddenly Max's beloved older brother once more. "We are all older and wiser than you are. That's why." His chuckle degenerated into a coughing fit.

Max waited. The congestion of the heart Julian suffered from frequently left him gasping for breath. If he tried, Max could just about remember his own father being the same, although that was a long time ago now. "I fail to see how advancing age equates with increased wisdom. Some of the oldest army officers I knew were less wise than the rank and file under their command." This last was tinged with bitterness. If his commanding officer hadn't ordered the much too late cavalry charge at Vimeiro, he might still be a part of his regiment, with two sound arms.

Julian chuckled again, with caution this time. Coughing fits took it out of him so he tried hard to avoid provoking them. "Touché, brother. But you need to look at this from my point of view. I've always felt guilt over our father having put that damned codicil in his will about your inheritance. I don't want to go to my grave knowing you didn't get what you were entitled to. Humor a dying man and do as we all want you to do. Lavington House was brought into the family by our grandmother. It would have gone to Papa's younger brother had he not died as a youth. Not for nothing were you named after him. Papa always wanted it to go to you."

Max sighed. "Then why did he not leave it to me, caveat free?"

Julian shrugged. "I have no idea. He didn't even tell me he'd done it. The first I heard of it was at the will reading, as you know. I tried to settle it on you then and there, but Old Hawksworth said our father had suspected I might try to do that and the will's conditions prohibited it. And of course, you were only sixteen then."

Max shook his head. "I know all of that. I'd like to know why he thought I was such a problem that I had to be forced into marriage by the age of thirty."

Julian leaned forward over the desk, his face thrown into shadow. "I can't help it, you know. If I could, I would have reversed it. But I can't. And it behooves me to inform you that if you don't marry by your next birthday, which is now barely four months off, you'll lose everything."

Max bit his lip. "What makes you think I haven't lost everything already?" The words were out of his mouth before he could stop himself, quickly followed by anger at allowing his tongue to run away with itself.

Julian's gaze went to where Max's right arm hung in its sling. "You mean that?" His eyes moved to meet Max's, his tone suddenly turned bitter. "You think losing the use of your arm is the end of everything for you? Is that it?"

Max stayed silent, fuming.

"Granted," Julian said, keeping his voice level, "you are maimed indeed, and it appears to be permanent. You can no longer continue in the army that you'd hoped to make your life. The only option for you would be a desk job, and you turned that offer down. For you it was in the field, or nothing. I understand that. You were always that way as a boy. Ready to leap up and take action at every possible turn of events. It's little wonder the army, the Dragoons, suited you so well." He shook his head. "Nor that our father thought you needed taming."

Max pressed his lips together, already anticipating what was coming next and wishing his own words unsaid.

Julian coughed again and spat. "But the rest of you is unaffected. You have two legs and one good arm that works. You have a strong and youthful body. A healthy body save for that one arm. If you find a young lady to marry when you go to London with Maria and Mama, you'll have children of your own and see them grow to adulthood, see them marry in their turn, become a grandfather. Die when you've been made old and gray by the passage of time, not illness."

He coughed again, his chest heaving as he fought for breath. "But I won't see this year out, little brother. If I'm lucky, I might see Arabella married, but I'll never see her children. Little Freddie will inherit the earldom, but I won't be there to guide him. Rupert will grow up to follow in your footsteps into the army, or perhaps go into the church, but I'll never see that happen." He sighed. "You have not lost everything, Maxim. Remember that."

"I'm sorry," Max said. "I didn't think."

Julian rubbed a hand across his chin. "Well, it's high time that you did do some thinking. On this, to start with. I will leave two sons, but they're both still in the schoolroom. Who's to say either of them will live to become men, hard as that is for me to consider? Or if they do, that either of them will marry and have sons? What then of Bratton Park and the title, if all they produce is girls? I need you to marry, Max. You are third in line to the earldom, and if anything should happen to Freddie and Rupert, you will have the title."

"I do know all of that," Max said, avoiding telling Julian that the last thing he wanted was the responsibility of the earldom. "It's just that I have an aversion to doing as I'm told by others."

The laugh that emitted from his brother's throat set him wheezing for breath for several minutes. When he finally recovered he fixed Max with an amused gaze. "And you think I've never noticed that? Good heavens, boy, I'd guess that's precisely why our father added that caveat to your inheritance. He knew you for the stubborn fool you are."

"Not so much of the fool, thank you. I'll own to being stubborn any day, but not a fool."

"Then marry and take your inheritance and let me die a happy man."

"You're not dying yet."

Julian pursed his lips. "Not yet, maybe, but one day soon. Very soon. And I'll be glad of the rest from this failing body that exhausts me every day when what I want to do is get up and run through the woods here as I did as a boy. Believe me, Max, I shall not be sad to leave this world and find my rest. Although I'll be sad for the family I have to leave behind. I wish I could have lived long enough to set Freddie and Rupert on the right path. You must promise me you'll guide them well once I'm gone."

Max shifted in his seat. This talk of dying had unnerved him. Julian had always been here, his rock, his admired older brother, who'd been almost like a father to him since their father died. Who, with the kindly, gentle Maria, had brought him up and set him on his path to what he'd seen as his life's goal. A goal that had vanished in the puff of smoke of a musket ball. "You're not allowed to die," was all he could think of to say.

Julian shook his head as though exasperated. "I'm afraid you have no say in that. But if you can agree that I cannot avoid what fate has in store for me, will you grant a dying man a wish?"

This was so unfair of Julian. How could he refuse? Max fidgeted under the directness of his brother's stare. If he agreed, though, was that not tantamount to admitting his brother's life was ending? Something he'd been denying ever since he'd returned from Portugal. Something Maria was also denying, perhaps his mother, too.

"Well," Julian said. "Will you?"

Max licked his lips, wary of commitment. "I will try."

Julian laughed, this time managing not to cough. "How typical of you to add your own caveat. You're more like Father than you think. No. That's not good enough for me. You have to say you will." His eyes sharpened. "And who knows but that you won't meet the woman of your dreams and fall in love? Now. Give me your promise and make a dying man happy."

Max frowned. "I will give you my promise if you in turn promise to stop talking about dying."

"I can do that. Now, promise you will grant me my wish."

"I promise."

"Good. You know what that wish is. I shall think of you in Town attending all the balls and soirées and routs and picnics. They're only a memory to me now, but I hold them dear in my heart because that is where I met Maria, twenty years ago."

"I daresay they've changed a bit since then."

"They'll still abound with hopeful mamas intent on securing a match for their daughters. I'm sure one of them will suit you well enough."

"That's almost what Mama said. I'm not sure I can marry a woman for financial gain, and definitely not one who is a fool, which most young society ladies appear to be."

Julian gave a rueful smile. They must both be thinking of his headstrong daughter who, truth be told, fitted all too neatly into that description. The girl was as empty-headed as a chicken, no matter how much her mother had tried to drum education into her. And common sense. She was not a good measure of what society young ladies might be.

Max returned the smile. "Although, as I have no desire to spend longer than I need in that melting pot of madmen and harpy-like women known as the Season, I shall in all probability affiance myself with alacrity to the first woman I meet who is neither a fool nor a shameless flirt."

Julian shrugged his bony shoulders. "Possibly an admirable sentiment, although I can't quite be sure, but don't forget; time is ticking past. Love isn't everything, although for me, it was. I could not have chosen a better wife than Maria."

Max refrained from comment on this. Julian had fallen in love with Maria the first time he'd seen her, something he'd confided to the ten-year-old Max, even though she was a widow in her early thirties. But Max was certain falling in love lay beyond his capabilities. However, the sooner he found someone to marry, the sooner he could be away from London.

"Very well," he said. "I'll do my best to find myself a wife so you can bestow my inheritance upon me. If that's what will please you."

Julian smiled. "Thank you. Now, perhaps you would be so good as to call Rumbold and Blewett to me, as I think I'd like to lie down for a while before my dinner is brought up to me."

CHAPTER THREE

TWENTY-TWO-YEAR OLD SERAFINA Gilbert was seated, as usual, furthest from the parlor fire and closest to the wintry draught that was inevitably finding its way in through both the sash windows and the heavy curtains that covered them. Ignoring the chill, she raised her eyes from her sewing to regard the rest of her family.

Araminta, Lady Gilbert, the wife of her half-brother Ogden, was holding forth as she was wont to do, her insistent voice enough to quell to silence anyone who tried to interject a word. "I know it isn't yet Christmas, Ogden, and you think it's early to be discussing Letitia's debut in society, but she'll be eighteen in January, and we need to plan ahead."

In fact, her whole appearance was enough to subdue all others in her presence, especially Ogden, who had long given up any pretense of resistance. She was a woman who Serafina remembered as once having been good looking, until her quest and winning of the seat of power in the Gilbert family had rendered her shrewish and hard-faced. She ruled her family with a rod of iron, and Serafina was used to keeping below the parapet where her sister-in-law was concerned. She'd long ago learned that antagonizing her was a terrible idea.

Ogden, whose whole demeanor shouted hen-pecked, but whose renowned parsimoniousness had nurtured that same characteristic in a wife who had taken it to the extreme, tweaked his side whiskers in the nervous habit he'd not had before he met Araminta. "Of course, my dear. But do think of the expense. Taking a house for the whole Season will prove an exorbitant outlay. Not to mention the gowns she'll require. Just for one girl."

"I have indeed been weighing up the expense," Araminta replied, her voice managing to be both tart and dismissive as well as smug and self-assured. "And with Letitia's outstanding good looks, I believe equipping her with the wardrobe she deserves will be money well spent. We will see a desirable return on our investment when she carries off the most sought after gentleman of the Season. I foresee her capturing the attention of earls and dukes, no less."

Letitia, their oldest child, who was ostensibly as industriously employed as her young aunt, raised her head slightly and caught Serafina's eye. She gave her a quick, triumphant, I-told-you-so smile, her blue eyes glittering with scarcely bridled excitement.

It had been Letty's idea to suggest a Season in London to her mother, and for this she'd engaged Serafina's support. This had been the easy part, as Serafina was fond of her numerous nieces and nephews and always happy to be of help to them, even if it involved running errands or putting up with discomfort on her own part. After all, she had no one else on whom to lavish her love and attention. So she'd taken no persuading to sing Letty's praises to Araminta, putting the idea into her sister-in-law's head that, with such looks, her oldest daughter could be the toast of the Season.

Which was quite true. Letty, despite her parentage, had recently blossomed into a true beauty, leaving behind the gawkiness of her youth. With just the rich russet hair of her grandfather, the late Sir George Gilbert, and the delicate features of his first wife, her grandmother, she would have been striking indeed. But her wide blue eyes, which hid an inner core of determination, lifted her appearance to the level of outstanding. Where she'd inherited the eyes from, no one knew. They must have come from some much more distant ancestor, as they were not to be seen amongst the portraits hanging on nearly every wall at Milford House. The Gilberts had been in residence there in Berkshire for hundreds of years, with a propensity for every member of their family sitting for portraits, so it was likely the blue eyes, had they been present, would have been recorded for posterity.

"Just so, just so," Ogden muttered. He was sitting with his feet on the fender of the blazing fire, a necessity in this house if you wanted to be remotely warm in winter, and his face, already somewhat choleric from his daily intake of large quantities of port, had achieved a ruddy glow. "I do admit that it would be most pleasing were Letitia to ally our family with a gentleman of note. As you say, my dear, an earl, perhaps, or even a duke. With her looks, I think I would prefer a duke. She should be instructed to turn down any lesser offers." He chortled to himself as though he were already the father of a duchess.

Letty, under cover of her sewing, waggled her delicate auburn eyebrows at Serafina.

Serafina bit her lip and stitched with increased ardor. As usual, she was employed in mending one of her little nephews' damaged items of clothing. "Your stitches are so neat," Araminta was wont to say, a sentiment echoed by Letty, who hated mending. "It would be a shame to allow one of the nursery nurses to ruin a garment with their clumsy sewing." So Serafina inherited all the mending for the five Gilbert children, as well as having to darn and repair her own limited wardrobe. Ogden didn't believe in buying new if old could be mended, even for his brood, and still less for his bothersome half-sister with whom he'd been burdened since she was six years old.

"A duke indeed," Araminta said, puffing out her chest as though a duke had already made her daughter an offer and she were responsible for Letty's looks. Which she wasn't, as nothing about Letty's beauty spoke of who her mother was.

Letty and Serafina exchanged glances again, and Letty gave a little nod. "Might I make a request, do you think? If I am to be allowed a presentation into society in the new year?"

Her parents' heads swiveled to regard her, surprise on their faces as though they'd forgotten the subject of their conversation was present in the room with them. Araminta's cold eyes narrowed. "It very much depends on what it is." Never one to commit herself.

Serafina lowered her gaze to her sewing, her heartbeat quickening. If she could have crossed her fingers, she would have, but she didn't want to give Araminta the opportunity to berate her for lack of industry.

Letty visibly heaved in a breath and sat up straighter. How brave she was, especially when her own comfort was involved. "Might Serafina be allowed to accompany me? I should be much more confident with her present, as you know how timid I can be."

Silence fell. "Serafina?" her mother repeated, as though she were wondering to whom Letty was referring.

Serafina dared a peep at her and nearly stabbed her finger with her needle. That wouldn't do at all. If Araminta saw a spot of blood on the sewing she'd be furious.

Letty nodded, patting her immaculately arranged hair. "Yes. Serafina. She is by far the best at doing my hair for me, and always knows what color suits me best. Her judgement and taste are perfect. She's far more a help to me than Roberts ever is. And she's been practicing with all the newest styles from my magazines, as I asked her. So I should be very much à la mode without any need for extra expense."

A masterly move to point out a saving of money to her parents.

"That's all very well," Araminta said, her upper lip curling in obvious distaste, as it did so often where Serafina was concerned. "But if Serafina comes to London with us, she will need at least one new gown as well. She can't very well go out in society in the drab things she wears here at Milford." Her expression belied her words. No doubt she'd be quite happy to send Serafina off in her patched and mended gowns if she possibly could. But apart from being as parsimonious as a church mouse, Araminta possessed a keen awareness of what others thought of her. Thank goodness.

"Gowns for her as well as Letitia?" Ogden's voice rose. "Impossible. Can't afford the expense and it would be wasted on her, anyway. Look at her. Plain as a pikestaff. Be like dressing up a broom handle. She has the misfortune to look just like her mother."

Serafina, biting back a reply in defense of her mother, who had died when she was less than a year old but whose portrait, hidden in a shadowy corner of the house, she liked to visit, swallowed her nerves down and looked up to meet her brother's eyes. "I have the money Papa left me. I could pay for the gowns myself."

This was a moot point. Sir George had indeed left her a lump sum of two thousand pounds, a veritable fortune, and a fact she'd only discovered lately and by chance, as he'd died when she was only six and too young to be told such things. Back then, Ogden, freshly married and also newly a new father, which event had been followed almost immediately by being installed in the baronetcy, had taken control of her money, for "safe keeping." Serafina had yet to see a penny of it, even though she'd turned twenty-one more than a year ago.

Ogden harumphed. "That's as may be, but my father didn't intend for you to fritter it away on frills and furbelows. He knew what girls are like and entrusted it to me to take care of." He cleared his throat. "And it stays with me until we can find you a man foolish enough to take you as a husband."

"Ridiculously unlikely," Araminta added. "No one would be desperate enough to want her. And besides which, she's lost what bloom of youth she ever had. She's destined to be a spinster all her life."

Serafina, cheeks blazing, bristled with indignation, experiencing an urge, not for the first time, to leap up and slap her sister-in-law's prune face. She didn't, however. The years had lent her caution. Rebellion had not been well received when she'd been an angry, bereaved six-year-old. Punishment had followed swiftly in its wake and Serafina, being an intelligent child, had rapidly worked out how to avoid it.

However, some small measure of protest was called for. She drew in a hesitant breath. "How am I supposed to meet any men while I'm here at Milford House? Whenever you entertain, I'm not allowed to attend. And even if I was, you never invite anyone of my age who might show an interest in me."

"What perfect nonsense," Araminta snapped. "A girl like you… an indigent girl… should be grateful for what she has and not have the temerity to complain. Isn't that right, Ogden? She's beholden to us for taking her in after your father died. Without a mother, we could have sent her off to the workhouse, but we didn't. We showed true Christian kindness by taking her in. She's only your half-sister, after all, not a true, full-blood relative."

Serafina ached to point out that she wasn't an indigent girl now, and she hadn't been then, and that if they'd only relinquish her two thousand pounds she'd be glad to leave Milford House and make her own way in the world. But for the children, that was, and especially Letty, who, despite her inclination to behave like a spoiled brat, she loved. So instead, she held her tongue on that point.

Letty waded into the fray. "Do say she can come with me. You know how I've always loved to have her with me—to fetch and carry for me, and of course to do my hair. I'd be lost without her."

Her parents regarded her out of sour, pursed mouths, as alike as two peas. For a long moment neither of them spoke.

Serafina held her breath. If she could just get to London, just see what the Season was like, even if it was from the shadows, and if she could make sure dear Letty didn't choose the wrong man for a husband, she would be content. Although she didn't agree with Letty's avowed intent to accept the first man who offered for her in order to get away from her parents. Something that had made Serafina all the keener to keep an eye on her niece.

Ogden patted his potbelly, where his waistcoat buttons were straining in a losing battle to hold him in. "I suppose we could take her with us, if just to please little Letty. And it would be an economy if she were to do Letty's hair, and yours, too, my dear. I've noticed she's a dab hand at hair. Otherwise we might have to hire another maid who understands the latest fashions."

"But what about the other children?" Araminta asked, her voice rising in indignation but perhaps suspecting that on this subject she was likely to lose. "Who will look after them while we're all away?"

Ogden waved an airy hand. "They have a governess, don't they? Miss Wychwood can look after them perfectly well. Anyone would think there were dozens of them instead of just four. Yes, I think it a good idea of Letitia's to take Serafina with us. She'll be very useful. To us as well as Letty."

Letty shot a triumphant glance at Serafina and bent her head over her sewing. "Thank you, Papa."

BEDTIME AT MILFORD House was always early in the winter months, because neither Sir Ogden nor his wife liked to waste unnecessary money on lighting and heating, even though they were not in the least bit poor. Sir George had left his oldest son comfortably off, as well as a good stipend to his younger son, the Reverend Eustace Gilbert, along with four parishes to administer. As a consequence of their father's abstemiousness, the children's bedrooms were never allowed fires, not even when snow covered the ground. As a consequence, when Serafina and Letty retired upstairs that evening, one candle between the two of them, they found their room was icy cold. As usual.

Roberts, Letty's recently acquired maid, was waiting for them, red-nosed, and already rubbing her hands together to restore the circulation. She bobbed a curtsy as the two young ladies came in.

Serafina shot a warning frown at Letty to abstain from discussion until Roberts had left, and they hurried through their ablutions and undressing into their thick flannel nightgowns. At least Roberts had put hot bricks in the big bed they shared.

As Roberts departed with their dirty water, Serafina blew out the candle, which was meant to last them all week, and snuggled down under the thick blankets with Letty.

"Every time I have to go to bed in the cold," Letty whispered, "I thank God for you. If it weren't for you I should have to go to bed by myself every night. And not only would that be much colder, but I'd also be so terribly lonely."

Letty's siblings were all much younger than her, and the next one down was Theodore, known as Teddy, who was only twelve. Consequently, she'd grown up with Serafina as her usual playmate as a child, and then as her confidante as she'd grown older.

"I can't help but think a fire would be nice, though," Serafina said, with a hint of wistfulness. "I remember when my papa was alive there was always a fire in the nursery."

Letty shivered. "That was before my mama decreed being warm was spoiling us children and making us feeble. I know she's my mother, but sometimes I do wonder if she loves us. Little Amy has chilblains on her fingers as if she were the child of one of the poorest of Papa's farm workers." Amy, the youngest in the family, was only seven and still slept in the night nursery with Laurence, who was eight and Charlotte, who was ten. No fire in there, either.

Serafina ignored this pronouncement as there was so little she could do about it. "Well done for asking if I could come. That was very brave of you."

Letty giggled. "I thought they were going to say no, though. And if they did, I was ready to have a fit of the vapors and declare I couldn't possibly go without my precious Serafina. You know I couldn't manage without all your help. And besides which, if I'm standing beside you at a ball, I'll look all the prettier."

Serafina flinched at this casual insult as she was well-used to Letty's lack of tact, and besides which, what she'd said was true. She'd had it drummed into her by Araminta that any girl standing beside her would look pretty. And of course, she could forgive Letty anything.

"I'd have loved to have seen their reaction if you'd had to resort to the vapors. Your mama would have had her smelling salts out in a flash."

"Thank goodness I avoided having to sniff them. They smell awful. I pretended the vapors once before when she was present, and she practically stuffed the bottle up my nose. Horrible. Couldn't get the smell out of my nostrils for days."

Serafina giggled too. "All the same, it was very kind of you to stand up for me like that."

Letty leaned over and planted a kiss on her aunt's forehead. "Darling Serafina, how could I possibly not stand up for you? You're my dearest friend and you know I spoke the truth when I said I couldn't go without you. I'm determined to find a husband and I need you to help me do that. Mama will be no help at all—she just wants me to marry someone with the most important title. Or perhaps with the biggest fortune." She gave a shiver as if of cold, even though they were now snug in bed. "What I want is a husband who lets his servants light fires in the bedrooms. I think that's on the top of my list of requirements."

Serafina smiled in the dark, even though Letty wouldn't have been able to see her. "An admirable trait in a prospective husband." She knew better than to criticize Letty's parents directly, but she was thinking how well Araminta had adapted to Ogden's penny-pinching ways. Although they had a fire in their own bedroom, of course. The warmest room in the house was always the kitchen, a place Serafina, and then her nieces and nephews, had spent a lot of time in over the years, getting under Cook's feet.

"And you never know," Letty whispered. "But we might be able to find you a husband as well." Although she didn't sound as though this was more than a sop to instill hope in her aunt.

Serafina shook her head. "You know that isn't going to happen. Who would want me? I'm twenty-three next year, have no looks to speak of, and no chance of offering my inheritance as an incentive, because your papa will never relinquish it. And besides, if I were to capture some old widower on the lookout for a carer for his motherless children, I might only find myself in a similar situation to the one I'm in here. Beholden to him for everything. And also with, an, er… different obligation I might well be expected to fulfill." She shivered, but not, this time, from cold. "I almost think I'd rather stay here than do that."

Letty, who could at times be practical, gave a shrug. "Well, if not a husband, perhaps we could procure you a governess's employment with a nice family? Where you'd be paid for the duties you perform here for nothing? There's always that possibility. And if you were employed, and paid, and found you didn't like your situation, then you could always up and leave and find another one." She paused. "But only once I'm married. I couldn't lose you until I'm safely married myself. So you're not allowed to marry before me."

One thing you could say about Letty was that she was ever the optimist. "I have no letter of recommendation to show anyone requiring a governess, and I can't see Ogden or Araminta giving me one. They like having me here at their beck and call to do all the jobs no one else wants to do."

Letty took her hand. "Stop being such a pessimist. You should do more looking on the bright side, like I do. I can assure you that doing so will improve your mindset. I am convinced that I'll be married before the end of the Season. To a man who has fires lit in every hearth in his house. All you have to do is think positive thoughts and they'll come true."

Serafina frowned, a little concerned at Letty's blasé view of her possible future. "I'm not precisely a pessimist. More what you might call a realist. We have to face it, Letty. I'm on the shelf. A spinster. Too old and too plain, and lacking any kind of dowry, and no one will want me like that. Besides which, I don't think I have it in me to fall in love with anyone."

Letty snorted. "What makes you plain is the way you do your hair, the awful gowns you wear and the sad look on your face all the time. You make nothing of yourself. When we get to London, I'm going to make sure you get a new gown, even if you only get one. And I'll get Roberts to do your hair for you so you look a bit more attractive. She's not as good at it as you are, but you can't do your own by yourself. Trust me, Fina, we're going to find your handsome prince for you."

CHAPTER FOUR

M ARIA HAD SENT servants on ahead to organize the opening up of Westbury House in Cavendish Square so, when the considerable equipage arrived from Wiltshire at the end of January, their London butler, Allsop, was waiting on the front steps to welcome them.

Julian had, without much difficulty, been persuaded to remain at Bratton Park under the care of Dr. Ellison, in whom Maria appeared to invest great faith. The dowager had decided, at the last minute of course and with Dr. Ellison's assurances that her oldest son would be well cared for in her absence, that she would accompany her daughter-in-law to Town in order to renew her acquaintances amongst the older ladies of the *ton*. Although Max harbored a strong suspicion that her real intent was to ensure he found himself a suitable spouse.

So the party consisted of the dowager, Maria, Max and Arabella in the largest carriage, as well as in a second, lesser vehicle, maids for each of the three ladies, Watkins, who was Max's ex-soldier-servant and now valet, and Mrs. Larkin, the cook from the Dower House at Bratton Park. This latter was because the dowager insisted she couldn't do without a cook she knew. And behind these two carriages trundled a vehicle containing everyone's luggage.

The servants' carriage delivered them to the mews at the back of the house, whereas the carriage bearing the family arrived at the front door just as evening fell and the typical London fog that Max remembered from his boyhood came crawling up the street and into the square.

A liveried footman hurried out to lower the step for the ladies, and Max waited inside the carriage while they descended. A number of weeks had passed since he'd committed himself to escorting the Aubrey ladies for the Season, and he'd grown a little more used to managing everything one-handed. The footman, who no doubt had been briefed by his mother, and possibly by Allsop as well, held out a hand to assist him, but Max waved him away. He wasn't an invalid yet, even if he looked like he might be, and it grated on him when he was treated as such.

The lamplighter was just in the act of lighting the lamps in the square, their golden light illuminating not just the cobbled road but also the wide garden in the center. Max had stayed here while he'd visited the useless London doctors his army surgeon had recommended to him last autumn.

Allsop, waiting beside the wide front door, bowed to him as he followed the ladies inside. "Good evening, Captain Aubrey. I trust his lordship remains well?"

Max pulled a face. "As well as can be expected, Allsop. Which is why I'm back again. It falls to me to take on his duties and escort the ladies about Town. And no doubt my mother will want to host something here as well." He heaved a resigned sigh.

Allsop's gaze lingered for a moment on Max's arm where it hung in its sling. "If I can be of any assistance, Captain?"

Max shook his head. "Since last I saw you, I've grown used to doing everything one-handed, thank you. And Watkins serves me well. I'll see the ladies settled and then dress for dinner, if you can send Watkins up to me, please."

Allsop bowed his grizzled head. "Very well, Captain."

Watkins, who'd been Max's soldier-servant throughout his military career and had risen to the heady rank of lance-corporal, had already laid out Max's evening wear on the bed. So Allsop didn't need to send him up.

"Everything to your liking here?" Max asked, as he divested himself of his sling and Watkins helped him out of his coat. Damn that arm, hanging there by his side like some unwanted appendage. He'd often thought the surgeon would have been better advised to just hack it off. Then it wouldn't keep on getting in the way. But the musket ball that had severed the nerves and damaged his right shoulder hadn't sufficiently damaged the arm itself, and the surgeon had worked hard not to have to amputate. "You're a very lucky fellow," he'd told Max. "Most musket ball damage I see ends in amputation. Or gangrene. Don't ever think you're not blessed by the gods." As if that could ever be true.

Watkins nodded. "Everything is shipshape and running smoothly below stairs, Captain. I'm pleased to say that Mr. Allsop runs a tight ship and keeps everyone on their toes. I foresee no problems during your stay." He helped Max into his breeches, something which Max had discovered was nigh on impossible to do one-handed. The ignominy of not being able to fasten one's breeches oneself wasn't lost on him.

Watkins, ever tactful, fastened the fall on the breeches for him and reached for his smart evening coat. He held it out for Max to thread his useless arm into the right sleeve using his left hand, then slip his good arm into the other sleeve. Max shifted his shoulders to make sure it was comfortable, and put his sling back on again. A glance at his watch told him it was time to go downstairs for dinner with the ladies.

LESS THAN HALF a mile away in Great Titchfield Street, and at very much the same time, the Gilbert family were arriving at the house Ogden had secured for them for the duration of the London Season. Theirs, however, was not quite such a well-orchestrated arrival. The party consisted of Sir Ogden and Lady Gilbert, Letty and Serafina, accompanied by just two maids and Sir Ogden's dour-faced valet, Moorcroft. Lady Gilbert had not thought to send any of their servants from Milford House on ahead and, when they arrived, they found the house shut up and cold. Clearly their landlord had not thought fit to provide them with any household servants to speak of, apart from an elderly and very deaf old lady dressed all in black who appeared to be the housekeeper.

"Where are all the other servants?" Lady Gilbert asked, in the tone of someone who was used to an army of them, which wasn't at all true, as they made do at Milford with as few as possible. To save money.

"Eh?" replied the old lady, one hand to her ear. "Speak up, can't you? I'm a little hard of hearing."

That was an understatement.

"I said," Lady Gilbert enunciated every word a little more loudly and clearly. "Where are the other servants?"

The woman, her gray hair scraped back from her wrinkled face in a neat bun, frowned in concentration. "Your servants are in the kitchen. I sent them down there."

Ogden stepped in. "Not our servants, my good woman. The ones that normally keep this house up and running. A footman at least, if not a butler, a few housemaids, a cook. Where are they?"

As he had a deeper voice than his wife, possibly the house-keeper could hear him better. Her eyes brightened in understanding. "Oh, my master doesn't keep a horde of servants here when the house isn't let out." She gave a dismissive wave of her hand. "He leaves it to whoever takes the house to organize their own staff. Didn't he tell you that in his letter?"

Serafina and Letty exchanged glances. "Home from home," Letty whispered. "I bet there aren't any fires lit."

As the house possessed the unlived-in chill of long emptiness, Letty was probably correct in that surmise.

Serafina looked about herself with a critical eye. The house was not large. That much had been evident from the street, with only a single sash window to the left and right of the front door, and three floors rising above that. Five altogether if you counted the basement that must house the kitchen and servants' hall. The empty servants' hall.

Araminta also looked about herself and tutted. She did not look impressed.

The tiled front hallway was not large, with doors opening to either side, and a less than magnificent set of stairs rising to the floor above. The house of a middling merchant once, perhaps. But Ogden had never seen the point in keeping a house permanently in London, as the family so rarely journeyed there from Berkshire. When he had occasion to visit himself, a few times a year, he stayed at his club every time.

"Tell her she will need to set about hiring servants for us. Immediately." Araminta's voice reflected the strain she must be feeling. "And that she will need to prepare dinner for us tonight. Tell her we're used to dining at six."

Ogden for a moment looked as though he might like to suggest that his wife should tell the housekeeper herself, as the woman was standing right there, but wariness got the better of him. He relayed this message to the housekeeper in as loud a voice as possible, and with a shrug of her thin shoulders and a resigned expression of annoyance, off she went to comply. Hopefully. It was always possible what she'd gone off to do was sulk at the imposition of having to cook.

"Goodness knows whether there's even any food in the house," Araminta snapped. "Now, girls. Upstairs to find your rooms and see if Roberts is unpacking your clothes."

Serafina and Letty took advantage of this command to absent themselves from the hall, hurrying up the murky staircase to the next floor. Visibility wasn't helped by the fact that the windows were all shuttered. A lot of the furniture was still swathed in dust sheets, as though no one had known which day they were to be arriving, if at all. Or that the housekeeper was lax in her duties, which seemed more likely.

"The parlor," Hetty said, peering inside the first doorway.

Serafina tried the other side of the landing. "Library. Lots of books. That's good." Having worked her way through most of the books in what had once been her father's library, a new set would be a boon.

Hitching up their skirts in a way Araminta would have condemned as unladylike, they ran up the next flight of stairs.

Hetty peered into a room on the right. "This must be Mama and Papa's room. They won't like the fact there's only one bed. Mama says Papa snores far too loudly."

Serafina pushed open the other door. Two beds. That would make a change. She and Hetty had been sharing a bed since Hetty had left the nursery six years ago. She crossed the room and unlatched the shutters. Folding them back revealed a long sash window with a view from the front of the house onto the foggy street below. The hired carriage that had brought them up from Berkshire had gone, but the street was busy with other types of vehicles, pedestrians and people hawking merchandise. Even at this time of day, it bustled with a vivid life that made her want to run outside and join in, only she had no pin money to spend on the gingerbread the girl across the road was selling, or the hot chestnuts a man further down was shouting about.

Hetty, who'd spent a minute bouncing on one bed after the other to test out their comfort, joined her at the window. "I can't believe we're actually here. London. And I'm going to go to real balls. I'm going to wear those beautiful gowns Mama had made for me and dance with handsome young gentlemen who will no doubt all fall head-over-heels in love with me." She clasped her hands together under her chin. "And if I'm lucky, I won't ever have to return to Milford and spend another winter nursing chilblains and looking forward to the hot brick in my bed at nights."

Serafina nodded. "But nevertheless, you must promise me that you won't accept the first offer you receive. If any young man makes an offer, you must tell me about it and we'll decide together if he will suit. A little research into their background will be necessary before you commit yourself. After all, you don't want to end up with a reckless gambler who never has any money to pay the household bills. Or a man who's so tight-fisted he squeaks when he walks."

Letty nodded with girlish vigor. "I promise. I shan't be like the girls in any of the novels I read. I shall act with the greatest of prudence. And don't worry. I have no intention whatsoever of ending up with a man like Papa."

Serafina returned her gaze to the street, where already darkness was falling. Despite Letty's promise, she had little faith in her living up to her words if she took a fancy to some handsome young man, suitable or not. Previous experience of her niece had led her to doubt she possessed much in the way of common sense. No one but Serafina knew, but Letty had nurtured a fledgling passion last autumn for the new young groom at Milford House, whose employment had perforce been very short-lived. Yes, he'd been abnormally handsome, but he'd also been a little too free in his manner, and Serafina had surprised him and Letty wrapped in one another's arms in the carriage house one afternoon.

She'd threatened the young man in question with revealing all to Letty's father if he didn't resign his job, and he'd believed her. Which was just as well as she wouldn't have told Ogden anything, as it would have entailed revealing Letty's part in the fiasco. Which would in turn have meant that Letty would never have succeeded in persuading her parents to let her have a London Season if they'd known she'd compromised herself with a lowly groom. Serafina was almost but not quite certain the relationship had gone no further than the furtive embrace she'd disturbed, but with Letty's impulsive, self-centered nature, one could never be completely sure.

A knock sounded on the bedroom door. Roberts came in holding a single candle, followed by Ogden's valet with the girls' trunks. Time to unpack and dress for dinner. Whatever that might entail.

CHAPTER FIVE

I N THE BRIGHT ballroom full of flamboyant gowns, ostrich feather head-dresses and smartly dressed gentlemen, Max stood out of the way, just behind where his mother had taken a seat with her friends, his face set in an expression guaranteed to put off even the most determined of conversationalists.

His mother had experienced no trouble in reacquainting herself with her old friends—for the most part elderly dowagers such as herself. Indeed, she was at present heads-together with two of the most imposing of these acquaintances, Lady Routledge and Lady Ponsonby. The latter happened to be their gracious hostess for the evening, but both of them fancied themselves as the utmost arbiters of the *ton*. No doubt they were picking apart this year's crop of young ladies and their ambitious mamas. Probably the young gentlemen too. But in all likelihood not his pretty niece Arabella, for fear of upsetting her grandmother.

Max had chosen a corner with a convenient pillar behind which he could shelter, in the hopes of avoiding the feeling of being exposed to the critical scrutiny of the assembled crowd. This ball had come as quite a surprise. He hadn't expected Maria and his mother to have settled into Westbury House so infernally quickly. But they had, and, within days, invitations had started flying in for balls and routs and masquerades and soirées. He'd failed to take into account how many people his mother knew. And all of them seemed keen to see her again after her self-inflicted retreat to the Dower House at Bratton Park, from where she'd been overseeing Julian's medical care.

This was the first ball they'd been invited to, and Arabella had been bursting with the most irritating excitement all day long. This, and Maria's similar girlish over enthusiasm, had driven Max into the library that had once been his father's, seeking refuge from all the women rushing around the house like demented chickens. Why was it women made such a fuss about what they were going to wear, how they should do their hair, what perfume was sweetest smelling, and what embellishments would look best with the gowns they only *might* have made their minds up to wear?

Much easier to be a man and just have to choose a different waistcoat and cravat. Although some men, and there were be plenty of them here in Town for the Season, obviously spent nearly as long as Maria and Arabella in perfecting their evening dress. Max wrinkled his nose as just such a dandy minced past. Ten years in the army had not been an adequate preparation for the vagaries of a London Season in full swing.

Thankfully, from his unobtrusive position, he was able to observe the dance floor without himself being much observed. Arabella, gorgeous in a green gown ornamented with Brussels lace, and with the long train caught up by a loop hooked over a finger on one hand, was at present dancing with a young Second Lieutenant in his scarlet regimentals and looking as though she were very much enjoying it. As Maria, ever the proud mama, had predicted, Arabella was proving a most popular dance partner. Aided, no doubt, by the fact that as the daughter of an Earl with a sizeable fortune, anyone making an offer for her could be sure of a handsome dowry. And of course, her fresh beauty was an added incentive.

Happy that his supposed charge was not in any way either compromising herself or in danger of falling prey to any aged fortune hunters, Max allowed his gaze to stray over the rest of the room. Despite winter still having a firm hold on London, inside

Highcourt House the air could even have been said to be a little too warm. A fair number of those present were rather ruddy about the face, and those dancing had foreheads where sweat stood out in a shining film.

Max tapped his foot in time to the music, remembering the adage his old nurse had been used to tell him. *Horses sweat, gentlemen perspire, but ladies glow.* There were a few ladies out there behaving very much like horses.

Where was Maria? Aha. There, standing with two other proud mamas, all of them closely observing their offspring while maintaining a garrulous three-way conversation. Why she'd insisted he accompany them to this first ball, he had no idea—she was clearly perfectly all right on her own. But she'd insisted he should start as she meant him to go on—by showing himself as available to the scheming mamas of the girls on offer. Nothing he'd said had persuaded her otherwise. She was clearly under strict instructions from Julian.

However, he'd succeeded in keeping to himself ever since they'd arrived, a couple of hours since, ostensibly attending on his mother in case she might need anything, but in reality camouflaging himself amongst those unlikely to take a turn on the dance floor. It would be time for supper soon, and he was even feeling a little hungry. He'd already decided he would escort his mother or Maria in, thus obviating the need for him to have to talk to any of the young women present.

He frowned. Why was it that amongst the dancers all spinning and skipping in the center of the room, the number of men in their scarlet regimentals seemed disproportionately large? Or was it just that they appeared more prominent and numerous because of his acute awareness that he'd never be among their number again?

A fair number of regiments must be back from the Peninsula and allowing their young officers time for rest and recuperation. A pang of jealousy stole through him. Not that he himself had ever been inclined to participate in the hurly-burly of the Season in his breaks from active duty. Rather that before too long they'd be returning to their regiments, possibly back to Spain or even Portugal, and leaving him behind. The army had been his life since leaving Oxford, and no matter how he tried, his soul cried out its melancholy at not still being a part of that camaraderie of brothers.

With reluctance, he pushed that thought out of his head. Nothing he could do about it and it didn't do to dwell on what he couldn't change. His arm was never going to recover and he would have to make the best of it. After all, Lord Nelson had done just that, only, as a much higher up officer, and in the navy rather than the army, he'd been able to continue with his naval career. Until it had ended abruptly at Trafalgar, of course, just three years ago.

Lord Nelson forgotten, his gaze roved on. One of his favorite things to do, even from boyhood, had been to people watch. And now he could no longer participate in the wider world, and never having had much of a London Season himself, being an onlooker to one was proving interesting. Of course, he didn't know who anyone was, although no doubt his mother could have filled him in, had she not been so busy gossiping with her two old friends. But that didn't matter. He could imagine for himself the backgrounds of the various people who drew his attention.

That dainty looking young blade with the much older henna-headed woman who was most definitely not his mother, for example. She had to be well over forty and had once been quite a beauty but now was definitely a little frayed about the edges. Judicious use of cosmetics was fighting a losing battle to maintain the illusion of youth, but the young man hanging on her arm didn't appear to have noticed. No doubt she possessed skills other than the obvious ones of graceful dancing and flirting, or the young man in question might have moved on to fresher pastures.

The dance was coming to an end. Arabella shot a questioning glance towards her mother who returned the slightest of nods giving her permission to perambulate the room on the arm of her dashing Second Lieutenant. She turned and smiled at one of the other young ladies who'd been part of her eight as though they'd formed some sort of rapport, and the two of them laughed together, making a pretty picture of enjoyment. How sweet it must be to be young and carefree. It felt like an inordinate length of time since Max had last felt young and carefree.

The girl Arabella had been with caught Max's attention. How could she not have, with her striking good looks. Like the woman with the hapless young blade, this girl had red hair, but hers was a natural russet, piled up on her head in artless curls to frame a dainty face with wide blue eyes the color of cornflowers. A beauty, much as Arabella was, but with entirely different coloring to Arabella's dark locks and eyes. If he'd been younger, and had an arm that worked, he might have ventured in her direction and asked for an introduction. Although only with the intention of enjoyment, not because she was of the sort he could ever consider countenancing as a possible bride. Far too young and frivolous for him, but great fun to dance with, no doubt. She seemed to have made friends with Arabella, though.

He watched the girl as her jaunty partner led her across the room to rejoin her family, idly curious as to who she was. He already had her down as the daughter of some nabob made rich on pickings from the East Indies.

Her family had clustered in a little group almost opposite where Max was standing. At least, he thought they might be her family. She didn't seem to resemble any of them at all, so perhaps she was a distant relation being launched into society by a kind aunt and uncle.

The man who might be either her father or uncle, or maybe just a distant cousin, was a portly, balding gentleman in a rather too tight coat and waistcoat, as though he'd put on weight since last he'd worn it, but been too parsimonious to have bought a new one or even let it out. Beside him stood a small, hard-faced woman in a puce dress that didn't suit her coloring, who surely couldn't be that beauty's mother. And behind them, lurking in the shadows just as he was, a taller young woman, head down, her chestnut hair austerely scraped back from her face. She was wearing the plainest gown he'd seen that evening. Dove gray and unadorned with any furbelows. A Plain Jane if ever there was one, so perhaps a paid companion to either the pretty girl or the hard-faced woman.

Even as he watched, another young gentleman approached the group, made his bow, and the pretty girl, who couldn't have been more than eighteen, smiled shyly up at him before taking his arm and letting him lead her onto the dance floor.

But in that moment, Max, ever the people watcher, had noticed something. As the young gentleman approached, the object of his attentions had looked a question at the Plain Jane. The woman had given her an imperceptible nod of approval, as though she were the one in charge of the girl. Definitely a companion. Perhaps a governess. And Max had seen her face more clearly. She wasn't as plain as all that, after all, but the way her hair had been done served to deprive her of any looks she might aspire to. That and the dress she wore, which would have been better suited to a country dance. However, there was sharp intelligence in her eyes. Eyes that matched the gray of her gown. Yes, the girl she appeared to be chaperoning was pretty, but something about this Plain Jane was infinitely more interesting.

His curiosity was more than aroused. Anything to assuage the boredom he was feeling right now.

His thoughts returned to working out her role in that family. A governess, as he'd thought before, perhaps? Allowed to attend the ball with her charge? How unobtrusive her presence was. Rather like his own. And the parents, if that was who they were, ignored her as though she didn't matter. Perhaps it was she who was the poor relation, not a governess after all—a distant cousin. The local vicar's sister? An orphan adopted into the family from the workhouse? Only neither of the parents, from the expressions on their faces, seemed as though they might be given to deeds of charity. His mind juggled stories that might suit the young woman for a minute or two.

His mother's voice interrupted his thoughts. "Max, my dear, I believe it's nearly time to go in for supper. Can I trouble you to take me for a walk about the ballroom first, so I can see who else I recognize? I fear I've monopolized my friends for long enough."

Lady Routledge and Lady Ponsonby made the sort of polite noises that indicated they'd not thought themselves monopolized, amid promises of further invitations and of calling on one another for afternoon tea. His mother seemed more than satisfied.

Max, his reveries disturbed, pushed the downtrodden girl and her position in that family out of his head and offered the dowager his good arm. "Of course, Mama."

ON THE FAR side of the room, Serafina had just watched Letty go off on the arm of a young man named William Wilton. As she'd predicted, Letty was finding herself popular amongst the young gentlemen present, and her dance card was almost full. Something Araminta had already taken full credit for.

Serafina had been a little surprised that an invitation had arrived so precipitously on their arrival in Town. But Araminta had disclosed, a trifle smugly, that she'd sent letters to some of her old acquaintances letting them know she would be coming up to present her daughter. As her late mother had been a friend of Lady Ponsonby's, the invitation to come to the ball at Highcourt House had arrived even as Araminta had been approving the servants their new housekeeper had hastily engaged for them.

Luckily, all their new gowns had been made before they left Berkshire by a dressmaker local to Newbury, their nearest town, including this plain gray one for Serafina. As it was the only new gown she'd had in a number of years, Serafina had decided not to turn up her nose but to make the most of it, subscribing to the 'beggars can't be choosers' motto. A few embellishments had turned it into something a little more festive. Some lace she'd had in her treasure box, cut from an old gown she'd outgrown, some ribbons Letty had given her. Until Araminta had seen her in the gown that evening and ordered her to remove every item she'd affixed to it.

"Who on earth do you think you are?" had been her scathing words. "You are not to put yourself forward, as I've already told you. Anyone would think you were out to catch yourself a man, if only that weren't so ridiculous a notion."

Serafina, seething but silent, and with blazing cheeks, had returned upstairs and deprived her gown of all the little extras she and Letty had so carefully stitched on, in a hurry lest Araminta decided not to wait for her. Who knew what naughtiness Letty might get up to if allowed the sort of free rein her mother might not notice.

Now, Araminta turned to her. "Serafina. Kindly go to the refreshment table and procure me a glass of lemonade. It's so warm in here, I declare I'm quite parched. Off you go. Hurry yourself. But don't spill anything."

Serafina detached herself from where she'd been standing just behind her brother and his wife, and slipped out into the throng of people promenading arm in arm: ladies chattering and gentlemen standing in small defensive groups, eyeing up the young ladies on offer but clearly wary of their matchmaking mamas. The heady perfumes of men and women alike filled the warm air, managing to overlay the unavoidable and singularly less pleasant odor of hot bodies sweating.

A little overcome by the heady feeling of sudden freedom, Serafina took her time as she edged between the press of people. And as she passed between the crowd she could never be one of, she caught snippets of their conversations.

"...and I said who on earth would have thought she would do that..."

"...I'll lay five guineas you wouldn't dare..."

"...how much did you say it cost?"

"...that horse of Buxton's is a flyer..."

"...did you see Westbury's brother? Back from the war with

his right arm in a sling. Stuck like that forever, so they say. Poor chap..."

"...that girl's a diamond of the first water, you mark my words...' She smiled a bit as she heard this last remark. The men in question were definitely not talking about her.

She made it to the refreshment table at last, where glasses already holding lemonade stood ready to be taken. Perhaps she'd best take two, as Ogden was likely to decide he too was thirsty if she arrived back with just the one. She picked up two glasses and turned.

Straight into the man behind her. The lemonade slopped over the top of the glasses and down not just the front of her gown, but also the front of the gentleman's brocade waistcoat and onto the sling his right arm rested in.

Serafina raised horrified eyes to meet his gaze, struck dumb at her own foolishness, but at the same time taking in how handsome the man was. He must have been over six feet tall, with wavy dark hair that might have been said to be a little too long to be fashionable but which gave him a rather swashbuckling look. He was looking down at her out of surprised dark eyes she could quite willingly have melted into.

"I'm so sorry." His voice was pleasingly deep. "I should be looking where I'm going."

Serafina found her voice with difficulty. "Oh no." She had to clear her throat. "It was my fault, not yours. I swung around most precipitously without first making certain no one was behind me. I'm afraid I've spoiled your lovely waistcoat."

The lady on his arm, old enough to be his mother, fixed a hard stare on Serafina. No doubt she was in agreement that it was her fault but was too polite to say so. "Come along, Max," she said. "Once more around the ballroom and it'll be time to go into supper. Good evening to you, Miss...?"

"Gilbert." Serafina's cheeks glowed with embarrassment at what she'd done, and to a man with his arm in a sling too.

"Miss Gilbert," the man said, in a way no one had ever said

her name before. "Captain Max Aubrey at your service. And this is my mother, the Dowager Countess of Westbury. I seem to have inadvertently caused damage to your gown. I'd be happy to pay for it to be cleaned. Or to pay for a new one if you think it past repair."

Serafina stared at him for a second, remembering what she'd overheard on her way to the refreshments, before letting her gaze drop to her gown front. The lemonade had left a dark mark over the pale gray fabric. "Oh no. It's nothing. I'll easily be able to get the mark out. I'm very good at cleaning. No need for you to do anything. It was all my fault. I'm so clumsy." She really couldn't let him take the blame for this. "I'm always being reprimanded for not looking where I'm going."

"Max." His mother sounded impatient.

The far-too-handsome Captain Max Aubrey, no doubt a wounded war hero, made Serafina a bow. "If you're certain?"

"I am." Was her voice shaking just a little?

"Then I must obey my mother and complete our tour of the ballroom. She's anxious to seek out her old friends. Good evening to you, Miss Gilbert."

And he was gone.

Serafina stood very still, a glass in each hand, staring after him as he walked away: at his straight back, the broad shoulders filling out his coat in the most satisfying manner, and his martial walk that he'd measured to match his mother's slower pace. That hair. Those interested dark eyes. That mouth. Good heavens. What was she thinking? A man like that would never be interested in a plain little mouse such as she.

Giving herself a little shake, she set off back to deliver the lemonade to Ogden and Araminta.

CHAPTER SIX

O F COURSE, NO gentleman came to offer to escort Serafina into supper, although Letty had by then quite a crowd of eager admirers vying for the honor of her company. Once Serafina had returned with their somewhat sticky glasses of lemonade, Ogden and Araminta reprimanded her for their state, then seemed to forget all about her presence. As soon as the last dance finished and supper was announced, without another word, nor even a glance her way, they departed into the supper room in a swish of Araminta's silk gown.

Serafina looked about herself, wondering if she should just follow them in, but the ignominy of going in alone put her off, and of course, she wasn't au fait with the etiquette of a ball and whether that would even be the right thing to do. Everyone else seemed to be going in with someone, even if it was only a friend of the same sex, and she would stand out if she went in by herself. People would stare and even perhaps pity her, something she couldn't abide. She glanced with longing towards the doors out onto the terrace.

A few people had been going in and out of them all evening, both ladies and gentlemen, often in the company of one another, so perhaps for a tryst or two. She'd been keeping an especial eye out to make sure no young man tried to take Letty out there, given Letty's propensity for indiscretions. But now everyone was busy with heading off to eat, she could perhaps try the terrace herself, in safety, and escape the fug of rich scent and hot bodies, and the noise of raucous chatter that could never include her. A little bit of peace, unobserved by any other guests, would be a pleasant change. A whole hour of peace seemed suddenly the most attractive thing in the world.

As unobtrusively as possible, head down to avoid eye contact, she slipped around the edge of the dance floor until she reached the nearest doors. It was going to be cold out there after the heat of the ballroom, but after all, she was well used to being cold at Milford House, so what would that matter?

No one took any notice of her as she slipped into the curtained alcove that contained the double doors, took hold of the handle, and let herself out.

Not so cold as she might have expected as spring could not be far off, but a dampness hung in the air that brought with it the unpleasant tang of coal fires from neighboring houses. Not really the fresh air she was used to in the countryside, but better than the shared, stuffy atmosphere inside the house. She inhaled some deep breaths, immediately feeling better.

A graveled terrace ran along the entire back of the house, with low stone balustrades that must overlook whatever garden, at present invisible, the house possessed. It being London, the garden would of necessity not be large. Half a dozen oil lamps on head-height iron posts illuminated the terrace with a soft golden glow, and a few ornate metal tables, their chairs empty, were scattered across the gravel. Not a single person with whom she might be forced to share her haven.

Good.

But ballgowns, however plain, were not made to keep their wearers warm and cozy while out of doors at night. She shivered as she closed the doors behind herself, and wrapped her arms around her torso. Anything was better than having to go into supper by herself, though. And being away from her brother and his family, even if just for an hour, was something to be savored. She so very rarely had any time to herself, as Araminta always kept her busy waiting on them all.

Indeed, if there was nothing for Serafina to do, Araminta delighted in making some useless task up. She'd been known to dispatch Serafina to make an inventory of the linen cupboard, to itemize what was stored in the lofty attic of the house, and to count the ducks on the lake below the house before now.

Curiosity about the garden got the better of her, and on wary feet she crossed to the far side of the terrace, the gravel crunching under her slippers. Two lamps stood at the top of a short flight of wide stone steps, leading down into the dark garden. Perhaps there might be a summerhouse which would be a little warmer? Nothing ventured, nothing gained, as her old nurse had liked to say. Before Araminta had dismissed her for being, in her opinion, too lenient with the seven-year-old Serafina.

The steps were wide and shallow, and as her dress had no flamboyant train, Serafina was able to negotiate them with ease. A wide path continued down into the gloom, past a circular pond that might have proved to hold goldfish had it not been so dark. Beyond that, the bright lights of the house played upon the many glass windows of what did indeed appear to be a summerhouse. What luck. An octagonal one of wood, with a conical tiled roof.

Shelter indeed. Supper should take at least an hour, and this might prove to be the warmest, most secluded spot to spend that hour. Out of the prying, embarrassingly sympathetic gazes of the house servants. The pity of the other guests would have been bad enough, but the pity of servants was something she could not stand.

Her eyes now accustomed to the lack of light, she approached the summerhouse with some confidence that none of the other guests would have felt the need to retire to such an inhospitable retreat, especially not during supper. She pushed open the door and stepped inside.

Despite the many windows, the darkness within was deeper than that of the garden, and an unused, musty smell tickled her nostrils. This being the tail end of winter, with spring only sniffing at the year, doubtless no one had been in here for a number of months, nor would anyone venture down here for several more months yet to come. A summerhouse was a thing for late spring and summer only.

There appeared to be a circular, cushioned seat around the circumference of the interior. Not that she could see all of it. The far side was thrown into almost complete darkness by the proximity of several tall trees that must overhang it. Undaunted, Serafina settled herself on the left of the closed door, smoothing out her skirts and uttering a sigh of pure relief. It was still chilly in here, but not as cold as the night air of the garden. She could definitely sit out here for an hour, and no one would miss her until supper was done with. Araminta would only then miss her when she discovered she was in need of her dogsbody to run some errand.

She leaned her head back on the window and closed her eyes, tiredness washing over her. Since their arrival, she'd been kept running about after everyone, doing the work of the servants no one had seen fit to take on in advance. She'd lit fires—only in Ogden and Araminta's room, of course, made breakfast and brought it on trays to the bedrooms, helped Mrs. Cottrell, the housekeeper with any of the tasks she was too old to accomplish herself, as well as spent hours perfecting the hairstyles for both Letty and her mother. She never minded helping Letty, who was always such a joy to prettify, but Araminta had proved to be the most exacting of subjects for whom her hairstyle was never quite good enough. Even tonight she'd had to spend over an hour doing her sister-in-law's hair and it still hadn't met with her satisfaction. A single word of thanks would have made it all the more bearable, but none had been forthcoming.

At least, though, she now had an hour to herself. A little nap might be nice, or just a little quiet contemplation. She breathed deeply and allowed her body to relax, ignoring the chill creeping up from the flagstones into her feet. This was better.

For a long minute, she noticed nothing but her own breathing and the gentle soughing of the branches above the summer-house. She smelled nothing but the musty dust and her own light perfume, lent by Letty in an uncharacteristic moment of generosity.

Wait. Was that a slight shuffle as of something moving across the flagstone floor?

She stopped breathing and listened, ears straining. Could there be rats in here, as there were in the stables at Milford? Or worse? What sort of wild animals might exist in a city? Something that had escaped from a menagerie? She knew those existed in London. Somewhere.

No. That wasn't the sort of noise scuttling rats made. And that second, less intrusive sound was of someone else breathing. Faint, but definite. She'd always had exceptional hearing. Or maybe of some*thing* else.

She swallowed, glancing out of the window behind herself at what now looked to be the very distant lights of the house. All the other guests would be in the supper room, chattering away, making so much noise of their own they'd hear nothing at all if she screamed. They'd be oblivious to the danger she might be in.

Sitting very still, and trying to keep her own alarmed breathing as quiet as possible, she listened harder.

That was definitely someone, or something, else breathing. Over there, in the darkest part of the summerhouse. If she jumped up now and flung the door open and ran, would she be able to get away from whoever or whatever it was? Suppose it was an escaped lion? She glanced down at her gown. She'd be hampered by long skirts and her flimsy little satin slippers, and a man, which she wanted to be almost sure this must be, would catch her in a few short seconds, possibly before she even got the door open. A lion certainly would.

It must be a person. She wouldn't think about the possibility it was an escaped wild animal.

It could be anyone. A homeless vagabond of some kind, per-haps, who'd wandered in here to get out of the cold. Or maybe a burglar out to spy on the house he intended to rob when everyone had gone home or to bed. Or just a plain murderer, lurking here with the intention of bludgeoning or stabbing or shooting the first party guest who was unwise enough to come his way. Just as bad as a lion. Logic had no place in her tumbled thoughts.

And she would be that unwise party guest, found dead in here in the morning. In a pool of her own blood.

She could hear him moving. Just the rasp of fabric, but it came to her as clearly as if he'd been shouting. And with it the faint scent of gentleman's cologne… a little hint of lavender and citrus, not unlike the cologne she remembered her dear papa as having worn. But… a villain wearing gentleman's cologne? How likely was that? And definitely not a lion.

Her thoughts strayed from the track they'd been following. The person lurking here so secretively was now no longer a villain of the lower classes, but some dastardly cad, some rake, as up to no good as a burglar would have been. And she still needed to get away from him.

The worst thing was, he must have seen her enter through the door and take a seat. He must know her for a woman. Perhaps that was what he'd been waiting for—some unwary woman to find her way to this summerhouse in the dark. To be ravished.

What on earth was she thinking? Anyone would conclude that she read the same lurid novels as Letty did, where young heroines were always getting themselves into danger and screaming and fainting. But she was not the stuff those hapless young heroines were made of. She was more than that. She was Serafina Gilbert, a young woman who'd had to fend for herself since she was six years old, and she refused to be afraid of whoever was sharing this summerhouse with her.

She drew in a silent but deep breath, albeit a little shakily. "Whoever you are, sir, would you please make yourself known to me?" Her voice, a trifle high-pitched, sounded far too loud in the screaming silence.

A sound of shuffling feet. "Good evening." The voice was deep and a little irritated, and even a little familiar. Where had she heard that voice before?

As he was being polite and sounded as though he was indeed a gentleman and not the vagabond she'd at first suspected, she'd best be polite in return. "Good evening." She paused, gathering her thoughts. "I had supposed to have this summerhouse to myself as the night is so cold."

"As had I."

Why hadn't the owner of this voice gone into supper like everyone else? The itch to ask him blossomed, but if she did, he might ask of her the same question, and she didn't want to answer that. Somehow it seemed important above everything that he shouldn't pity her. "I am sorry if I disturbed you."

Light glimmered over a profile as he leaned forwards out of the darkness, but he retreated almost as swiftly so she saw nothing of his face save a long and slightly aquiline nose and a determined chin. He cleared his throat. "I suppose I too should apologize for disturbing you."

"You were here first. I should leave you to your reflections." She rose to her feet, unsure where she would go if she had to leave, but determined to do so.

"Please don't leave on my account."

She hesitated. Did he mean that or was he just being polite? Deciding to take his words at face value, and not wanting to return to either the cold terrace or the ballroom, she sat again and resmoothed her skirts. "Very well. But I should prefer it if I could see the face of the gentleman I'm addressing."

He was silent for so long she thought she might have offended him. But at last he cleared his throat again, and there came the sound of him standing. "Do not be anxious. I will sit as far away from you as possible."

A tall and shadowy figure emerged from the darkness and took a seat in the gloom. A figure which unmistakably carried its right arm in a sling.

"Good heavens. Captain Aubrey. I had no idea it was you."

Captain Aubrey was staring at her as though as surprised as she was, although it was hard to make out his exact expression in the dark. "Miss Gilbert. I also had no idea it was you. All I saw of your arrival was a silhouette against the lights of the terrace."

She managed a little laugh. "I certainly wasn't expecting to meet anyone at all down here."

Captain Aubrey laughed in return, but his wasn't a pleasant laugh, being mirthless and bitter. "We, the outcasts of society, have found our niche in life it seems."

He'd divined why she was out here alone all too easily. Thank goodness for the sheltering gloom that would hide her embarrassment. And yet, he'd included himself in this sweeping statement. Why was he, the brother of an earl, an outcast of society? His mother was a dowager countess, so he must be from a far more exalted family than her own and surely a richer one. Definitely not a poor relation. Although, as she well knew, money did not necessarily make one happy. She herself had managed to find small things that made her happy throughout her life, without having a penny to her name, despite her situation and her withheld inheritance. She was surely a happier person than Araminta, despite all of her and Ogden's money.

Still, she wasn't prepared to admit to being an outcast. "You mistake me, Captain. I came out here solely for some fresh air."

He smiled, a fraction too knowingly. "As did I. Of course."

Why did she get the feeling he knew exactly why she'd ventured out in the cold dark, all alone? Most irritating of him, and bad mannered to imply so.

Silence fell between them. He broke it. "You are here with your brother and his family?"

And how did he know this? She frowned. "I am."

"Your niece has been quite the success."

She nodded, realization dawning. Ah, that was it. He was interested in Letty and wanted to use her to get an introduction.

Oh well. "She is a very pretty girl, so that is no surprise."

"And I would say that hopefully she is possessed of a lot more pleasant a disposition than her sour-faced mama."

Serafina's eyes widened at the same time as her heart plummeted into her boots. She was unused to hearing anyone, especially not someone she'd taken more than a passing fancy to, speak their mind so boldly. What was she supposed to say to that? She scrabbled about in her head. "She is indeed a pleasant-natured girl." If he had intentions towards Letty, then she'd better sing her praises and not mention Letty's selfish side. Finding her a suitable husband, after all, was what they were in London for. From what she'd seen of Captain Aubrey so far, he might suit Letty well enough.

"And I am sure her head is as empty of wit as the fish in that pond out there."

Serafina gaped at him. "That is a most unkind thing to say." But it was true. Apart from reading her rather lurid romance novels, Letty had never shown any inclination toward things intellectual. Serafina had overheard Araminta assuring Ogden that no man wanted a girl who might know more than he did. She'd been referring to Serafina herself, of course, whom she classed as bookish, but had held up Letty as an example of the sort of girl a man would prefer to marry. A girl who could paint a neat watercolor and play a pretty tune on a piano, but not one who could discuss Egyptian antiquities with a man. "Letty is a lovely girl and will make an exceptional bride."

He chuckled. "Lovely girls don't interest me."

Serafina's heart started to creep up out of her boots. "They don't?"

He shook his head and let out a rather heartfelt sigh. "I'm only here in Town to act as escort to my sister-in-law and her daughter. To accompany them to dances and such like. My brother is not a well man, and my mother and sister-in-law have prevailed upon me to perform the duties he would normally have undertaken. I can assure you, Miss Gilbert, that a girl like your niece would not be to my liking."

Should she be angry at his turning up of his nose at Letty? Or should she be glad? The suspicion that he was hiding something from her arose.

Two could play at that game. "I too am here in the position of escort. For my brother's wife says I am too old and plain for the marriage mart, and even if I were not, I don't think I would like to find myself married to a man who didn't want an intelligent wife with a mind of her own."

He snorted with laughter, which annoyed her some more. "Well said, Miss Gilbert. A woman after my own heart. Then perhaps, as neither of us are at this moment required for our squiring duties while our charges are at supper, you might sit here a while with me and talk of what it is that does interest you and what it is you wish for in life. I'm all agog to hear."

Was he teasing her? No. Perhaps not. Perhaps he did want to hear about her interests. It would be refreshing to talk to someone else about them, as all she had at home was Miss Wychwood, her nieces' and nephews' governess, whose knowledge of Egypt was minimal. She settled herself more comfortably on her cushioned seat. Somehow, the darkness surrounding them made baring her thoughts and wishes all the easier. "What I would really like, is to go to Egypt and see the pyramids and the Valley of the Kings for myself."

CHAPTER SEVEN

Before the call to go into supper came, Max had rather neatly managed to steer his mother towards one of her old beaux, the widowed Duke of Dunbar, a handsome, white-haired, lion of a man he'd heard her mention more than a few times in passing. How handy it had been to have come across him standing all alone, and with a somewhat forlorn expression on his face. This had been vanquished the moment he'd set eyes on Lady Westbury, and Max hadn't felt in the least bit guilty at abandoning her to the elderly gentleman's attentions. She even seemed quite flattered by them.

Having returned to check with Maria that Arabella was to be escorted into supper by the polite young man she was at present dancing the cotillion with, and that Maria was to go in with one of her oldest friends and had no need of his chaperonage, he'd beaten a hasty retreat onto the terrace.

With the music of the cotillion sending him on his way, he crossed the terrace and headed down into the garden, content in the knowledge that no one else was likely to resort to the summerhouse even for a romantic tryst, as it was still so chilly. At least there was as yet no fog hanging in the air. The bane of London nights.

He'd just been settling himself for some quiet reflection, when a movement outside on the path had caught his eye, and the door swung open to allow entry to the figure of a woman. By her silhouette, which showed her as tall for her sex but slender and graceful, he concluded that she must be young. She closed the door behind her with decided firmness and sat down on the bench beside it, the sound of her smoothing her gown carrying through the night air. That she couldn't see him had been obvious.

Whatever was she doing here when she should be inside, on the arm of some beau? Or, heaven forbid, had she arranged a tryst here with her lover? Should he show himself before something that would lead to acute embarrassment on all sides occur?

He'd never for a moment suspected she would turn out to be the same rather plain young woman who'd spilt her lemonade down his waistcoat. The young woman he'd been wondering about ever since that moment, for a reason he couldn't fathom. And now, here she was, pouring out her dearest wish to him as though they were old friends, perhaps made the more willing to confide in him because they were partly obscured from one another by the darkness. And her dearest wish had turned out to be something he would never have guessed. She wanted, above all things, to travel to Egypt and see the remains of that ancient civilization.

And the strangest thing of all was that this was something he could talk to her about, because he'd been there himself.

"It is infernally hot there," he said, by way of a starter. "Unlike this summerhouse. Too hot for most young ladies."

She chuckled. "I imagined it would be. You will find, Captain, that I have done my homework. I have studied many books on the subject and also pored over maps to spot out the places I would like to see. If, one day, I'm lucky enough to go there, which sadly seems unlikely."

"I was there myself, last year."

Her eyes widened and sparkled in the feeble light. "You were? How splendid. You are so lucky to have visited. I envy you."

He couldn't help but smile. "It was not under the most ideal of circumstances, I can assure you. I couldn't recommend that you should hope to have the same experience as I had. Although I did manage to return with one or two mementoes for my brother, who is writing a book about Egyptian antiquities."

"Oh." Realization must have dawned. "I suppose, now I think about it, that you went there with the army?"

He nodded. "I did. I served until quite recently in the Third Squadron of the 20th Light Dragoons. We were stationed for a short while in Messina, which is in Sicily. The island at the foot of the Italian Peninsula."

She nodded. "I know where Messina is." Her tone had turned a little sharp as though offended by his assumption that she lacked geographical knowledge. This was a girl who seemed to pride herself in her learning. Unlike Arabella.

He ignored the rebuke in her tone. "Under Major-General Mackenzie-Fraser, we embarked as part of a six thousand man expedition, plus us, the cavalry, of course. But our cavalry only numbered seventy-four men and four officers, so we were but a small part of the force involved. I was a mere lieutenant back then, serving under Captain Delaney, our commanding officer."

"Where in Egypt did you land?" Her eyes had lit up. Did he have her enthralled already? The feeling was heady. To have someone, a young lady in particular, even if she was plain, hanging on his words when he spoke of his army service was a new sensation. Not that he'd ever spoken of it much before. It was a past he'd always steered clear of bringing up, so strong was his longing to be able to return to it.

"Alexandria, but with only fourteen of our thirty-three ships at first. I remember it was the sixteenth of March. We had a rough sea, and it was hard to get ashore, but we got a thousand men disembarked, plus us Dragoons, and we set to and assaulted the city, which was being held by three hundred Turks. When the missing ships turned up, and we were up to full numbers, the Turks capitulated and we occupied the city."

Somehow, with her in the quiet privacy of the dark summer-house, it felt quite natural to be recounting his lost days in the

20th. He'd put them out of his mind for so long now it felt almost a relief to be able to talk about them. He had a sudden vision of the cloudless blue skies burning down on the flat delta land of the River Nile, and of the endless, green, irrigated fields stretching away towards the far horizon.

Her next question brought him back to the chilly present. "What did you bring back for your brother?"

He shrugged. "Small things only, that were easy to carry with me. I had to buy them from street vendors as I had no opportunity to search for them myself. He was particularly pleased with the blue glazed shabti that would once have been in a tomb, and the scarabs, as well as some old papyrus covered in hieroglyphs. Unreadable, of course, but he was pleased with his gifts. The locals make money from digging up old tombs and the like and selling off the contents to any who ask."

She nodded. "What was it like? I mean, what was it really like? Being there. Seeing the land. The remains of that civilization." She was leaning forwards now, as though his words held real interest for her, and the sensation that he liked her interest settled over him like a warm blanket. Hard to imagine any of the other young ladies present tonight as being so enthralled.

"Hot. Hot as I imagine hell to be. The sea was azure blue, and the sky matched it. The city walls shone bright enough to dazzle the eye, as did the walls of the houses. Heat rose up in visible waves from the ground, making the air shimmer, despite the earliness of the season. Summer lasts forever in Egypt."

She frowned. "I have read it is so. But the natives all wear loose clothes the better to keep themselves cool, do they not?"

He smiled again, and nodded. "They do indeed. It might not have been so bad for us had we imitated them, but we wore our British uniforms as a badge of pride." How good it would have been to have donned the flowing robes of an Egyptian instead of the stifling wool of his own cavalry uniform.

"And you saw action?"

"I did. But very little at first. As I said, the Turks surrendered

Alexandria to us the moment our other ships arrived and they knew themselves outnumbered. We were inside the city for a good while."

She gave a little sigh. "What was it like? What was Alexandria itself like? I've read so much about it. Did you attempt to discover the location of Alexander the Great's lost tomb? See where the Pharos stood? Visit Ptolemy's Serapium?"

She seemed remarkably well-informed on the sights of Alexandria. "I saw the remains of the Serapium. There are wonders there, on every street, that I don't have the words to do justice to. But the Pharos is long gone, tipped over into the sea, I was told. And as for Alexander's tomb—I believe none alive know its exact whereabouts, although many seek it."

She clasped her hands. "I should like to be the one who finds it. My dream has always been to study the ancient remains of Egypt at first hand. Every epoch interests me—from the earliest pharaohs right through to Ptolemaic Egypt and beyond."

He shook his head, further surprised by how glibly the correct terms slipped off her tongue. "It would be better for you to study it from afar. Visiting it would not be a safe undertaking. Especially not for a woman."

She fell silent for a long minute as though digesting this warning. "But how else am I to see such wonders as the Pyramids of Giza and the Sphinx? And the River Nile—how can I live without ever having laid my eyes on that mighty waterway?"

Such enthusiasm. And from a woman.

She leaned forward a little more. "Tell me. Did you see the pyramids for yourself? They are a sight I would give anything to lay my eyes on before I die. Indeed, I believe I could die happy if I'd seen them."

He shook his head. "Sadly, no. I admit I would have liked to, but our stay in Egypt was a military one, and our purpose to drive out the Turks and secure for Britain a base from which to operate against not just the Ottomans but also the French." He paused. "Something I'm ashamed to say we failed at."

She sat back as though disappointed in him. Most people, especially women, knew very little of the details of the war Britain was fighting. He had the feeling that despite her apparent knowledge of Egypt, her interest was confined to its past and not its present.

"Where did you fight, then?"

"We attacked Rosetta…"

This brought her forward again. "Rosetta? Where they discovered the famous Rosetta Stone? The stone which even now resides in the British Museum and some say will be the key to understanding hieroglyphs?"

He nodded.

Her eyes sparkled in the dim light. "That is something I would also give anything to go and see." How wistful she sounded. "But even though we're in London for the Season, I doubt very much if my family will allow me to do so. None of them would want to go, and they certainly wouldn't allow me to go alone."

Curiosity overtook him, encouraged by the companionable dark. "Why would they not wish to go and see something as interesting as that?"

She sighed. "My brother, who is in truth only my half-brother, and his wife are here solely for my pretty niece to make her debut in society and find herself a suitable match. That is also the only reason I'm here. They've brought me because Letty insisted. She persuaded them that I should come too as I am so useful to her. To all of them, I suppose." She paused. "Well, to both Letty and Lady Gilbert, as I'm very good at running errands and doing their hair, but not so much to my brother, who I think sees me as a nuisance he is forced to tolerate." Her voice trailed off.

For the first time in a long while Max felt a twinge of sympathy for another human being. He might be hampered by his arm, but this girl was hampered by her family, as he'd initially suspected on observing them from afar, and also from judicial enquiry of Maria, well out of his mother's earshot. "And you? What do you want?"

She chuckled, her momentary melancholia brushed aside. "What I want is immaterial. But, as you have so politely asked, what I would like, as I cannot up sticks and bolt to Egypt, is to visit the British Museum and see what they have on show in their Egyptian rooms. Particularly, I would like to see the famous Rosetta Stone. That would be the next best thing to traveling to Egypt myself."

He slapped his left hand on his thigh. "Then you will do that. And I shall take you there. I don't think your brother and his wife can object to you having a gentleman caller who wishes to take you out walking. Accompanied by your maid, of course. Can they?"

This silenced her again, for a full two minutes this time. Her whole body, silhouetted against the pale light of the windows, had stiffened.

Max waited as the silence stretched on.

Eventually, she found her voice again, suddenly almost timid, as though she couldn't believe someone would want to do something for her alone. She must have spent a long time at the beck and call of her brother's family. "You-you would do that? For me?"

He nodded. "I would. To encourage a fellow scholar in their studies."

"But everyone says a woman cannot be a scholar. Ogden has told me so many times. Whenever he catches me with a book, in fact. And Araminta says it is unmaidenly to study foreign civilizations."

He huffed. "Of course a woman can be a scholar, and it makes her all the more interesting and not at all unmaidenly. A woman who can talk of nothing but the weather or what hat she should wear is as insipid as..." He groped for a simile and failed. "Well, she's insipid, and that's all there is to say about that. I think an outing with you to the British Museum would be anything but insipid. And besides, my own sister-in-law, who is altogether too solicitous of my welfare, would see a visit by me to anywhere as progress." Especially if she thought he was going in the company of a young lady. He indicated his arm. "I have been a little self-conscious of my disability, you see, and didn't want to come up to Town at all." Why was he even admitting this to her? He certainly wasn't about to confide in her that this was also a quest to obtain a suitable bride just so he could inherit his estate.

She turned her head and the light caught her smile. "I would be delighted to accompany you to the British Museum, Captain Aubrey. And proud to do so with a war hero."

Whatever had given her that idea? He shook his head. "I'm no hero, so please don't think I am. Everything I've done in my life was just my duty to my king and country."

She smiled again. "You may say that, but to me you are my hero, if only for the fact that you have offered to do something for me that will make me happy."

She didn't need to tell him no one had ever tried to make her happy before. He'd guessed that already.

Max got to his feet. "Now, I think it might be an auspicious time for us to return to the ballroom. But not together, or tongues will wag. If you like, I will go first, and brave the curious stares of the servants. You, perhaps, should wait here for ten minutes or so before returning. I wouldn't want to give anyone cause to gossip about you."

She nodded. "Thank you, Captain Aubrey. I shall look forward to renewing our acquaintance when you come to call at Great Titchfield Street. My brother has taken a house there for the Season. You will find us at number thirty four."

He bowed. "Until tomorrow, then. Or perhaps I should say until later today, as midnight has passed. I wish you goodnight, Miss Gilbert."

CHAPTER EIGHT

T HE NEXT MORNING, Serafina was up early as usual, even though they now had the servants Mrs. Cottrell had hired, and Ogden and Araminta had been coerced, with great reluctance, into paying for. After a late return from the ball, no one else was as yet up, of course, so she had the house to herself. With no duties to perform, and breakfast being attendant on Ogden's rising, she took the opportunity to retreat into the sanctum of the small library. The shutters had been opened and the dismal light of a foggy London morning was creeping in through the long windows.

Of course, no fire had been lit, but as she'd donned one of her warmest old gowns this morning and augmented it with a thick shawl about her shoulders, and a pair of fingerless gloves, that hardly mattered. A short perusal of the shelves provided her with a book, which she took to one of the two high-backed chairs in front of the cold hearth. She could pretend, as she'd so often done before, that a cozy fire burned in the grate. Pulling the shawl more closely about her body, she opened the book, the musty scent of its many ignored companions tickling her nostrils.

But she couldn't read. Well, she could, but she found she kept on having to read the first few paragraphs over and over again, as their content had made no impression on her brain. Why was she finding it so hard to concentrate? An easy answer to that. She was thinking about her fascinating encounter last night with Captain

Max Aubrey. A man whom she might also classify as fascinating in person.

She'd never met anyone like him before. Well, she'd hardly ever met any men at all, ensconced as she'd been for all of her life at Milford House in deepest Berkshire, and certainly none of them had been young and handsome. The fat old physician came to mind, followed by Ogden's balding man of business, then the widowed vicar of St Mary's who, with his long, thin legs and lank gray hair, closely resembled a heron strutting about in the shallows of the river, or in his case, the churchyard. Of course there'd been that handsome young stable lad she'd caught Letty with, but he'd been no older than her niece and with eyes only for Letty's obvious attractions. She wasn't such a fool as to have thrown herself at a servant. Ogden and Araminta would have relished the opportunity to throw her out on the street for that sort of indiscretion.

Captain Aubrey's dashing good looks had not been lost on her, and nor had his polite interest in what she had to say. Despite her long-ingrained opinion of herself as not likely to be the object of any gentleman's attentions, a girl could dream. She closed her eyes for a moment, and he appeared in front of her, not cloaked in darkness as he'd been in the summerhouse, but in the full light of the ballroom, when she'd spilled the lemonade on him. So tall and slim, yet with broad shoulders beneath his tight-fitting tailcoat that suggested immense strength. And his hair. Oh goodness, his hair. She'd never been a girl given to romantic nonsense, but Captain Aubrey possessed hair she'd quite definitely like to run her fingers through, preferably while held tightly in his arms.

And those eyes, like peaty pools... she gave her head a little shake but couldn't rid herself of the image of his eyes, nor of those lips... Even though she'd never been kissed, the thought of pressing her lips to his sent a shiver of excitement coursing through her. Kissing was supposed to be a pleasurable activity, and she nurtured a forlorn hope to one day try it out for herself.

Even if it were just once.

She pulled herself up sharply and opened her own eyes, dispelling the alluring image of the captain. Whatever was she thinking? Just because a man had been kind to her, kind enough to offer to take her to visit somewhere she'd been longing to see, it didn't mean a thing. He was the son and brother of an earl, a war hero despite his denial of it, and, as far as she was concerned, the handsomest man at last night's ball. So, despite his kind words, he would not be interested, at least not in the way she would have liked, in a plain spinster without a penny to her name and who was definitely too old to be considered for matrimony. Araminta had told her so often enough.

No, if he decided at some point to marry, it would be to the daughter of a peer from a higher level of society than a baronet's impecunious half-sister. And he would choose someone young and pretty. There'd be plenty of young ladies overjoyed to have his attentions. He would never cast his eyes in the direction of someone as plain as she was. Not at all. She'd better get used to that and modify her vivid imagination.

He was just being kind. And polite. As any gentleman would be.

The morning crept by as though someone had applied a strong brake to it. After what seemed an interminable length of time, Ogden and Araminta appeared downstairs and breakfast was served in the dining room. 35 Great Titchfield Street was too small a house for a dedicated breakfast room. Serafina joined them but found she had no appetite, something which no one seemed to notice. Letty had not yet risen, and was, according to her proud mother, 'resting after her successful debut last night and her popularity amongst so many eligible young men'. In that moment, if Letty had not been her only friend, Serafina could have almost hated her.

After breakfast, Serafina went upstairs to the room the two of them were sharing before Araminta could find a chore for her to do. The room was gloomy, and Letty was just a hump under the covers, her auburn curls spread across the pillow. Time for her to get up. Serafina needed someone to talk to. She drew back the curtains and the feeble London daylight filled the room. So different from a morning in the country.

Still no movement from Letty.

Serafina gave her dainty shoulder a shake. "Wake up, can't you, Letty? It's nearly midday. Aren't you hungry?"

Letty rolled over and squinted up at her out of bleary blue eyes. "That's still morning. I'm not getting up until it's afternoon. You know how I hate mornings."

"Well it soon will be afternoon," Serafina said, sitting down on the edge of Letty's bed. "You're not usually such a slugabed."

Letty rubbed her eyes. "I haven't usually been up until the early hours of the morning dancing. I'm quite exhausted, my feet hurt and my legs ache. I had no idea having fun could be such hard work. I need my sleep. You should know better than to wake me up." She pulled a cross face.

Serafina bestowed an admonitory frown on her niece. "I'd say you've had enough sleep. After your success of last night, you need to be up and dressed because some of the young gentlemen you danced with, and no doubt charmed, are going to be calling on you before very long. That's what happens after balls. And you don't want to still be lying in bed when they arrive, now do you?"

Letty sat bolt upright in bed. "I forgot about that." Her hand went to her mouth. "I'm sure I invited far too many of them. All of them, in fact. And they're bound to want to come and see me. They were so attentive and every single one of them practically begged me for invitations." She patted her disarrayed curls. "One of them told me I was the prettiest girl in London. And another said I was a diamond of the first water, whatever that might be. But of course, it must have been something good. No one could say anything bad about the way I look."

Serafina ignored Letty's burst of self-congratulation, and smiled, content for now to bask in the radiance her niece was throwing. "Of course they all will come if you invited them. I believe that's the whole point of going to balls and soirées. You go out and are seen, and then would-be suitors come calling." At least, that was what she'd been led to expect. She was no expert herself.

Letty's blue eyes flew wide. "Suitors? I wonder how many of them might be thinking of offering for me? Even though we only met last night, and I only danced with each of them once, I do think several of them were quite smitten by my looks. I did manage to make friends with another girl, as Mama advised, although she wasn't anywhere near as pretty as me. Lady Arabella Aubrey. Her papa is an earl, she told me. Unfortunately, though, her brother, who'll be the next earl, is only twelve, or I should have set my cap at him. That would have pleased Mama no end."

Might this Lady Arabella Aubrey be the niece whom the handsome Captain had said he was escorting to balls in lieu of his brother? Serafina shrugged. She'd think about that later. For now, she was beginning to tire of Letty's unbounded self-confidence. "Who can tell how many might be considering proposals? But best for you to be prepared, I always think. And everyone else has already taken breakfast. I'll ring the bell and ask Roberts to fetch you up something to eat. How does hot chocolate and toast sound?"

Letty pushed back the covers. "Perfect. Now, where's my peignoir?"

Five minutes later the two girls were seated at the small round table in the window while Letty ate her toast with gusto. Roberts, taking advantage of the fact they were in a new kitchen with servants who didn't know Araminta's penny-pinching housekeeping methods, had brought two cups of hot chocolate, and Serafina was savoring the unlooked for bounty.

"Did you see how many gentlemen danced with me?" Letty asked, between bites of toast. "My dance card was full to bursting. There must surely be one amongst them I could envisage spending the rest of my life with. And more than one who allows fires in every room. So hard to choose though, as they were all so handsome, and they all gushed about my beauty. It was most satisfying." She patted her curls again, as she was wont to do whenever she found herself considering her own good looks.

Not so handsome as Captain Max Aubrey, but Serafina didn't volunteer that information.

"Was there one amongst them whom you liked more than the rest?" she asked, pushing another vision of Max out of her head.

Letty gave a shrug. How very beautiful she looked with her hair mussed up from sleep and the excitement of the night before making her eyes shine and her skin glow. She was only five years younger than Serafina, but the age gap had never gaped more widely. Almost as though she came from an entirely different generation. She set down her toast, only partly nibbled. "One dance isn't enough to form an attachment, I don't think. At least, not for me. Although I did rather enjoy the company of Lord Grey's younger brother—Mr. Herbert." She dimpled. "He asked me to call him Louis."

Serafina frowned over the top of her chocolate cup. "That was very forward of him." Letty, who had never been backward at coming forward herself, had to be kept a strict eye on. "And he's a younger brother, so perhaps won't have much of an inheritance. Younger brothers are wont to be the spendthrifts of the family, with money they so rarely have, so I've been told. You would do better there to set your cap at his older brother. He's a viscount, I believe, with a small estate in Hampshire."

Another dimple showed. "But Louis is so much more hand-some than his older brother. With whom I also danced, of course."

Thinking of Captain Aubrey again, Serafina frowned once more. "Looks don't mean a thing. It is steadfastness you need, and reliability of finances. I thought both those young men a little on the boisterous side—perhaps too young to be considered suitable husband material." She smiled. "We have to remember that young men take much longer to achieve sensible adulthood than we women." Not that Letty had reached that stage herself yet. Not by a long chalk.

Letty waved a dismissive hand. "I have the whole Season to find myself a husband. I know I said I would accept the first man who offered for me, but I've changed my mind. I would rather not settle for one particular gentleman too soon. Now I've been to one ball, and I know what they're like, I want to have as much fun as possible before I tie myself down to anyone. It's such fun having a crowd of men clamoring around me for the next dance or to fetch me a glass of lemonade or to fan me."

Serafina's heart sank. This did not bode well. How very like Letty, the girl who'd indulged in a romantic tryst with a lowly groom, to take to London society in this wholehearted manner. Thoughts of seeing her safely married off retreated. This was not going to be as easy as she'd hoped.

THE FIRST CALLER arrived in the early afternoon, and he was not, after all, a caller for Letty.

Araminta had ordained that she, Letty and Serafina should occupy the small parlor, maintaining an image of industry for when the expected gentlemen callers for Letty should arrive. Consequently, Serafina was employed in doing some mending, while Araminta and Letty held pretty embroidery on their laps, although neither of them was much good at it, and the bulk of the neat work had already been done by Serafina. But it looked good, Araminta said. Ogden had retired to the library, now with a fire lit in the hearth, 'leaving you ladies to yourselves'.

Joseph, the new young footman Ogden had taken on, who had to also serve as butler, as Ogden said hiring a butler for so short a time was an unnecessary expense, brought the first caller to the parlor.

It was Captain Aubrey.

Even more devastatingly handsome in his blue topcoat and

hessian boots, and with his dark hair swept carelessly back from his forehead, he filled the doorway with his presence.

Serafina's heart bounded within the confines of her stays, but she managed to keep her face a calm blank. It wouldn't do to betray her feelings in front of Araminta.

Captain Aubrey swept a bow to that lady. "Captain Aubrey, at your service, Lady Gilbert."

Araminta was looking at him in almost but not quite open mouthed astonishment. No doubt she knew quite well that Letty had not danced with him, and probably she also knew exactly who he was. And who his brother was. She'd made it her business to compile a list of all the Season's eligible men with their titles, or the titles they might inherit, and their monetary worth. The cogs in her brain must be whirling as she turned over the prospects of an earl's younger brother for her daughter. "Please," she said a little faintly. "Do sit down beside my daughter." She'd positioned Letty on a chaise longue with a handy space next to her for ardent suitors. "How very kind of you to call."

Letty was also regarding the captain with an astonished expression, the acquisitive glint in her eyes betraying the fact that she was finding him more than pleasing to look at, despite, or perhaps because of, the sling. It further enhanced his rather swashbuckling appearance.

Captain Aubrey surveyed the room, his gaze coming to rest on Serafina, whose chair was pushed back a little out of the way of the suitors Araminta and Letty had foreseen arriving. A smile lit his face.

Letty's brow furrowed.

Araminta's frown deepened to almost scowl-like proportions.

Serafina's heart nearly burst, and heat crept up her neck to her cheeks, but she kept her face emotionless.

"Miss Gilbert." He bowed to her, a deeper bow than he'd bestowed on her sister-in-law, to whom he now turned. "You mistake my intentions, Lady Gilbert. I am here for Miss Serafina Gilbert, and not Miss Letitia." And he took a seat close to

Serafina.

He must be able to hear her heart hammering.

Araminta's face was a picture of thwarted shock. Serafina experienced a longing to capture that moment forever. Astonishment, anger, jealousy—all flashed across Lady Gilbert's face before she had it under control again. "I had no idea Serafina had made your acquaintance." Her words were frosty cold. Icy. Threatening. Serafina's already upset heart quailed. There'd be trouble over this. For her if not for the captain, who seemed all oblivious to the volcano fulminating on the far side of the fireplace.

"We became quite good friends last night, as neither of us were dancing," Captain Aubrey said, with a smile. "In the course of our conversation, we discovered we share a common interest."

Araminta's pencil-thin brows rose towards her hairline. "Indeed? And what might that be, pray?"

The captain still seemed not to have noticed her frostiness. No, her glacial attitude. He smiled. "Why, our love of antiquities. I promised Miss Gilbert I would call today to escort her, accompanied by her maid, of course, to the British Museum. She tells me she has long desired to explore its many exhibitions."

Letty got her furrowed brow under control, but the flash of her blue eyes betokened clear disfavor that not only was the first caller of the afternoon not for her, but that he was both handsome and eligible and not interested in her. Serafina had been on the receiving end of Letty's jealousies once or twice before, and it had not ended well. "How nice for you to have your own gentleman caller," Letty said, her voice nearly as cold as her mother's. "And to have met someone who shares your odd passion for old bits and bobs. I'm so pleased for you." She did not sound as if this was remotely true. The mean streak, which Serafina hadn't experienced for some time, was clawing its way to the surface at speed.

"The British Museum?" Araminta pronounced the three words as though they were alien to her. Which they probably were.

Captain Aubrey nodded. "It's a wonder of the modern age. I've been there before, of course, but not for some years, as I've been overseas with my regiment. And I've been lucky enough to procure tickets for us. For today. They're quite sought after, I gather."

Araminta's gaze settled on the arm he held in the sling. "I see you have received a wound." Her lip curled. Perhaps she was dismissing anyone with a useless arm as beneath her notice and therefore also beneath appearing on her list of possible sons-in-law.

Itching to be away from Araminta's scorn, Serafina seized her courage in both hands. "May I go, please?"

Araminta's eyes narrowed, hard as a pair of diamonds. She was going to say no, and then everything would be over. She'd probably never see Captain Aubrey again. In fact, she was more than surprised that he'd actually fulfilled his promise to her. All morning she'd been imagining that he wouldn't come, and now here he was. In their parlor. If Araminta now said no, she would have successfully chased away the only person, apart from Letty, with all her drawbacks, she'd ever consider calling a friend. And she'd be back to being alone, because Letty was bound to capture some handsome gentleman of the *ton*, and never return to Milford for another freezing winter.

Captain Aubrey must have suspected the same, because he stepped in before Araminta could reply. Standing up, he reached out and took Serafina's hand. "I promise you I won't keep her out late, Lady Gilbert. The British Museum is somewhere that can be explored over many days, and I hope to have the privilege of escorting Miss Gilbert there more than once, if I can again procure tickets." He smiled, his dark eyes dancing a challenge. "And I can assure you that my intentions are of the most honorable."

Serafina, rising to her feet to stand beside him, had to stifle the impulse to look smug as she caught sight of the new expression on Araminta's face. Pure fury at being bested. "She does not possess her own maid," she snapped, as though this would prevent the excursion.

Letty, perhaps anxious to meet her own callers without Serafina and her beau present, was quick off the mark, though. "That's quite all right, Mama. She can take Roberts. I have no need of her until I have to dress for dinner this evening." She managed a smile. Perhaps her mean streak had been vanquished. "Have a lovely time, Fina." She sounded as though she might mean it.

Araminta's mouth shut in a thin, angry line. Bested, now, by her own daughter as well. Letty was going to be in almost as much trouble as Serafina. But that would be later, and right now, Serafina didn't care. A visit to the British Museum with Captain Aubrey would be worth all the reprimands afterwards.

Captain Aubrey released Serafina's hand and held out his good left arm. "That is settled then. We shall progress to the museum in the company of the redoubtable Roberts." He bowed to Letty. "Thank you for the loan of this sterling escort, Miss Letitia."

Serafina drew in a deep breath, avoiding Araminta's gaze, and slipped her hand into the crook of his arm. "Thank you, Captain Aubrey."

CHAPTER NINE

I N THE CHILLY hallway, Max watched Serafina as she donned a shabby pelisse and bonnet, brought to her by a middle-aged woman whose black outfit gave her a rather austere appearance. This must be the aforementioned Roberts. It dawned on him that the maid was possessed of what appeared to be a newer dress than her charge—no doubt because she received remuneration for her services and Serafina did not. What was this strange feeling of protectiveness that was inching its way over him since he'd encountered her in the summerhouse last night? Most uncharacteristic.

And what sort of household didn't provide a young lady of Serafina's age, who was a member of their family, with a maid of her own? He'd done a little of his own surreptitious research, and had discovered further information about the Gilbert family. More than Maria had been able to tell him last night, anyway. Not that he would have enquired further of her, anyway, as that would only have aroused her hopes for him.

He'd discovered Serafina was the daughter of the previous baronet, and only half-sister to the portly man he'd seen her standing with, and that this was the first time the family had come to Town for the Season. His informant, an older acquaintance he'd known in Spain and whom he'd bumped into at the ball, had told him that the present baronet, Sir Ogden, rarely frequented London and when he did, he stayed at his club as he was renowned for his tight-fistedness. Something Max could have guessed from the appearance of the baronet's sister.

The fellow, an ex-cavalry officer, on being casually questioned, had proved quite forthcoming. "Sir George Gilbert was a friend of my father's. A good sort, but that son of his is nothing like him, I'm afraid to say. I remember meeting him as a boy and thinking he would not make a good lord of the manor at Milford. I pity his tenants."

Max, uninterested in Sir Ogden's unfortunate tenants, had steered his friend towards talking about the family. He seemed quite happy to oblige. "Well, I met that stick of a wife of his when she was a debutante. Must be nearly twenty years ago." He frowned. "All I can say about her is that they're well-matched. And as for their daughter... I suspect she's rather a selfish young woman from what I've seen of her tonight. I'd steer well clear of them if I were you. If that woman gets you in her sights she'll be determined to have you for the girl. You being third in line to an earldom." Although Max itched to enquire about Serafina, he held himself in check, content to have discovered the composition of their household.

However, he hadn't missed the way Lady Gilbert had looked at her niece, as though she were less, even, than one of the servants. One thing he couldn't abide was anyone who treated their servants as though they were lesser mortals. The army had done that for him. And for someone to treat a relative even worse than they treated their staff made the blood rise in his veins. A cold anger he was unused to experiencing coursed through his body, accompanied by an absurd inclination to snatch Serafina away from her family and into safety. An inclination he really ought to curb. Unless...

Serafina pulled on a pair of faded gloves, the fingertips betraying where they'd been carefully darned, and smiled up at him as though her shabby ensemble meant nothing. Her whole face shone with an anticipation that rendered her beautiful. How had he ever made the mistake of thinking her plain? "There. I'm ready."

He held out his arm as the footman opened the front door for them, and Roberts hastened in their wake. Outside, any vestiges of the morning's London fog had cleared, and the afternoon promised to be fair, with even a hint here and there of blue in the sky. Max's spirits rose, and he pushed the anger he felt at Serafina's poor treatment to the back of his mind. Today was for giving her some pure enjoyment. And for relishing her reactions. He couldn't deny to himself that if she were happy, then he would be too. And no, he wasn't about to analyze the reasons for this.

He looked down at her. "I thought we would walk, as the museum can't be above a mile distant, and the day bids to be a good one for late February. I hope that suits you."

Her candid gray eyes met his. "Very much so. I have a fondness for walking and do it often when we are home at Milford House. The countryside in Berkshire is most beautiful."

Probably that sour-faced sister-in-law of hers didn't allow her the luxury of travelling in a carriage. Nor even the lowliest of pony carts. Max was happy to mentally accuse the woman of all sorts of crimes against Serafina. But it was good to be in the company of a girl who liked exercise. He matched his stride to hers, and found she set a good pace.

They walked in silence for a short while, Max watching Serafina as she gazed about herself in wonder at the streets they were passing through, drinking in the vendors on street corners hawking hot chestnuts, gingerbread, matches, pies, and suchlike. Had she not been out in the streets before today? Did her family keep her immured within the house in Great Titchfield Street, at their beck and call?

Perhaps he should tell her a little about where they were going. He cleared his throat. "The British Museum stands in Great Russell Street in what was once called Montagu House." Good heavens, he sounded like a guidebook.

She nodded. "I know. As I already said, I've done my research. I believe a new gallery has been opened there quite recently—the Townley Gallery?"

His turn to nod. "You're well informed. I've heard it houses Charles Townley's excellent collection of classical sculptures. Something I'm anxious to see for myself." Keeping the conversation to what they both hoped to see seemed easiest. He wasn't used to making polite conversation with gently bred young ladies. The mess room or a tent on campaign with his fellow officers was more his cup of tea.

"As am I. But I have to confess that I'm deriving almost as much pleasure just from being out walking along the streets of this great city. I've peered out of the windows, of course, and watched what goes on in Great Titchfield Street, but it's nothing compared with being amongst the throng of people, breathing in the life of the city. I really must thank you for taking pity on me and taking me out, although you must think me a terrible country bumpkin."

Max's heart swelled with something he couldn't identify. "Nonsense. It's my pleasure to be able to initiate you to the wonders of London." And he meant every word of it.

She laughed, a throaty chuckle, rather than the sort of girlish giggle that would have annoyed him. "You can have no concept of the joy I'm feeling to be able to explore these streets. I've grown quite fed up with being inside all the time and, as this is my first ever visit to London, I've been itching to get out and see it for myself. The carriage ride last night to the ball was simply not enough."

How refreshingly honest she was. "Is it that bad at home?" The words were out of his mouth before he could stop himself, and he could have kicked himself for his audacity.

Her brow puckered in a frown. "Please don't take my words to mean I'm ungrateful to my brother and his wife. They took me in when I was an orphan of barely six-years-old, and I'm beholden to them for that. I had no other relations in the world, and they have been most...kind... in providing me with a home all this time. I owe them a great deal."

He noted her hesitation over the right word to use to describe their behavior towards her. "I'm sorry. I shouldn't have implied I thought anything of the sort. It was very impolite of me. I'm sure you're very lucky to have had their care." Did he mean that? No. Of course not. She was anything but lucky to have fallen prey to such heartless people. His dander well and truly up, he could have cheerfully drawn Sir Ogden's cork right now if he'd popped up in front of them. Only one arm or not.

She seemed to accept his words, and a small frown settled between her eyes. "I have not been the easiest of charges for them. My sister-in-law has been very patient with me. And I love my nieces and nephews with all my heart. Being with them and being able to help them gives me great joy."

They walked on a few more steps while Max digested this. That behind her words lurked something unspoken, that he'd suspected from the start, went without doubt. But he wasn't going to get her to admit this, at least not while he remained a stranger.

"I myself have four nieces and nephews," he said, by way of lightening their conversation. "And two step-nephews—at least that's what I suppose one would call them. They're not a lot younger than I am, but are inclined to behave like a pair of schoolboys still. And I think you might have seen my oldest niece, Arabella, at the ball, as she seems to have made a friend of your niece."

"The pretty girl with the lovely green gown?"

"The very one. She and your niece are a well matched pair— the belles of last night's ball. I know Arabella was expecting a number of young gentlemen to call on her today. I was glad to be out of the house before that occurred. I can't bear the niceties of socializing with people I don't much care for." Again, that last just popped out, as though her easy company had provoked him to speak his mind. Had he gone too far in his honesty?

Serafina laughed again. "A wise move, I think. I, too, am not fond of having to make polite conversation with people I don't know. And Letty, my niece, was expecting a similar experience this afternoon. I believe her mama, Lady Gilbert, was a little put out that our first caller was here for me." She'd disguised her own satisfaction well, but he caught a small hint of it in her voice. The petulant expression on young Letitia Gilbert's face at her aunt having beaten her to having the first caller leapt into his head.

"In that case, I'm glad I was the first to call. And it shouldn't be a surprise to Lady Gilbert that gentlemen should wish to call on you."

Color surged up her cheeks, and her grip on his arm stiffened for a moment. "It is very kind of you to say so, Captain Aubrey, but I fear Lady Gilbert is correct. I'm not here in London expecting any kind of romantic interest. I'm here merely to assist Letty and assure myself that she makes no mistakes. My future lies at Milford, caring for my nieces and nephews, and eventually, I hope, for their children. I believe I shall live my life out in deepest Berkshire."

He smiled, deciding to ignore her disclaimer of not wishing to garner romantic interest. "Is Miss Letitia likely to make a mistake, in your opinion?"

She pursed her lips. Was she hiding something? "Letty is very young and inexperienced, and a little willful and unwise." She certainly sounded as though she were choosing her words with care. "She sometimes has been known to make the wrong decision. I don't intend to allow her to choose a potential husband who will not suit her."

The urge to cover her hand with his useless right one swept over him, an urge he'd never experienced before. Impossible, despite the longing. Instead, he squeezed her hand with his elbow. "And you consider yourself equipped to guide her?"

She peeped up at him, her gray eyes sharp. "I am no fool, Captain Aubrey, despite my lack of experience. But I am a full five years older than Letty, and I like to think with more calm commonsense than she will ever have. Fortunately, she has always looked to me for guidance, and I trust she will continue to do so in this matter. Her mother is keen for Letty to secure a husband with a title and money, whereas Letty and I have agreed that he must above all be kind—and also have at least *some* money. A title is immaterial to us. We have made a pact."

He smiled, not at all sure this was going to be the success she anticipated. "A good idea. If it works. You seem so sensible, that I myself would value your assistance with Arabella. Her mother, whom I love dearly as a sister, has far less commonsense than you appear to possess. Although the fact that my own mother, the redoubtable dowager, has taken it upon herself to join us in Town is a comfort to me."

They'd nearly reached the gates into the museum, and her footsteps slowed. Max looked down at her, a little puzzled. "Is there something amiss?"

She shook her head, letting her breath out on a sudden huff, as though she'd been holding it in. "Nothing at all. I'm just so excited that I'm about to enter a place I've longed to see. At last. I can't tell you enough how much this pleases me."

Nothing can rival causing someone else pure pleasure, and Max was not immune to the sense of satisfaction that crept over him at the sight of her face, shining with anticipation in the pale morning sun. As before, he was struck by how beautiful her happiness had rendered her. His heart, so long unused, had occasion to soar. He swallowed. Better not let her see the effect she was having on him, although, as he had to marry someone, why not a girl like this one? He shook himself. He mustn't confuse the pity he was feeling for her circumstances with anything else. And besides, surely a young woman as sensible as she so obviously was would not want to ally herself with a man such as he was. Disabled by having only one arm of any use. He cleared his throat. "Is there anything in particular you would like to see first?"

She nodded with determination. "I should very much like to see the famous Rosetta Stone—from that same city in Egypt you told me you besieged. I believe it's on display in the Townley Gallery amongst the other Egyptian antiquities the museum now possesses. That would be my dream come true. I've read everything I could find about it."

He nodded, amused by her description of seeing an old, inscribed stone as being her dream come true. "I believe you're correct in your assumption. But first we should look at the main part of the museum. The Townley Gallery is in a new wing to the rear."

With her hand holding firmly to his arm, he led her through the gates into the museum's spacious courtyard. At the far side, a wide flight of stone steps rose to the enormous front doors of the main building.

Serafina caught her breath as they stepped out of the shelter of the splendid gatehouse. Before her lay what remained of the original Montagu House, a vast brick and stone building stretching all the way across the far side of the courtyard. Down either side, lesser buildings ran that perhaps might be accommodation. The house itself, however, rose to four lofty stories, and was something in the way of French in architectural style. She'd never seen anything so big before. It made Milford House, that had belonged to her father and was now her brother's seat, seem tiny.

Beside her, Captain Aubrey paused, an almost proprietorial smile on his handsome face. "I'm pleased to see it lives up to your expectations." She couldn't be certain, but he sounded as though, perhaps, he was enjoying this outing. That anyone, any man, that was, might do so while in her company astounded her. And that the man doing so was the most handsome man she'd ever set eyes on astounded her even further. She still couldn't quite believe she was there with him. A warm sensation that had kindled in her very core tingled out to the extremities of her body. She resisted the impulse to jump for joy. He might have been startled.

Instead, she kept her reply businesslike. "It surpasses them. But what will really impress me will be the contents." In truth, what was really impressing her was coming here with him, with her hand on his arm, feeling the muscles beneath his coat, and with his tall, masculine presence so close. But she wasn't about to tell him that. How embarrassing it would be were he to divine the real reason for her delight. A man such as he could never be interested in such a plain little nonentity as she was.

She let him escort her across the large, square courtyard, where other people were already heading in the same direction as they were. Mostly men, in ones and twos, with very few ladies present. Of course, the British Museum had been founded fifty years ago to enhance learning and was intended for the perusal of scholars. Not many of those to be found amongst the fairer sex. Feeling a little like a pioneer, Serafina matched Max's confident stride, her heart making leaps and bounds within the confines of her stays, and not just at the thought of seeing the Rosetta Stone.

Up the wide stone steps and through the front doors of the main building, and the captain steered her to the right, through an archway. Before her lay the most impressive staircase she'd ever seen, climbing with grace towards the first floor. But it was not the staircase that held her breathless. It was the sight of what stood at the top of the stairs.

Not one, not two, but three giraffes. A family group, perhaps. She recognized the exotic creatures from a book she'd found in Ogden's library, a book that had once belonged to her father. One of eight books in a series, in fact—George Shaw's *General Zoology or Systematic Natural History*. Books she'd devoured with fervor since her childhood, poring over the beautifully executed copper engravings of animals she'd never hoped to see.

She sighed. "I never thought to see a real giraffe in all my life."

Captain Aubrey looked down at her with a far too attractive twinkle in his eye, and for a moment Serafina had a brief insight into why women were wont to swoon when faced with such masculine perfection. "I see your interests extend to the world of nature, and with that I can help you as well. Do you know of the Exeter Change at all?"

She shook her head, a little apologetic and humbled by her own lack of town polish. "I'm afraid I know nothing about London apart from a few details about this museum."

"Then if Lady Gilbert will allow it, I'll take you to see it one day. To see live animals, not stuffed ones. I think you might find it diverting. I haven't been myself since I was a boy, and I've a hankering to see it again."

If Araminta would allow it. That was the question. But wasn't she a woman grown who'd passed her majority? Did Araminta have any right to stop her? Guilt that she was even considering this small rebellion washed over her. They'd not needed to take her in after her father died, but they had. She must be eternally grateful to them for that. And now they'd brought her to London, and she'd met Captain Aubrey. That in itself was something she should appreciate them for, rather than considering how to disobey them.

They were now continuing up the stairs, approaching the little family group of giraffes, that someone, somewhere, had lovingly stuffed. She couldn't help but be impressed by their industry. They were huge. How did anyone go about stuffing something as big as that?

She came to a halt again, staring up at them. "Do they have giraffes at the Exeter Change?"

He smiled, and her heart did another painful leap. "Not as far as I know, as they are so tall and might not fit, but they do have an elephant, I hear. And a zebra and some big cats—at least one lion and a tiger."

Good heavens. Was there no end to the wonders of London? "Then I should very much like to go. If, of course, my sister-in-law can spare me."

That oh so charming smile again, that melted her heart to sticky goo. "Then we shall just have to make sure she does, won't we? Come. Let's go inside the first gallery and see what they have on show."

Feeling like a princess, she let him lead her past the giraffes and through the large doorway into the body of the museum, Roberts still trailing behind them. This was going to be the best day of her life so far.

＊

CHAPTER TEN

T RUE TO HIS promise to Lady Gilbert, Max had Serafina back at the house in Great Titchfield Street before evening fell. They'd spent a joyous two hours viewing the entire contents of the museum with particular attention to the Egyptian antiquities, and he'd been rewarded for his efforts by the enthusiasm with which she'd studied every object in great detail, uttering little cries of excitement at each new revelation. He'd decided to steer well clear of discussing her home situation, and had divulged nothing of his own, as she seemed intent on keeping their conversation confined to things historical.

And now, alas, they were back at her brother's house. However, before they could reach the door, Serafina ground to a halt on the pavement. Not difficult to sense the apprehension coursing through her and guess the reason for the suddenly tightened grip on his arm. She looked up at him out of those beautiful gray eyes that now held a mixture of anguish and apprehension. He could have drowned in those eyes. How had he not noticed how thick and long the eyelashes that framed them were.

Good heavens, he must stop thinking like that immediately. But he couldn't help it. Julian's words, and those of his mother, echoed in his head. They wanted him to marry, in order to secure his inheritance, so what was holding him back? Marriage to a young woman like Miss Gilbert would surely not be difficult. She would be a most interesting companion—unlike those pretty, empty-headed debutantes whose mamas were so keen for them to secure advantageous marriages. And as for her, might she be grateful for being rescued from her present situation? Although… even if he cared for her, what sort of basis for marriage was mere gratefulness on one side? He brought himself up short. No, she could never care for a man who might just as well have only one arm, and not once had she bestowed anything but friendly interest on him. In short, she clearly did not find him an attractive proposition.

He had to clear his throat before he could speak. "Is there anything amiss?"

Her small white teeth drew her bottom lip in and a slight frown marred her pale brow. "I confess to being just a little uneasy about returning home after such a wonderful afternoon…" She gave an almost dismissive shrug, as though to belittle her feelings. "If I'm to be honest with you, I'd have to admit that I'm loathe to have this afternoon end, for it's truly been one of the best I've ever spent."

Discussing the possibility of someone one day using the Rosetta Stone to decipher hieroglyphics, smiling together at the sight of how the sarcophagus of the pharaoh Nectanebo had been turned into a bath, complete with drain holes, exclaiming over the mummies on display, wrapped in their bandage shrouds; those were the things which had held her rapt. Not his company, Max was even more certain now than he had been before.

He felt heat warm his cheeks. This admission, much as he'd like it to be for a quite different reason, must surely be due to where he'd taken her and what she'd seen. His acute awareness of his own disability resurfaced, as it was wont to do at inopportune moments. A woman as fiercely intelligent and sweet natured as Miss Gilbert wasn't about to throw herself away on a man with only one good arm. But he could be of assistance to her. "You have no need to worry. I shall be coming in with you. Of course."

She blinked. Were those tears forming on her lashes? "Thank you. That will make me feel more confident. You're very kind."

Kindness be damned. To his surprise he found he didn't want the afternoon to end, nor to wish her goodbye. Coming inside would put off that moment a little longer. How had discussing long dead Egyptians made him feel so protective towards her? Was it perhaps because she was the first woman who'd shown him any interest, even though it had been entirely directed at where he'd taken her? Was he that needy?

He pushed his own feelings out of his head, albeit with some difficulty, and focused instead on hers.

Once more he found himself wondering what kind of a home her brother had given her that she should feel such apprehension after a perfectly acceptable outing with a gentleman who, did she but know it, found her a most interesting companion. He balked at using the word 'attractive' with all its connotations, even in his head, and even though, in his opinion, she undeniably was. Despite her having made it obvious she didn't see herself in that way. That they could continue as friends was suddenly the most important thing in the world to him.

"Come. Let us brave your lion's den."

A small smile formed. "It would be best if you didn't refer to my brother's house in that way in front of him."

He chuckled. "Have no fear. I shall be the soul of discretion."

The family were still assembled in the drawing room, although this time accompanied by the patriarch, Sir Ogden, whom so far Max had only observed from afar. They presented a no doubt contrived tableau when the footman opened the door to usher Max and Serafina inside.

Sir Ogden was seated closest to the fire, the newspaper he'd been reading lowered to his lap, and an expression of stern disapproval on his flushed and fleshy face. Lady Gilbert sat opposite him, her upright chair drawn back from the heat as though she abhorred it, a piece of embroidery lying unheeded in her lap. Her cold eyes fixed with accusation on Serafina just for an instant as though she were something she'd trodden in by mistake and needed to wipe off the sole of her shoe. And, by contrast, there was the pretty niece, Letty, who'd stopped her piano playing in the middle of a piece to fix Max and her youthful aunt with a decidedly resentful stare. Altogether a rather forbidding reception party. Perhaps no one else had come to call that afternoon and Miss Letitia was seething with jealousy. Max found himself hoping so.

He made a careful bow, encompassing the room. "Good evening, once again. I hope I haven't incommoded you by keeping Miss Gilbert out too long. I believe the clock in the hall was just striking five as we entered the house."

Sir Ogden rose to his feet, puffing out his chest like a turkey-cock, and returned Max's bow. "Not at all, not at all. Five is a most reasonable hour to return. Most reasonable. So kind of you to have offered to escort my sister to..."

"The British Museum," Max said.

"Quite so, quite so." Sir Ogden rumbled. "Somewhere I my-self should visit, I'm sure. Very enlightening, so I hear." He gave a short guffaw at laughter, but whether it was at the idea of going somewhere like that himself, or for some other reason, was not evident.

His gaze slid past Max and flicked sharply over Serafina for a moment before returning to study Max a little further. "Delighted to make your acquaintance, Captain Aubrey." He held out his hand. His right hand.

Whether it was deliberate or not, Max couldn't be sure. He took it in his left hand, as he'd been having to do for some time now, and they shook, a little awkwardly. "Sir Ogden." The color darkening on Sir Ogden's cheeks implied he'd suddenly realized the error of his actions.

He cleared his throat. "Won't you take a seat, Captain? My wife and I would very much like to further our acquaintance with you. You are the brother of the Earl of Westbury, I gather. My wife is like an encyclopedia of knowledge regarding the *ton*. She knows who absolutely everyone is related to."

Lady Gilbert, having shot her husband a quelling glare, bestowed her most ingratiating smile upon Max. "Indeed, it would please me to invite you to take some tea with us. Serafina can go and organize that. Do, pray, sit down near the fire." Without waiting for a reply, she waved a hand at Letty. "Whatever have you stopped playing for, child? Continue. I'm sure Captain Aubrey would be charmed to hear such a skillful rendition."

Max turned to Serafina. "Please don't organize tea on my account, Miss Gilbert. I'm afraid I'm unable to stay, as my sister-in-law will be expecting me for dinner in Cavendish Square." He turned back to Lady Gilbert. "I just wanted to make sure Miss Gilbert arrived home safely, and that you were in no way put out by the length of time I've kept her out." He beamed around at them, keeping his expression guileless and friendly, which took a Herculean effort. "I would very much like to return, if that is convenient, and take her out again. She is a most rewarding companion with all her knowledge of historical facts."

There, get out of that if you can.

Oh, how hard Lady Gilbert was struggling to keep her expression affable. Sir Ogden, his face even redder than before, seemed at a loss what to say. Only young Letty, who had played just a few jumbled notes on her piano, seemed at ease. She swung around on her piano stool, her wide blue eyes, which anyone could have taken as guileless and sweet, instead diamond hard. "How lovely for you, Fina. Someone who shares your passion for history." The spite behind those words almost made him take a step backwards.

Her mother shot her a look that would have quelled someone with more sensitivity, something young Letty seemed devoid of.

Bypassing Lady Gilbert, who would be trawling for any excuse to say no, Max directed his most commanding stare at Sir Ogden. "I was thinking perhaps in two days' time—this Thursday, if you have no engagements that day which involve Miss Gilbert?"

"I wanted Serafina to come shopping with me on Thursday," Letty put in, her tone plaintive, before her mother shot her another quelling glare. This time it worked.

Max could almost see the calculations going on in Lady Gilbert's head. Was she thinking she could entrap him into taking an interest in her own daughter? She was the sort who would never imagine how he could prefer Serafina over Letty. She certainly knew who he was. Or was this just an attempt to court an association she might deem useful with his family?

Max raised his eyebrows at Sir Ogden, waiting for a reply.

The man's eyes slid sideways towards his wife.

"If the weather is suitable, I would very much like to take Miss Gilbert out in my carriage to Hyde Park," Max said, drawing his prey's attention back again.

Sir Ogden squirmed, but he was trapped. "That would be most kind of you. I'm sure my sister would be honored to accompany you to the Park on Thursday afternoon."

Hiding his satisfaction at having extracted such a promise, Max made the family an overly flamboyant bow, which they would probably have taken at face value. "Then I'm afraid I must leave you." He turned to Serafina. "But I shall be back on Thursday in the early afternoon." He took her hand, and, before she could draw it back, planted a firm kiss on it. "Until then, adieu." Before anyone could suggest a reason to cancel this arrangement, he swung on his heel and, opening the door for himself, departed.

"LETTY, GO UPSTAIRS. Now." Araminta directed a fierce stare at her daughter, who, for once, must have read it correctly. Closing the piano, she rose from her stool and, with a glare aimed at Serafina, stalked out of the drawing room.

Serafina, who'd remained standing near the door after Captain Aubrey's departure, drew in a deep, fortifying breath and straightened her spine. She didn't need a man to stand up for her. She could do it herself, although the years of mistreatment had left an indelible scar on her psyche.

The door closed behind Letty with a bang that brought a

frown to her mother's brow. Letty was a girl who liked people to notice her actions, especially when in a huff.

Silence reigned. Both Ogden and her sister-in-law fixed disapproving gazes on Serafina.

"I, for one, would like to know what is going on here," Araminta snapped, her cold eyes running up and down Serafina's dowdy clothing as though she were looking for signs of incipient depravity. "You have clearly been putting yourself forward like a hussy when you should not have been."

Serafina bit back the response she would have liked to have made. Whatever happened, she mustn't anger Araminta any further or she would be bound to find a way to scotch Max's visit on Thursday. She couldn't bear it if that were to happen. She so rarely rode in any carriage, the thought of taking the air in Hyde Park itself, with him in his private vehicle, had already proved intoxicating. She schooled her face into equanimity. She'd learned from painful experience that the more Araminta thought she might enjoy something, the more she would try to prevent it. Trying to appear contrite, she hung her head, clasping her hands in front of her until the knuckles whitened.

"Well?" Araminta continued. "What do you have to say for yourself? How have you had the temerity to make the acquaintance of an earl's brother when you were supposed to only be here to care for Letty?"

The truth would not do. The very thought of admitting to Ogden and Araminta that she'd spent nearly an hour out in that summerhouse with Captain Aubrey, completely unchaperoned, made her stomach curdle. They'd lock her up at Milford and never let her out again, or worse, they might try and blackmail poor Captain Aubrey into marriage, and that would be too humiliating for words. But what to say instead of the truth? She didn't like to lie, and prided herself on not doing so, but here, if ever there was one, was a moment where a lie would be expedient.

She kept her voice subdued. "We met at the ball yesterday.

He was kind enough to speak to me, and we discovered we had a mutual liking for Egyptology." There. That was no lie. No need to specify exactly where they'd met. If further questions followed she would have to steel herself and make something believable up. The last thing she wanted was Araminta finding out how she'd really met him. She'd put a twist on it that would forever render it unpleasant and sordid in her head.

Araminta, however, had not given up. When she seized upon something that irked her, she could be like one of the grooms' terriers with a rat, shaking it until it was long dead. "I told you specifically not to put yourself forward last night. You were there only to act as a chaperone to Letitia, and nothing else. Your place was in the shadows, behind me, not out chattering to eligible young men who might otherwise be interested in Letitia."

So that was it. Araminta thought Captain Aubrey, as the brother of an earl, should have been focusing his attentions on Letty. An enormous urge arose to tell her sister-in-law that a girl like Letty, much as Serafina loved her, was not the sort to attract Captain Aubrey, but she resisted. Mainly due to her acute awareness that she was also not the sort of girl to attract so handsome a man. "I'm sorry, Araminta. I don't know what I was thinking of. I met him when I went to fetch you a glass of lemonade." That too was true. How easily this subterfuge was coming to her. And the amazing thing was that she didn't feel at all guilty about it. Araminta did not deserve the truth.

Araminta turned to Ogden. "I don't understand what some-one as eligible as Captain Aubrey could see in your sister. Even with his arm like that, he could have the choice of any pretty, well-connected girl this Season. He may be only a second son, but I believe he stands to inherit a sizeable fortune of his own and a large house in Wiltshire when he turns thirty."

Why did Araminta always do this? Talking about her as if she wasn't present and didn't matter. Serafina itched to point out that she was standing there while she was being discussed and at nearly three and twenty should have some input into the conversation. Common sense, a skill she'd learned early on in the company of her brother's wife, kept her silent.

"Do you think he means to offer for her?" Ogden asked, his tone implying the surprise that would be if the captain did, and also a hint of smug satisfaction at the thought of allying his family with that of an earl.

Araminta looked back at Serafina, her lip curling. "Look at her, Ogden. Of course he doesn't. He must feel sorry for her as she has no hope of securing an offer of any kind. Who would take a girl as plain as her off our hands? Perhaps some elderly nabob in need of someone to care for his motherless children. Not a man as handsome, well-bred and rich as Captain Aubrey, you can be certain." She gave a little, scornful laugh. "No, you can be sure he's calling on her for a quite different reason. Pity, perhaps for a bet, or for a jest with his friends." She sneered. "Out to make a fool out of her and his give his friends amusement."

Serafina's blood chilled as Araminta's words sank in, and for a moment her knees wobbled, but she stayed valiantly upright.

Of course. Why hadn't this occurred to her before? That was it. Captain Aubrey must have called on her for one of the terrible reasons Araminta had just suggested. She'd been a fool to even give credence to the tiniest hope that he might like her. She only needed to look in a mirror to know the reason why he wouldn't have done it for that sort of a reason. She'd never have Letty's sweet good looks nor petite vulnerability. And she'd talked only of history, which might well have made him think her nothing but a boring bluestocking. For a short while this afternoon, she'd been foolish enough to think he might be interested in what she had to say, but it must all have been for show. Kindness on his part perhaps. Or maybe he'd gone back to his friends now and was laughing with them about her.

She must not cry. She could feel the tears waiting to be shed and dug her nails into her flesh where her hands were clasped in front of her. She must not give Araminta the pleasure of seeing how upset she was.

Ogden laughed as well, every bit as scornfully as his wife. "You have it right, my dear, I'm sure. My plain little sister is destined to remain at Milford House an old maid, as I've always feared. She'll be the aged aunt to our children's children all her life."

This was so close to how she'd described herself to Max that Serafina struggled to control her breathing as a tear slid unbidden down her cheek.

Araminta waved a dismissive hand without bothering to look at her. "You may go, Serafina, and see if Letty needs your help in changing for dinner. She'll need you to do her hair. And be warned, she's not happy that you usurped her position with such an eligible gentleman. You will need to apologize to her."

Serafina turned on the spot, reaching blindly for the door as more tears followed the first down her cheeks, unseen by Araminta. Outside in the hall, thankfully empty of servants, she leaned against the wall, heaving in great breaths and fighting off the urge to break down and sob. She had to keep herself under rigid control, as she'd always done. She couldn't let anyone, especially not Letty who would be bound to tell her mother, know how much she hurt inside.

For a brief moment she'd glimpsed the way her life could be. She'd spent such a wonderful afternoon with Captain Aubrey, a recipient of his gentle charm, his interest, his apparent kindness. But he was a gentleman, and all of that came naturally to him. None of it had betokened any kind of interest in her as anything more than someone with whom to share the treasures of the British Museum. He hadn't seen her as a woman, but merely as someone who was lonely and who happened to like Egyptology. She could just as well have been a child he felt sorry for, or an elderly dowager, or even a male friend yet to visit the museum. He hadn't seen her in the way she'd seen him at all.

She wiped her eyes on the long sleeve of her gown. She'd better go upstairs and help Letty or she'd be in even more trouble.

CHAPTER ELEVEN

L ETTY WAS ALREADY dressed in the gown she'd chosen for dinner that evening when Serafina reached their room. She'd taken a few extra minutes outside on the landing to compose herself and wipe away the vestiges of her tears, not wanting Letty to be able to see just how upset she was.

But her eyes must have still been red, because Letty shot her a sharply penetrating look and waved a dismissive hand at her maid. "You may go, Roberts. Fina and I will dress each other."

Roberts, poker-faced and giving nothing away, slipped out of the room. She'd been a housemaid for years before being promoted to lady's maid and suffered no illusions about the way Lady Gilbert treated Serafina, who'd been the recipient on more than one occasion of her commiserating glances.

The moment they were alone, Letty turned to Serafina, ignoring her obvious distress and with a somewhat triumphant expression on her face that deprived it of some of its prettiness. She probably needed to look in a mirror when she was feeling this vindictive. The old adage about not pulling faces in case the wind changed and you got stuck like that came to mind. "You're probably itching to ask me how many gentlemen callers I had, I assume. Well, it was a lot more than your measly one, and one of them was a viscount. So much better than just the brother of an earl. Although I believe he's somehow related to Captain Aubrey, or so Mama informed me after he'd left. How handy it is that she knows who everyone is related to and what they're worth."

Serafina, who was used to her own feelings being disregarded, fixed an interested expression on her face. Sometimes Letty's self-centered personality grated, but this time she was glad to have the attention switched away from herself. "Of course I am. Was it great fun for you, and were they all doting on you?"

Letty's expression softened now she was assured she had Serafina's unwavering attention. "It was quite wonderful. You'll never guess how many young men called on me. No, don't even try. I was never more astonished to receive no less than *eight* callers, for I suspected that even though they'd expressed the desire to call, most of them would have forgotten by the time they rose this morning."

She flicked her auburn curls with a suspicious air of nonchalance. "Although how they could forget me, I have no idea. Lord Simon Rosebery arrived first. He's very handsome in a washed out sort of way as he's so fair-haired. No sooner had he taken a seat then he was followed by the Honorable Matthew Lytton, whom I'd taken to be something of a bore and not at all interested in me when we danced at the ball. Even though he has the most delightful dark curls. For some reason, all he wanted to do was talk about farming. I have no idea why someone like him would even be remotely interested in things like plows and… and seed drills, I think he called them." She giggled and shrugged. "I can only suppose he must have thought it a subject in which I was interested."

She dimpled and warm color rose to her cheeks. "Luckily Rosebery and I didn't have to suffer being told about the latest developments in agriculture for too long because two more gentlemen arrived." The offhand way in which she said this seemed at odds with her previous words.

Serafina's ears pricked at the change in Letty's tone. "And who were they?" she asked, observing Letty's somewhat shifty gaze.

"Lord Grey and his brother." She paused. "I was never happier to be interrupted than by their arrival."

Of course, Lord Grey's brother was the one she'd intimated she'd found attractive. More needed to be discovered about this young man.

"You said eight. Who else called?"

"Two army officers, in their splendid regimentals, as well as a slightly older gentleman who Mama said was more desirable as he's a cit which means he's made his money in trade but is horrendously rich, so although he doesn't have the breeding, I encouraged him, as Mama instructed."

"Goodness." Serafina schooled her face into an expression that conveyed how impressed she knew she ought to be, even though she was quailing inside. Despite Letty's increasing high-handedness and selfishness, Serafina remained very fond of her oldest niece. These young men would all require research to ascertain whether they would make Letty happy if they were to offer marriage. Araminta, whose sole measure for suitability was by title or wealth, could not be relied upon to do that.

"Do you favor any of them?" Serafina enquired, as that was who she needed to begin with.

Letty gave a tinkling little laugh. "Last night I thought it was Lord Grey's brother I preferred, but today, after seeing them all again, I think I am leaning towards preferring Mr. Oliver Talbot, the cit. After all, Louis Herbert is just a younger brother, and only of a mere viscount. Younger brothers are not at all desirable. Mama says. And Mr. Talbot is so very rich."

Serafina pursed her lips, ignoring the dig at Captain Aubrey's status as a younger brother. "I should like to meet this Mr. Talbot then, before you decide to encourage his suit. We need to know a bit more about him. Whether he would be a kind husband to you, should he make an offer and you accept."

Letty, who before they'd left Milford had been sweetly ame-nable to Serafina's assistance in choosing the right husband, gave a rebellious toss of her auburn curls. "Oh pooh to that. You have no experience whatsoever where men are concerned, Fina. Mama does, and she very much likes Mr. Talbot."

"You said he was older. How much older than the other young men is he, then?"

Letty pouted as though she might be hiding something. "A few years." This emerged as an unwilling mutter.

Serafina was not to be put off. "How many is a few?"

Now Letty scowled. "I suppose perhaps twenty…"

Serafina's mouth fell open. "He's twenty years older than your other callers? Is he older than your papa? I didn't see you dance with anyone that age last night."

Letty scowled. "Well I did, straight after supper. I don't know where you'd got to, but you weren't there to stop me. And I'm glad you didn't, because he was so nice to me. So charming. He said I was the prettiest girl at the ball." She giggled. "In fact all of them told me that, I think, so I know it to be true."

Serafina opened her mouth to speak, but then closed it again. Maybe this was the right move for Letty. A mature man could be what was needed to keep her in check, and surely someone that age would dote on a girl as young and pretty as she was. Plus he'd be unlikely to stray. Although, of course, he might have no intention of offering for her at all. She dismissed that final thought—a man of mature years would surely not be calling on a pretty debutante just to flirt. He would have marriage in mind.

"And you were indeed the prettiest girl at the ball," Serafina said, as this was a sure way to mollify the vain Letty. "But we mustn't count our chickens, my love. That was but the first ball you've been to. Best not to jump at the first man who catches your eye."

Letty brightened. "You always say the right things, darling Fina. And you're quite right about that. I shall encourage Mr. Talbot, of course, but if he makes an offer, I'll think of some way to delay my reply. Who knows what might be waiting for me at the next ball, or the one after that." She patted her curls again. "With my looks, Mama says, I would be able to snare a prince, were there one of the right age available."

Serafina nodded, heartily relieved that the king's sons were all too old. "And your mama is quite right." At least this was taking her mind off what Araminta had said to her. Letty could be such a child at times, and her selfishness and vanity could be laid entirely at the door of her parents. Trying to iron these disastrous traits out of her was like banging your head against the proverbial brick wall. Perhaps what she needed was an older man who could persuade her into once more becoming the pleasant girl she'd been a few short years ago.

Serafina stalwartly refused to acknowledge the uncomfortable fact that all of the Gilbert children treated her in the same way— as someone not quite a servant but also not quite a member of the family, whom they could order about at their will. Following the lead shown to them by their parents, of course. Shunned by Araminta and Ogden and left to grow up uncared for, Serafina had found in the five Gilbert children, especially Letty, someone to lavish her love on, ignoring their faults. And in their way, they all loved her back.

Letty appeared sufficiently satisfied by her responses to turn her attention to Serafina. "Now, you'd better hurry up and change into your own gown for dinner," she said, nodding to where Roberts had laid out a plain brown dress on Serafina's bed. "And you can tell me about your afternoon with the Earl of Westbury's younger brother."

As she slipped out of her day gown, Serafina bit back a smile at Letty's deliberate classification of Captain Aubrey as a mere younger brother.

"We'd better hurry," Letty said. "Or Mama will be angry with us. You can tell me about your afternoon while you change. I want to know everything."

But what to tell her? Araminta had expertly changed the way Serafina now saw her afternoon's excursion with her hateful words, and no doubt Letty didn't really want to hear that it had been the best day of Serafina's life. Nor did Serafina want to tell her that. The shine had gone off the day, and she almost couldn't bring herself to talk about it.

But Letty was a determined girl, possibly due to her inveterate selfishness and blindness to anyone else's feelings. As Serafina pulled on her gown for the evening, she continued where she'd left off. "Did he really take you to a stuffy old museum?" Her tone implied that she didn't think this a suitable location for a visit with a gentleman. Letty was not an intellectual by anyone's standards. The only reading she did was of romantic novels that had filled her head with fanciful notions of true love that were probably far from the truth of reality. She'd recounted a few of the intricate plots to Serafina during some of the long cold nights at Milford. So Serafina was sufficiently au fait with the way her niece's brain worked.

She turned so Letty could fasten the back of her dress. "Of course he did. That was the whole point of the outing. He knew I wanted to go there."

Letty snorted with badly disguised disgust as she did up the buttons. "What a strange thing to want to do. In fact, you are such a strange thing yourself, it's a wonder any man would want to call on you and take you out anywhere. If a man were to offer to take me to a museum, I would immediately cross him off my list of eligible suitors."

She tutted over the gown. "I sometimes wish we could get you some nicer gowns to wear, you know. Goodness knows what Captain Aubrey thinks when he sees you in these dowdy things." She stepped back. "Do you want me to try and do your hair or shall we just leave it like that?"

Serafina patted some stray curls back into place and peered into their dressing table mirror. "I think it will do like that. No one will notice me anyway."

Letty giggled. "You're quite right. Your hair hardly matters, does it?" She seemed to recall her previous question. "And as the captain did indeed take you there, was the museum as good as you'd hoped it would be? Although I'm sure I would be bored to tears if I'd had to go."

Serafina nodded as she slipped her stockinged feet into a pair of worn slippers, suddenly glad to be able to talk even just a little bit about her afternoon, even though she knew Letty wasn't really interested. "It was every bit as fascinating as I'd imagined. We went all over, but the best bit was the gallery with all the Egyptian antiquities in it. I saw the Rosetta Stone. Can you imagine? Something that old—over two thousand years old—and I saw it. Touched it. Put my fingers on the stone that real Egyptian hands had carved their language onto."

Letty was unimpressed. "A stone? Really?"

Serafina nodded with vigor, finding it easier to talk about what she'd seen than to dwell on the reason for the outing. "It's an important find. Someone French discovered it at a place called Rosetta, but after a treaty of some kind they had to hand it over to us, and we brought it back here to display in the museum." She herded Letty to their shared dressing table. "Sit down and let me do your hair. Time is pressing on, and your mama is bound to notice if your hair looks messy, unlike mine."

Letty sat down in front of the mirror, for once seeming interested. "Why is a stone so important?"

Serafina began to pin up her curls. "Because it has three sorts of writing on it. It has demotic script, which is an old Egyptian way of writing, Hieroglyphs which are symbols, like little pictures, rather than writing, and Greek on it. Scholars think that one day they'll be able to work out how to read the Hieroglyphs thanks to this stone. Because they already know how to read the Greek bit of it and they think all three bits say the same thing but in different languages."

Letty shrugged her slender shoulders. "Whatever do they want to do that for? It's bad enough having to read in English without people thinking of new ways to read and write." She was not a great scholar herself, nor even a mediocre one, and had no real mastery of the one her governess had tried to teach her – French. She twisted on her stool. "But tell me about Captain Aubrey. Hurry, before we have to go down to dinner."

Was this interest more because Letty knew Louis Herbert was related to the captain? Probably. However, she couldn't resist the invitation to talk about him. Just a little.

She got the last curl secured. "There, I think your hair will do. There's not much to tell about Captain Aubrey. He was most kind and polite."

Letty jumped up. "Fina, that's not good enough. Do you like him is what I want to know." Clearly Serafina had been forgiven, for the moment, for having upstaged Letty by receiving the day's first caller.

Serafina's legs suddenly gave way. Luckily she was near enough to the stool Letty had just vacated to land on it. She put her hands up to cover her face. "I liked him very much."

Letty pulled her hands away, her face for once devoid of any hint of jealousy. "But that's wonderful. If you can find someone as well as me, neither of us need ever return to Milford House and suffer another winter of chilblains. But most importantly, do you think he likes you?"

That was the question. Serafina bit her bottom lip. What to say? "I don't know. I thought he liked my company. He was so solicitous and kind, and a most pleasant companion. He has a great deal of interesting knowledge..."

Letty stamped a foot in impatience, her hands on her hips. "Fina, stop hedging. Tell me if you think he liked you?"

Serafina raised sorrowful eyes to meet hers, remembering Araminta's words. "I did think that perhaps he did, but now I've changed my mind. I fear that perhaps he was just being nice to me out of kindness." She couldn't mention Araminta's other suggestion—that he'd taken her out for a bet with his friends. She gestured at herself with a resigned hand. "Look at me. Why would any man be interested in me, looking like this?"

Letty, careless of her coiffured hair, threw her arms around Serafina and hugged her tight, reminding Serafina of the impulsive child she used to know. "Because men are not all the idiots we think they are. Because your goodness and kindness shines out of you, dearest Fina. That is why he would like you. Because you're the best person I know."

Serafina took an unsteady breath, moved by the reappearance of her childhood friend. "Careful, Letty, or you're going to make me cry. But thank you for saying that."

Letty released her hold but didn't step back. "If your captain has the sense he was born with, as our old nurse used to say, then he'll have seen beyond these drab gowns Mama makes you wear. And he doesn't look like an idiot to me." She planted a kiss on Serafina's cheek. "Now, come on. We'd better hurry or we'll be in trouble for keeping dinner waiting."

She caught Serafina's hand and pulled her towards the door.

Serafina, her confidence rising, went with her.

CHAPTER TWELVE

MAX WALKED THE short distance between Great Titchfield Street and Cavendish Square in just a few short minutes. Lamplighters were already out, working fast to dispel the gathering gloom, but the streets were no less busy. The enticing aroma of hot chestnuts induced him to stop where a man was selling them and buy himself a few, wrapped in a twist of old newspaper. He'd eaten nothing at noon and his stomach was protesting at his neglect.

As a soldier, he'd often had to eat while on the move, wherever he'd come across available food. Uncaring of what anyone might think at seeing a gentleman eating on the street, he shelled them quickly as he walked, relishing their sweet flavor. Just for a moment, he was back in Portugal with his men again, before Vimeiro, and the world was the right way up.

He pushed the memory away, and his thoughts returned unbidden to Serafina. Had she ever tasted the delights of street food? Most likely not, with the way she was kept under such close lock and key by her family. Next time, he'd initiate her. Next time... The expression on Lady Gilbert's face swam like an unwelcome specter into his head, and he saw again the way she'd looked at Serafina as though she were the lowest of the low. His blood heated with indignation. He could take Serafina away from that life, show her something more existed, keep her safe. Marry her.

What?

His thoughts so shocked him, he ground to a halt, and the man who'd been walking behind bumped into him. Words of apology wafted into the night air from both sides, but Max's thoughts were still on Serafina. What had he just thought? Were they not the musings of someone with the intention of... fulfilling his brother and mother's wishes?

People flowed past him like the water of a river does around a rock. If he had to marry someone in order to please his brother and inherit his estate, which, since his wound, he couldn't have cared less about, then why not a girl as out of the ordinary as Miss Serafina Gilbert? A girl who could talk of things other than the gown she was wearing or the tittle-tattle of the *ton* and the current *on dits*. A girl who wouldn't bore him within a few weeks of their marriage. But he was fooling himself. How could a girl like her ever see him in the light of a suitor? Could any girl, in fact? With this arm? Of course not. He was just dreaming of something that could never happen. She wasn't interested in him or what he could or couldn't offer, and she'd made that very clear. She'd accepted his invitation merely to satisfy her curiosity about the contents of a museum she'd longed to visit. Her conversation had been proof of that, having been entirely about the exhibits they'd seen. Her enthusiasm had been for the long dead Egyptians, not for him.

Damnit. How had he allowed his head to be overruled in this way? Hadn't he vowed after the condition of his arm had been diagnosed never to marry, nor even to take any interest in a woman again? Despite the promise Julian had coerced out of him. And yet, here he was, in Town for only a few days, and at the very first ball he'd escorted the Aubrey ladies to he was considering the first woman he'd had occasion to converse with as a possible wife. Of course, he'd told his mother and Julian that he'd offer for the first woman who wasn't a fool who happened to cross his path, but he hadn't really meant it. Had he? And this one was a woman who so clearly wasn't interested in him as a man, and who no doubt saw him as something less than that, thanks to his arm. Was he that weak willed and foolish? No, she might become his friend, but she would never look at him as a possible husband. Would any woman?

He came back to his senses and started walking again. Ahead, on the eastern side of Cavendish Square, he spotted the front door of his brother's town house. He'd better hurry or he'd be late for dinner. And if he was late, he'd suffer a catechism from both his mother and sister as to where he'd been. And it would come out that he'd taken a young lady out for the afternoon, a fact they'd pounce on like bees on honey.

Having successfully sneaked inside and up the stairs without being spotted by any of his family, he found Watkins, his valet, waiting for him in his bedroom. His evening apparel was already laid out on the bed, and Watkins had a slightly agitated air about him, as though he'd been waiting some time. He probably had. However, as Max's soldier servant, he'd become well acquainted with his master's atrocious timekeeping and was not above administering a reproving stare, or even a few words. On this occasion, he confined himself to merely a pursing of the lips and a slight frown.

Max sighed. "I know, I know. I couldn't help it. The streets were crowded and I could hardly shoulder my way through and send redoubtable matrons flying." He gave Watkins a rueful smile, which was returned with a diminishing of the frown. He was a few years older than Max, and it was easy to tell from his wiry build and the tough, careworn set of his features that he'd until recently been a soldier.

"We'd best make haste, Captain," Watkins said, his reproving tone redolent with the accent of the wilds of Yorkshire where he'd grown up on a small tenant farm. "Her ladyship the dowager informed me we have guests for dinner."

"Guests?" Max raised his eyebrows. Damnit, though. The last thing he wanted was guests. He was not feeling very sociable tonight. Not that he ever felt particularly sociable with people he didn't know.

"I believe Viscount Gray and his brother are in the drawing room," Watkins said, flicking an imaginary speck of dust off Max's shoulder. "Allow me to assist you out of your coat."

After nearly ten years in the army and only a few months out of it, Max resented having to be helped to dress and undress by his valet, but there were some things two hands were essential for, such as knotting a cravat. And buttons.

"Thank you, Watkins. You're right, as usual. I'd better hurry or my mother will reprimand me for being out too late and keeping her waiting. Mothers never seem to think of their sons as anything more than small boys."

"Very true, sir." Watkins, his expression inscrutable, helped Max out of the buff-colored coat he wore during the day. Did the valet possess a mother somewhere, who fussed over him the way the dowager did over Max and Julian? Max had never thought to ask him, mothers not having been a much discussed subject amongst the military. Hard to imagine Watkins with any family at all. He had the air about him of having sprung fully formed into life as first a soldier servant and then a valet.

Max's hand went to his cravat, but in vain. Undoing a cravat was as hard as knotting one with only one hand. Without a word, Watkins came to his aid. He had a subtle way with him that diminished the feeling of helplessness Max hated.

Half an hour later, resplendent in his full evening dress of navy blue tailcoat, over a white shirt and a navy waistcoat, and white silk breeches, stockings and black pumps, Max descended to the drawing room. Where he encountered his mother and sister-in-law's visitors. His two nephews, offspring from her first marriage to the late Viscount Gray, Henry and Louis Herbert, were already ensconced on comfortable seats and in the middle of some racy story of their adventures that was making Arabella, their impressionable half-sister, giggle uproariously and the dowager frown in vain disapproval.

Of course, everyone stopped in their tracks when Max came

in, as all heads turned towards him. Another thing he hated, as whatever their intention, he now always took it to mean they were looking at his bad arm. On occasion it felt as though the arm itself must be about ten times its normal size, and the only thing anyone noticed about him.

"Uncle Max!" Arabella exclaimed. "Look how lucky we are that my brothers have found time to call on us. It feels such an age since we last saw them."

Henry, who'd held the title of Viscount Gray since his father died when he was only six years old, let out a bark of laughter. "Heavens, Bella, but you saw us last night at the ball. Have you quite forgotten?"

Arabella pouted. "But that was at a ball, and, as you're my brothers, you paid me no attention whatsoever. You were far too busy flirting with the other young ladies present to even notice me."

"Oh but we did notice you," Louis, two years younger than Henry, put in. "Who could not have with the crowd of assiduous suitors you had clamoring to have their names written in your dance card. You were quite the success, as you well know, and we couldn't get anywhere near you."

The dowager, seated near the nicely blazing fire, modified her frown and managed to smile with unaccustomed benevolence on her step-grandsons, of whom she was fonder than she liked to let on. "I noticed you two dancing attendance on the young Gilbert girl."

What? Max's ears pricked. Had he missed something?

Louis grinned at the dowager, irrepressible as usual. "How could we not have, as she was by far the prettiest girl present." He caught Arabella's eye. "After you, of course, Sis."

Henry nodded. "Although she was under the protection of some kind of female guardian, a veritable dragon, who seemed to be vetting all of us young men who attempted to press our attentions on her. I had the feeling the woman could see straight through me to my very heart. Unnerving."

Louis snorted with laughter. "And when I think of what's hidden in your heart it's a wonder she didn't expire on the spot. But worth her scrutiny to secure a dance with La Belle Miss Gilbert. We've been this afternoon to call on her. Not a sign of the dragon, thank goodness, and her mama was kind enough to leave her alone with her callers. Although unfortunately we had to share the room with no less than six others, one of whom was a far too rich cit of advanced years. He obviously fancies his chance with her due to his fortune."

Oh. Of course. Max heaved a metaphorical sigh of relief. They were talking about Letty Gilbert, not Serafina. A certain amount of indignation arose that they'd not only ignored the attractions of Letty's youthful aunt but dismissed her as nothing but a guardian dragon. Although he was fond of his two nephews, they'd never ranked high in his estimation of their qualities, and now they sank even further.

"Letty Gilbert is such a nice girl," Arabella put in. "I believe I can count her amongst my friends now. We were able to converse in between dances while we sipped our lemonade, and I found myself growing fond of her immediately."

Max's estimation of his niece's assessment of character dropped a notch as well. From what he'd seen of Miss Letitia Gilbert, he would not, so far, have classed her as 'a nice girl'.

"Does that mean you can invite her here?" Louis asked. "Because if you do, please let me know, so I can call by chance to see you."

Henry guffawed with laughter. "Not just him, but me as well. I won't have him taking advantage of me. He is the younger brother, after all. I'm the one with the title which must make me much the more attractive of us two."

"But I'm the most handsome," Louis put in, with a grin that was enough to dispel any bad feelings in his brother. These two had always vied with each other in this playful manner and it had never amounted to much angst.

Arabella pouted. "Perhaps I will, but perhaps I might prefer to spend an afternoon in girlish chatter rather than being interrupted by two hapless young men intent on stealing away my new friend."

"Max," Maria said, patting the vacant seat beside her. "Come sit beside me and tell me about your afternoon before we have to go into dinner. I've had my fill of the prattling of young people."

He took the seat with relief, a little insulted that she didn't consider him young any longer, and determined not to think about the slight on Serafina. After all, she was nothing to him. Wasn't she?

"I paid a visit to the Egyptian antiquities of the British Museum. It's a long time since I was last there, and they've vastly improved the displays. I saw the Rosetta Stone—an object that interests me because, as you know, I've been to Rosetta. It wasn't there when I last went. In fact, there were a lot of new exhibits and a whole new gallery to explore."

Maria sighed. "Dear Julian would love to go there, I'm sure. Such a pity he's not well enough to have accompanied you. He could have found a lot of new material for his book, I imagine. Although why you gentlemen find dusty old remains from years ago so interesting, I have no idea." Her face fell a little. "And there I was, thinking you might have been doing something fun."

He chuckled. "But it was fun. For me, at any rate." More fun than he was ready to share.

She brightened. "Perhaps it would do my boys good to spend an afternoon in such an intellectual pursuit rather than passing their time in drinking and gambling at White's." She followed this with a frown. "Not to mention pursuing flirtations with pretty girls they have no intention of offering for. As the mother of a daughter, I abhor the fact that young gentlemen pay court to eligible young ladies with no intention of anything further than enjoying themselves at their expense."

Max smiled. "So you see why I don't advocate an afternoon of fun, then."

She laughed. "Touché. And now I think it must be time to go

into dinner."

Max offered her his arm, while Henry escorted the Dowager and Louis accompanied Arabella, and the party proceeded into the dining room.

It was a cozy, intimate meal, with the two younger men, both born raconteurs, holding forth with further tales of their adventures in Town, where they shared rooms. Max was able to sit for the most part in silence, reflecting further on his afternoon with Serafina.

Not that he wanted to think about her. Rather that it was occupying his brain to the exclusion of all else. Most confusing. He tried listening to Henry and Louis but just could not concentrate. Was this what it was like to feel an attachment to someone? Or was he just intrigued by a bluestocking of a girl who seemed so deserving of a better life? Most likely he was confusing the pity he felt for her with warmer feelings of friendship. How could a girl he'd met only twice, and who had talked on both occasions only of history, have captured his thoughts so completely? And so easily. If that was what had happened.

He tried again to listen to Louis's latest tale, but failed.

Was he feeling like this just because of an inclination to help her escape a life that must be less than pleasant? If anyone could be described as a dragon, it was not Serafina but the intimidating Lady Gilbert. Who probably already had her eye on Henry as a possible, titled of course, spouse for her lovely daughter. Not nearly so intelligent and interesting a girl as Serafina though. Why was he having to repeatedly go over how he was feeling like this? Why couldn't he get that young lady out of his head? He huffed a deep, disgruntled sigh.

"Max, you're not eating," the dowager said, her tone a mix of anxiety and reproof. "I've been watching you, and all you've done is push your food around your plate. Are you ailing?"

Max stared down at his plate. She was right. He'd rearranged the food but not touched it. What to say to avoid alerting her? "I have a megrim, I suppose, after little sleep last night followed by a day in the overcrowded streets of London, and it's making me feel out of sorts. I'm not hungry. It's nothing. I'll take a headache powder before I retire, and I'll be fine in the morning."

His mother's hand twitched as though she would like to lay it on his forehead to check for fever as she'd done when he'd been a child. "You're sure that's all it is?"

He nodded. He couldn't blame her for her worrying. With her husband long dead, her older son such an invalid, and Max himself now war-damaged, it was little wonder she interpreted every uneaten meal or pallor of cheeks as a sign of imminent demise. "Nonsense, Mama. Of course I'm sure. I'd tell you if I were truly sick, rest assured."

She nodded, but the worry in her eyes told him she wasn't totally convinced. To show her he was telling the truth, he took a mouthful of the now nearly cold dinner and chewed. For some reason, it was tasteless and took forever to reduce to a consistency he could swallow. But the reward for that was her mollified expression and a small smile. "That's better."

Conscious of his mother's continued scrutiny, he managed to eat a little of the dessert that followed, but it sat leaden in his stomach as though he had no taste for it at all. Which in itself was strange, as normally he possessed a healthy appetite. It must have been those chestnuts. That was it. They'd filled him up. It was a relief when the meal ended and the ladies retired, leaving Max with his two nephews and a bottle of his brother's best port.

"I gather you've been to Great Titchfield Street," he said to Henry as he passed him the port. "Do you intend to make an offer for the girl? Your mother would be more than happy if you were to provide an heir for your title. She worries about it as your father died so young."

Henry took the bottle. "Heavens, no. I went to keep Louis company. He's the one smitten with the girl. And our papa died racing his curricle with another young buck, not from any illness. So I think we're quite safe from inheriting that."

Louis, hand out waiting for the bottle, had the grace to blush.

"I wouldn't quite say I was smitten." But he sounded insincere in his denial.

Max sipped the port. His brother kept a fine cellar here in his townhouse, although not so extensive as the one at Bratton Park. "You could do worse."

"She's a diamond of the first water," Louis said, the blush deepening. "Every young man at the ball was chasing after a dance with her, as they were with Arabella, of course, but when she looked at me…" His voice hoarsened. "It was as though only she and I existed in that whole ballroom."

Henry burst out laughing. "I had no idea you were such a poet, Lou."

Louis scowled at him. "I think I must be in love."

More derisive laughter from his older brother. "That's what you said only last year about that actress of yours."

Max held out his hand for the port bottle. "How do you know when you're in love then?"

Henry shrugged. "No idea. Never been in love. Unlike Lou. He's been regularly in love ever since he went up to Oxford."

Louis scowled a bit more. "Those were mere dalliances. This time it's real. And as to how I know… well… I can't sleep, I can't eat, I think of her all the time. That's how I can tell it's true love." He bestowed a beaming smile on Max and Henry. "I fear I shall have to make an offer for her before the week is out. She tells me she's going to the Hadleigh ball on Friday, and she even intimated she hoped to see me there. I'm confident my feelings are reciprocated."

Henry leaned back in his chair with a grin. "They'll need to be, with your lack of fortune. That mama of hers has 'fortune hunter' stamped across her forehead if I'm not mistaken, with underneath that 'title hunter' in smaller letters. To get to the daughter you'll have to get past the two guard dogs—the mama and the dragon."

Max frowned. "I wish you wouldn't refer to any lady as a dragon. You know full well how mothers need to guard their daughters from the likes of you two. And it's impolite when you don't know the lady concerned."

Louis and Henry turned surprised expressions on Max. "Who made you the defender of old spinsters?" Henry, who'd always been the more outspoken of the two, asked.

Irritated now almost to the point of wanting to plant a facer on his nephew's physiog, Max resisted that impulse with difficulty. "Good manners have made me so," he said, a little stiffly. "And if your mother had the sense she was born with, she'd have instilled better manners in the pair of you." He stood up. "And now I'm going to join the ladies."

As he closed the door he heard Louis's voice, strident with amazement. "Whatever's got into him tonight?"

CHAPTER THIRTEEN

WATKINS HAD JUST helped Max out of his coat and cravat and was laying out his nightshirt for him when a timid knock came at the bedroom door. Watkins opened it to reveal the sallow visage of Willis, Maria's middle-aged lady's maid. "If you please," she said, bobbing a curtsey to Max, "but Lady Westbury has asked if you would be kind enough to come to her room."

Max glanced at the clock on the mantlepiece, a mahogany and fan inlaid eight-day timepiece by John Horn. Just gone ten. Well, he wasn't tired yet, and it appeared Maria wasn't either. What might she want to talk about at this hour? He'd better go.

Watkins, who must have been hoping to be able to retire to bed soon, passed him his banyan, and, wrapping it one-handed about his torso, Max strode along the landing in his stockinged feet to the room that Maria shared with the absent Julian's.

A fire was blazing in the hearth making the room cozy and welcoming. Maria, sitting up in bed looking jaunty, with a warm peignoir about her shoulders and a lacy cap on her graying curls, waved Willis away. "I won't need you again tonight, thank you, Willis. Max can blow out the candles when he leaves."

Willis, luckier than Watkins, departed.

Maria waved an airy hand at a rather-too-pink upholstered chair by the window. "Bring that over here by the bed and sit down, Max." She sounded very much as she had done when he'd been a boy of eleven and she'd wanted a heart-to-heart with him about his unwise decision to let the sheep from Home Farm into the churchyard and one of them had fallen into an open grave and needed rescuing by Old Rushworth, the sexton.

Should he feel worried? Had he done something last night that he shouldn't have? Good heavens. What was he thinking? He was a man grown now, not a small boy.

His curiosity aroused, as well as a sort of nameless guilt that insisted on returning him to his childhood, he did as he was told, and settled himself in the seat, a little annoyed that he'd forgotten to put his sling on in his haste to obey her summons. His right arm hung like a dead weight that he had to physically pick up so he could lay his hand in his lap, something that made him acutely self-conscious of his disability, even in front of Maria. "What can I do for you?" The words emerged a little more gruffly than he'd intended.

Maria glanced down as she smoothed the bedcovers with dainty fingers, before raising her eyes and fixing him with something that could easily have been described as a hard stare. "How did your afternoon go?"

Immediately on the defensive, Max bridled. "I spent an interesting few hours at the British Museum. As I told my mother."

Maria's eyes twinkled. "Come now, Max. Tell me the truth. You went there with a young lady."

How on earth did she know? Did she have psychic powers? He'd once had a discussion along those lines with a friend at school, and they'd come to the conclusion that mothers and schoolmasters could well have been possessed of magical intuition. But he'd been a boy then. However, even now the urge to deny everything was strong. Luckily, honesty got the better of him. "I did." He wasn't about to impart more than that though. It wasn't any of her business who he went where with, after all.

She smiled, her resemblance to her pretty daughter noticeable. "There's no need to look so forbidding, you know. I'm a woman, and we have our ways of finding things out."

A mind reader, too.

Max heaved a sigh. "I can believe that. How on earth did you find out, though? You have to tell me." Was he going to be questioned about everyone he met here in London? Every woman, that was. If he hadn't been so fond of Maria he'd have thought her intrusive. That her interest was purely due to her concern that he should receive his inheritance, he acknowledged, but it didn't make her nosiness any more bearable. Nosiness had always been something he'd found abhorrent.

She chuckled. "Louis told me, of course. Have you forgotten he and Henry went to call upon the Gilbert girl this afternoon? She told them where you'd gone. Or rather, she told them where her aunt had gone and in whose company. I don't think she knew they were related to you. Not at first, anyway. I imagine the younger Miss Gilbert was glad to share such a juicy piece of gossip."

Of course. No use denying it now. Best to come clean. "I encountered her at the ball last night, and discovered our mutual interest in all things Egyptian. She told me she'd never been to the British Museum, but had always longed to visit. So I said I'd take her." His words came out in more of a hurry than he'd intended. A little flustered by the defensive way he was feeling, he frowned in an effort to put Maria off further enquiry.

It didn't work.

Maria, who'd long suffered the vagaries of her husband where Egyptology was concerned, wrinkled her nose. "Not a very romantic place to take a young lady."

Max shifted in his seat. "It was not meant to be romantic."

She sighed. "Oh, Max, you ask a lady to step out with you and then you take her to a stuffy old museum? How very like dear Julian you are. If I didn't know you were brothers before this, I most certainly would now. She must surely have been expecting something a little less dry and dusty?"

Max laughed. "You're mistaken, I'm afraid. It was Miss Gilbert, Miss Serafina Gilbert, who told me she'd always wanted to go there. So I said I would take her. I had no intention of our outing being in any way romantic." But was he telling her the truth? Heat he couldn't control rose to his cheeks. He had nowhere to hide. Maria pounced.

"Aha. I see you have found her company felicitous or you would not now be blushing like a maiden."

This only made him blush more furiously. Max scowled at her. "Thank you for drawing attention to my condition."

Maria chuckled. "It seems even the most hardened and experienced of soldiers cannot hide their feelings when pressed."

Max stayed silent. Denying he had feelings would play into her hands.

She blew out her lips. "Well, perhaps you could tell me a little about your Miss Serafina Gilbert. Julian will be expecting to hear all about her in my next letter home to him."

Clearly he wasn't about to escape Maria's clutches until she'd extracted every detail of the afternoon from him. Max sighed. "She is a nice girl but from a not so nice family."

Maria huffed. "Such an evocative turn of phrase. And Louis already told me his opinion of the family, gained from an afternoon spent with the niece. And of course, I'm aware that Miss Serafina is only a half-sister to the present Baronet. If you imagine I will not know your young lady's connections, then you are very wrong."

"She is not my young lady."

Maria tapped the side of her nose and bestowed her most knowing smile upon him. "So you say, my dear Maxim. So you say."

Deciding to ignore her intimation that she didn't believe him, Max shifted on his seat uncomfortably, groping for something else to say to distract her, and failing. What he itched to do was to question her, but he controlled himself. Raising a false hope in her would raise a matching one in him, and as far as he could make out, Serafina was not attracted to him. Although… perhaps Maria might be the one who could give him some advice. He'd confided in her on numerous occasions throughout his youth, and every time she'd fulfilled her promises not to share his secrets, small though they might have been. Unlike his mother who'd been known to announce them to all and sundry at dinner parties and the like. He'd learned early on not to confide in his mother. She had no sense of what should remain private.

"Maria…"

Her gaze sharpened. "Yes?"

He fidgeted. Confiding in anyone came hard to him nowadays. He was no longer a hapless boy. "I'm very aware that if I don't marry, I won't receive my inheritance, as you know."

She nodded.

"And I think you know that I feel I have little to offer a young lady with my arm like this. It makes me feel…" He paused. "It makes me feel like I'm only half a man. And on top of that, I don't think I have it in me to fall in love. Not now, at any rate."

She opened her mouth to protest this, but he held his hand up, wanting to continue before his natural reticence silenced him. He'd heard her and Julian's arguments to this before.

"I cannot deny that Miss Serafina Gilbert interests me. We have our love of Egyptian relics in common, at least. She is most knowledgeable on the subject. I think Julian would love to converse with her. But… I don't think she's interested in me." He glanced down at his arm. "Why would she be? When I am like this."

Maria pursed her lips for a moment. "Max, she is a girl in a difficult situation. She's an orphan who has lived in the household of her brother for a number of years, and from her appearance—yes, I studied her for a short time at the ball—it does not appear that it is a happy home for her. She has more the appearance of a governess, or perhaps even a lady's maid or unpaid companion. She's too young to be condemned to that sort of life. Her niece, Arabella's new friend, I had more leisure to observe, and a more spoilt and demanding young lady I've yet to meet."

"She loves her niece unconditionally."

Maria shook her head. "That's as may be. I doubt the girl has any true affection for her aunt. Really, I'm quite surprised Arabella has taken to her like this, but they were somewhat thrown together at the ball. A superficial acquaintance I suspect, not to be continued."

"And what did you think of Serafina?" Max asked, keen to shift the subject back to her, his tongue loosened now he'd found someone with whom to talk about her. He didn't give a jot about the niece.

"I think she needs to escape that house and that family who are sucking her dry like a set of leeches, or she'll end up a dry, withered husk of an old lady treated like a servant all her life. I've seen that happen to unmarried sisters before. It's a half-life only, and from the look of her, she doesn't deserve that."

One thing you could rely on with Maria was her tendency to speak her mind, at home if not in public. A small smile twitched the corners of Max's mouth. "I think you have it there."

"Then why not offer for her?"

Yes, why not? "A lot of reasons, the main one being my arm, or rather my lack of it. Also throw in the fact that neither of us love each other. Although you might say that is the most important point."

"A problem that's entirely in your head," Maria retorted. "And it's also a problem, if you want it to be counted as one, that will be exactly the same with any young lady you consider. At least you like this one and have found common ground. And if she is interested in Egypt and its history, surely that means she is a girl in possession of a brain?"

Did he like her? Or was there something more? "I don't know if she likes me though."

"Did she talk to you?"

He nodded.

"Smile at you?"

He nodded.

"Did she enjoy herself?"

He nodded a third time. "But you can't equate those reactions with her having liked me."

Maria sighed as though she were dealing with a recalcitrant puppy. "Tell me, Max, do you look in the mirror when you shave in the mornings?"

Max frowned. "You know I have to have Watkins shave me nowadays."

She frowned back at him. "I forgot. What about when you do up your cravat? Or comb your hair? Surely you look in the mirror when you're doing that?"

"I do when I comb my hair."

"Well then. What do you see? No. Don't answer me. The man looking back at you is one of the handsomest men in London. Forget your arm, for once. You wear it like a ball and chain and need to get out of that habit. Having it in a sling gives you the attractive air of a wounded soldier."

"I *am* a wounded soldier."

"Exactly. Just because you find your arm unpleasant does not mean women will. You're tall. Taller than Julian and much more handsome." She pulled a wry face. "Especially now he's got so bald and fat. Not that I love him any less like that, but one has to be realistic. You, on the other hand, are a positive adonis."

Max burst out laughing. "An adonis I am not, I can assure you."

She shook her head. "Nonsense. You are making the mistake of considering yourself from the point of view of a man. I see you with a woman's eyes and I find you most attractive."

Max fidgeted. "Should I be worried?"

She laughed. "No, you shouldn't. A woman can find a man attractive without following through. My love for your brother is steadfast, but I can see what other women must see in you. And I can assure you that your Miss Gilbert, Serafina, will not have been blind to your attributes."

He frowned. "I don't know. Perhaps you're right. She was charming company." He remembered her nervous demeanor as they'd neared the house in Great Titchfield Street. "And she's clearly unhappy in her situation. But whatever you say, I don't think she would agree. And not just because of my disability."

"Your mama and I would very much like to see you married, Max, and I know Julian has asked you to marry before he… before he has to leave us." Her voice faltered. This was the nearest she'd ever come to saying Julian's time was limited.

Max reached out and covered her hand with his own. "I know I have to marry. I'm not such an idiot as to deliberately give up my inheritance out of contrariness. And I do like Miss Gilbert, but I feel knowing her for such a short time, I'm not in a position to decide whether to offer for her. And nor is she in a position to decide to say yes or not. In fact, what I fear is that she might choose to accept my offer just to escape her situation and then regret it afterwards."

Maria shrugged. "She might, but an arranged marriage can develop into true love, you know. And I'm well aware that you don't wish to attend the 'marriage mart' as other eligible gentlemen do."

He nodded. "Not being able to dance is a handicap to begin with."

She chuckled. "That and being as miserable as sin. Your expression last night was enough to put off anyone from approaching you. You didn't circulate but instead kept close attendance on your mama. It's a wonder you didn't frighten off Arabella's possible suitors."

"I can't help it if I feel as though everyone is staring at my arm."

Maria huffed. "For goodness sake, forget about your arm. It means nothing. If you want my advice, you should pursue your Miss Gilbert. And invite her here for tea, but without her dreadful sister-in-law if possible. I'd like to meet her."

He snorted. "Inspect her, you mean."

"That as well. When are you seeing her next?"

He rubbed his forehead. "Thursday. I said I'd take her out in the carriage to the park. For some air."

Her mouth widened in a triumphant smile. "Perfect. I see you need no directing from me. Perhaps you could bring her here for tea afterwards?"

He couldn't be angry with her. She was far too well-meaning and loveable for that. "Very well, but no inquisition. Just be friendly."

"As if I was ever anything else. Now. Off you go to bed and blow out my candles on your way out. I need my beauty sleep." She dimpled at him. "And so do you in your new role as suitor."

CHAPTER FOURTEEN

T HURSDAY AFTERNOON TOOK a long time arriving. Despite her conviction that Captain Aubrey had only asked her to go for the carriage drive out of pity or for a bet, Serafina couldn't help but look forward to it with growing anticipation. An anticipation that allowed her to float over the mundane jobs Araminta found for her to do, and the constant jibes from both her and Ogden. Closing her ears to their voices helped, and conjuring up an image of the captain's handsome face while she carried out her chores made light of the work she had to do. A girl could dream, couldn't she? Even if she knew in her heart it could lead to nothing.

Letty had further callers on Wednesday afternoon. Serafina sat with her sewing making herself appear unobtrusive, but all the while keeping a wary watch on how forward these young men might become, and noting their names so she could discover their worthiness as potential suitors. The sort of job Araminta, with her knowledge of the *ton*, was far better equipped to carry out but had deigned to do. She would be quite happy if the husband that Letty secured was an inveterate old lecher, so long as he was either rich, titled or both.

To Serafina's interest, Mr. Oliver Talbot, the cit, returned, arriving a full half hour before anyone else and giving her ample opportunity to assess him. And what she saw, she had to admit, she liked. Araminta had let slip during breakfast that she'd already discovered Mr. Talbot to be a widow of several years, with no children—something Araminta appeared to see as a distinct advantage. "No heirs waiting to dispossess you once he dies," she informed a slightly shocked Letty, to whom early demise of her suitor had probably not occurred. "Any children you might have would be his sole heirs."

Letty had wrinkled her delicate nose at the mention of children, no doubt because she'd once told Serafina that she never intended to have any because she wouldn't be able to tolerate being the size of a house for months on end. She'd been ten when little Amy had been born, and could recall with clarity her mother's constant moans about how she was suffering and how awful carrying a child was.

Despite herself, Serafina found herself agreeing with Araminta on this point. It would suit Letty admirably if she were the only point of attention in any gentleman's gaze, and if he'd had children, that would necessarily not have been the case. However, his age might be considered a barrier to a happy marriage where the bride was so much younger—and so immature with it.

When she met Mr. Talbot in person, though, she was pleasantly surprised. He was not handsome, but nor was he unpleasant to regard, with a pronounced solidity about him that spoke of ancestors who might have performed manual labor for a living. But he had about him an air of practicality, and a twinkle in his kind eyes as he regarded Letty that spoke of a desire to spoil that already well-spoiled girl. If Araminta and Letty could ignore his less than noble roots in the face of his considerable fortune, then so could she. And the fact that he appeared to be smitten by Letty after only two meetings had to be a good thing.

He spoke with a cultured voice of his estate in Warwickshire and a play he'd been to see a few nights since, and Letty, encouraged by a nod from Serafina as well as her mother's obvious approval of Mr. Talbot, chattered away to him in the most artless fashion. Despite her propensity for selfishness, Letty could be the sweetest and most charming of girls when she wanted to be. Until she was crossed, of course. Luckily for Mr. Talbot, he did not cross her but was most attentive to her every word. Serafina began to think of him as the ideal suitor for the flighty Letty. He might even be able to curb her less attractive traits.

When several new callers arrived, Mr. Talbot wisely bade Letty good afternoon, perhaps not keen to be viewed beside the youthful, downy countenances of the eligible young men who seemed so enthusiastic to capture Letty's attention. If he was not there, she could not compare him.

Letty, hardly seeming to miss the man Serafina had half-decided should become her husband, basked instead in the rapt attention of so many handsome new callers. She had to keep herself in check over dinner that evening, but by bedtime all she could do was chatter to Serafina about the various merits of each young man. Nonstop. Serafina, with a thought for the staid and sensible Mr. Talbot, steered the conversation his way whenever she could.

"They were indeed a very attractive collection of young men," she said as she and Letty prepared for bed. "Handsome and well-dressed. However, appearances can be deceiving, I fear, and at least two of those who called on you today are inveterate gamblers and have limited funds."

Letty bounced into bed, still buoyed up by her obvious success. "Really? Which ones? And how do you know?"

"Your mama told me."

Letty pulled the covers up to her chin. "Brrr. No hot brick. I shall have to talk to Roberts. She's slacking. I bet she's put one in her own bed, though. And how does Mama know?"

Serafina climbed into her own bed. Letty was right. The sheets gave her a chilly welcome. "She's made it her goal to discover all there is to know about every supposedly eligible young man of the Season. Mr. Topham and Mr. Ryder, who are friends, have more in common than their friendship. Your mama told me she's found out that they both go far too deep when playing cards. And when backing horses. And anything else they can wager on, which includes, so I'm told, beetle racing and snail racing at White's."

"Really? I think I should like to see beetle racing." Letty giggled. "Oh well, I wasn't considering either of them, anyway. Mr. Topham talks about himself the whole time, and Mr. Ryder, despite being passably handsome, has a squint."

Coming from a girl whose favorite topic of conversation was herself, this criticism of the unfortunate Mr. Topham seemed a bit rich. Serafina forbore from saying so, though. And she was right about Mr. Ryder who had an unnerving ability to look cross-eyed, which in itself shouldn't exclude him from consideration, although his propensity for gambling did. She heaved an inward sigh of relief at not having to steer Letty away from either of those two. "Today was the first time I met Mr. Talbot," she said instead. "He seems a most charming gentleman."

Letty nodded. "And tactful too, departing so I could enjoy myself with all my other callers. I should think at his age he's past all the fun young men love so much." Her tone was dismissive.

"I gather he's very wealthy. Your mama told me that too."

Letty giggled. "He is indeed, much of it gained by trading, though, which isn't at all the same as inherited money." She frowned. "Although, I do think I might be able to overlook his background as he's so rich. One of the richest men in England, so I'm told."

Hooray for Letty's acquisitive heart. Serafina just might be able to trust her to make the right choice. She blew out her candle and snuggled down, rubbing her cold feet together in an attempt to get warm. "An admirable decision. Goodnight."

Letty blew her own candle out. "Goodnight, Fina."

The only light in the room now was the faint glow of the streetlights filtering in from behind the curtains over the long window. Serafina turned onto her side, determined not to think about tomorrow. Faint hope. Would Captain Aubrey remember he'd invited her to come out driving in the park? Or would he have put her out of his mind as he'd left the house to return to his own life, with no intention of ever seeing her again? That seemed more and more likely as she lay thinking about it in the quiet dark. A vehicle of some sort rumbled over the cobbles in the street, and, far off, a dog barked. At least she'd had that afternoon in his company. Something she could hold in her heart forevermore.

IT WAS WITH more than a little relief that on Thursday, Serafina saw Captain Aubrey escorted into the drawing room even before the afternoon round of gentlemen callers on Letty had begun.

Letty, to Serafina's surprise, had remembered the captain was calling. A mixed blessing, as if he didn't call, everyone was going to know she'd been forgotten, which added to Serafina's growing anxiety until she laid eyes on him. Also to Serafina's surprise, Letty had fussed around Serafina's choice of gown and insisted on Roberts doing her hair for her and applying some of the scent on Letty's dressing table. "You want to look your best for the captain, don't you?" she'd said, a little accusingly, when she'd seen the gown Serafina had picked out. "I know Mama never lets you have new dresses, apart from that plain one you wore to the ball, but if you wear this one…" Here she flourished the least dowdy inhabitant of Serafina's wardrobe, "…instead of this old one, it will bring out the lovely gray of your eyes. You have such beautiful eyes and you should make the most of them at every opportunity. Unfortunately one couldn't say your face is your fortune, but your eyes might well be."

"My eyes are nothing compared with yours," Serafina had retorted, but Letty had poohpoohed that disclaimer. Also unusual in a girl who normally basked in praise. She must be feeling very confident in herself.

And now here Serafina was, wearing the dove gray dress Letty had chosen for her, conscious of the disapproving glare of Araminta, which no doubt was due to her hair being done in the elaborate style Letty had also insisted on.

Captain Aubrey's eyes went straight to her, as though, dare she hope, no one else in the room mattered to him. But surely that was her imagination.

"Miss Gilbert." He bowed to her first before turning to Araminta, Ogden not being present. "Lady Gilbert and Miss Letitia."

Araminta bestowed a somewhat condescending smile on him that didn't reach her stony eyes. "How charming to see you again, Captain Aubrey. Do sit down and I'll send for tea."

Captain Aubrey returned her smile, his not reaching his eyes either. "I must unfortunately refuse your hospitality, as I've left my carriage outside with my groom, and my horses are impatient, hot-blooded creatures who don't like the cold, and I'm particular in their comfort. I'm afraid I can't keep them waiting. Perhaps another time?"

Araminta's already sour expression soured still further. No doubt she'd been anxious to secure the attentions of an earl's brother to improve her standing in society even if she couldn't secure him for her daughter as a suitor. Serafina set down her sewing, a warm, and unaccustomed feeling of superiority burgeoning in her breast. She was the one going driving with the captain, and she felt certain Araminta was bitterly jealous. After all, Ogden was but a lowly baronet. Not that this had ever crossed her mind before, as her papa had also been just a baronet, but the thought once broached now wouldn't vanish. She was unused to feeling anything but subdued and wary in Araminta's presence and suppressing all rebellious thoughts. There were a lot in her heart clamoring to be let out.

Captain Aubrey held out his hand and she set her own in it, managing to smile up at him. "I will make haste as I don't wish to incommode your horses on such a cold day." She met his gaze and saw an unmistakable twinkle in his eyes. Was he finding this amusing? For a moment, the urge to giggle was enormous and only just held in check. How shocked Araminta would be by a show of levity.

"Have a lovely time," Letty said, her blue eyes wide and

guileless. No doubt she was already anticipating the return of the smitten Mr. Talbot and whoever else had fallen under her charms. Possibly Louis Herbert.

"Letitia," her mother snapped. "Continue with your sewing." A ridiculous command, as Letty had never really been sewing at all in the first place.

In the hallway, Roberts, who seemed to have materialized from nowhere, helped Serafina into her pelisse and bonnet and handed her a pair of gloves and her reticule. A pair of Letty's much smarter gloves, also an unusually given loan. Truly, today Letty must be in a very good mood indeed. What a miracle three days of gentlemen callers could wreak on a girl.

A few moments later, and Max and Serafina were out of the front door, where a thin, wintry sun was trying its best to brighten the day.

A spotless, shiny barouche, drawn by two matching bay horses, stood in the street with a liveried driver seated on the high box seat. Serafina had never seen such a splendid outfit in all her life. The family had journeyed up to London from Berkshire in a hired carriage, and at home at Milford House her brother kept only one vehicle of his own—a much smaller, less impressive carriage than this one. There'd been a lot more horses in the stables there when her papa had been alive, but that was sixteen years ago now.

This was going to be fun.

CHAPTER FIFTEEN

M AX, ACUTELY AWARE of his one-armed limitations and the task he'd set himself that day, let down the carriage step for her. "This is my brother's outfit, I should explain. Before he was taken ill, he was a great fancier of horseflesh and a noted whip. They're his horses, although he allows me to treat them as though they're mine." He was gabbling, but it was almost impossible to shut up. The void between them needed filling with words, and he seemed incapable of preventing his mouth from running away with itself. What sort of a fool would she take him for?

With a little awkwardness, he handed her into the body of the barouche. "As you may imagine, I'm limited as to what vehicles I can use nowadays." He climbed in and settled himself beside her, not quite close enough that their legs might touch. "There's an impressive curricle in the mews behind Westbury House which I long to take out, but I can only use it if I take a groom with me. And that's too frustrating." Why couldn't he just shut up? It was as though he had some sort of death wish and wanted to draw her attention constantly to his disability. As if she wouldn't have noticed it long ago.

She bestowed a gentle smile on him. "I'm perfectly happy with a trip out in this fine equipage, Captain. I'm not a great admirer of speed, and I believe, that once in the park, we're confined to making a decorous progression."

More at ease, Max managed to smile back at her, although he remained irritated with himself for behaving more like a green schoolboy than a seasoned army officer. Despite his limitations, as he'd put it, and her professed preference for sedate travel, it would have been fun to take Serafina out in the racy curricle and perhaps driven along the Great Bath Road into the not-too-distant countryside. The number of things you needed two hands for never ceased to grow.

Serafina smoothed her skirts as the estimable Badger, Julian's coachman who was now standing in as groom and driver of the barouche, clicked his tongue at the two horses, Bella and Bonny. The carriage moved off into the as yet quiet traffic.

She drew in her breath. "I've never been for a carriage ride with a gentleman before." She peeped up at him from beneath her straw bonnet, her gray eyes brimming with enjoyment. For an instant, his heart warmed at the sight of her pleasure, before the thought that offering for her just because she was convenient rose to stick in his craw. He'd professed himself prepared to do just that to the first woman who was remotely pleasing, but somehow, doing so to Serafina seemed wrong. He couldn't quite work out why that should be. He'd think about that later.

However... for now he would have to overcome these inexplicable feelings. She was intelligent, good company, and although not pretty, pleasing to the eye. What more could he hope for in a bride? She might even be able to overlook his glaring problem. Possibly out of politeness. Yes. He would ask her today, while she was feeling grateful to him for having taken her out, and while she was away from her brother's family. At least if she said yes, he wouldn't have to look further for a bride.

However, she had a question for him first. "Might I ask you something, Captain?"

"Of course you may." He swallowed, a little wary of what she might ask, due to the direction his own thoughts had taken. Small talk with young ladies did not come naturally to him. An idea dawned. "But as this is our second outing together, perhaps you would do me the honor of addressing me as Max?"

Color rose to her cheeks, rendering her suddenly almost pretty. "I would like that very much... Max. And perhaps you could in turn call me Serafina, for that is my given name, chosen for me by my dear Papa."

Warmth suffused Max's chest to dispel those lingering feelings of guilt, and he couldn't help but smile, conscious of heat rising to his own cheeks. Ridiculous. However, he was a gentleman and a reply rose unbidden to his lips. "A beautiful name, and one that should be spoken aloud as often as possible... Serafina." Her name rolled off his tongue, and he suppressed the urge to repeat it. Several times. She might be a little surprised if he did. He was a little surprised himself by that urge.

He hesitated, searching for something else to say and feeling a bit of a fool. Why were soldiers so much easier to talk to than women? "Named for the highest of angels—the seraphim. The fiery ones." Whatever had made him think that about her? And what was more, say it out loud.

She laughed, shaking her head. "I suspect the name doesn't really suit me. I am much more of a mouse than a fire breather, by necessity."

The barouche turned into Oxford Street and headed towards the park. "I don't see you as a mouse at all." Which was true. Despite being ruled by her horrendous family, she had about her the air of one suffering in an enforced silence maintained only because she possessed such good manners and common sense.

She had to be strong to have dealt with that family all her life and emerge undaunted. Since she was a tiny child, in fact. Well, practically undaunted. A lesser woman would have buckled. A lesser woman would most likely accept his intended offer with alacrity. For a moment he hesitated, unsure of what her response would be. She wasn't like those girls his mother had tried casting in front of him so far. She'd already told him in no uncertain terms that she wasn't here in London to find a husband. But surely that had only been because she didn't think of herself as suitable marriage material?

"You have a gentle exterior but with the strong heart of your namesake." He'd nearly said a heart of granite, but on reflection had amended his words, as they didn't sound a good descriptor of a lady. And he didn't want her to jump to the conclusion that he thought her hard. Which she wasn't. Or at least, he didn't think she was, which was a different thing altogether. And really, he didn't know her well at all, as yet. So what was he doing thinking of proposing to her?

She patted at a stray strand of hair, loosened by the breeze generated by the progress of the barouche, away from her face. "I like to think I'm strong. In the face of adversity, I do not give in to weakness, unless common sense suggests I should do so. I have had to bow to common sense on many occasions in my life. It is almost always wise to do so, I have found."

"An admirable sentiment and advice you could do well to pass on to both your niece and mine. Wise words for young girls debuting in society."

They passed a carriage bearing someone Max knew, and their exchange of nods gave him a moment to compose himself. If he was going to make her an offer, he needed to explain to her what it entailed. He glanced at Badger's broad back, far enough away and with his attention too much taken by his horses and the other traffic to be listening. Hopefully.

"Serafina," he began.

She turned those luminous gray eyes on him. "Yes?"

This was far worse than waiting to go into battle against the French or the Turks. "I would like to explain myself to you."

"Do you feel a need to do so?"

He indicated his bad arm. "I do. You see before you a man who is only, in truth, half a man."

"An arm does not make a whole half of you, surely?"

He pressed his lips together and drew in a breath. "It might just as well. There are many things I can no longer do, because all of them require the use of two arms and two hands. Being unable to perform those tasks and having always to have help for simple things like shaving makes me feel as though I'm but half a man." The temptation to reveal to her how impotent he felt at not even being able to dress himself arose, to be discarded. Too much, too soon. She might interpret his offer as a desire for a nurse, and that was the last thing he needed. The last thing he wanted her to think. The ignominy would be too much for him.

"I can assure you, I do not see you as even three quarters of a man, but rather as a complete man." She was smiling still, her lips forming a perfect bow. What would it be like to press his own lips to them in a kiss?

Promising.

"And yet I am here before you, unable to take your hand in mine." As she was sitting on his right, this was true.

Her cheeks reddened, but in a most attractive manner. She bit her lip, keeping her eyes down to regard his right arm where it hung in its sling. Damned thing. "Might I enquire as to how you came by the injury to your arm? And if it is… permanent?"

He glanced down as well. Best to be honest, Julian would say, and lay your cards upon the table, face uppermost. "You may ask indeed, and I have no reason not to tell you. I was shot while involved in a somewhat reckless cavalry charge at the Battle of Vimeiro in Portugal. The nerves are damaged beyond repair." He paused. "I've seen every doctor in London, I think, and they all say the same. I'll not be able to use it again. I have no feeling in it from the shoulder down."

She reached across and laid her own hand on his useless one. "I am truly sorry."

Unable to feel her touch, he found his heart unaccountably aching for want of it. Such a small thing, touch, but so important. More important than he'd ever given it credit for.

To cover his discomfort, he shook his head. "What for? You didn't pull the trigger. And there's nothing anyone can do to undo the damage. It's been six months, now, and I'm growing used to my limitations." He sighed. "But I wanted you to be fully aware of my disability."

"I had guessed it, but it makes no difference to our friendship. You are not diminished by it in my eyes. I am not about to shun you for it."

Badger maneuvered the barouche through the busy gates into the park and they set off, most decorously, down Rotten Row, in the company of a whole host of other equestrians both in carriages and mounted. The brighter weather had brought them all out. Over in the distance Max caught momentary sight of the distinct form of Mirza Abulhassan Khan, the Persian ambassador in his colorful national dress, cantering sedately along the Row.

Was this the place for him to continue in the direction he had planned? He took a deep breath. "Serafina, you told me you weren't here in London looking for a husband. That you were here for Letty, alone. There's something I didn't tell you. I'm here not just to escort my sister-in-law and my niece, but also to find myself a bride."

Her face fell.

"No, no, you misunderstand. I am twenty-nine-years old. On my thirtieth birthday I will inherit a substantial fortune left to me by my father. Property and funds that came into the family from my maternal grandmother and so are not entailed. But only if I'm married by that date."

Her eyes widened, still confused. He was bad at making himself clear.

"I have been away in the army until very recently and marriage was far from my mind. My brother has made it known that he wants me to marry before he… before it is too late, and I am in agreement. But I'm not easy to please and I don't find any of the girls my mother has thrust beneath my nose in the least bit attractive." He shrugged. "And I doubt any of them found me to their taste either, as I'm unable to dance with them, and that is all girls like that want to do—dance and flirt."

She opened her mouth to speak, but he held up a hand. If she interrupted him he'd never get it said and the moment would be gone. "No. Let me finish. I need a bride who will not bore me in a month. I need someone who is sensible and intelligent, not some feather brained girl straight out of the schoolroom. And I must marry very soon or I'll lose my inheritance."

Her gaze sharpened. "You wish me to help you find a bride?"

He almost laughed. "No. Not at all. I wish for you to be my bride." There. He'd said it.

Damnit. A carriage going in the opposite direction to them pulled in close. It held the impressive Lady Routledge and one of her many similarly impressive daughters. She waved imperiously at Badger to stop, and he did.

Serafina shot Max a hunted look before composing her features into bland politeness. Max forced himself to smile. "Why, Lady Routledge, how unexpected." She would choose this very moment to appear, as if out of the blue. The woman had an altogether uncanny nose for gossip. His eyes slid sideways to check Serafina wasn't about to give everything away and found her face still expressionless.

"Captain Aubrey, good day to you." Lady Routledge's beady eyes fixed on Serafina, a touch of confusion in them. She must be sorting through her memories to fix upon exactly who Serafina was. "Ah," she finally exclaimed. "Miss Gilbert. Lady Gilbert's... young relation. I thought I knew you." She raised her exquisitely painted-on eyebrows at Max. "Out with Captain Aubrey, I see."

Max ground his teeth. The last thing he wanted was one of the worst gossips of the *ton* seizing upon him as a subject. "My sister-in-law is acquainted with Lady Gilbert," he lied, although probably it wasn't as much a lie as he was thinking. "We're out taking the air."

Lady Routledge raised just one single arched eyebrow at him this time. "Remember me to dear Lady Westbury, Captain Aubrey. Good afternoon, Miss Gilbert. Captain."

Her driver clicked to his horses and her carriage moved away.

The moment she was out of earshot, Serafina turned to face Max, her gray eyes brimming with accusation. He'd rather hoped they'd be brimming with excitement at the prospect of marriage to him. "Was that a proposal?"

Feeling less confident, if that were possible, he nodded. "It was. You need to escape your family, and I need a bride in order to receive my inheritance. Perhaps it's a little more along the lines of a business proposal." Good God, had he just said that? But there was no unsaying it now.

"Oh." Nothing in her tone gave away what she was thinking but her eyes had not lost their accusing expression. Had he somehow insulted her?

"You would gain significantly. I will inherit a house and estate in Wiltshire, not too far from my brother's estate at Bratton Park. I'll keep a house in Town as well, if you wish. And you'll have a generous allowance for... your attire. I know from Maria and Arabella how much ladies like to spend on gowns and such like." Was this the right thing to say? From her appearance she didn't look like a girl who spent money on clothes, but he might be wrong about that.

Why was she not looking pleased?

"You will have your own carriage and as many servants as you require." What else might a young lady require on marriage? He was scraping the bottom of his barrel of knowledge now, but felt more as if he were digging himself a deep hole to fall into.

Her eyes narrowed. "Pray tell me what it is you would expect in return?"

Aha. The nub of it. She was a virgin, of course. She had told him she didn't want to be married and was probably worried she might have to partake in one of the consequences of the marital state. Despite his fondness for her, or perhaps because of it, he felt sympathy. "Nothing. Nothing at all. Merely that you will be hostess for any social gathering I might wish to hold." But was that really all he wanted? Dealing with young ladies was so much more confusing than dealing with soldiers.

"Nothing?" Did she sound a tiny bit disappointed? Or was he reading into her tone of voice something that wasn't there?

Perhaps, on the other hand, it indicated relief?

He nodded. "A marriage strictly in name only, so that I may receive my inheritance. And so that you might escape your brother's house." The longing for her to fall into his arms and declare that she would love to be married to him rose from nowhere. Wasn't that what was supposed to happen when one made an offer for a young lady? Even if love were not involved. He pulled himself up short.

What was he? A romantic hero from a novel? He swept that thought away, to where it belonged. Even though she'd claimed she didn't find his useless arm unmanly, the certainty that she didn't have feelings for him remained. And of course, he didn't have feelings for her beyond those warm ones of friendship. And as his mother would say, many a good marriage was based on friendship alone.

She nodded. "Oh. Of course. How very kind of you to wish to take me away from Milford House." Her tone had flattened.

"An arrangement that should suit us both. I imagine we could spend many evenings discussing Egypt together." This wasn't quite how he'd wanted his proposal to come out. In his head, her reactions had been quite different. She didn't even seem pleased.

What had gone wrong?

They were approaching the Kensington Palace end of the Row now, where Badger swung the carriage around. A weak winter sun shone down on them and the breeze ruffled Serafina's hair.

She gazed at Max out of troubled eyes. "Thank you very much for your offer, Max. But if you don't mind, I shall have to take some time to think about it."

What? She was considering saying no? Was he so awful that staying on with her brother as an unpaid servant was a better option than he was? Max slumped back in his seat, speechless, his ego well dented. He'd rather imagined she'd be grateful to be removed from the frosty confines of her brother's house and shown just a little pleasure in his proposal. It was going to be an awkward drive back to Great Titchfield Street.

CHAPTER SIXTEEN

THE JOURNEY BACK to Great Titchfield Street seemed to Serafina to take at least three times as long as their journey out had done. Having escorted her inside, Max took his leave, and she made haste to excuse herself from the parlor as suffering from a megrim. She made her way upstairs, leaden-footed with disappointment.

The empty bedroom, however, felt like the quiet haven of peace she'd been in search of. Sitting in the parlor with Araminta and Letty, and the lovesick young man who was still in residence, would have been intolerable. His obviously smitten expression coupled with Letty's air of self-satisfaction would have been too much to bear.

Without bothering to remove her pelisse, she sat down on her bed and wrenched off her borrowed gloves. Was she, could she but bring herself to admit it, just a little bit jealous of Letty? The thought brought guilt flooding over her. Despite their two very different positions within the household at Milford, she'd never felt any jealousy towards Letty or her sisters and brothers. Yet now, here it was, raising its ugly green head in her heart.

Since Letty had been a rosy-cheeked baby, just learning to walk, and she'd been a motherless six-year-old orphan, there'd been an unbreakable bond between the two of them, although perhaps that bond was stronger from her side. With no mother to care for her, she'd showered her love onto the one creature who loved her back without question. Pretty little Letty, a child who'd been so easy to love and so willing to be loved. Letty's younger brother Theodore had arrived much later, when the two girls had been ten and five, and although Serafina loved him and his three younger siblings, she cared for none of them as much as she cared for Letty.

And now she was feeling jealous of her beloved niece, a fact that proved disquieting in the extreme. Why would she suddenly feel like this? Perhaps because of all the eligible young men who were calling on Letty with nothing but love in their eyes. How ridiculous was that? It wasn't as if she'd seen this trip to London as being anything other than centered around Letty and the requirement that she find a husband. And she'd known men would fall at Letty's dainty feet as soon as she smiled at them, and that Letty would bask in their attention as though they owed it to her. She was that sort of girl, to whom everything came easily and who treated that luxury as an unassailable right.

No. She, Serafina, knew her place, and it was to wait upon the increasingly demanding Letty and make sure she married the right man. Because she loved her. And envied her… This last sentiment came as a surprising revelation she'd rather sweep under the rug and deny.

But she couldn't. The ugly sentiment kept rearing its equally ugly head. And it was all because she'd met Max. His fault. She'd never for one moment expected to meet a gentleman she herself might like. Until she'd laid eyes on him.

And there she was admitting it to herself. The truth was, she wanted Max to look at her in the way men looked at Letty. Only he never would. She wanted Max to want to marry her because he loved her, not so that he could claim his inheritance. But no, she was nothing but a convenient step to gaining what he wanted. She was useful to a man who saw himself as unattractive to women. Because he thought she'd be grateful for the attention. Because she was plain and badly dressed and well past the first flush of youth. Because he felt sorry for her. And as for her, she was probably just suffering from an infatuation with the first man who'd ever shown her any interest. The first man who'd done anything for her. The first man she'd ever liked. That was it. She was ridiculously infatuated like a schoolgirl.

A tear trickled down her cheek, and she swiped it away with the back of her hand. Much good all Letty's primping had done, even if it had proved that somewhere in Letty's self-centered heart lurked a girl who could care for others. Although Letty might see the primping as having been a success. Max had offered for her, after all.

Another tear followed the first at the realization that what she truly wanted was the same romance in her life as Letty appeared to be receiving. She wanted someone to gaze into her eyes with open adoration and tell her they loved her. Before they asked for her hand in marriage. But that was never going to happen. No one was ever going to love her. She didn't list the reasons again but they were there, nevertheless, lodged in her aching heart. No matter how infatuated she might become of any man, none of them would ever give her a second look. She just wasn't falling in love material.

More tears ran down her cheeks, unheeded now. What hurt the most was the way being with Max made her feel, and knowing he didn't reciprocate those feelings. She sniffed. She could never let him guess at how she felt. Never. It would be too humiliating. If she accepted his offer, she must maintain the illusion that she was accepting a business contract. That she was agreeing to be the means to him inheriting his estate. That was what he wanted and that would be what she would give him. She would lock this silly infatuation away in the deepest recesses of her soul and never take it out again. She would be what he'd said—sensible, educated, practical.

Where was her handkerchief? Unable to find it, she resorted to wiping her eyes with the sleeve of her pelisse, which reminded her she was still wearing her outdoor clothes. With rather shaky fingers she removed her bonnet and slipped out of her pelisse, laying them neatly on the bed beside her. With precise care, she laid Letty's gloves on top of the pelisse.

The fact that she had allowed her thoughts to wander in the direction of acceptance of his offer brought a new shock. Was she so mercenary that she would resort to using him to escape her brother's household? The money he professed to be about to inherit meant nothing to her, didn't it? What did she care for pretty gowns and fancy carriages? What she'd never had she could do without. All she asked for was a fire in every room in winter and an end to the chilblains she'd grown so used to. Yes, if she had that she'd be content. And the infatuation would wane.

He'd promised more, as some kind of incentive, no doubt, but material wealth meant nothing to her. The memory of how she and Letty had laughed together as they'd listed the attributes required of a suitor, and how wealth had featured highly on that list. Bittersweet. That now, when her heart had engaged, if with reluctance, she had to acknowledge that it no longer seemed nearly so important. Nowhere near so important as fires in every room, and they came in at a poor second to being loved.

She heaved an unsteady breath just as the door burst open and Letty came bouncing in, as full of energy and enthusiastic good cheer as ever. She threw herself down on her own bed and bestowed a wide smile on Serafina. "What a day. I can't believe how successful my debut in society has been." She paused, head tilted to one side in a coquettish manner. "Well, I suppose I can. I knew I was pretty, of course, but knowing that yourself and having others say it to you, many times, are quite different things. And as so many of them have said it, I'm certain they must be right."

Hidden by the gloom in the as yet unlit bedroom, Serafina pulled herself together with a huge effort and nodded. "Of course they are right, dear Letty. You are quite the prettiest girl of the Season, as far as I can tell from just the one ball we've attended. And I'm sure also that you're the most successful. You deserve to be." Only this time when she said it, a little voice nagged at her asking why Letty should get all this praise heaped on her just for the way nature had favored her. Not a thought that had ever crossed Serafina's mind before. Not until she'd discovered jealousy, that was.

Might Max have professed some kind of love for her had she been as beautiful as Letty?

Letty's pretty face took on a smug expression that wasn't all that attractive. Better warn her not to let slip that look while there were gentlemen around, nor at the next ball they were to attend, which she remembered with a start was tomorrow night. They might get the wrong idea. However, she couldn't bring herself to point this out just now. "Did your Mr. Talbot return?"

Letty's face lit up. "He did indeed. I was so pleased to see him. Mama says he is the one I should encourage, on account of his enormous fortune, and also because as yet no one properly titled has shown any interest in me. She says there aren't any available dukes as there are so few of them in the whole of England. Which is most annoying." She giggled. "Although there is one, she says, the Duke of Dunbar, but he's very old—older by far than Mr. Talbot—and a widower with children older than Mama herself. And he walks with a stick and has white hair." She paused, her brow wrinkling. "Mama told me she would have considered him had he not already been provided with a son and heir and grandchildren by his first and second wives. I'm quite glad he has been, to be honest, as I don't fancy being married to someone that old."

How like Letty not to notice someone else's distress, although the room was growing gloomier by the minute as evening fell outside. However, it gave Serafina the chance to regain her self-control. There would be no point in sharing her own doubts and fears with Letty. The feelings of someone else had never mattered to her self-centered niece. She cleared her throat. "I must say that I too am glad your mama has dismissed this elderly duke from her list of possible candidates for your hand." She managed a smile. "Although whether he would have been in agreement had she decided you should set your cap at him, I have no idea."

Letty chuckled. "Before Mama's determination, I fear he would have been putty in her hands. Unable to resist." She paused and patted her curls, as she was wont to do when thinking about her looks. "And of course, once he'd seen me…"

"A lucky escape," Serafina said, trying hard to keep the irony out of her voice. "For you and him."

Letty rose to her feet. "But it's almost dinner and neither of us are changed. Come, Fina, and you can help me choose a pretty gown to wear and do my hair for me."

Serafina heaved a sigh and, pushing all thoughts of matrimony out of her head, if with a little difficulty, as they steadfastly wanted to remain, rose to her feet. She would concentrate on Letty, and how best to ensure her mama didn't marry her off to someone in his dotage, just for a title, and not think about Max at all.

After Max had bid goodbye to a silent and subdued Serafina, Badger drove him home in the barouche. Back to Cavendish Square, that was. His aim had been to sneak inside and upstairs to his room, where he could ruminate on the unexpected reaction of Serafina to his proposal, much as she was doing in Great Titchfield Street. However, Maria happened to be in the hallway outside the parlor and she hailed him as though she'd not seen him for weeks.

"Max, wherever have you been? I had a letter from Julian this morning and he specifically mentioned you in it."

Uh oh. Max had a good idea in what context. He made a polite bow to the countess. "I've been out driving in the park. Or rather, Badger has. I was just the passenger. Of course."

Her eyebrows rose. "Oh? By yourself?" This remark was made with the implication that of course he'd not been alone and he ought to admit this to her straightaway or she'd tease it out of him.

Max steeled himself. He might as well grasp the bull by the horns and tell her. She'd give him no peace if he didn't. "With Miss Gilbert."

Maria's expression brimmed with triumph. "How lovely. And how is she? Shall I issue an invitation for her and Lady Gilbert to call for tea?"

Max gave a determined shake of his head. "Please don't. I doubt you'd find Lady Gilbert good company, and I fear to do so would be to play into her hands, as by her demeanor each time I call, it appears she would like nothing better to be on friendly terms with an earl and a countess. Or at least a countess, as Julian is not here."

"But Miss Gilbert is not like that, I trust?"

Why were women always so nosy? If he'd gone to his club instead, none of the men there would have asked him a single question about how he'd spent his afternoon. "No," he said in a tone that indicated, he hoped, his desire to end the conversation here. "She is made of different materials to her sister-in-law, thank goodness."

Maria opened her mouth for another question.

Max held up his hand. "I need to go and change for dinner, Maria. It takes me longer than it did, on account of my arm, and I wouldn't want to keep the family waiting." The one thing he didn't want to have to disclose was Serafina's obvious lack of enthusiasm for his marriage proposal. If she decided to refuse him, he didn't want anyone to know he'd even asked. It was bad enough having one's ego knocked without having one's family know that it had happened. So the less Maria knew about Serafina, the better.

Maria's face betrayed her disappointment at failing to glean any further information on his outing with that young lady. "Very well. Shall I ring for Watkins and send him up to you?"

"Thank you." And with that, Max hurried up the stairs out of her way.

Watkins joined him a few minutes later, puffing a little as

though he'd been running.

If he was going to share his predicament with anyone, it would be with the sensible Watkins, who could be relied upon to keep it to himself. His valet was several years his senior, and, having traveled extensively while in the army, probably would have described himself as a man of the world. He'd been known to share details of his amorous past with his master on a number of occasions. Mostly around campfires in Portugal and Spain, it had to be admitted, when differences of class had seemed far away and unimportant. But nevertheless, that easy camaraderie still existed between the two of them, and Watkins had on occasion corrected Max when needed.

Watkins pulled Max's boots off for him, revealing his thinning hair and a burgeoning bald spot as he bent.

Max stretched his legs. "Watkins…"

The valet was slipping the trees into the boots. "Yes, Captain?"

Max bit his lip. "You're a man who knows women, are you not?"

Watkins had the grace to blush. "I like to think I am, sir." He came to help Max out of his coat. "A clean shirt and cravat, sir?"

Max nodded. "Might I ask you a rather awkward question?"

Watkins brushed imaginary dust from the coat. "Of course you may, sir."

"Have you ever proposed to a girl?"

Watkins' bushy eyebrows rose. "As a matter of fact, I have. A long time ago."

Max pulled at his cravat and failed miserably to get it undone. Watkins came to his aid. "And did she answer in the affirmative?"

Watkins undid the top buttons of Max's shirt. "She did indeed, sir. And we were married forthwith, once the banns had been called."

This was news indeed to Max. Watkins had never mentioned a wife in all the time he'd known him, and if he had one now, he was keeping her well hidden. "Did she give you her answer straightaway?"

A faraway look came into Watkins's eyes. "She did, sir. She said yes straightaway. And we was married, like I said, as soon as the banns had been read. Happiest day of my life."

So Watkins's mysterious wife had known her mind immediately, and had in fact been in such a hurry they'd waited only the requisite three weeks to wed. What had he done wrong that Watkins had clearly done right?

Max rubbed his chin, which had grown stubbly during the day, uncomfortable at this catechism to which he was subjecting poor Watkins. "And did you love her?"

Watkins, who seemed not in the least bit uncomfortable, nodded. "I did, sir. I loved her with all my heart." The sincerity of his words rang true.

Max wriggled out of his dirty shirt, with Watkins' help. Damn this arm. "Might I ask where she is now?"

Watkins had the clean shirt ready. He helped Max into it before he replied, his voice solemn. "I was already in the army, you must understand. As you know, I joined up as a boy. I was home on leave when we decided to marry. We'd been sweethearts before I joined up. We married and had a few weeks together before I had to rejoin the regiment." He cleared his throat. "While I was gone, she caught the typhus fever. I never saw her again."

Max stared at his valet, a man who'd served him for nearly ten years, but who'd never revealed how he'd been married and widowed. "I'm sorry, Watkins. I feel this is something I should have known about you."

Watkins shook his head. "Nothing to be sorry about, Captain. Weren't your fault she caught the typhus fever. No one could've prevented it. Things like that just happen. But for a short while, she were mine, and we was happy. I've got that here." He patted his chest. "In my heart forever. I gets it out from time to time and it's still all warm and fresh, despite all the other women I've had doings with since then."

Max fell silent as Watkins helped him into his breeches and a fresh cravat. At last, attired suitably for dinner with the family, and his arm back in its sling, he turned to Watkins. "I wanted you to know, as I can trust you not to tell anyone else, that today I made an offer of marriage to a lady."

Watkins's eyes widened in genuine surprise before a gleam of pleasure lit them. "You did, sir? Please accept my congratulations, sir. I'm very pleased for you. Indeed I am."

Max shook his head. "That, I'm afraid, is not all. She hasn't given me an answer yet."

Watkins shrugged. "I'm sure she's just overwhelmed by your proposal, sir. Women, I mean young ladies, seem inclined to fits of the vapors when emotional. And I gather they're also fond of keeping gentlemen dancing on strings."

Max shook his head. "I don't think it's that, Watkins. I fear I've messed up my proposal and now she thinks I've made it just because I need my inheritance."

Watkins's eyes sharpened. He knew all about the details of the old earl's will. "Forgive me for asking, sir, but was it indeed only because of the inheritance that you made the proposal?"

Max compressed his lips, suddenly unwilling to admit the truth even to Watkins. If it was the truth. "Well, in a way I suppose it was. But I like the girl. I think we could rub along together well enough. I wouldn't have asked just anyone. She's not a vapid miss. She possesses a keen intellect."

Watkins smiled. "And am I to presume that because you're telling me all this, you require my advice?"

Max nodded. "I do. You're a sensible man and we've known each other a long time. You've been married, even though I didn't realize it. I value your wisdom."

Watkins sighed. "In my experience, Captain, a girl likes some romance in her life. Your young lady might not be a 'vapid miss,' as you say, and in possession of a keen intellect, but that doesn't mean she hasn't dreamed of true love. Did you, might I ask, inform her of the conditions of your father's will at the time of your proposal?"

Max nodded. "In the interest of honesty, I did. Full disclosure. I didn't want her to be ignorant of it."

Watkins shook his head, possibly in exasperation. "Perhaps not such a good idea. Honesty has its place, and I find in dealing with women—ladies—it is a somewhat unnecessary trait. Women like to hear what they want you to say, not what you want to say."

"So you're saying I shouldn't have told her why I have to marry?"

"I am, sir."

Max ruminated for a few seconds. "Damnit. I think I might have messed up."

Watkins flicked a speck of dust from Max's shoulder. "I think perhaps we might be able to undo your mistake. Go down to dinner and give me time to think about this."

Max sighed. "If you can get me out of this spot, then you're a miracle worker."

CHAPTER SEVENTEEN

SERAFINA DISCOVERED, TO her secret delight, that Ogden had been forced to hire a carriage to take his party to the Hadleigh Ball on Friday. And in fact, he'd also engaged both the coachman and the groom for the rest of their stay in Town. "We have to keep up appearances, my dear, whatever the expense," she'd overheard him saying to Araminta, "when our Letty is attracting so much attention. We don't want Mr. Talbot thinking we are not well off, with all that might entail."

Araminta had agreed with him, which in itself was unusual, as she was usually the more miserly of the two. "You are quite right, my dear. We certainly don't want Mr. Talbot to think we are out merely to catch a man with a fortune for Letty."

Probably she hadn't seen the irony in her statement. But whatever the cause, they now boasted a fine hired carriage in which to pay calls on people in Town or for rides out to the park for Letty to be seen by the beau monde, which of course meant her suitors. For this reason, the carriage possessed hoods that could be lowered in clement weather, although, for the outing to Hadleigh House, which stood in Berkley Square, the hoods were up. A fine wintry drizzle was falling, dispelling any inclination spring might have had to show its delicate nose.

Letty, beside herself with excitement at the thought of another ball and all the handsome young men who were about to fall at her feet, had already been reprimanded by Araminta. "Young men do not like young ladies who are too forward," she snapped, as her daughter settled her diaphanous skirts onto one of the carriage seats. "You do not wish to be thought of as fast. That would never do." Letty was wearing another new gown and, Serafina had been forced to admit, looked quite ravishing.

A ridiculous longing to be able to look ravishing herself had settled in her bosom and refused to relinquish its hold on her. However, a quick glance into the mirror in their bedroom before she'd descended the stairs had told her that she herself did not look in the least bit ravishing, but rather plain and boring in a gown she'd owned for several years now. Admittedly it was made of cream silk, accounted for by the fact that it had once belonged to Araminta, but nevertheless it was not the height of fashion as gleaned from Letty's magazines, and nor was it new. A little mischievous voice inside Serafina was busy complaining that if she were to see Max tonight, she would have liked to have been more strikingly attired in order to make a better impression on him. She hushed the voice.

The journey to Hadleigh House took very little time, despite the roads being busy with other carriages all heading in the same direction. The Earl and Countess of Hadleigh, Araminta informed them as they joined the throng waiting to alight at the doors, were amongst the most influential members of the *ton*. A kind word from Lady Hadleigh could be the making of a girl and lead to the forging of a very advantageous marital state.

Not that she was likely to have a kind word for Serafina, who had no illusions of grandeur. However, despite her avowal to lock away her infatuation, she couldn't still the wild beating of her heart at the thought she might be going to see Max again, and that he might renew his request for her hand. Time, and much mulling over of his offer, had produced in her, amongst other things, a realization that she was unlikely to receive any other offers, and that if she had to marry someone, then surely marrying a man she was already infatuated with might be for the best. Even if he wasn't similarly infatuated with her.

The alternatives, once carefully considered, didn't bear thinking about. Suppose, for example, Ogden and Araminta found someone like that old duke Letty had mentioned to marry her off to? Not a duke, obviously, as they would be reserving one of those for Letty, but possibly an old man in need of a nurse for his twilight years, or as a stepmother for his brood of children, who would, of course, be unmanageable. Both possibilities were abhorrent and depressing, so she'd come out tonight almost convinced she could accept Max's offer. Despite her continuing inner sadness that the offer hadn't been made out of something more than practicality.

Their driver maneuvered the carriage into place by the large doors into Hadleigh House and a liveried footman stepped up to let down the step and open the door for them. Ogden descended first and handed first Araminta and then Letty out onto the pavement. He then turned his back on Serafina. But a gloved hand was extended, and in surprise Serafina took the young footman's hand as he helped her out. However, the look in his eyes as his gaze ran over the parlous state of her gown had heat rushing to her cheeks. The pity of a servant was not something she could ever become used to.

Biting back her embarrassment, she smiled and nodded to him and followed her family into the house, her head held high as though she were Cinderella in her fine, fairy-godmother-made gown about to meet her prince.

If anything, Hadleigh House was more splendid than the Ponsonby's, being constructed on a larger scale, with higher ceilings, wider rooms, bigger chandeliers, more people and what sounded like louder music. Already, a fug of warmth filled the air, bringing with it the inevitable aroma of exotic perfumes worn by men and women alike and smothering any scent that might have clung to the displays of hothouse flowers in every alcove.

Serafina gazed about herself in consternation. If Max were here, how would she ever find him?

Araminta seemed certain of where they were going, and led

the way through the crowds of chattering people towards the source of the music. A veritable orchestra was seated on a raised dais at one end of a large ballroom, diligently plying their trade. Clusters of people lined the edges, some seated at small round tables, others on upholstered benches and still more standing about and watching the dancing going on in the center of the room. No sign of Max though. Nor his formidable mother.

Like bees to an exotic flower, young men flocked to Letty's side, clamoring for her attention and vying with one another for the honor of leading her out in each dance. Serafina edged closer to her niece, putting a gentle hand on her shoulder and dropping her voice to whisper a warning in her ear. "Do not forget to leave a dance spare for Mr. Talbot. Your mama wishes you to encourage him and I have to agree with her advice."

But Letty shook her off. "Pooh. If he's not here to claim his dance then he's going to miss out. I can't possibly dance with everyone, can I?" Unlike Serafina, she didn't keep her voice down, and several of the young men crowding around her seemed encouraged to press their suits further.

"One dance only for each of them then," Serafina added. It would not do at all to allow Letty to dance twice with any gentleman. Not even the as yet unseen Mr. Talbot. Well, perhaps they could make an exception for him, if he asked.

Letty shot her a discouraging frown and returned to flirting with her entourage of admirers. Amongst whom the two young gamblers Serafina had warned her about seemed much in prominence. Hopefully, Letty would remember what she'd told her about them and not allow them a dance at all. The naughty girl turned her back on Serafina with determination, and her laughter rose towards the chandeliers.

Well, if she wanted to behave like that, who was she, Serafina, to stop her? As this was a totally new thought, it brought her up short. Everything she'd ever done up until this point had been with Letty's welfare in mind. And until now Letty had been reasonably biddable, as long as Serafina hadn't crossed her, which of course she'd tried hard to avoid. However, here in London, she seemed to have suddenly got the bit between her teeth intent on bolting out of Serafina's restraining company.

Serafina compressed her lips. Tonight, for once, she was going to do something for herself. Instead of putting Letty before her own concerns, she was going to put herself first. Letty couldn't come to any appreciable harm here, and she did have her mother to keep an eye on her. She could leave her to indulge herself with all her many admirers, and try to enjoy the ball for what it was. Perhaps someone might even ask her to dance if she wasn't hiding in a corner all evening.

And perhaps if she perambulated about the room, she might find Max.

Leaving Araminta and Ogden smiling fondly over their daughter's obvious success, she slid away from them and headed towards the refreshment room. A glass of lemonade would give her something to do with her hands, and make her feel as though she stood out less as alone amongst so many people in groups or couples.

She reached the table where a footman was serving glasses of lemonade to warm dancers and made her way to the front of the press. She was just extending her hand to take a glass when a voice sounded from behind her. "Allow me to get you a glass, Miss Gilbert."

Max. His deep voice was unmistakable.

He'd spotted Serafina from his secluded vantage point on the far side of the room the moment she'd entered with her brother's family, and watched her careful detachment from the crowd around Letty and her progress into the refreshment room. Buoyed up with Watkins' advice, he'd headed after her to cut off any possible idea she might have of returning to Letty's side. He wanted her to himself tonight.

Now, she swung around to find him standing a mere foot behind her, and their eyes met. She managed a small smile. "Why

Captain Aubrey, what a surprise you have given me." Somehow, here in public, it hadn't felt right to call her by her first name, and she seemed to be of the same mind. If anyone had overheard such familiarity, gossip could start.

He picked up a glass and handed it to her, then took one for himself. "I had hoped to see you here, but after our last meeting I couldn't be sure you would come."

Warm color rose to her cheeks, bestowing a healthy and attractive glow to their normal pallor. "I am here to attend on my niece, of course."

He raised his eyebrows. "I don't see her with you."

She looked flustered as though uncertain how to answer this. Inspiration, and a fleeting look of relief, came to her. "I was just fetching her some refreshment."

He smiled. Watkins had suggested he should smile a lot to make sure she knew he liked her company. It wasn't hard, as after all, he did find her company interesting. A little intriguing, even. "Then why are you sipping it yourself?"

It must have been a natural reaction to taste the lemonade as he handed it to her. Her color deepened, and she glanced about herself furtively. "I shall drink this one myself and then fetch her another."

He smiled. "I would rather you didn't return to wait upon that rather spoiled young lady, but instead spent a little time with me."

Let her know you want to spend time with her, Watkins had said. *Make sure she knows how much you want to please her.*

Serafina flustered was a sight to behold, with flushed cheeks and widened eyes, her breasts rising and falling as though she were finding it hard to breathe. Max had never truly learned to flirt, as his previous associations with women had been with ladies of a different class during his time at Oxford and in the army, none of which had begun in a ballroom. However, Watkins seemed to have a natural instinct for how to engage the feelings of a young lady of class.

"Perhaps you would care to promenade around the ballroom with me, as I cannot ask you to dance?" Max said, as this was another of Watkins's suggestions. Did the working classes do much the same at whatever dances they might hold?

Serafina shot him a puzzled look, but when he set down his untouched lemonade and held out his good left arm, she slipped her hand into the crook. "That would be most agreeable." She appeared to have herself back under control. It occurred to him to wonder what might have been going through her mind since that drive in the park and his rather ham-fisted proposal. He wasn't used to putting himself in the shoes of another, at least, not unless it was another soldier on the battlefield. And especially not seeing inside the head of such an alien creature as a woman.

He steered her slowly around the dance floor, conscious of the curious stares of more than a few of the other guests. Let them stare. What made him more of a spectacle than all the other gentlemen doing exactly the same thing? His arm, of course, and the fact that he was escorting a young lady none of them would recognize.

"I fear I might have offended you yesterday afternoon," he said, sticking to his plan to grab the proverbial bull by the horns. Not that Serafina remotely resembled a bull.

She looked up at him, her gaze direct. "I was not offended."

Well, that was something. What next? "Perhaps I was a little too blunt in what I said to you."

She gave a small shrug of her slender shoulders. "You were honest, and I admire honesty in a person."

All good so far. "But in matters of… marriage, I fear total honesty is something less than romantic."

She smiled. "On the contrary, honesty is to be admired and sought after where marriage is concerned. I would not want to enter into any contract where honesty was not at the forefront of the arrangement."

His vow to approach her in a more romantic fashion, as advised by Watkins, seemed to rapidly be disintegrating. And she was doing the demolition. "You didn't mind when I told you why I need to marry?"

She shook her head. "Always best to be frank from the very start."

As this was how he'd felt himself only yesterday, he couldn't argue with her reasoning. However, he had to inject romance in here somewhere. "But I neglected to tell you why I want to marry."

Her brow furrowed. "Why, you wish to marry because if you don't you won't receive your substantial inheritance. Plain and simple. I believe there is nothing more to say on that subject."

For a moment Max was lost for words. He'd been planning to tell her that he wanted to marry her rather than anyone else because he admired her, because he liked her, and because he found her good company, but she'd forestalled him there. Probably Watkins would have protested that those were not romantic reasons. Damn Watkins. This was not going the way he'd predicted.

She, however, was not at all lost for words. "Am I being presumptuous in thinking that the reason for your approach this evening is to press your suit?"

He nodded. "It is." Not much else he could say.

She halted, turning slightly to look up at him, her gray eyes veiled and her expression unreadable. "Then I shall set your mind at rest. You may have my acceptance, Captain Aubrey. I agree to marry you so that you may receive your inheritance and that I might become the chatelaine of your estate. Your conditions of marriage suit me well. I shall escape my brother's house and endeavor to perform my duties as hostess for you whenever required." She drew a breath. "It will be, as you said, a marriage of convenience, and we will both continue to live our lives as we see fit."

Max stared at her, all thoughts of how to smooth the way between them flown. Her demeanor had changed to businesslike, her words were calm and sounded well rehearsed. That she'd been planning how to accept his proposal seemed evident. So why wasn't he feeling pleased?

Pushing his worries out of his head, he bowed over her hand, then lifted it to his lips. "I shall be honored to have you as my wife... Miss Gilbert." Their easy intimacy as friends at the museum and in the park had vanished.

She nodded. "And I shall be honored to have you as my husband, Captain." She paused. "And now, perhaps, we had better go and inform my brother and his wife. I fear my niece will not be happy that I have received and accepted an offer of marriage before her. She may need some mollification."

CHAPTER EIGHTEEN

THE MARRIAGE OF Captain Maxim Aubrey and Miss Serafina Gilbert was to take place three weeks later, to allow for the reading of banns in the churches adjacent to where they were both living. As predicted, Letty had been far from amused that the aunt everyone considered plain-faced and unmarriageable had succeeded in securing a proposal before she had. And from the brother of an earl, no less, with, as a prune-faced Araminta pointed out, only a sicky brother and two small boys who could all too easily succumb to any childhood illness before they reached adulthood between him and the actual earldom.

As Max had been the one to inform Ogden and Araminta of his proposal to Serafina, and he'd done so in public at the ball, they'd been unable to express anything other than rather tight-lipped congratulations. And they maintained this silence all the way home in their hired carriage, most likely in case the driver overheard them and gossiped. He was only a hireling, after all, and would have no loyalty to them, and it was well known that with servants you get what you pay for, or so Araminta said later. However, once they were home and a somewhat subdued and sulky Letty had been dispatched upstairs to bed, they both rounded on Serafina in the cold parlor.

"Have I nurtured, no, loved like my own and cared for like a mother, a viper in my bosom?" Araminta began with, the moment the door had closed behind the departing footman.

Serafina stood her ground but remained silent. Three weeks and she'd be away from this house. She began to see the wisdom in having agreed to accept Max's offer. Not that she hadn't before, just that Araminta's reaction was successfully hammering it home.

"Has he compromised you?" Ogden almost snarled. "Is that why he's being forced to offer for you? Did you set out to snare him? Like the wanton hussy who called herself your mother did with my father? I've always thought you cut from the same mold as that woman and now we have the proof before us."

Serafina bit her lip at both the insult to the mother she'd never known and the absurdity of his accusation, but maintained what she hoped was a dignified silence. What she'd really like to have done was fly at him with her fists and claw his eyes out. One of these days, she'd not be able to hold onto her temper. For now, she grit her teeth and pretended to feel nothing.

Araminta, however, seized upon the idea that she'd done something untoward to secure this offer like a terrier with a bone. "I should never have allowed you to go driving with him without a maid." Her eyes narrowed. "Did you lure him into compromising you? Is that it? For I cannot see that a well-connected man such as Captain Aubrey would ever consider importuning a girl like you voluntarily. Not one so plain and with alarming tendencies towards being a bluestocking." She pronounced this last word as though it were the worst of all insults one could throw at a girl.

Serafina's cheeks warmed, not just with embarrassment, and behind her back she clenched her fists. The notion that she would like to plant her sister-in-law a facer with one of them burgeoned. "No, Captain Aubrey did not compromise me. He is far too much of a gentleman to do so. And I confess myself shocked that you think I, whom you have so diligently brought up to know right from wrong, would ever consider luring a gentleman into a compromising position." She widened her eyes deliberately. "As you know, I have no experience with young men whatsoever. I have no idea how one even becomes compromised." That last bit wasn't entirely true. The memory of the incorrigible Letty clasped in the arms of her lusty stableboy arose. If that wasn't getting oneself compromised, Serafina wasn't sure what was. How shocked would Araminta and Ogden be if she were to reveal their own daughter's dreadful behavior. But she couldn't do that to Letty. Annoying as she could be, it would be so unfair. Luckily for her niece, she was a girl who rarely acted on impulse.

Ogden spluttered in what looked like amazement before joining in again. "If you ask me, you have ambitions above your station in life, my girl. I cannot possibly believe this offer to be genuine. To the mere half-sister of a baronet."

The irony of his words, bearing in mind he and Araminta had been considering the merits of that ancient duke for 'the mere daughter of a baronet' must have been lost on him, because he didn't blink an eye as he said this.

"I can assure you his proposal is genuine." Serafina bit her lip again, determined not to disclose the reasons behind the proposal. How Araminta would laugh if she discovered it to be a marriage of convenience with money at its heart. She must never know. Too humiliating. "And I have already accepted it. Captain Aubrey came to you as a matter of formality. I am of age and am able to make my own decisions." As she had been for some time. She forbore from adding that on her marriage she would like control of the legacy from her father that Ogden had been hanging on to. It wouldn't do to rile him too much. His face already had an apoplectic hue to it.

Araminta's eyes flashed. "While you are in my house, you will do as you are told, miss."

"My brother's house," Serafina retorted. "And we are not in his house at the moment but merely in a rented property in London."

"Ogden!" Araminta gasped, fanning herself with her hand as though she might be about to suffer a fit of the vapors. "Stop her from talking to me like this. Immediately."

Serafina, her confidence growing by the moment, fought to keep herself under control. The inclination to spill every grievance she'd ever felt rose within her breast, but she must not allow her emotions to run away with themselves. Not at this late a date. What was it her old nurse had said to her on more than one occasion? *Discretion is the greater part of valor.* She was finding it difficult to remain discreet.

Ogden wagged a pudgy finger at her. "You ungrateful hussy. You should remember who it is who took you in when your father died. Who it is who's fed and clothed you. Who it is has brought you to London where you've had the luck to meet with someone foolish enough, or blind enough, to take you on. Apologize to my wife immediately."

Serafina compressed her lips. She did, after all, have to live with them for another three weeks so she'd better comply. "I am sorry if I offended you with my words, Araminta, but I only spoke the truth. I am no longer Ogden's ward and am free to do as I wish." She drew a breath. "I didn't intend to sound rude, only to point out my standing."

Araminta's brows met in a furious scowl. "Your place is to do as you're told and to remember how lucky you are. We could have sent you off to the workhouse if we'd been less generously minded."

Less generously minded? Images from Serafina's childhood almost spun before her eyes. Thin bread and butter in a cold nursery, the sleeves of her dresses always too short as she grew, holes in her shoes that she'd had to line with paper, watching the nurses doting over little Letty while she was ignored in a corner by all except for Agnes. And then Agnes being turned away, all because she'd had the temerity to ask for a new gown for her small, threadbare charge and an extra blanket for her bed. Generosity had never been at the forefront of Araminta's treatment of her. Serafina had at times wondered if the woman took pleasure in causing her misery. Well, she'd soon be away from them now.

Still, she couldn't say any of this. Yet. If ever. "I very much appreciate the way you took me in when I was orphaned," she said, keeping her voice as low and humble as possible, which turned out to be more difficult than she expected. "I'm very grateful to have been brought up in such circumstances. Grateful and lucky."

Her tone of voice must have worked. Araminta harrumphed and smoothed down the skirts of her new puce gown. "And so you should be. I can't abide ungratefulness and this engagement smacks to me of just such a thing. You've done it to spite me. And to spite our dear little Letty, who you know is the one for whom we are here."

Serafina kept her eyes down. "I am sorry if you feel I've acted ungratefully, but I thought you might be glad to get me off your hands and lessen the outlay you have to make for me. I'm sure I've been a terrible expense over the years."

Ogden snorted, completely missing her sarcasm. "And you've been very expensive indeed. I've a mind to ask that suitor of yours to contribute something towards my costs in having to bring you up."

As Serafina couldn't think of anything much they'd ever spent on her, all her clothes having been secondhand, and her meals as a child having consisted of mainly leftovers in the kitchens with Cook, she held her tongue. Wisely. One thing she'd learnt from life in her brother's household was when to do that.

Araminta tutted loudly. "I'd very much like to do that too, Ogden, but I fear it's not the done thing, even when one has had the generosity to take in a foundling." She turned her stony gaze on Serafina. "But we will miss her help with Letty and the other children. We might even have to hire in another nurse. That will be a dreadful expense." She looked back at Ogden. "Perhaps we can delay her marriage for a year. A long engagement would suit me and be helpful with the children."

This had to be stopped. "No," Serafina said, a little amazed at her own bravery. "Captain Aubrey has explicitly said that we are to wed as soon as the banns have been read. He does not want to delay… and neither do I."

Araminta's gaze fell to Serafina's flat belly, and her lip curled. "You don't want to delay? Are you certain you haven't been compromised?" Her thin cheeks flushed. "Did you allow him to take… liberties with you in the privacy of his carriage? Has he touched you anywhere he shouldn't have?"

Ogden's piggy eyes sprang wide open. "You don't mean that she…?"

Serafina controlled the urge to stamp her foot. "I am not with child!"

That shut them both up. For a few seconds.

Araminta found her voice first. "Serafina! We do not mention such a condition in the presence of a gentleman. Have you no decorum?"

This was too much. "You broached the subject by suggesting I might be."

Araminta's mouth opened and closed a couple of times but no words came out.

Ogden took advantage of his wife's shock to interrupt. "Enough. I have heard quite enough for one night. Go to your room, Serafina, and leave us to discuss your possible engagement alone."

"My engagement," Serafina said, emboldened by her previous bravery. "Nothing 'possible' about it. I am engaged."

"Go," shrieked Araminta. "Go now, impudent girl. Now."

Serafina, her breathing coming fast as though she'd been running, and already repenting on having allowed herself to get so uncharacteristically carried away, lifted her chin, turned on the spot and stalked out of the room without even a 'goodnight'. That would have rather ruined her exit.

LETTY WAS SITTING up in bed wearing her nightgown and a fetching lacy nightcap, and sipping a cup of chamomile tea when Serafina arrived.

Serafina closed the door and leaned against it, struggling to control her breathing after her headlong flight up the stairs. She'd been rather hoping to find Letty asleep.

Letty set down her cup and stuck out her lower lip in a sulky fashion. "I must say, I never thought you would try to upstage me, Fina. That's a little unfair of you." Then her face slipped and she giggled, for she was not, at heart, a spiteful girl. At least not unless she was crossed. "But I must say it's worth being upstaged to have seen the expression on Mama's face when Captain Aubrey announced that you two were engaged. If only there were some way to preserve that image for me to take out every now and again to laugh at. She looked as though she'd just bitten into a large and very bitter sloe in mistake for a sweet plum. So funny."

Serafina managed a rueful smile. "I suppose perhaps you are right."

"Right? Of course I am. And Papa's face was nearly as bad. I must say, I was glad to be sent to bed because I was having such a hard time preventing myself from laughing out loud." She stuck her lower lip out again. "Although I do think you might have waited to make your announcement until I had formed an attachment of my own. Until Mr. Talbot has offered for me."

"Do you think he will?" Anything to distract Letty from discussing the engagement.

Letty's face brightened, her favorite subject being herself. "I do think so. He seems most taken with me and was very annoyed that I had no dances left on my card when he came to ask me." She tittered. "I had to tell him that I'm finding myself very much in demand and that if he wants to dance with me in future then he must arrive earlier. And with that he invited me to come out driving with him in the park tomorrow. I haven't told Mama yet. She's been too taken up with your news." She frowned. "When she should in all truth be concentrating on me. Unfair of you to dominate her attention like this."

This was something Serafina could deal with, and agreeing

with Letty would keep her on track. "She should indeed be focusing on you. I am of no importance whatsoever. My future is settled. We must all concentrate on you." She abandoned the support of the door and came to sit on the edge of Letty's bed. "Driving in the park, you say? You'll enjoy that."

Letty frowned again. "A drive in the park seemed to convince Captain Aubrey he wished for your hand, so perhaps Mr. Talbot will feel the same about me when we are driving together. Apparently he has the most dashing horses to draw his curricle." A smile lit her face. "And everyone who is anyone will be there in the afternoon and all the other gentlemen who've been paying me court will see me out with Mr. Talbot in his curricle and be jealous. That will be most satisfying."

Why Letty wanted to create jealousy between her suitors escaped Serafina, but she nodded in agreement. "And you will have the most wonderful time. I saw this evening how Mr. Talbot, despite not dancing with you, kept in constant attendance, fetching you lemonade and fanning you when you grew hot from dancing. I think he must indeed be going to offer for you soon."

Letty pulled a cross face. "I wish he'd make up his mind, or I might change mine. Sir Arthur Dawlish asked me to dance tonight and he is as handsome as… as a Greek god."

The fact that the unstudious Letty had any idea of what a Greek god might look like took Serafina by surprise, but she glossed over that. Sir Arthur Dawlish, she already knew, had a reputation as a bit of a rake. If he were plying his suit with Letty it might very well not be with marriage in mind. "I'd stay clear of him if I were you."

Letty giggled. "But I rather like him. He's a bit more… fun than Mr. Talbot. And a lot younger."

Serafina sighed and got up off the bed. "Fun is probably not what one wants in a husband. If you remember, we had a list of attributes we were looking for in a suitor for you, and fun didn't figure in that list."

"Not being boring did though."

"Mr. Talbot isn't boring, is he? I thought he seemed very pleasant."

"He's boring compared with Sir Arthur Dawlish."

Serafina, who by necessity was adept at getting herself out of gowns and petticoats unaided, began to undress. "Don't compare Mr. Talbot with a rake. How do you think rakes get to be so popular and gain that reputation? Because they are fun to be with and ladies like that. But fun does not mean reliability and we want a reliable indulgent husband for you. Like Mr. Talbot. I'm sure he will dote on you. I doubt very much that Sir Arthur Dawlish is on the hunt for a wife."

Letty snuggled down into her bedclothes. "I suppose you are right." She paused. "Is Captain Aubrey reliable, do you think?"

That was a question. Serafina hung up her evening gown to give herself time to think. Was he? He'd asked her to marry him just to inherit a fortune. Was that the action of a reliable man? A fortune he'd had plenty of time to acquire in the past by marriage but had neglected to accomplish until just a few months before the deadline. Did both those actions not make him impulsive rather than reliable? Still… "He's the most reliable man I know." Not a lie, as she only really knew him and Ogden.

She wriggled into her nightgown and jumped into bed. Hooray. Two hot bricks wrapped snugly in cloth down at the foot of the bed to keep her feet warm overnight. Leaning over, she blew out their one candle. "And now I'm very tired so I'm going to sleep. Goodnight, Letty."

CHAPTER NINETEEN

O N THE FOLLOWING afternoon, Letty's carriage drive failed to produce the required proposal but, afterwards, Letty professed herself as quite content as she'd had the most wonderful time waving to acquaintances in the park. Gentlemen, of course, and her new friend Lady Arabella Aubrey who'd been out driving with a young man who'd also had the temerity to call on Letty the previous day and express his undying love. However, this had not marred Letty's pleasure, as Mr. Talbot's horses were far better than "the pair of bone-setters Lady Arabella was being driven around the park behind". Letty could, in fact, have been described as unattractively smug. Mr. Talbot possessed a pair of "beautiful steppers", or at least he'd informed Letty, who had no eye for horseflesh, that they were.

The early spring weather had been almost balmy, so the carriage hood had been lowered and she'd been able to stop and chat to numerous people, including several of the other young gentlemen who had been her callers, all having to control their expressions of resentment at seeing her out in Mr. Talbot's company.

"It was such fun, Fina," she confided on her return, while well out of earshot of her mama. "I saw Sir Arthur on his horse, a fine blood chestnut that made him look so dashing. Almost like an old-time knight in shining armor." She giggled, no doubt at the memory. "And he was quite green with envy that I was in Mr.

Talbot's carriage. So I waved to him, and Mr. Talbot had to stop so we could speak, and when we parted, it was Mr. Talbot who was the envious one, for I shamelessly flirted with Sir Arthur just for that reason." She giggled again, those blue eyes dancing with mischief. "I've decided that my favorite pastime is flirting. In fact, I'm not sure I want to become engaged. At least not yet. For it would prevent me from flirting with all the gentlemen who seem to like me so much. That would be boring."

As she'd already worryingly expressed a similar sentiment, for a moment, Serafina couldn't think of a reply to this confession. At least not one that wouldn't send Letty off into a sulky huff. She took the time to perform several more neat stitches on the embroidery she was doing. One that Letty would be required to sit holding and pretending to sew whenever callers could be expected, so they would see her as the perfect image of feminine industry. Araminta knew all too well that were Letty to sit holding her own embroidery, no one would be fooled into thinking her accomplished in that direction. A ridiculous notion, as surely men were not attracted by the sewing skills of their intendeds.

Having composed herself, Serafina poked her needle into the edge of the embroidery and looked up. "I can quite understand why you find talking to all your young gentlemen so much fun. But we need to remember the purpose of our visit to London, Letty. Your mama and papa, who love you dearly, are keen to see you married well." She managed a smile. "You're young, and this is your first time in London." As it was her own, of course. "And the excitement of it must be intoxicating for you, especially as you've already been such a success. However, it might be wise to fix your interests on one gentleman, although of course it doesn't have to be Mr. Talbot." She paused to let that sink in. "However, it should perforce be a gentleman who is likewise looking for a spouse, not someone who merely wishes to flirt, or more, with a young and pretty lady."

"Or more?"

Serafina frowned. She was groping in the dark here due to her own lack of experience, but she had observed a few love affairs amongst the servants and tenants at Milford, albeit from a discreet distance. "Yes. More. Not all gentlemen are… true gentlemen. It behooves us to make sure we do not associate with their like. To do so could be disastrous for a young lady."

"Do you mean to imply that Sir Arthur is not a gentleman?"

Serafina nodded. "I fear he is not.'

Letty's turn to frown. "But he's very handsome." She dimpled. "Like a Greek god. He has such broad shoulders, and the sort of hair a girl could run her fingers through, and the most kissable lips shaped a little like a Cupid's bow, and…"

"None of those things featured on the list we made before leaving Milford, and I fear they are all the things that make him a successful rake."

"But he's so very handsome…"

As was Max. And yet Serafina was sure he was a gentleman in every sense of the word, if one didn't take into account his desire to marry purely to inherit his estate. That didn't sound all that gentlemanly when she thought about it. If he hadn't been so handsome, would she have considered agreeing to the arrangement? If he'd been old and fat, or short and bald? Or ancient like the Duke of Dunbar Araminta had dismissed as unsuitable for Letty. She wouldn't think about the possibility that her agreement had anything to do with his looks. She stiffened her spine. "Being handsome and charming is part of the weaponry of the ungentlemanly gentleman, I fear."

Letty leaned in close, keeping her voice low, even though they were alone in the parlor. "Like Will Masters?"

Will had been the stableboy she'd had the dalliance with. Who knew how long it had been going on before Serafina had surprised them in one another's arms in the stables? There was, after all, ample room in a hayloft for all sorts of misdeeds. Serafina had not grown up in the countryside without gaining a reasonable knowledge of procreation. "He was not a gentleman at all," she said, with determination. "Not in any sense of the word."

Unabashed, Letty dimpled. "But he was very handsome, as well as decidedly charming and excellent at kissing."

Serafina nodded. "He was indeed, and I suspect that he is the sort of young man who uses his looks to his advantage wherever he works. Just like a rake does in society ballrooms. That young man took advantage of your lack of experience, which was unforgiveable, and he paid for it by losing his position. I fear Sir Arthur is cut from the same cloth as young Will, but had the luck to be born with more advantages in life. However, I'm certain he intends only the same outcome."

A whimsical expression stole over Letty's face as though she were remembering with fondness her brief association with young Will. "Do you think so? Do you think he will want to kiss me? I think I'd rather like that…"

Good heavens. Did the naughty girl actually want to be seduced by a rake?

Serafina sighed. "I do indeed, and you can stop simpering about it because it's not good. Not at all." Letty had to be weaned from this rather disturbing propensity to encourage the most unsuitable of admirers. "And if you were to behave in such a way with any of the young gentlemen who call on you, straightaway you would be ruined. Men like Sir Arthur have no intention of marrying, even if they have compromised the lady in question, and once compromised, men like Mr. Talbot, or even octogenarian dukes in search of a nurse for their old age, would never consider you for marriage. You would have to remain an old maid at Milford for the rest of your life, with all that entails."

Letty's face fell as the enormity of this outcome settled over her. "Oh my goodness. I don't want that to happen to me." She sounded properly frightened, which was just as Serafina had intended. Now the prospect of that fate had been removed from her own future, she felt at liberty to use it as a stick with which to castigate Letty.

Better rub it in just a little bit harder so her charge wouldn't forget it in a hurry. "No, you don't. Imagine all your life in that house with no fires in the bedrooms and chilblains every winter, because Teddy will grow up to be as tightfisted as your papa, you mark my words." One of the best things about her niece was the ease with which she could be manipulated. Possibly due to her distinct lack of brain power.

Letty nodded with vigor. "You are quite right. I can assure you that dear Mr. Talbot looks more attractive by the minute. I shall dismiss Sir Arthur and his deceptive good looks from my mind immediately." She turned a bright smile on Serafina. "I'm so glad I have you, Fina. I did think that when I was married I might take you with me to my new home, to help look after my children." She sighed. "But now I won't be able to, and I shall miss you dreadfully. Are you sure you want to marry Captain Aubrey? Might you not be happier to come and live with me? I promise you that you'll have a fire in your room all year around."

Serafina put an arm around Letty's slender shoulders. "I'm sorry, my darling, but I do wish to marry Captain Aubrey, and even your tempting offer of a fire all year round in my room won't sway me. However, when we are both in charge of our own households, we can visit each other whenever we like. I shall look forward to that." And she planted a kiss on Letty's forehead. "I think if your Mr. Talbot offers for you, you'd best say yes."

NEWS OF MAX'S engagement received a far different reaction in Cavendish Square. Both his mother and sister were pleased for him, eventually, Maria a little more so than the dowager.

"That's wonderful, Max," Maria said, a genuinely relieved smile on her face, when he met her at breakfast. "I shall invite Miss Gilbert to call on us forthwith. Your mama will wish to become acquainted with your intended."

His mother, who hadn't been at the Hadleigh ball, reacted with slightly less enthusiasm much later in the morning when she deigned to rise and descend to the parlor. In fact, she looked down her long nose at him with a distinct air of reproval to start with. "Miss Gilbert? Do you mean the rather fast hussy who has been attracting all that attention to herself and has all the young men of the Season queueing at her door? Throwing herself at my grandsons, too, so I hear." By this she meant Henry and Louis, who were really only her step-grandsons but of whom she had become very fond over the years.

Max shook his head. "No, Mama, not her, for goodness sake. Do you think me mad? Her aunt."

His mother's thin eyebrows shot towards her hairline. "Her aunt?" Her voice rose in astonishment. "That girl has an aunt? How old is the woman? You need to marry someone young enough to bear you children, Maxim, not some dried up old maid."

"Mama," Max said, his tone even more reproving than hers had been. "You are jumping to unnecessary conclusions, as usual. Miss Gilbert is a very young aunt, being only a few years older than her niece. Quite young enough to produce children." As he said this last sentence, heat swarmed up his neck to his cheeks, impossible to control. Because there would be no children, as this was purely a business arrangement, and she didn't want his attentions. She'd made that very clear.

His mother, her sharp eyes on his warm cheeks, harrumphed. "You are certain she's not lying to you about her age?"

"Absolutely certain. Her father was married twice. The first marriage produced her brother. The second produced Serafina. She was a small child when her father died."

"No mother?"

"No mother."

"Gilbert. Let me see. I'm sure I know the name. Are they from Hampshire?"

"Berkshire. Her uncle, Sir Ogden, owns a small estate there. I believe it is called Milford."

She stared past him towards the window, for a moment far away. "She can't be related to Sir George Gilbert, can she by any chance?"

What was that wistful tone in her voice? Unsure, Max could only shrug. "I don't know. She might be. Why?"

A smile crept over his mother's face. "He was a young man I once knew, that's why. When I was a girl. A long time ago now." She shook her head but Max didn't miss how misty-eyed she'd become. "I came out when I was just seventeen and he was one of my many admirers." She patted her graying hair. "You might not think it now, but at seventeen I was considered quite a beauty."

"I've seen your portrait, don't forget. And Arabella takes after you." He paused. "And of course, you're still a beautiful woman now, Mama. You know you are."

"Age leaves its indelible mark, Max. I'm no longer a girl of seventeen. But when I was, one of the young gentlemen who came calling at my father's house was called Sir George Gilbert. Older than me of course, but devastatingly handsome with his auburn hair. Hidden under a wig, back then of course, and cut very short, but given away by his beautiful brows." She chuckled. "I quite fell for him, I confess, my heart being that of an impressionable girl. And he for me. But your own dear papa was also pressing his suit, and of course, my parents preferred an earl to a mere baronet for me. In those days, one had to do what one's parents instructed, not like the lax approach nowadays." She shook her head again, eyes even more misty at the memory. "Don't mistake me. I had a very happy life with your papa, but I've never forgotten George and his auburn brows. Never. That must be where the young Gilbert hussy gets her striking coloring from."

His mother so infrequently revealed anything about her inner feelings that Max could find nothing to say in return. That she might have married Sir George herself was a revelation, but if she had, they would all have been different people.

His mother reached out and took his hand. "I think you should invite your Miss Gilbert to call on us. I would very much like to find out if she is George's daughter and see if there's anything about her that reminds me of him."

Max nodded. "Maria was before you in this. I believe she's already issuing an invitation." He sighed. "However, I fear we'll receive not just Serafina but also her brother and his wife."

His mother looked pleased. "Wonderful. I should very much like to meet them if they are related to Sir George. I wonder if the present baronet is as handsome as Sir George was?"

She was going to be sadly disappointed when she met Ogden, and Max couldn't help thinking she might also be disappointed in Serafina. Yes, he could see beneath the plain exterior, and she had beautiful eyes which perhaps she'd inherited from her father, but she was nothing like her pretty niece. It seemed more than likely that there was a close relationship between his mother's old beau and Serafina's family, but that did not mean they were going to please her.

CHAPTER TWENTY

W HEN THE INVITATION came to call on the Dowager Countess of Westbury and her daughter-in-law, the present countess, Araminta could barely conceal her satisfaction. The missive arrived at breakfast, which was being taken at ten in the morning as Araminta's habit was not to rise until that advanced hour. The footman she'd engaged on their arrival brought the note in on a silver tray and presented it to her with some aplomb for a young man being paid the lowest amount possible. He must have been desperate for a job.

Ogden, whose head was buried in his morning copy of *The Times* newspaper, ignored this arrival.

Without a glance for her husband, who should have been the one opening it, Araminta unfolded the sheet of paper. As she read, her face, which had been wearing its usual sour expression, took on the appearance of the cook's cat having her bowl filled with the unexpected largesse of cream. Her normally pebble hard eyes shone with triumphant excitement for an instant, before something must have dawned on her and she veiled them in a hurry.

Serafina, who'd been nibbling a piece of toast as she wasn't at all hungry for some reason, glanced sideways at Letty, to find her gazing at her mother in expectation. She was clearly thinking this might be a missive of some kind from Mr. Talbot. Or possibly one of the other young gentlemen who seemed so taken with her. Although surely none of them would offer for Letty in such an unexpected manner.

Araminta refolded the letter with precise care and slipped it into her reticule, something she carried with her at all times. No doubt for purposes of concealment like this.

Letty set down her cup of hot chocolate. "Is it an important letter, Mama?" It must have taken a certain amount of courage to pose that question to her intimidating parent. But with her sojourn in London progressing, she was becoming bolder by the day. Not always a good thing.

Serafina swallowed her mouthful of toast, ears pricked. Something had affected her sister-in-law and she was now struggling to hide this fact.

Araminta compressed her already thin lips as though having to force herself to remain silent when what she would rather do was shout her news from the rooftops. Well, perhaps not quite that, but something similar. From the look she was having trouble hiding it had to be something good.

Ogden lowered his paper. He must have been listening after all. "What is it?" he grunted. "What's going on? Something important, my dear?" His tone was casual, but with a hint of warning that she'd better not be hiding anything. Proof that on occasion, when necessity arose, he could get the better of his wife.

Araminta's face contorted in indecision for a long moment before she heaved a sigh and withdrew the letter from her reticule. "We have an invitation to call on the Countess of Westbury at her house in Cavendish Square." She was clearly having difficulty maintaining a balance between smug self-satisfaction and annoyance that this invitation had only been forthcoming due to Serafina's unexpected engagement and impending marriage.

Good.

Serafina lowered her gaze to her half-eaten toast and kept her face as expressionless as possible. Difficult. If she could have chosen a betrothed for herself, out of all those available, she could not have chosen one whom Araminta would envy more, unless perhaps an actual duke or earl. Max might only be the son and younger brother of an earl, but it was obvious Araminta considered him the next best thing.

"We do?" Letty almost squealed. "Do you think Louis Herbert will be there? I do hope so."

So much for encouraging her towards less flirting and more consideration of one suitable man.

"All of us?" Ogden asked, folding the paper up and laying it on the table. "To an earl's residence?"

Araminta must have been fighting hard to suppress her smile of triumph, because it suddenly defeated her and sneaked across her face. "Yes. It will give Letty so much more credence if we let it be known that we are friendly with the Westburys. Of course all of us. This invitation will be the making of our family."

Letty clapped her hands. "How perfectly splendid. I shall wear the new white gown with the roses embroidered on it." She threw a glance at Serafina, who'd looked up. "But what about Fina? She can't go to an earl's house in any of the old gowns she has, can she? And she's already been seen in the one new gown you bought her. And besides, that one is so dull and boring. She can't wear that either. Not when she's engaged to the earl's brother."

A stony silence fell in the dining room.

Serafina kept her head down, with a wary eye on her sister-in-law. A struggle was going on beneath the surface. Satisfaction that their family had received such an exalted and much desired invitation must be vying with Araminta's innate desire to keep her young sister-in-law firmly under her thumb and in the shadows. Given Serafina's new status, she was going to find that nearly impossible.

Ogden glanced at Serafina, brows furrowed. "She could wear one of your gowns, Araminta. She's the same size as you are. A little thinner, perhaps..." He picked up his newspaper again as though he wished the matter closed. "I'd think the blue one would suit her well enough."

Araminta's mouth opened, but for a long moment, no sound came out. When she found her voice, it was as squeaky as Letty's had been. "But that's one of my new ones. Even I haven't worn it yet."

"All the better," Ogden said with a snort that betokened a definite end to the discussion. "They won't have seen it before, and they'll think the gown is hers. That should do nicely." He fixed his wife with a hard stare. "After all, we have only received this invitation because of her. We don't want her future in-laws thinking she's a poor relation, now do we?"

Only of course, she was.

ALTHOUGH CAVENDISH SQUARE was but a short distance from Great Titchfield Street and easily walked on a fine afternoon, Araminta insisted on taking the carriage. "No one," she pronounced, "goes anywhere in London on foot, unless they are of inferior birth, of course." Whether this was true or not, Serafina had no idea. But from the number of well-dressed people she'd seen on the street both on her visit to the British Museum and in the park, she concluded Araminta might well be wrong, and perhaps just lazy.

So, that afternoon, with Serafina feeling both overdressed and out of place in Araminta's new blue gown, the whole family took the short journey to Cavendish Square. Letty, who'd been fairly bubbling with excitement, had required a stern talking to about how she should comport herself, and a reiteration of Serafina's earlier dire threats of what might happen to her, were she to behave in too forward a fashion. Consequently, she sat with unusual decorum all the way to their objective.

A butler showed them into the magnificent interior of West-bury House and up a wide marble staircase to a drawing room on the upper floor. He opened the door for them and announced their arrival in stentorian tones. "Sir Ogden and Lady Gilbert, my ladies, Captain. With Miss Letitia Gilbert and Miss Serafina Gilbert."

Serafina did her best not to stare around herself in too awestruck a fashion, but this room was so much more magnificent than either the one in Great Titchfield Street or the one at home in Milford House. Everything about it was more sumptuous and luxurious, from the heavy curtains over the long windows to the thick Persian rugs and the upholstered seating. Paintings of people who must be Max's noble ancestors festooned the walls, and elaborate ornaments sat on every available surface. What a room. She almost didn't want to sit in it.

The two ladies seated near the blazing fire were on par with their surroundings. The dowager dountess, whom she'd already briefly encountered, was a tall, gray-haired woman of imposing demeanor, dressed in a gown that could only be described as flamboyant, while her daughter-in-law, the present Countess, was a plumpish, much more approachable looking woman with a ready smile on her face and brightly sparkling eyes.

Max was sitting on a chair opposite his two ladies, wearing topboots and a navy coat of immaculate cut, and with his hair teased into a Grecian of artistic proportions. He looked as self-conscious as she felt.

He rose to his feet as they entered. "Sir Ogden, Lady Gilbert. How charming to see you again." He swept a bow. "And the Misses Gilbert as well."

Serafina suppressed a smile at his guessed discomfort at having to be polite to two people he'd made clear to her he didn't like. Such were the exigencies of society.

Ogden shook his hand with relish, and Araminta held hers out palm down, clearly expecting to have it kissed. Max obliged, brushing his lips across the back of her hand in a perfunctory fashion. As he lifted his head, his eyes met Serafina's, and he winked.

A sudden sensation of camaraderie washed over Serafina. She wasn't alone in this alien parlor having to face Max's family with the handicap of her own family hanging about her neck. She had a partner who understood how she was feeling and would support her. A partner.

Everyone sat down.

The dowager opened the conversation. "Now that I have met you, I'm curious to know," she said, her sharp eyes lingering on Ogden's corpulent form, "whether your family is related in any way to Sir George Gilbert?"

Ogden cleared his throat. "Sir George was my father, Lady Westbury."

Her severe face lit up, making her appear both younger and gentler. "I thought you must be some connection of his. Sir George and I knew one another when we were quite young." She looked across at Serafina, sitting stiffly upright beside a disappointed Letty, this being due to the absence of either of the young Herberts. "And so Miss Serafina Gilbert is also his daughter, I take it?"

The countess clapped her hands together. "So they are all related to your old friend, dear Mama. This is so exciting."

Ogden nodded. "She is but my half-sister, I'm afraid. My mother died when I was fifteen and my brother, who is a clergyman of some standing, was only ten." He paused as though considering how to word the following. "My father, ahem, chose to marry my brother's governess, and that marriage produced Serafina." He was doing a poor job at hiding his dislike of his father's second wife, and his oft repeated scorn for her having been nothing but a lowly governess. Serafina bit her lip to make herself stay silent. If she burst out with what was in her head right now the dowager and the countess would be so shocked they'd immediately veto the marriage.

The dowager looked directly at her. "And does your mother still live, Miss Gilbert?"

Serafina shook her head, a pang of sharp pain stabbing at her heart. "I'm afraid she died when I was only a baby. I don't remember her at all." Something that had been a constant source of regret.

"And your father?"

Was that a hint of sadness in the dowager's suddenly hoarse voice?

Serafina shot a glance at Ogden, to find him looking affronted that she'd had the temerity to include herself in the conversation, but as the dowager had addressed her directly, she had no other recourse but to reply. "He died when I was six."

The countess's smile faded, commiseration in her eyes. "How sad that must be for you."

The dowager sighed. That was definitely sadness in hers. "And do you remember him, Miss Gilbert?"

Serafina nodded. "I do." A tall, gray-haired man with a hearty laugh who'd catch hold of her and swing her up into the air until she squealed with delight. A man who'd taught her to ride on her own little pony in the park that surrounded Milford House, who'd read stories of the Ancient Greeks to her as she sat on his knee, and who'd brought gifts for her every time he'd had to be away from home. But she wasn't about to say all that.

The dowager rose to her feet. "We have a much admired garden here at Westbury House. Not large, but a pleasure to walk in when the weather is fine as it is today. I think I would like to walk in it with Miss Gilbert. I will leave my capable daughter-in-law to entertain the rest of you." Her voice had that crisp quality to it that commanded instant obedience, as though, indeed, she was used to that deference in everything.

Max made to rise.

"You should stay here too, Max," said his mother with an imperious wave of her hand. "I should like time alone with your betrothed, so that we may talk without interruption. Come, Serafina. I may call you that, may I not? It is such a pretty name."

What could she do but acquiesce to this autocratic demand? "I should like it very much if you did." Not that she was about to ask to be able to do the same.

Max sank back into his chair, a slightly worried frown on his face, but the countess seemed unperturbed by her mother-in-law's absconsion with their chief guest. However, both Araminta and Ogden's faces betrayed open indignation at Serafina being singled out for such attention. Only Letty, absently twiddling a strand of her hair, appeared unaffected. Probably still sulking that the young Herberts were not present.

Walking alone in the company of Max's imposing mother was not something Serafina had envisaged herself doing when they'd set out from Great Titchfield Street. But there was no way she could politely refuse. She stood up and smoothed down the skirts of the lovely blue gown, and the dowager held out her arm for her to take. With some trepidation, she slipped her hand into the crook of her elbow, and together they left the drawing room.

"We'll go out through the parlor doors," the dowager said, leading the way into another magnificent room. One which boasted double doors out onto a stone-flagged terrace and beyond that, a walled garden. Outside, the air was bracing, but the sky was still clear. Snowdrops filled the nearest flower beds in a welter of green and white.

The dowager must have seen the direction of her gaze. "I like the town to remind me of the countryside. We don't come here very often, but my son keeps a full staff to maintain the house in our absence, as his father did, and two gardeners. It was his father who engineered the planting of wildflowers in the beds especially for me."

This seemed a safe topic of conversation. "They're lovely. I thought I would miss them this year as we had to be in London for the Season."

The dowager smiled. "Then I am glad I have brought pleasure to George's daughter."

She was right that the garden wasn't large. The rest of the rear of the house must have been taken up by the necessary mews. From what Max had told her, the stabling here had to be extensive. "This garden would have brought pleasure to him, as well," Serafina said. "He used to take me out in the spring and we would pick little bunches of snowdrops, then primroses in the woods and, later, bluebells, campion, stitchwort and lent lilies. He always had room in his study for my little bunches of wildflowers."

The dowager patted her hand. "Tell me about your papa, my dear. It must be nearly fifty years since I last saw him and it would give me pleasure to hear his daughter's memories of him."

"You might be better asking my brother. He knew him far longer than I did."

The dowager shook her head. "I am in the habit, my dear Serafina, of forming an opinion of people the moment I meet them. I do not wish to converse with your brother or his wife any more than I have to. I feel he would have quite different memories to you."

Promising. How awful would it have been if the dowager had liked Ogden and Araminta? Serafina could have lived with that, but she would always have known her future mother-in-law lacked wise judgement.

"My father was a gentle person," she said. "I loved him very much. He died a long time ago now, but I have some very clear memories of him."

"Might I ask you to share some of them with me?" Her voice was gentle.

Serafina, who had expected a walk in the garden with the dowager to be a severe trial, smiled at the old lady. "I remember when he took me on his horse, riding on the pommel in front of him, down to the little river that runs through the park at Milford. We tied the horse to a tree and took our shoes and stockings off to paddle together in the shallows. He'd brought a fishing net and showed me how to catch sticklebacks."

The old lady swallowed as though she might have had a lump in her throat. "He was always a kind man."

"You knew him well?"

The dowager nodded. "I knew him during the Season when I came out. He was one of my suitors. My parents dismissed him as a mere baronet, and I married Max and Julian's father instead." She cleared her throat. "I have no regrets about my marriage to their father, of course, but I do have regrets that I lost George. We never saw each other again after my wedding."

A revelation indeed. Serafina struggled to remember if her father had ever mentioned Lady Westbury, but failed. Why would he have to a six-year-old? All her memories were of warm summers' days by the river or in the park and gardens. It was impossible now to even recall her father's voice. Only his face remained to her.

The dowager seemed to snatch herself out of the reverie she'd fallen into. "If you are to marry my younger son, I would like to know you better, Serafina. Perhaps you might like to visit Bratton Park before the wedding? It would be quite respectable as I would accompany you. And you could also visit the house that will be yours after your marriage. It lies within a few miles of Bratton."

Get away from Ogden and Araminta? Now? Before the wedding which was to be set in three weeks' time? Of course she would like that. "What about the Season? Aren't you here to accompany your daughter and granddaughter? Don't they need you?"

The dowager chuckled. "Maria gives the impression of being empty-headed and vaporish, but in truth, she's as sharp as any knife in the kitchen cabinet. She will be perfectly all right here with Arabella on her own." She met Serafina's eyes, which must have been holding hope. "And besides, I would like to see you away from your family, and have the fun of providing you with a trousseau. I was never blessed with a daughter..." her voice trailed off for a moment. "Not one out of petticoats, that is. I should derive a great deal of pleasure from outfitting you for your wedding."

Serafina hesitated. If she agreed to this, she would have to abandon Letty, whom she was all too aware could not be trusted to choose the right man for herself. She would revert to flirting again and encouraging rakes to hang about her. But... the wedding was to be in three weeks, and after that she would have had no further influence over her niece, anyway. What harm could it do to bring that forward by those three weeks and acquiesce to the dowager's request? And it would mean escaping from not just Great Titchfield Street and Milford House, but also from Araminta and Ogden. A far too tempting proposition.

The dowager must have divined the direction her thoughts were travelling in. "You could even be married from Bratton Park, in our local church. You will like it there—the woods and fields are full of snowdrops and will soon break out in all manner of other flowers as well. You will make a beautiful spring bride."

Throwing caution to the wind, Serafina nodded, ignoring the suggestion that she could ever be beautiful. "I should like that very much, thank you, Lady Westbury."

CHAPTER TWENTY-ONE

Needless to say, neither Araminta nor Ogden were enamored of the dowager's proposal to sweep their helpmate off to the country. However, in the presence of both the countess and her determined mother-in-law, all they could do was agree, stony-faced, to the arrangement. It was agreed with false smiles of pleasure, that Serafina would leave for Bratton Park in Wiltshire on the following day, in order to make the acquaintance of the earl himself and to be married in the family chapel. This last so the earl could himself attend his brother's long-awaited nuptials.

On the return journey from Cavendish Square, neither Ogden nor Araminta spoke to Serafina about what had occurred at Westbury House. Perhaps they feared to air their views in the face of what now seemed certainty where the forthcoming marriage was concerned. They probably wouldn't want to alienate the countess and her mother-in-law, now they'd established a connection with her family. However, once they'd returned to the house in Great Titchfield Street, a strong air of disapproval clung with steely determination to the very air, prompting Serafina to make herself conspicuous by her absence.

Letty came upstairs a little later to find Serafina packing for the journey that was to take place the following morning. "Well," that young lady said, plumping herself down on her own bed and regarding her aunt with, it had to be said, open admiration. "If anyone had asked, I would never have guessed this outcome to my first Season in London."

Serafina looked up from where she was carefully folding her threadbare linen. "Neither would I, if that's any consolation." She couldn't help but smile at Letty, who at least seemed to have gotten over her annoyance at her coming wedding. If she was leaving her behind, then it would be preferable for her last memory of her to be a pleasant one.

Letty matched puzzled brows with a smile and a shrug. "To be upstaged by someone who looks like you do, though. Although I suppose he is only a younger brother… but of an earl, no less. I wish Mr. Talbot had a title." She frowned a bit more. "Although I daresay he might be able to buy himself one with all the wealth he supposedly has. Like Lord Clive of India. He wasn't nobly born, was he?"

Serafina, surprised by Letty's sudden historical knowledge and unsure whether it was right to imply the late Lord Clive had bought his peerage, ignored the insult. Long experience had taught her that Letty didn't mean her words to be hurtful even if that was how they came out. "I have to say that I agree with you. I didn't for a moment imagine this would happen to me. I'm as surprised as everyone else."

"And you're going to visit the earl's estate, where you'll meet the earl himself, who Mama says is not at all well. And you'll stay in their enormous house, which is the next best thing to being a castle. Indeed, Mama says it once was a castle. Of sorts." There was about her voice a definite tinge of envy, even though she was being so friendly. She sighed, probably wishing that Mr. Talbot had a castle.

Serafina shrugged as well. "But I shan't be living there once I'm married. Max, Captain Aubrey, will inherit his own estate and we will live there." She smiled. "Have you managed to discover where Mr. Talbot's house actually is?"

Letty frowned more deeply. "I have, and I'm a little dissatisfied. While it turns out that he owns a smart townhouse here in

London, he told me he doesn't see the point in having a house in the countryside. Because he's not interested in country pursuits, and living here in London enables him to attend to his matters of business." The frown vanished like a cloud revealing the sun. "I suppose, if I were to marry him, it would mean I should always be in Town where the best parties are, and the best dressmakers and young men to flirt with." She paused. "If he offers for me, that is. He's being such a slowcoach, I begin to suspect he just likes to be seen at the park with me, or at a ball. Perhaps he's not after a wife at all."

"There will always be plenty of other young men for girls as pretty as you," Serafina said, as she laid her old gowns with infinite care into her trunk. "You are blessed with your good looks, you know. Whereas for me, only the one chance will ever come. A chance I truly never thought I'd have."

Letty dimpled at the praise. "What do I care if Mr. Talbot never proposes? You're quite right. I'm sure there are lots of other men who are more interesting and more handsome who will be happy to make me an offer. Younger men." She fiddled with her hair. "It's just that you have already received a most respectable offer, and that makes me nervous that I never will. I still can't quite understand why you have had such success without even looking for it, while I, with all the callers I've had, all the admirers of my beauty, have so far received nothing but fine words. It's most puzzling." She wrinkled her nose and sighed, as baffled as only someone with such a high opinion of herself could be.

Serafina added her last gown to the trunk. "Perhaps you haven't yet met the right man?"

Letty shrugged. "I suppose that's possible…"

Serafina had to smile at her niece's inability to contemplate anyone else receiving attention before her. "And when I'm gone to Wiltshire, please don't forget all my advice. Do not encourage any men your mama says are rakes, nor those you yourself suspect of being so, exciting as they might appear. Do not push yourself forward, as nothing is more damaging to your reputation than being known as fast. You may flirt, but in moderation. And never be alone with any gentleman. That is completely forbidden to respectable young ladies."

Letty sighed. "Yes, yes, I know all that. My life must be conducted in the most boring of ways. No need to keep reminding me."

Yes there was, because her mother certainly wouldn't be doing so. She would probably like nothing better than to force a titled and rich gentleman into marriage after her daughter had been compromised. A good thing she didn't know she'd already been compromised by the stable boy. "I can't help being anxious for you without me. I almost think I shouldn't go."

Letty's face crinkled in thought. "I was thinking that too," she said. "At first. But when I considered the matter more deeply, I decided that I mustn't stand in your way. You may trust me to follow your instructions to the letter, Fina dear. And if Mr. Talbot can muster the courage to ask me, I shall accept his offer on condition that he buys me a house in the country, preferably in Wiltshire, so that you and I may call upon one another whenever we wish. A castle, I think, if he can find one. I wonder if there are plenty of them in that county?"

Serafina laughed. "Splendid. When I'm at Bratton Park, I shall await a letter from you announcing your engagement with bated breath."

Letty bounced up and down on the bed. "It's settled then. I shall be sad when you leave, but I shall also endeavor to be pleased for you."

THE DRIVE DOWN to Bratton Park was a long one, that could only be accomplished by a private carriage in a minimum of two days. Having broken the journey in the excellent hostelry of The George Inn in Reading, Badger, Max's brother's coachman, brought the carriage in through the impressive gates to Bratton Park just as the sun was setting on the second day of their journey.

Serafina, who'd passed the entire trip having to answer questions from the dowager about her father, was feeling more than a little jaded by this time. She'd managed to glean enough information from the old lady to work out for herself that her attachment to her father had been an emotional one. The dowager had been guarded, but her constant questions had given away a deep-seated sadness that endeared her to Serafina and made replying easy, if tiring. And a little melancholy, as some of the memories were ones she'd not taken out and studied for some time as they were too painful. Once or twice she and the dowager had shed a few tears together.

Max had accompanied them in the carriage, because, he told her, with only one arm such a long journey on horseback would have been difficult for him. From the wistful expression on his face, she guessed he would have preferred to have ridden, but with one arm, a journey of over eighty miles would have been too much. Knowing he was an ex-cavalryman, her heart went out to him, for riding would have been more congenial than being cooped up in a carriage for two long days, no matter how comfortable it was.

She would have relished the fresh air herself, despite there still being a chill left over from winter in the air. However, she'd not ridden since she was a child. Araminta had seen to the selling of her pony—"to pay for your keep." Riding again after so long would probably not have been as comfortable as she hoped.

With the dowager in full flow and occupying all of Serafina's attention, he'd contributed only a few short contributions to the conversation, and for the rest of the time sat quietly in his corner, a lot of the time with his eyes closed as though he were sleeping, although Serafina wondered if it was just a ruse to avoid having to talk.

Leaving the twin gatehouses behind them, the road wound up through woodland on either side, with here and there a track leading off to left or right between the trees. As they neared the top of the rise, the parkland opened up before them, stretching away towards a slight dip where the vast slated rooftops of the substantial building that was Bratton Castle glimmered in the pale wintry sunlight.

Serafina leaned forward in her seat to better peer out of the carriage window as they approached their destination, taking in the tree-lined avenue that led towards the front of the house, and the creamy-golden stonework of the façade. It was enormous, dwarfing Milford and making it appear a mere cottage in comparison.

She glanced at Max, to find him regarding her with a quizzical expression on his handsome face. He must, of course, be well used to living in such a place, although he'd been away much of his adult life in the army. Perhaps he didn't take it for granted after all. "It's magnificent," she said, feeling as though some comment were warranted and wishing to distract herself from the fluttery feeling in her chest when he looked at her like this.

He nodded. "Too large for one family, I always think."

His mother snorted. "Nonsense. A perfect size. You have the most bizarre opinions, Max, so please keep them to yourself."

His eyes met Serafina's, twinkling with amusement, and he winked. Was he deliberately baiting his mother? For a brief moment Serafina felt an almost irresistible urge to laugh, but managed to hold herself in check. It would never do to laugh at the dowager.

The carriage drew to a halt on the wide gravel forecourt of the house, in front of an imposing door that, even as the wheels ceased to turn, swung open to reveal not just a butler but two liveried footmen as well.

Luckily, the dowager didn't seem to have noticed her son's amusement. She laid a hand on Serafina's. "Welcome to Bratton, my dear. I shall, of course, be staying here with you rather than returning to the Dower House in order to maintain propriety. Shall we go in so that you can meet my older son?"

Trying her best not to gawp and look like a country bumpkin in such hallowed surroundings, Serafina descended from the carriage and followed the dowager and Max inside the house, which was even more splendid on the inside than the out. The marble tiled entrance hall contained a wide, oak staircase leading to the floors above, and a stone archway led through into an enormous space that rose to a domed, ornately decorated ceiling where high, unreachable windows let in the light. All around the upper floor a balustrade ran, mirroring the ground floor arches, and decorated with stucco and coats of arms. Were they perhaps the coats of arms of other families the Aubrey's were related to? Might one day her own coat of arms join them?

"This way," the dowager said with confidence. "Upstairs. Julian will be in his library at this time of day. He always is."

She was quite right. After mounting the stairs to the galleried landing, and passing through a wide doorway, they found the Earl of Westbury in residence in his library. But what a library. A slightly faded Turkish rug of epic proportions covered the wooden floor, and every wall, save of course for the long curtained windows, was covered in bookcases. At one end a cluster of comfortable chairs clustered welcomingly around a fireplace in which a fire blazed, and at the other, seated at an impressive dark oak desk, sat the man they sought.

It didn't take much common sense to realize that Julian, Earl of Westbury, was not a well man. He sat at his desk in a red banyan and a gaudy turban over loose clothing that might have been his night attire. His countenance, bloated by what was probably excess water in his body, had a grayish tinge. Similarly bloated, and heavily ink stained, fingers rested on a book that lay on the table before him, and beside that lay an untidy pile of papers. The only vital thing about the man before Serafina was his eyes, bright and dark and not unlike Max's. But they were the only part of him anything like his brother.

He made to rise out of his seat, his breath wheezing.

The dowager waved him back down. "Be seated, Julian. We come bearing glad tidings. Your brother has an announcement to make. He is betrothed."

Julian Aubrey, Earl of Westbury looked past his mother and brother at Serafina, those brightly intelligent eyes studying her with open interest. "I take it you are the lady concerned?" he said, with a slight smile. His voice was thready, as though he didn't have enough breath to give it volume. "I confess myself delighted to make your acquaintance. You will forgive me for not rising."

Max, who had hung back, stepped forward. "Julian, I would like to introduce you to Miss Serafina Gilbert. We are to marry as soon as the banns have been called. Serafina, this is my brother, Julian."

Leaning forward, Julian held out his hand to Serafina. When she set hers in his, he bent his turbaned head and kissed it. "Excellent. A wedding will give me something to look forward to. I have precious little like that at the moment." He emitted a deep sigh. "My little brother is to marry." His smile widened. "And you have brought her here to meet me. I am touched, Mama, by your consideration. And by yours, Max." His eyes twinkled much as Max's could do, making him suddenly appear much younger and giving him a fleeting look of his younger brother. He must once, before sickness had ravaged him, have been a handsome man.

Serafina made a respectful curtsy. "My lord."

Julian sank back into his seat again, breathing heavily as though the effort had been too much for him. Absent mindedly he began to draw together the papers on his desk. "You find me employed in my study of Greek antiquities, Miss Gilbert. Please forgive me for not being able to be more welcoming." He looked at Max, his eyebrows rising. "You never cease to astound me, little brother, as I clearly lacked enough faith in you. But may I offer you my hearty congratulations."

Max nodded. "Thank you. I thought you'd be pleased."

So Julian was party to Max's reasons for offering marriage in such a hurry. He must be a very magnanimous older brother if he wanted to make sure Max inherited what would perhaps have otherwise been part of his own estate, and that he could have passed on to his own children. How many had Max said he had?

Was it not two girls, Arabella being one of them, and two younger boys?

Julian smiled. "Now, pleasant as this tête-a-tête is, I can see Miss Gilbert is as fatigued as I am. If you ring the bell, Max, I'll have Larkin show her to her room. Let it not be said that taxed as I am, I cannot offer a welcome to my brother's intended."

The dowager nodded her approval. "Shall we ask your valet to come and take you to your room for a rest?"

Julian bowed his head. "I feel that would be appropriate. I would have liked to dine with you this evening, to properly welcome Miss Gilbert into our family." He coughed, his chest battling for breath. "But I fear I am too tired and I do not wish to be carried down the stairs this evening like a baby. I have my pride. I will dine in my room."

Max moved towards him. "I can help you."

But Julian shook his head. "With your one arm? No, brother, you're as incapacitated as I am, nearly. And Rumbold knows my habits and needs far better than you do. No. You should escort Mama and Miss Gilbert to their rooms. Dinner can be delayed until seven tonight, to give the ladies time to prepare themselves. I would not want to be an inattentive host to a young lady who is about to become a member of my family." He coughed again.

Max bowed to his brother. "And Larkin will have to provide Miss Gilbert with a maid as she was unable to bring hers with her."

He was being very tactful in avoiding mentioning that she didn't possess her own maid. Would that have shocked the dowager or the earl? Never having had the luxury of a maid of her own, Serafina had no idea.

As a butler, Larkin must have been trained to show no reaction no matter how odd the request made to him, and his face stayed impassive at the revelation that Serafina had arrived without a maid. Probably the servants all knew she was Max's betrothed. Word like that would spread like the proverbial wildfire in a country house. Although it was most likely the driver, Badger, who'd told them. Or Max's valet, Watkins, who had travelled in a second carriage with Mrs. Howard, the dowager's housekeeper, her maid and the luggage, and gone to take care of it the moment they arrived. One of them at least was bound to have confided everything in the servants' hall. Even at Milford, with its comparatively few servants, gossip was known there well before it arrived upstairs.

"The blue room, I think, sir," Larkin said. "I'll have Miss Gilbert's luggage sent up immediately and inform Elsie that she is to be promoted to lady's maid for the duration of her stay."

Max turned back to Serafina. "Best to let Larkin decide which room, or he'll get in a huff. Can't disturb the smooth running of the house, and he's the key to it. You'll like the blue room. And I believe Elsie will make you a personable and useful maid." He hesitated. "Perhaps you too would like to lie down for a while? As we're not dining until seven, you might manage a short rest before dinner."

Serafina bowed her head. After the long journey in which she'd had to entertain the dowager, followed by the overwhelming splendor of the house, a short rest would be wonderful.

CHAPTER TWENTY-TWO

JULIAN, AS HE had said earlier, did not dine with them that evening. He sent his apologies to his mother and to Max, and in particular to Serafina. A nice touch. However, this didn't allay Max's inevitable anxiety about his brother, as only a few weeks earlier, he'd been up to walking downstairs unaided. He seemed, if anything, to have deteriorated in the short time they'd been away in Town, even though Maria remained convinced he would overcome his ill health. His cheeks had grown flabbier and hung in pouches from his face, the color of his skin had faded even further, and his breathing had worsened. Max had few memories of his father's illness, as he'd been away at school throughout much of it, but servant gossip had given him what he assumed was an accurate report. And despite none of the family wanting to admit it, Julian was rapidly heading in the same direction.

With dinner over, the ladies withdrew to the drawing room, and Max, being the only gentleman, took a glass of port from Larkin. As he leaned close to pour, the butler, who'd been at Bratton Park since he'd been a twelve year old bootboy, coughed discreetly.

Max glanced up, eyebrows raised in expectation. "Yes?"

"His lordship has requested that you visit him in his chamber, Captain." He paused. "This evening."

Armed, now, with two glasses of port, Max climbed the stairs to Julian's room. A pang of guilt at abandoning Serafina yet again with his mother troubled him, but it couldn't be helped. Julian was his brother and needed him.

A tap on the door produced Rumbold, Julian's valet, a man built on the same proportions as a bare-knuckle boxer, who always managed to look as though he'd been poured into clothes that were a fraction too tight, and might, if he were to flex his muscles, burst apart. He wore his grizzled hair clipped short as a convict, something that only added to the overall impression of a back-street heavy. Yet he was a man of unwavering loyalty and kindness.

"Captain Aubrey." He opened the door a little wider, managing to make a stiff bow as he did so. "His lordship was hoping you might come up.'

The room smelled of sickness, and the close air was redolent of the embrocation Julian's nurse had to rub onto his chest in an effort to ease his respiration. All to no avail. Nothing was ever going to improve it, but Max couldn't bring himself to tell his mother or Maria that. He had to let them hang onto hope. They had so little else.

Julian's nurse, Blewett, a woman of indeterminate age, was tidying the room. She was built along the same lines as Rumbold, having wide shoulders and impressively bulging biceps beneath the tight sleeves of her uniform gown. Useful for a woman having to nurse a man who had once been over six feet tall. Her gray hair, that was customarily scraped back into a face-stretchingly tight bun, had, by this time in the day, had the temerity to allow a few untidy tendrils to escape. She brushed these out of her sallow-skinned face as she straightened up and made Max a bow. "Captain Aubrey."

Max nodded to her briefly, before crossing the thick rug to the large, canopied four-poster bed. Julian lay propped against the pillows, his drawn face haggard and his skin mottled as though bruised. If anything, he now looked worse than he had done earlier. With Blewett moving about so quietly, his breathing sounded harsh and loud.

Julian's red-rimmed and bloodshot eyes followed Max as he crossed the room and took a seat on an upholstered stool beside the bed, but he said nothing.

Max studied his brother's haggard face for a few moments. Up close, he looked worse than he had done from the doorway, if that were possible, and Max's heart gave an uncertain lurch. Death had its unmistakable hand on Julian's shoulder. Unable to think of anything to say that wouldn't sound trite, he remained silent, waiting for Julian to speak.

"I only briefly saw your Serafina," Julian said at last, his voice thready. "But she looks a nice sort of girl to me. Well done, old chap."

Max nodded. "She is. And she's interested in Egyptology and all things historical. I rather think you might like to talk with her about that." Not that Julian was ever going to get the tome he was working on finished.

Julian shook his head. "I've not the energy for that, I'm afraid to say. My end creeps ever closer. Something I've come to accept, so don't try to convince me otherwise." He paused, his chest laboring for breath, and Max said nothing. After a few moments, he seemed to have regained his strength. "Maria and our mother keep advocating new treatments, and I agree, just to let them feel they're doing something. But I know my end is near and I'm ready to meet my maker. But for one thing."

Max raised his eyebrows in a question.

But, once again, Julian had to stop, a red spot forming on each gray cheek. This time, Max would have spoken, but Julian held up a restraining hand and shook his head. He clearly wanted to have his say. "Two things, in fact. Firstly, as to your marriage that I've long wished to see. For that, I think you're going to need to apply for a Common License rather than wait for the banns to be called. I'd like to see you wed before I die, and be content that I've done as our father wished." He licked his pale, dry lips. "As it seems I might not be able to do anything else right."

An odd addendum.

Disregarding that final self-criticism of his brother's, once more Max found it hard to find anything to say. If he agreed with Julian it would be tantamount to admitting his beloved older brother was dying. Soon. Which even though both of them knew this to be true, he balked at saying aloud himself. But if he argued, he would be turning a blind eye to the truth, and be as self-deluded as his mother and Maria. "We can do as you wish," he said, instead. "I have no objections to a Common License and a hurried marriage within the week." He chuckled. "Although that always causes gossip of the most salacious kind."

His brother gave a weak smile and coughed into his handkerchief. Spots of blood brightened the thin cotton lawn. "I think you more than able to weather a little gossip, Max. And we can make sure the truth is spread. That I wished to attend your wedding before…" He coughed again. "Before I go to meet my maker."

Max frowned. "Perhaps the wedding could be held in our private chapel here at Bratton? That would be easier for you. Rumbold could help you down the stairs."

Julian pulled a disgusted face. "Like a babe in arms, I'm reduced to this."

Max mirrored his expression, but moved on, anxious to distract his brother from his incapacity. "And I believe I've heard it's necessary to wait a week after we obtain the license…" His words hung in the air between them. Would Julian still be alive in a week's time? He had about him a look of impending death. Max had seen this often enough in wounded men, and now he recognized it in his brother.

Julian, who must have read his mind, shrugged. For a man so bloated with dropsy, he possessed bony shoulders beneath his nightshirt. "But that is not the only reason I wanted to see you." He had to pause to catch his breath again, as his efforts at conversation appeared to be draining him. "I wish to ask your help in quite another matter. A more important one than your wedding, I'm afraid." He coughed. "It is fortuitous indeed that you arrived today, for I have no one else to turn to but Rumbold, and his modus operandi leaves a lot to be desired."

A grunt emanated from Rumbold.

Max leaned forward, the better to hear his brother's reedy words. "What is it? You know I will always do my utmost to help you with anything." And he meant it. Julian, eighteen years his senior, had always been his idol as a boy, a man he'd striven to emulate, and who'd inspired lifelong admiration in him as a younger brother. That he'd been reduced to this husk of a man pierced Max to the heart. If he could help him, he would.

"Send Blewett down for her supper. Rumbold may stay." Julian's eyes closed.

The nurse, who seemed to have finished her tidying, departed without needing further instruction. Rumbold went to stand beside the door as if to guard it from intruders. No one would get past that ox of a man. If Julian had a secret he didn't want Blewett to know, it seemed Rumbold was already party to it. Max looked back at his brother.

Julian's eyes opened and his hand disappeared beneath his sheets. Paper rustled and the hand emerged holding what appeared to be a small sheet of crumpled notepaper, covered in spidery writing. "This came earlier today. I didn't know what to do about it until you walked into my library this afternoon." He made to pass it to Max, but his hand fell back onto the covers as though it were too heavy. Max reached out and took it from his slack grip.

Smoothing out the creases, he read in silence.

"My deerest Julian, I am writing to you to draw your Memory back to the days of your Youth. We were both young and in love. I have no intenshun of Upsetting the Woman you call your Wife and Countess, but that should always have been my po-sishun in life, not hers. For you will Recall that when you were at Oxford, we met, and went through a Wedding seremony before a Preest. Only afterwards, when you wished to Repudiate me Unkindly, did you tell me that the Preest had been just a Frend of yours got up make Pretense to me, so that I would

surender my Maidenhood to you. And I in all Foolishness had beleeved you and lived with you as your Wife.

But having tired of me and thinking to better yourself, you told me that Lie and cast me Off, as I have only Recently discovered. That so-called false Priest was not false at all, and you and I are truly Wed. Your Wife is not your Countes, but I am. And I have a Son. Your Air. We shall call on you on the 14th inst, trusting to find you in Agreement.

Your ever faithful wife, Abigail, Countes of Westbury.

Without looking up at Julian or Rumbold, he read it a second time, and then a third, scarcely able to believe his eyes. Finally, he raised his eyes to meet Julian's. "Is this true?"

Julian nodded. "It is, in part."

"Which part?"

"When I was a boy at Oxford, when you were just a babe in arms, I met a beautiful actress, Miss Abigail Lewis." He paused for breath, chest struggling. "Being inexperienced, I was quite carried away with her, and couldn't believe she would be interested in me, for I was but a callow youth at that age." He coughed into his handkerchief. "She professed true love for me, and I counted myself more than lucky. I'd had a few liaisons before her, but all had been with young women of easy virtue." He stared into Max's eyes, almost in accusation. "You'll understand, no doubt having done that yourself." He paused and his wheezing breath rattled in his chest.

Max waited in silence, the letter's contents turning over and over inside his head. It couldn't be true, could it? This must be an opportunistic letter from some spurned lover of his brother's, or a fraud. Julian would never have gone on to marry Maria knowing their union was bigamy. Would he?

"The letter is reasonably well-written as though by someone with some level of education. Is what she says true? Did you tell her the marriage had not been legal?" He hesitated as a thought came to him. "Wait. Perhaps it wasn't ever legal. How old were you? If you hadn't reached your majority, it would be invalid."

Julian shook his head. "I was twenty-one. I bought a Common License. There was no false priest. We were married in a small church in Oxford." A coughing fit took him and it was some time before he regained his breath. "And she does not lie. I was with her a brief six months before it dawned upon me that I'd made a huge mistake. Our father would have killed me if he'd found out. To bring an actress back to Bratton to become its chatelaine…" More coughing.

Max nodded slowly. "So it is all true, not just part of it?"

Julian wiped bloody spittle away from his mouth and nodded. "Hard to imagine now I'm so frail, but back then I was young and virile and my blood ran hot for that girl. She was beautiful beyond all imagining. I can see her now, if I close my eyes. I was so desperate to have her and she said she was a virtuous girl and she'd only give herself to me if we were married." He had to pause for breath again, his face now an alarming shade of mottled gray. "But the gloss wore off very quickly, due no doubt to my youth. I'm ashamed to say I fooled her into thinking it had been no true marriage, and we parted company." Another coughing fit took him, and it was a minute or two before he could speak again. "I married Maria some seven years later, having never heard another word from Abigail. I suppose I thought her dead, or lost, or just run off."

"And you thought yourself free to marry Maria?" The fact that his brother had deceived the woman who'd been like a second mother to him was rankling Max the most.

Julian shrugged. "No need to look at me like that. I know I've been selfish and stupid. And now my youthful folly has come back to haunt me." He sighed, breath wheezing. "But I promise you I never knew she had a son." He paused. "My son."

Max straightened his back, regarding his brother with a more than troubled heart. Hard to believe his brother could ever have been as duplicitous as this. He'd married Maria, who'd been a widow with two small boys, when Max was ten, and all Max's memories were of his big dependable brother and his pretty wife, as though nothing had gone on before that. As though Julian had sprung fully formed into being as his solid and sensible older brother. Thinking of him as a lust-filled student at Oxford was impossible.

"You were together only six months?"

Julian shrugged. "Until I had my degree. Then we went our separate ways. I returned to Bratton Park and our father, to learn the ways of estate management. She to other theaters, or so she told me. She was angry when we parted. I offered her money, but she refused." He paused again. "I am not a monster, Max. I didn't want to leave her destitute. She had her acting skills. She could earn a living. I wanted to help her but she refused me."

"And she says she has a son…"

Julian frowned. "She does. She implies the boy is mine… but I knew nothing of any child. I'm certain she would have told me if she'd been with child when we parted. I was offering money and she would have needed it. We told each other everything."

Clearly not everything, or Julian's departure would not have provoked such an angry reaction. Max heaved in a deep breath. "It does seem as though you find yourself in a bit of a mess." An understatement.

Julian nodded, leaning his head back on the pillows and closing his eyes. "And I am too tired to untangle such a problem." He coughed, his breath whistling. "I must rest. Now you are here, you will have to do it for me."

Max glanced across at Rumbold, who remained expressionless and silent by the door. What was it Julian expected him to do? If he'd been legally married to this woman, then what was there to be done apart from accepting her into the family? This wasn't something that could be brushed under the carpet. If they'd truly been married and never divorced, then she was the rightful Countess of Westbury and her son the heir. Maria's children would be rendered illegitimate. He sighed, his shoulders slumping. He had enough to do with organizing his own marriage in such a hurry. How was he supposed to untangle the web of deceit his brother had just unrolled before him?

Julian's head had sagged forward, his chin on his chest, his breathing stertorous.

Rumbold tiptoed forward, his feet silent on the rug. He kept his gruff voice low. "His lordship is sleeping now, Captain. Perhaps you would like to take the letter and retire to consider your next move. I will be at your service for any task you require of me. Please rest assured. Nothing is beyond my remit. Nothing."

Good God, was the man offering assassination services? It certainly sounded as though he might be. And Max would put nothing past his brother's enormous valet. He rose to his feet. "I'll take the letter, as you suggest. Let me know if my brother worsens." He kept his voice as low as Rumbold's, and Julian never stirred. Only the labored rising of his chest told them he still lived.

Outside, in the paneled corridor, he leaned against the wall and drew in some steadying breaths. The repercussions of this letter could be like an earthquake through the family. If Julian had indeed married this woman, and it was clear she still lived, then his second marriage to Maria was illegal. Bigamous. Little Freddie would no longer be Viscount Lavington, his father's heir, and Arabella and Lucinda would be frowned upon by polite society rather than feted by it and find it impossible to make good matches. Maria would be dishonored.

What did Julian want him to do? Right now he had no idea. What he needed was someone to talk to about this. Someone he could trust.

The only person who came to mind was Serafina.

She had shown she was blessed with common sense beyond her years. Yes, he would go right now and see her. Two heads would be better than one. And he couldn't tell his mother this dreadful news. But first he'd best dispatch someone to get that damned Common License, before it entirely slipped his mind.

CHAPTER TWENTY-THREE

MAX ENCOUNTERED ELSIE, the sometime parlor maid who had been elevated to a new position as Serafina's maid, walking away from the Blue Bedroom carrying a jug of used water. He slowed his pace and waited for her to descend the stairs and vanish from view. Then he knocked on the door of the bedroom.

"Come in," came Serafina's voice. She probably assumed Elsie had forgotten something.

Oh well, they were to be married in just over a week, so what did it matter if he entered her bedroom and put her in a compromising position? Not that he intended any compromising behavior. She'd made it all too clear she wouldn't welcome that, even after they were married. He pushed open the door and stepped inside.

She was sitting up in bed with a shawl about her shoulders, reading a book by the light of one of Julian's new Carcel lamps, which he'd introduced a few years ago due to his love of reading when he couldn't sleep at nights. Her dark hair had been confined by Elsie in a long braid that right now rested on her left shoulder and breast. Something rather beguiling clung to her in this tranquil situation.

She looked up as Max closed the door behind himself and just for the briefest of moments, alarm flashed across her face. One hand went to the high neck of her nightgown.

Max remained by the door. "You are quite safe. I've not come to see you with anything in mind other than obtaining your advice. I have no one else I can turn to on a matter my brother has thrust before me. And you are the most level-headed person I know."

Her expression softened. "If that is so, improper as your arrival is, you had better fetch that chair over and set it beside the bed. I shall endeavor to live up to your expectations." She laid her book down on the bed covers and linked her fingers together.

Max did as he was told, setting the chair a good six feet back from the bed, in case she should feel intimidated. He was a big man, after all, and she was just a slip of a girl already in her night attire. That she was brave enough not to send him off with a scolding and his tail between his legs impressed him. This couldn't wait until the morning, not with the 14th and the promised arrival of this interloping woman so close.

Where to begin, though? Perhaps with the letter. He took it out of his pocket and passed it over to her, having to rise in order to do so. Then he retook his seat and crossed his legs. "My brother showed me this letter this evening and has asked me to help him with the problem it entails. It arrived earlier today and he confessed to me that he didn't know how to deal with it until I arrived home. Lucky for him that I did."

By the bright light of the Carcel lamp, she read it through, then, like him not so long ago, she read it a second time. She looked up, those lovely gray eyes wide with shock. "Oh my goodness."

He nodded. "You see my predicament. Julian's predicament. He could not have dealt with this himself, and I'm heartily glad he hasn't been forced to ask Rumbold, his valet, to do so. He is a good valet, but describing him as heavy-handed is a gross underestimation."

She nodded in return. "I have yet to encounter the estimable Rumbold. I take it the letter is true?"

Max shrugged. "As far as we know. Julian has admitted to

marrying the girl. They were together only six months when he was twenty-one, before parting unamicably and she vanished from his life. He admitted to me that he lied to her in order to abandon her. He says he assumed she'd disappeared, or even died."

"Until now."

"So he tells me." He paused. "I have no reason not to believe him on that, dishonest as he has been with poor Maria, and dishonest also with this poor young woman. He married Maria when he was twenty-eight, having heard nothing from this Abigail in the previous seven years. I suppose one could say it was reasonable of him to have assumed she had died, or emigrated to the Americas or some such place and that he would never see her again."

"Nevertheless, emigration would not have rendered the marriage invalid. He would still have been committing bigamy."

Max nodded. "He would, but it would never have come out."

She pressed her lips together. "And you have come to me for advice?" Her brows rose.

Max bit his lip. "I have." Feeling more than a little despondent, he shook his head. "I have so little time. She says she's coming here on the 14th. That's only in three days' time. I have no one else to go to but you. I can't tell my mother. She has enough to worry about with Julian's declining health. Maria is busy in London with Arabella—who, if she succeeds in making a worthy match, will no doubt be spurned the moment this comes out. I have to act quickly and discover if this woman is who she says she is. And deal with it." He paused. "I would very much value your help in this matter."

A small smile lit her face, combining with the glow of the lamplight to render her almost pretty. "I am very flattered that you have turned to me. And if, as you say, time is of the utmost importance, we must make a plan of action." Her eyes glittered for a moment with something else he didn't recognize, but he'd have to think about that later.

For now, relief that he wasn't alone in this fix flooded over Max. He might have been a commissioned officer in his regiment, but he was not used to having to work out a puzzle of this sort. And doing so with the help of someone else, even if it was a woman, was a boon. He had to admire her staunch commonsense. Any other woman would have had a fit of the vapors at such a scandal about to materialize in the family she was marrying into and perhaps run a mile. Not Serafina.

He managed a wary smile. "What do you suggest we do first?"

Serafina leaned forward, her eyes now alight with something that might have been possible to construe as excitement. Was she enjoying this? "First of all, we need to find, if we can, where the letter was delivered from and where this woman is at present."

Max reached for the letter and turned it over in his hands to reveal the reverse. "Sent from London according to the markings. So I'd assume she must live there."

Serafina nodded. "So she has a good distance to travel to be here in three days' time. If this letter came by mailcoach then it could have been sent barely a day since." She paused, her brow furrowing. "And what of her son? How old would this boy be now if she had him perhaps a year after her marriage to your brother?"

Max frowned as he did the maths in his head. "Fully grown by now. At least twenty-five, I'd say."

"What we need to do is look for information about his birth, and find out if there are papers recording any marriage between your brother and this woman. She can only claim this marriage if there is a record of it."

"He says he did marry her. He doesn't deny that."

"Nevertheless, we need to check all the facts are correct. Starting with discovering which church they were married in. Did he tell you that?"

Max shook his head, more than ever in admiration of her cool-headedness in the face of what seemed to him to be insurmountable obstacles. "He's sleeping now. His illness makes him very tired. I'll have to ask him in the morning. But I do know it must have been in Oxford." Then he recalled what else his brother had said. Perhaps he'd better let Serafina know her wedding was being brought forward by two weeks. She had a right to know something as vital as that.

Her eyes widened at the news, but he detected no displeasure in them. "You seem to be in a great hurry to marry. I thought you had until your thirtieth birthday."

Now came the crunch. He needed to tell her why. "You understand that my brother is ill, don't you?"

She nodded. "A congestion of the lungs, I suspected. He seems to have great difficulty in breathing."

Max bit his lip. "He suffers from an insufficiency of the heart, which his doctor says affects his lungs. The same thing my father had. Died from." He shot her a quick look. "It runs in our family so perhaps you might wish to reconsider my offer now you know this."

She smiled and shook her head. "You look perfectly healthy to me, and besides, were you to die, I should be left a wealthy widow, would I not?" She dimpled, making her look far younger than her twenty-three years, and he found himself smiling back at her.

"I shall endeavor not to succumb to the same affliction, if only to deprive you of a spendthrift widowhood."

She chuckled. "It would please me if you could manage that. But why does this mean that we must marry in such haste?"

"I fear he's dying. Well, nearer to dying than my mother and Maria will admit. It seems very unfair that this woman has raised her head in what might well be the last few weeks of my brother's life. If she knows he's ill, she can have no consideration for his comfort. I noticed today how much worse he's become since I last saw him so short a time ago. I assume it can only be because of this letter. I owe it to him to set his mind at rest before he dies, and reassure him that Freddie will inherit his title. And also to marry and secure my own inheritance, as he's long wanted. He wishes us to marry in the estate chapel so that he might attend. It is allowed, as it is consecrated, of course. Some of our tenants have married there in the past."

She gave a slow nod. "You wish us to marry before he dies."

"Yes. I know you're probably thinking that his behavior shows him to be a cad of the worst kind, a man who left one wife after telling her a lie, because she wasn't good enough for him, then conveniently forgot about her and took another. A man who has fooled that second wife into thinking herself lawfully married and her children legitimate. A man too weak to admit he was already married, who should first have tried to annul that prior contract." He paused. "I'm thinking all this myself, I can assure you, but he's my brother, and I love him. He has many other qualities that outweigh his shameful behavior, and I still admire him for those."

Serafina shook her head. "No. That's what you're thinking. I'm not. I'm thinking he was a very young man as foolish as many an heiress in her first London Season. He was lured into marriage by a seductress who recognized in him a way to better herself. I'm just surprised she allowed him to escape her clutches. What puzzles me is that she must have known he was an earl's son. He would have had some sort of title as the heir, wouldn't he?"

"Viscount Lavington, as Freddie does."

She nodded. "So she would have been a viscountess. And she would have known, as I said, that her husband was due to inherit an earldom with all that entails. So why did she allow him to get away like that? I find that very odd indeed. She just went off and abandoned life as a potential countess? Without a single glance back?" She waved her hand at the room. "She gave up life here at this enormous house surrounded by its enormous park and farmlands?"

Now she'd put it like that, Max could see she had a point. "Perhaps she didn't want all of this?"

Serafina gave an unladylike snort. "You think? And now,

twenty-five years later, she's decided she does want it all? She's decided she wants this life, and the earldom, for her son? The son she's deprived of this life for twenty-five years. I'm not so sure about that. And think of this. She's only sent this letter to your brother when he's on the point of death. She must know. It can't be a coincidence. That in itself is strange. I can't work out why she should leave it so long, but I'm certain it's significant. There's a mystery here, Max, and I think it will be a pleasure to solve it."

Of course there was. Why hadn't he seen it beforehand and why hadn't Julian? Because they'd been blinded by such a shocking revelation. He'd been right to coopt Serafina—she had the luxury of looking at this from the outside, whereas they were firmly on the inside, with all the problems that would lead to.

Serafina seemed suddenly to recall the wedding. "I believe you will have to obtain a Common License if you wish us to marry sooner."

He nodded. "Correct. I'm sending for one in the morning. But, at the risk of appearing insensitive to your needs, I feel that's of the least importance right now. This other matter pushes it aside."

"I won't argue with you about that. I think that tomorrow, we will need to go to Oxford and find that church and look at the records."

"We?"

"You don't think I'll let you go alone, do you?" She chuckled. "You probably wouldn't find them on your own. And now I have a maid, courtesy of your family, we shall be quite respectable. We'll take Elsie with us." She glanced at the door. "And now, if you don't mind, I need to go to sleep, if we are to set off bright and early tomorrow morning to Oxford. I have no idea how far it is from here, nor how long it will take to get there."

Max rose to his feet. "A good thirty miles, I'd say. But we'll take the fastest vehicle and the fastest horses. My brother maintains an excellent stable of horseflesh, despite being unable to use it himself." He poked his good-for-nothing arm. "However, due to my blasted arm, we'll have to take Badger as well."

She chuckled again. "We'll be quite a party. You, me, Elsie and Badger. I look forward to it."

He was by the door now, and as he opened it, he looked back at her. "Thank you for this, Serafina. You've no idea how much I appreciate your help."

All she did was smile in return, and pick up her discarded book. Curiously deflated, but with no idea why, Max let himself out of her room and headed for his own chamber.

CHAPTER TWENTY-FOUR

"D ID YOU MANAGE to ask your brother which church he was married in?" Serafina asked Max at breakfast. They were the only ones present save for a footman, but she kept her voice as low as possible, all the same.

Max, who was in the process of picking at a plateful of unappetizing devilled kidneys, nodded, his gaze flicking sideways towards the expressionless footman where he stood beside the breakfast buffet. "I did. We can talk about this later. When we're alone."

Serafina nodded back in understanding. If the servants picked up on any of this then it would fly around not just this estate but probably all the surrounding ones as well. That didn't bear thinking about, especially as a little voice at the back of her mind was busy warning her that none of this rang quite true. Something about it wasn't right, she was almost sure, but as yet she had no idea quite what. Hopefully, that would be made clearer as their investigations progressed. She returned to picking at the scrambled eggs and bacon she'd helped herself to from the huge variety of breakfast alternatives on offer in as desultory a way as Max was with the kidneys. She didn't quite have the appetite for food.

Elsie, her newly acquired maid, was over the moon when Serafina informed her they were to make a trip to Oxford that day, and that she would have to come too. "Ooh, Miss, I've always wanted to see Oxford and them smart buildings, but never been. I've not been nowhere really, to tell the truth. I'm that excited."

Serafina smiled at this double negative and pondered how she would manage to talk in private with Max with the voluble Elsie in tow. There must be a way to avoid this. She frowned. They might be about to be married, but it would not be the done thing to undertake this journey with just Max and his driver, especially as it would be necessary to spend a night in an Oxford hostelry. Whereas driving alone with Max had been acceptable in Town, in an open carriage, it would not be in the countryside in an enclosed vehicle.

Inspiration came to her as she and her maid descended the stairs into the hallway, Elsie hauling a bag for each of them. "If you want to see more of the countryside, Elsie, you may travel with Badger on the front seat. So you'd best be wrapped up warm as it'll be cold."

Elsie's face lit up. "That'd be a rare treat, Miss. Are you sure you don't mind?"

Serafina shook her head. "Not in the least. It's a fine day and you'll get to see all sorts of things, I'm sure. I refuse to stand in the way of your education."

Max, waiting in the hall attired in great coat, hat and boots, smothered a smile. "Neatly done," he muttered to her as they stepped out of the large front door and onto the front steps. Below them, drawn up on the gravel, stood a landau drawn by four perfectly matched grays, both hoods of the vehicle in the up position.

She couldn't help but comment. "What beautiful matched horses."

Max smiled, a touch of pride in his dark eyes. "My brother has always had a penchant for good horseflesh." And he handed her up into the luxuriantly upholstered interior. This was how the other half lived. Araminta would be frowning at the extravagance of the whole equipage, particularly for a man who was housebound, but she would nevertheless have been almost overcome with envy. Let her be. Serafina had no intention of dwelling on what her sister-in-law would be thinking. Today she was going to enjoy herself being useful to the man she was rapidly beginning to think she cared a lot for. If she couldn't have him care for her back, then she would accept his admiration, and the surest way to that was by helping him with this enormous problem.

He settled himself beside her on the forward facing seats and as soon as Elsie had been helped onto the seat beside Badger, the carriage moved off.

Serafina peeped out of the window at the wide expanse of parkland they had to cross before sinking back into her comfortable seat and turning to look at Max. "You said you'd tell me later."

He was looking particularly dashing this morning, with his dark hair tousled and his eyes bright with anticipation. If only he could be wearing that expression because of her. "I did, but we'd best keep our voices down even though we're alone." He glanced out of the window as though gathering his thoughts. "I saw my brother this morning before breakfast. He was a little improved, perhaps because he thinks I might be able to get him out of this mess. I can only think his brain must be as addled as it was when he bigamously married Maria, knowing full well he shouldn't be doing so. If this comes out, he would risk jail, or even transportation if he were not at death's door."

Max seemed to still be convinced of the veracity of this claimant. Serafina ignored most of what he'd said. "Which church do we need to find, then?"

"Saint Michael's at the North Gate. I was up at Oxford myself before taking up my commission, and I know where it is. It lies where the old north gate used to stand in Oxford's city walls. An ancient church but one much frequented by undergraduates seeking to marry, so I understand. Or that's what Julian told me. Without a hint of shame about him."

"We must go there first," Serafina said, resigning herself to being the chief investigator in this affair. "And verify if a marriage truly took place." She paused. "It's possible your brother thought it a marriage when it might not have been a true one."

Max's brow unfurrowed. "I doubt it, but we can hope you're right. He seemed sure a real priest had married them, and he'd only told the lie to the girl to rid himself of her."

The carriage rumbled down the drive towards the twin gate-houses.

Serafina kept her gaze on Max. Not a difficult thing to do. "Where does your mother think we're going today?" At least the dowager had not been up for breakfast so she'd not had to face her and tell the old lady a bare-faced lie.

A brief smile lit his face, and his eyes twinkled with mischief. "To visit friends of mine. The Callingtons. I told her we might stay the night. She was very annoyed as she wishes to lavish the attentions of her dressmakers on you to equip you for this hasty marriage. I fear she was feeling frustrated."

"She will not think it rude of me to depart so precipitously? I wouldn't want to offend her."

He shrugged. "You won't. She'll blame it all on me. And who knows? We might find a trail to follow in Oxford and our return might be delayed for a second night."

He might have told her this before they left. "I've only brought luggage for one night, as has Elsie."

Another shrug, as though this rather important point didn't matter. "As have I. If it becomes necessary, we'll manage." Elsie might find it a bit odd though.

They rumbled on for a few minutes in silence. From up above, came the indistinct hum of chatter, mainly by the sound of it from Elsie. She must be enjoying her sojourn into the big wide world. "Would you mind if I asked you about your time in Portugal?" Serafina said. "You've told me about Egypt, and now, as I'm to marry you, perhaps you'll tell me how you came to lose the use of your arm." A little daring, but she was curious.

He rubbed his freshly shaven chin. "How much do you know

of the Peninsular War?"

At least he didn't seem offended by her blunt curiosity. "Not a huge amount. Ogden has the *Times* every day, but he never lets me read it. Only what I've heard mentioned when I've been to church. When we've prayed for our soldiers." She frowned. "We lead… led… a very reclusive life at Milford and attending church was one of the only times I was able to meet other people."

"Good God. They kept you incarcerated? I surmised from what you've told me, and how Sir Ogden and Lady Gilbert behave towards you, that they don't consider you of any importance, but I had no idea they kept you shut away."

She shook her head, managing a little chuckle. "Pray don't think that they did that only to me. No one except Ogden goes anywhere while at Milford. As I said, only church. So not only I, but poor Letty as well, has been kept very much away from society."

"No balls?"

"Very few, and neither she nor I were allowed to attend. She was too young, of course, and I was considered… as you say, unimportant. Letty's brothers and sisters were too young to feel the lack of social life and have a governess so no need to go to school. Perhaps that accounts for how Letty has seized upon the Season's events with such gusto."

"I had noticed."

"Don't think badly of her. She cannot help the way she's been brought up. She's a lovely girl, really. Blame her parents for allowing her to be so selfish and demanding."

"Only of you, I imagine."

"Perhaps. But I love her, Max, so I excuse her because I know she knows no better. And she can be very kind." She shook her head. "But what about Portugal? You started to tell me before we were sidetracked."

He smiled, and her heart did a little uncontrollable flip. Sitting this close to him she could smell the musky masculine scent he must have applied this morning and it was almost too much to bear.

"Do you want me to start at the beginning? We have a long journey to make and it might pass the time." To her nod, he continued. "I was a captain in the 20th Light Dragoons, commanded by Lieutenant Colonel Charles Taylor, and last year we were sent out from England to Portugal to reinforce Sir Arthur Wellesley's army. Our squadron joined with the rest of our men who'd been in South America, in Maidstone in Kent, while we waited embarkation orders."

Never having had the opportunity to speak with a soldier, Serafina listened with interest as he spoke of his former life. She could, she realized, keeping her smile hidden, have listened to him reciting a list of imports and exports, or a shopping list. So listening to him speak of something close to his heart was no trouble at all. "Go on," she said in encouragement, in case he might think her bored by his talk of manly things.

He rewarded her with a smile. "In the end four troops left for the Peninsular. Thirteen of us officers, three-hundred-and-sixty-eight men and two-hundred-and-fifteen horses. Sir Arthur, our Lieutenant General, had shipped from Cork with eleven-thousand men and was joined by four-thousand from Gibraltar, in Mondego Bay." He eyed her a little suspiciously. "I'm not boring you, am I?"

She shook her head with vigor. "No. Not at all. Go on. I'm finding this very interesting."

"It's just that I've never met a lady who was interested in the affairs of war."

She smiled. "Well, you have now."

He returned her smile, once again making her heart do that delightful flutter and this time her stomach turned to water. Good heavens. She must make sure she hid the way she was feeling lest it unsettled her betrothed. After all, he wanted this to be a marriage based strictly on business. Didn't he?

He cleared his throat. "They were reinforced by a squadron of the Lisbon Mounted Police, so with our cavalry included, we were quite a formidable army. Our first battle was at Rolica on the 17th of August, although we cavalry weren't involved as the ground was unsuitable for a charge."

Serafina watched his mouth as he spoke, finding it more and more difficult to concentrate on what he was saying by the minute. Perhaps she ought to go and sit in one of the rear facing seats opposite, just for the sake of her equilibrium. A fine sheen of moisture covered his brow, even though it wasn't warm in the carriage. Might he be sickening for something?

"So what happened next?" she asked, determined to distance herself from how terribly distracting his presence so close beside her was. When she'd agreed to this trip, she hadn't taken into account in how close a proximity they might have to be. For a long period of time. Hadn't he said Oxford lay thirty miles off? How fast could horses go? No more than six miles per hour would be five hours. There and back. And they were to stay the night somewhere. Of course, having her maid would make that acceptable, but nevertheless…

"The French retreated, covered by their cavalry who were more numerous than ours, so we were still not put into the field. Then, a few days later, we took up position at a village called Vimeiro, near the mouth of the river Maceira, to allow two brigades of reinforcements to disembark." He paused, a heavy frown on his face. "And with it came Sir Harry Burrard who outranked Sir Arthur—an arrival which turned out not to be a good thing."

They had left the park well behind now and the carriage was rumbling down a narrow lane, the horses maintaining a spanking trot that made the scenery fairly rush past the window. Perhaps they'd arrive in Oxford sooner than she'd thought. "Why was that a bad thing?"

"Because he took over from Wellesley, a man of far greater experience than Burrard. We, the 20th, were bivouacked on Vimeiro Hill, watching out for the French advance from Torres Vedras, with the rest of Sir Arthur's army hidden behind two ridges to the north of the hill. We were in the valley with the village on our right. The French arrived and battle commenced." His eyes took on a faraway look, as though he were seeing that battle again. Not something Serafina could come anywhere close to imagining.

"Then what? Did you fight them?"

He shook his head. "Not us. Not at first. We were left to stand and wait as our infantry met theirs." He shook his head. "The frustration of standing idle while you see the battle going on is something I can't explain. We all wanted to be at them, but even though Colonel Taylor rode up the hill to plead for us to go into battle, Brigadier Fane refused."

Frustration was something Serafina could comprehend, so she nodded. Although not of the type a soldier might feel in battle. "Then what happened?" He must have been in the battle eventually, in order to have been injured.

"At last Fane shouted to us, 'Now we want you, 20th! Forward and charge! And show them what you are made of.' Those were his exact words. We needed no other command. Every horse was fighting for its head, each man was keyed up for the charge. We galloped up the slope to the sound of cheers from the rest of the army and in columns of half-squadrons, with the Lisbon Policemen on either flank, we charged at the French grenadiers." His eyes were alight now and a real passion filled his voice. This was something he remembered with pride, even though he'd been wounded. Serafina felt her own heart, already deeply embroiled, begin to quicken. He told a good story.

"The Grenadiers were in retreat, and we galloped through them and out the other side to find we were facing over a thousand of the enemy's cavalry—Dragoons and Chasseurs. We ploughed into them, as well, our swords cutting and hacking until they broke and bolted in every direction." He shook his head and chuckled. "The trouble with a charging cavalryman and his horse, is that they don't know when to stop. The light of battle seizes you, and your horse is like a galloper in the Derby, hooves flying across the ground. Out of control of our Colonel now, we kept on going in pursuit of the enemy. In fact, our Colonel was in the lead, so I doubt if he wanted to stop either." He shook his head again. "Unfortunately for him, someone shot him dead. But it was an honorable death. A soldier's death. Serving his king and country."

That faraway look was back in his eyes. Would he have preferred to have died a soldier's death himself, instead of having to return to Britain, wounded? That anyone might think like that had never occurred to Serafina before, and her heart went out to him. If she could do nothing else, she determined to make him happy.

"We ended up in a field, surrounded by the enemy, which was when I took a musket ball in my shoulder. It nearly knocked me from my horse, but I had my soldier servant with me, Watkins, who's my valet now, and he kept me upright. I thought we'd all be killed for our recklessness, but we were saved by the intervention of the 50th. As for those Portuguese Policemen—they were spotless while we were drenched in blood—ours and our enemies'. Those cowardly bastards hadn't lifted a finger to help us. Sorry. I shouldn't have used that word, but...'

"That's quite all right. I think you were justified. I'm not shocked, have no fear. I'm not easily shockable."

"We lost fifty-five men, including our colonel, and some were missing but rejoined us later. Those ungrateful locals, whom we were defending from the French, stripped our colonel's body naked. So not such a glorious death as it might have been."

"But you won?"

He nodded. "We did, but that idiot Burrard didn't allow our Sir Arthur to follow up on our success. Not that I could have joined in. By then I was in a hospital tent. Instead, they allowed the whole French army to take transport back to France. Taken by our own navy, no less. Along with all their loot and guns and equipment. That's not how to fight a war and I think the powers that be have realized. I believe Sir Arthur's back in charge in Spain and Portugal. As he should have been all along."

"And your arm?"

"The doctors tried, but the musket ball had severed the nerves. I have some feeling here and there, but I can't use it." He lifted his right hand with his left. "See here? I can feel with my little finger. How useful is that?"

Before she could stop herself, she'd reached out and touched his little finger. Under her hand, it twitched. "It moved."

"I know. It's about all I can do." His voice had gone a little hoarse and color flared on his cheeks. Might he possibly like that she'd touched his hand?

Serafina swallowed. "Thank you for telling me your story."

"And now," he said, "you'd better tell me yours. We still have a long way to go."

CHAPTER TWENTY-FIVE

"THERE'S NOTHING MUCH to tell about me," Serafina said, dropping her eyes from Max's piercing gaze. He almost looked as though he wanted to dig into her soul and set free her deepest secrets. Not that she had many. Well, apart from that one she never wanted him to find out about. Too embarrassing.

"I would disagree. You may think you've led a reclusive life, but you still have much to share. One of things that makes me curious is why you're still with your brother's family when you're past your majority. You could have left them more than two years ago, could you not?"

A question she'd asked herself on more than one occasion, but what was the answer? She gave a shrug. "I couldn't leave the children. They needed me." And besides which, he'd refused to hand over her inheritance. With no one to turn to for help, and no money to sustain her while she tried, she'd been unable to either leave or obtain her rightful dues. She'd begun to think that Ogden never intended to let her have the money.

"Yet you can leave those children now. Do they no longer need you?"

An excellent point. "I suppose they do… but one can only go on so long before having to change, be it for the better or the worse." He was prodding her where it hurt. She didn't want to tell him about her withheld inheritance. And thinking of Letty left to the avaricious clutches of her mama was like a nugget of anxiety in her heart. And as for the other children, at home with their governess… "I never for a moment imagined I should be able to leave Milford and get married."

He smiled, that heart-wrenchingly charming smile. Was he aware of how he looked when he smiled? "I should admit that I too had never thought to find someone to marry, even though Julian had instructed me that I had to. Our meeting in the summerhouse was a fortuitous occasion."

She nodded. "I suppose it was, for we could have happily attended ball after ball with our families and never would our paths have crossed. With both you and I waiting in the shadows as we were, we might never have even seen one another from afar." Best to keep their conversation to his aforementioned business-like mode. She must give no hint of how much she found him attractive. It was plain he could never reciprocate.

"Tell me about your life before your father died. He can't have been all that old, can he?"

In her mind's eye, her father's face smiled down at her as he kissed her goodnight, having read her a story from one of his books of mythology. Greek, or her favorite tales of Egyptian gods, nurturing in her the longing to visit that distant land. Ogden, thank goodness, had inherited nothing physical from their father and looked nothing like him. "My father was the kindest man I know. The sweetest, and the most just. My brother was much older than me, and already married to Araminta, but they kept away from me, so much so that I hardly noticed their existence until my father died." The truth was they'd looked down their noses at her, the "governess's brat."

The sudden lump in her throat forced her to halt. "It was very sudden. We were outside in the gardens, and he was playing with me. Chasing me between the flower beds and making me squeal with laughter. He staggered, I remember, with his hand to his heart, and as I turned to look, he buckled at the knees." This image was more indelibly printed on her brain than his laughing face had ever been, but it had been an image she'd not wanted to revisit. Suddenly, for Max, she felt she could. "He fell forward onto the gravel path, for a moment his breathing was loud in the suddenly silent garden, and then it was gone." She swallowed, hearing it anew. "The servants found me there, crying across his body, trying to get him to wake up and play with me again."

He reached out with his left hand and covered hers where they lay clasped in her lap. "I'm sorry. I didn't mean for you to have to tell me how he died." He sounded awkward. "It must be difficult for you…"

She looked up. "It's all right. I want to share this with you. I've not been able to do so with anyone before." She hesitated, frowning again. "Ogden told me it was all my fault. If he hadn't been playing with me, running at his age, which wasn't old, I see now, but to me then it was, he wouldn't have died. They said it was his heart—like your brother but a different type of heart ailment. A quick one." How warm and comforting his touch was.

"He had no right to do that. It was a cruel thing to say to anyone."

"I know that now. But then, as a frightened child, I believed him. My papa had been playing with me when it happened, so it must have been my fault. The guilt I felt was crippling."

"You know now that it wasn't your fault? No more than it's anyone's fault Julian is so sick. There was nothing you could have done to change it. He would have died anyway."

Words as comforting as his touch. "I do know that now, but at the back of my mind there's always that nagging doubt that if he hadn't been playing chase with me he might have lived just a little longer."

Max bowed his head, but he didn't remove his hand. The carriage rumbled on, now on a wider road, although its state was little better than the lane they'd been traveling. Serafina leaned back against the soft upholstery and closed her eyes, conjuring up her father once again, unseen this time, but his warm body there behind her as he held her on the pommel of his saddle to canter across the wide Milford parklands. A tear slid unbidden down her cheek. Hopefully Max wouldn't notice.

MAX WATCHED HER as she leaned back in apparent repose. An effective way of ending their conversation which must be about matters that still hurt. He'd been wary about asking her about her father, but now, the feeling that she'd confided in him warmed his heart. To his surprise, an overwhelming feeling of protectiveness filtered through him, and a strong desire to hurt the people who'd told a tiny, grieving child that it was her fault her father had died.

She'd closed her eyes, but he was sure she wasn't asleep. A tear trickled down her cheek and she made no move to wipe it away. The urge to do so for her was strong, quickly followed by the urge to take her into his arms and hold her tight against his chest and allow her to cry her sadness away. If that were possible.

How strange was that? What had prompted such a feeling? He frowned. Most unlike him to respond to someone, anyone, like that. Particularly not a woman. He'd been so sure his heart was unbreachable, and yet, watching Serafina's feigned sleep, he began to question how he felt about her. Might it not, after all, be a more productive match than he'd at first foreseen? He shook his head. She didn't feel like that about him. How could she, when he was so incapacitated?

Annoyed with himself for his momentary sliver of hope of a normal life, he too settled back into his corner of the carriage and closed his eyes. But sleep did not come.

THE RATTLE OF wheels on a cobbled road roused Serafina from a restless sleep. She opened her eyes and peered out of the window to see their carriage was entering a sizeable town. It must be Oxford, surely. On each side of the wide street tall buildings rose up, built of mellow golden stone, and people thronged the pavements at the side of the thoroughfare, many of them wearing the distinctive gowns of students. That this was a university town was obvious.

Max was taking out his fob watch. "It's well past midday. If we go to The Star on the Cornmarket we can find stabling for our horses and refreshment for us all before we head to the church."

"Don't you think we should go to the church first?"

He shook his head. "No. Food first. And…" He looked at his watch again. "It's later in the day than I envisaged so I'll procure rooms for us for the night and accommodation for the servants. We can return to Bratton tomorrow, unless anything untoward should occur." He held up a hand. "No need to worry. My mother is not expecting us back this evening."

She hadn't been going to protest. On the contrary, she was quite enjoying the unaccustomed sense of freedom this enterprise was providing. Never before had she been able to follow her instincts and set out with no goal in sight of what she was going to do next. The effect was positively intoxicating, especially when added to the fact that she was in Max's company.

The Star proved to be a substantial coaching inn which was happy to provide them with rooms, and, at Max's suggestion, Elsie was to sleep in her room with her on a pull-out bed. "For propriety's sake." She'd wanted to point out that they were soon to be married, but had held her tongue, secretly reveling in his attention to detail. Although in reality she might also have liked it if he'd behaved with a little less propriety. Not that he was likely to with a plain young lady he was only marrying out of conven-ience.

After taking luncheon in a private parlor at The Star, they set off to locate St Michael-at-the-North-Gate. Elsie, eyes wide with amazement at her first view of a city, followed dutifully ten feet behind them, in the direction in which Max assured her the church lay.

He was right. Having pointed out to her Jesus College oppo-site the inn and told her that no, it wasn't his alma mater, but Christ Church, which lay to the south was, and had also been Julian's place of education, he nodded ahead to where an ancient church stood on the corner of a side road named, rather oddly, Ship Lane. Its tall, ivy-covered, square tower appeared far older than the body of the church. But they were not here to study its architectural merits or origins. Together they pushed open the door and stepped inside the nave.

Out of the bustle of the busy street, a blessed silence descended as Max closed the door behind them.

"I believe the parish registers will be stored in the vestry," Serafina said. "If we're lucky. This church doesn't look as though whoever the vicar is will be living close by. His residence could be anywhere in this town."

"City," Max said. "You must remember Oxford is a city. She has a cathedral and that makes her a city, about which she's very proud."

"City, then. No matter. What we need to do is find those records."

The vestry was easily located, as was the iron bound chest that contained the church records. One book each for marriages, deaths and baptisms. A quick perusal found the one they wanted, and they laid it on the small table that occupied the center of the vestry. Serafina opened the heavy, leatherbound tome to find it full of closely packed lines of faded writing. "I think this goes back for years. What year are we looking for? Do you have the exact date?"

Max shook his head. "I have the year—1782—but not the date. Julian thought it was May or June but he couldn't be sure." He shook his head. "He was not himself this morning, and it was hard to elicit the information we needed. I think yesterday took more out of him than he would have liked to admit."

Serafina turned the pages until the correct year was reached, a good three quarters of the way through the enormous book. The writing was still spidery and difficult to read, as though whoever had inscribed the names of those being married hadn't meant anyone else to be able to work out who they were. The whole book was like that, in fact.

She ran her finger over the pages, Max leaning over her shoulder as though to follow her every move. Nothing in May, save a whole host of people she'd never see and who might even be dead by now, but June produced something. "There." She jabbed her finger on the page. "Look."

With difficulty, she read aloud what had been written by the then vicar of this church on the 14ᵗʰ of June, 1782.

"Julian Aubrey, Viscount Lavington, lawful son and heir to John Aubrey, Earl of Westbury, of Bratton Park in the county of Wiltshire and Abigail Lewis, spinster of this parish, lawful daughter of Amos Lewis, of Taunton, were joined in marriage this day the 14ᵗʰ of June by Common License by Thomas Abraham, Vicar of St Michael-at-the-North-Gate, in the City of Oxford."

Max let out a deep breath. "So he did marry her. It's written here in plain English."

"Did you ever doubt his word? I wonder if the same vicar is still here?" Serafina peered at the signatures of the married couple and those of two witnesses—Robert Trubshawe and George Paynter. "Or at least one of the witnesses. The trouble is, it's such a long time ago now. We need to talk to at least one of those three, if any of them are still living. If only to get a description of the married couple to verify if they were indeed your brother Julian and this mysterious Abigail."

Max nodded.

"Excuse me?" A refined and yet troubled voice sounded behind them.

Serafina and Max swung around as one, like children caught out in some naughtiness. The man standing behind them was elderly and wore the black uniform of his trade—vicaring.

"Oh, you made me jump." Serafina put a hand to her throat. "I'm so sorry if we shouldn't be in here, but we have something very important to do."

The vicar harrumphed. "Well, you could have come and

asked me. I would have been quite happy to assist you. What is it you are searching for?" He didn't sound all that friendly.

"Were you the incumbent here twenty-seven years ago?" Max asked.

The vicar shook his head. "Alas, no. I have been here but twenty years. A long time, I concede, but not so long as my predecessor who died whilst in office here. I think perhaps he would be the gentleman you are enquiring about. The Reverend Abraham."

Serafina couldn't help the frown. No chance of questioning the vicar then. But that left the two witnesses. She put her finger on their names. "What about these two men? Robert Trubshawe and George Paynter? They give their origins as 'of this parish.' Do you know if either of them might still be living here in Oxford?"

The vicar stepped forward and read for himself the record of the marriage. "You are making enquiries about this marriage? That seems more than a little strange." He raised his rather bushy gray brows. "What is it to you, might I ask?" His tone remained cold and forbidding, as though they were requesting something clandestine.

"You might ask, but I might not tell you," Max said.

"Then I might not divulge the whereabouts of either Robert or George."

So he knew them by their first names. They were likely then to be members of his congregation, or to have been members, once. Twenty-seven years was a long time and they might not have been young when they'd acted as witnesses to this marriage. But why did he find their request strange?

She put a hand on Max's arm to restrain him. "Could I ask you why you're so surprised we're enquiring about this, Father?"

The old man narrowed his eyes as though considering whether to divulge anything to her. "Because you are not the first to come here asking me about this marriage."

Serafina and Max exchanged glances. So that was how the woman had found out her marriage had not been false. She'd come enquiring at the church to see if they had any record of it—and found the same thing they just had.

"It is a matter of inheritance," Serafina said, frowning at Max again to keep him quiet, as she could feel the tension in his arm. "My companion is the brother to the man in question, who is now the earl himself, and on his death bed. You will understand how important this matter is, and how quickly we must resolve it."

The vicar's brows did another wiggle upwards. "Aha," he said, sounding perhaps a little less stern. "A lost heir, perhaps. Then that is different. But I'm sorry to say that Mr. Trubshawe, who ran a respectable inn, is no longer with us. I conducted his funeral myself, some five years since."

"And George Paynter?"

"Still living, but in a parlous condition. He has fallen on hard times since his wife died and old age took him. I do what I can for him, but he spends much of his money on liquor. You will no doubt find him in *The Malt Shovel*, Mr. Trubshawe's old place of business. Just down the lane from here."

Serafina bestowed a grateful smile on the old man. "Thank you so much for your help." Then she thought of something else. "Was the other person who came here enquiring about the marriage a woman?"

The vicar nodded. "She was."

"And did she ask to speak to the witnesses?"

"She didn't mention them at all, so I refrained from drawing her attention to them."

That was odd. "Could you tell me why you did that?"

He shifted uncomfortably as though not at ease with further revelations, but it seemed honesty got the better of him. "She did not seem to be a lady," he said, with infinite care. "And I did not care for her attitude."

Max held out his hand. "Thank you very much for your assistance."

The old man took it. "Don't give George Paynter any money," he warned as Max opened the door back into the nave. "He will only pour it down his throat. If you wish to reward him in any way, buy him food."

"We will," Serafina called as she hurried after Max.

CHAPTER TWENTY-SIX

THE MALT SHOVEL Inn, when located, appeared to be an establishment of less than salubrious appearance, despite the vicar's description of it as respectable, and was clearly frequented in the main by an eclectic mix of impoverished students and surly looking locals. A volatile mix of Town and Gown if ever there was one. Not that Max had ever been here himself in his student days. He wasn't at all sure he should be taking a gently bred young lady into the gloomy interior of this inn.

Heads turned in their direction as if drawn by a powerful magnet. A group of students, identifiable from their habitual and possibly inflammatory sporting of their gowns, were gathered at a large table by the small-paned window at a game of dice, a game which halted as half a dozen pairs of eyes ran over Serafina's slim form. Three men who might well have been merchants of some kind sat in a shadowy corner, heads together as though arrested in some clandestine deal. Two other men looked up with unwelcoming scowls on their jowly faces from their card game, pewter tankards on the table in front of them. The landlord, a youngish man who had nevertheless lost almost all his hair leaving only a few straggly strands that for some reason he'd combed over the top of his shiny pate, fixed them with the sort of glare that said they weren't welcome here.

The only inhabitant of the inn who took no notice of their arrival was the brindled hound lying in front of the smoky fire.

Max had fought his way around Spain, Egypt and Portugal though, and wasn't about to be intimidated by the landlord of a backstreet English inn. With a guiding hand on Serafina's back, he marched up to the bar. It was only a few planks of seasoned timber laid upon barrel tops. Best to spend some money in here first. "Good day to you, innkeeper. A pint of your best cider for me." He looked at Serafina with his eyebrows raised, waiting for her to tell him what she would drink.

After a moment she must have realized what he meant, for she shook her head as though in a hurry. "Nothing for me." Despite her assurances of being made of strong stuff, she'd clearly never been in this sort of establishment before. Perhaps she was wise in her decision not to partake of any fluid from the innkeeper's none too clean receptacles.

The landlord supplied a pewter tankard of the requested beverage, and Max took a long draught of it then handed over a few coppers in payment. "Excellent stuff."

Mollified a little, the landlord gave him a nod. "Thank'ee, sir."

The clientele, such as it was, had lost interest in them by now and returned to their previous occupations. No sign of anyone who might be George Paynter though. None of them looked old enough to have acted as witness to a marriage twenty seven years ago.

He was just about to broach the subject when Serafina got in before him. "I wonder if you might be able to assist us," she said, bestowing what must be her most innocent and sweet expression on the landlord. "We've come here looking for a Mr. George Paynter. The vicar of St Michael's directed us here."

The landlord made a pretense of straightening his few strands of hair before answering. It seemed Serafina's polite enquiry might have worked. She might not be as pretty as Letty or Arabella, but any young lady with a smile like hers could be assured of gaining whatever she was asking about.

"Well, miss," the landlord said. "Then you've come to the right place. Thass him over there in that high backed seat by the fire. Everyone knows not to sit in that seat—it's been his since before my old dad died." No wonder they'd not noticed him before, as his seat almost completely hid him from view.

"You're Robert Trubshawe's son then?" Max interjected before Serafina could. She was rather taking over this enquiry. Not that he really minded. It was a much more enjoyable enquiry thanks to her participation.

Young Trubshawe nodded. "Aye, I am that."

Serafina seemed disinclined to small talk, for she was already heading over to the fireside. Max followed, nursing his tankard. This time the dog did open a sleepy eye for a moment, but only to close it again and go back to sleep. Not much of a guard dog.

Serafina took the only other seat, as high-backed as Mr. Paynter's, so Max took up a position behind it, feeling somewhat secondary. For some reason though, he didn't mind.

From the stubble of white hair that covered his head and his equally white beard, George Paynter looked to be at least seventy years old. His skin had a deeply corrugated appearance to it that spoke of years spent out of doors, although a distinct pallor also hinted that those years had been some time ago now. He peered at them out of faded blue eyes that were also decidedly blood-shot. However, he appeared to be reasonably sober.

"What are you drinking, Mr. Paynter?" Serafina asked.

The old man blinked at her. "You offering?"

She nodded. "My companion will fetch you a tankard of whatever it is you like best."

A chortle emitted from the old man. "I like best a whisky, my dear, but I don't think I'd best have a tankard of the stuff."

Max nodded to the landlord who poured a generous measure into a small glass and brought it over. George knocked it back in one. "Thass better. Thank'ee kindly. Now, no one goes round giving out free drinks lessen they wants something. So what is it you fine folks want of me?" He fixed them with a keenly intelligent eye.

Once again, Serafina got there first. "You were a witness to a wedding at St Michael's some twenty seven years ago, were you not?"

His already heavily wrinkled brow furrowed still further, but his eyes, bloodshot or not, held distinct canniness. "Aye, I was that."

She kept going. "Do you remember it?"

He nodded. "I do that. What's it to you?" A grin crept over his face revealing his startling lack of teeth. The one he still owned in his upper jaw stood out like a sentinel. "Do you want me to do it again? For you two? I'm a bit over the hill nowadays, but not averse to standing up as witness for a wedding. Got paid well for that first one, mind, so I'll be wanting the same again."

A blush rose up Serafina's cheeks. "No. We don't want to marry today. But we do want to know what you remember of the wedding twenty-seven years ago. If you can recall the details."

The man was a drunk though. Would he be able to recall anything that would help them? Was he even telling the truth when he said he remembered something that had happened that long ago?

But the old man was to prove a surprise. "I c'n remember it like it was yesterday," he said, with another practically toothless grin. "Not going to forget being paid ten whole guineas for half an hour's work, now am I? Me and young Bob's old dad did it. Got ten guineas each out of it. The young man as wanted us to act as witnesses were in a tidy hurry to get the job done, and seemed to have plenty of money to splash out." His eyes rose to meet Max's and he winked. "Looked a lot like you, sir, if I may say so. A lot."

Serafina twisted in her seat to look up at Max. "Did Julian look like you? When he was young?"

Max nodded. "He did. Not now of course. But my mother has always said how alike we are. That I remind her of Julian when he was my age."

She turned back to old George. "Did you know the gentleman's name?" Perhaps she still didn't quite trust his memory.

George frowned again, as though this question annoyed him. "'Course I did. He was getting married, weren't he? You have to give your name when you gets married or you ain't married. But I can't rightly recollect it now, I'm afraid." He paused. "But what I do know is that he weren't one of the regular students what comes in here. He was a young lord of some kind. Don't ask me what though."

"A viscount," Max said. "He would have been Viscount Lavington then, as my father was still living."

"Thass it," George said with relish. "That were his name."

So it looked indeed as if the young man who had married back then had been Julian. But what about the woman?

Serafina nodded to George. "And what about the young lady he was marrying? Do you remember anything about her?"

Again George grinned. "Not likely to have forgotten her, neither. She were a sight to behold. Prettiest girl I ever did see. All golden ringlets and frills and furbelows for her gown what she was wearing." The grin became a puzzled frown. "But I don't think she was no lady. He'd not have been marrying her in such a hurry with me and old Robert as witnesses if it hadn't been a bit dodgy. I reckon she were a bit below him, so to speak, and he didn't want his family to know. Not till it was done and dusted, that is."

"Can you recall exactly what she looked like?" Serafina asked. "What color were her eyes, for example? Anything distinctive about her?"

The old man frowned in concentration. "You don't often see a girl that pretty, I can tell you. Like I said, prettiest thing that ever come in here, if you don't mind me saying so. I'm pretty sure as her eyes was blue. Matched the dress she were wearing, I remember noticing. The dress were blue like you see on them flowers out in the cornfields—cornflowers, they're called, and I remember thinking as how everything matched on her, from her blue bonnet and shoes and gloves, to her bonny blue eyes. Yes, I'm certain sure they were blue now I thinks about it."

"Do you remember how tall she was? Her build, perhaps?"

The old man looked up at Max again and Max straightened. Although he was taller than Julian now, before his brother had succumbed to illness, they'd been of a height. "Up to your shoulder, sir, I'd say. Maybe a bit above. Tall for a leddy."

About the same size as Serafina then, who, for a woman, was on the tall side.

Max put his hand on her shoulder. "We have a good description now, and I think Mr. Paynter guessed rightly when he said she was from a lower social order to Julian. An actress would be. Ladies do not take to the stage."

Serafina nodded. "Thank you so much, Mr. Paynter." That smile came out again. It rendered her face beautiful in a different way to the beauty of girls like Letty and Arabella. As though her inner core of goodness had manifested itself on her face. She looked back up at Max. "I think my friend will stand you another drink for your useful information."

Obedient, Max nodded to the landlord who brought another generous tot of whisky to the old man's corner. Max handed over some more coins, drained his cider, and leaving the old man to his tot, they left the inn.

The sun shone down on the narrow cobbled street. "Food," Max said, with determination. "But not in *The Malt Shovel* I fear. A more salubrious establishment on the main street, I think. You must be hungry and tired. I know I am."

Serafina slipped her hand into his arm as though it had always been meant to be there. "An admirable idea. I have never fainted in my life, but if I go much longer without sustenance, I fear I might join the ranks of the young ladies I've always despised. Lead on."

And so they repaired to the main street and went in search of the not too distant *Star Inn*, where Badger had already stabled the horses and a fine dinner and their rooms must be awaiting them.

*   ⚜   *

CHAPTER TWENTY-SEVEN

THE STAR WAS a much superior establishment to The Malt Shovel, being one of Oxford's premier coaching inns. Badger had already sorted out their rooms for them, and Serafina heaved a silent sigh of relief at discovering she would not be expected to sleep top to toe with some strange woman in a crowded bedroom that night. Elsie had waited there with Badger, the horses and the landau, so when Serafina was shown up to her room by a chambermaid who looked only about twelve years old, she found Elsie had unpacked her bag for her and even had a jug of water and a basin ready to wash the dust of travel off her hands and face.

"I'm right sorry, miss," Elsie said, clasping her own reddened hands in front of her. She didn't look much older than the chambermaid, although Serafina had been reliably informed she was eighteen. "It were nice warm water when I had it brung up here. If I'd'a known you was going to be such a long time I'd've waited on your arrival a bit longer."

"That's perfectly fine," Serafina said as she dunked her hands in the tepid water. The grubby feel of that back street tavern needed washing off her skin. Nobody in it had looked very clean, and she'd turned down a drink when offered one. No way of ascertaining the receptacle it arrived in would have been washed since it was last used. She could only assume that Max, as a soldier, possessed a robust health up to dealing with the stray infections one might encounter in a less than clean hostelry. Why the vicar of St Michael's had described it as respectable, she had no idea. Perhaps it had been until the old landlord had died.

That was better. With still wet hands she removed her pelisse and bonnet and attacked her face with her flannel. A mirror would have been useful, but none were apparent. With hands made skillful by many years of having to look after herself, she adjusted her hair, tucking in any stray strands that had been able to escape in the course of their adventure. "Does my hair look all right?"

"Miss, you look beautiful."

Serafina had to laugh. Elsie could not have very high standards if she thought her new mistress was beautiful, or maybe she was courting favor. "Thank you, Elsie. You may go down to the kitchens and get them to feed you. I'm dining with Captain Aubrey but will be back up for you to help me out of my gown in an hour or two. Mind you're up here waiting." How odd it felt to be ordering a maid about. She'd never presumed to tell Letty's maid to do anything, and of course had never had one of her own. What a luxury to have someone to help her for once. She bestowed a grateful smile on Elsie lest the girl assumed she'd been told off.

A few minutes later, feeling a little lightheaded, both from the sensation of having a maid all to herself and also from undoubted hunger, she descended the stairs to the private parlor Max had again commandeered for their repast.

He was already there, looking little different from how she'd left him, although perhaps he too had taken a wash as strands of his hair looked wet, which, if it were at all possible, rendered him more handsome than ever. She quelled the pang of regret that theirs was not to be a true marriage and stiffened her spine. She mustn't think about that.

He held out a chair for her with a little ham-fisted awkwardness. "I hope you're hungry. I ordered three courses and the fare at a coaching inn is inclined to be stodgy and filling."

She took her seat, smoothing her skirts down and reflecting that it would be her first meal in a coaching inn. First time in one, to be exact, never having been out of Milford that she could remember. Not until that fateful journey to London. "That will suit me well, as it feels as though it's a long time since luncheon. I think I was too nervous about our investigation to have done justice to the food presented to us then."

The twelve-year-old maid came in bearing a tray with two bowls of brown soup. It tasted faintly meaty, but what it consisted of remained a mystery, and even the girl couldn't say when asked. For a short while they ate in a companionable silence.

Max broke it. "Now we've discovered the wedding did indeed take place, and was between my brother and this Abigail woman, and on top of that appears to be legal, what do you suggest we do next? You seem to have about you the makings of an excellent investigator. Better than me, at any rate. I don't think my soldiering career has prepared me in any way to fathom out a mystery. If that's what you could call this. Although so far, it seems quite straightforward."

Serafina set her spoon down, wishing his presence were not quite so distracting. No matter how much she told herself to think about him differently, she couldn't. The man exuded some kind of physical aura that she was finding increasingly hard to ignore. She pulled herself together with a huge effort. "I think our next call is upon the lady in question. We don't know where her son was born, so we can't check the birth records in the parish register for that place. And besides which, it would only have his baptismal records, so it wouldn't give us an accurate birth date. He could have been baptized any time from straight after birth until he was at least a year old. And I think we have to assume that he was born and baptized in London, which is a huge place with hundreds of possible churches. We could search for a year and not find him anywhere." She nodded with determination. "No, we must concentrate on the woman calling herself Countess of Westbury." She refused to give her the title properly.

Max nodded. "But how do we find her?"

"You said she's threatened to come to Bratton to visit your brother. Well, if she wants to do that, she must come first to your nearest town and stay in some hostelry or another. I doubt she would travel down and try to see him on the same day. And you said she was intending to meet with your brother three days after the letter came. Which is the day after tomorrow. So, in the morning, we should return towards Bratton. Where is your nearest town? I'm afraid my geographical knowledge of the British Isles is not good."

"The town of Marlborough lies about five miles south of Bratton. It's on a good coaching route to the West Country with a number of excellent inns. I would think she would be staying there. If she catches the mail coach in London, she could be down there in not too many hours. Far more quickly than our journey from London."

"That sounds likely. And if she intends to travel five miles north, then she will be arriving tomorrow by stagecoach, and will need to arrange transport for herself for the following day. We need to be in Marlborough to welcome her, I think." Plotting their next move proved to be almost the distraction she required. She took another spoonful of the soup.

Max nodded. "A wise move."

They finished their soup, the empty bowls being removed by the girl, and started on hearty plates of roast beef and Yorkshire pudding. To her surprise, though, Serafina discovered that her appetite had died to nothing, despite the quality of the food. She picked at the meat and potatoes in an effort to look as if she was eating, but could barely swallow a thing. And to her further surprise, Max seemed afflicted in the same way.

Eventually, he pushed his plate away and leaned back in his seat. "I don't know what's the matter with me, but I find my hunger has vanished." He shook his head in what might have been perplexity. "That's not like me at all. When you're a soldier on the march you learn to eat at every opportunity that presents itself. And eat everything that's put in front of you." He regarded her out of troubled eyes.

As she was feeling the same, a sudden thought flashed into her mind. "I feel similarly afflicted. Might we be sickening for something? Could we have caught some dreadful disease in that back street inn? It did seem to be a very dirty place." The thought of Max falling ill sent a chill to her heart, only to be assuaged when it was followed by a much more comforting image of her tending him in his need and nursing him back to health. For which he would be eternally grateful and fall in love with her on the spot.

She shook her head to clear that tantalizing image. If he had contracted something, then so had she, for they both had the same symptoms. And if both became ill, it would fall to Elsie and Badger to tend to them.

"I suspect if we had caught something at The Malt Shovel, then it would not have manifested itself so swiftly." He reached across the table and put his hand on her forehead.

She nearly jumped backwards out of shock, only the fact that she'd been longing for him to touch her all evening prevented this. How warm his hand was. How gentle.

"No fever," he said, dropping his hand. A flush of color had appeared on his cheeks though, that she suspected might match the heat flaring on her own. On an impulse, and before she could stop herself, Serafina reached out to lay her hand on Max's forehead in return. Cool and dry. "No fever here, either." Oh, how she didn't want to drop her hand but keep it pressed to his skin. However, she did, more heat rising to her cheeks. And his.

Dessert, when brought in, was undertaken in a rather awkward silence.

As soon as she'd pushed the dessert, which was apple pie, around her bowl a few times in a token attempt to pretend she was eating it, Serafina excused herself, careful not to look Max in the eye. "I'm sorry, but after such a long day, I confess myself tired and in need of my bed." How formal she sounded, but after the awkward moment when they'd touched one another, she couldn't stay any longer. The silence stretching between them gaped too wide and uncrossable.

He, in return, was stiffly polite, the easy camaraderie of earlier vanished. "Of course. I must apologize for tiring you. I wish you a goodnight, Serafina."

The girl had brought in a bottle of brandy, and as she left, Serafina saw Max pouring himself a goodly measure and draining it in one gulp. She could have done with one of those herself, but it was too late now. Besides, she was indeed exhausted, and they had an early start in the morning.

WHEN SHE'D GONE, Max poured himself a second generous measure of the brandy and knocked that back in one as well. A third followed. He had a mind to drink himself into oblivion tonight. Already he felt as though he were floating on a warm, somewhat brandy-scented, cushion. He didn't want to think about Serafina and the way she'd touched his face but, of course, he did. How could he not?

In an attempt to remain objective, he decided to try assessing her attributes. That should keep any other disturbing thoughts at bay. She was the cleverest woman he'd ever met, of that he was certain. Not only did she have a proven deep knowledge of all things Egyptian, but she also possessed a mind astute enough to formulate an investigation such as the one they were pursuing. In fact, she was far better at it than he was, and he didn't care. That in itself endeared her to him. If only it might endear him to her, but the more he got to know her, the less he felt he could offer.

He poured himself another generous brandy but this time only sipped it. They did have an early start the next morning and he didn't want to oversleep or have a hangover—or both. Not the impression he wanted to give to the woman he was becoming increasingly attached to. That was it. He was attached to her as he would become attached to a dog. As he had indeed become attached to that cur dog he'd found in Egypt. She was like a particularly clever dog. He would tell himself that every time he found his thoughts wavering in her direction.

The thought that she might not approve of being compared to a dog raised its head. He wouldn't tell her, of course, so she would never know. He'd loved that dog. He'd found it roaming the streets of Alexandria with a string tied to its tail in such a way that it was trailing a load of rubbish behind it. How grateful it had been when he'd rescued it. So grateful it had followed him back to where he had his accommodation. So he'd fed it, and it had been his for the few months they'd been in Alexandria. And he'd had to leave it.

He wouldn't think about that. He had, in fact, found a street boy who used to hang about asking to polish the English soldier's boots, and asked the boy to look after Dog. Whether the boy had continued to do that, he had no way of knowing.

But unlike Dog, Serafina was going to belong to him forever. If one could use the word belonging. His heart did a little unexpected leap. No penance in that. He'd done what his brother had asked of him, he was engaged to be married, the Common License would have arrived at Bratton by the time they returned, and he rather liked the young woman he'd asked to be his wife.

But was that all? Did he perhaps have feelings for her that he'd never expected? Never thought he could have. Was he not enjoying this trip with only her for company more than he'd thought he would? She was indeed good company, and he had to admire her intellect. Might it only be those two things that were attracting him? Or was there something else as well? Might he, beyond all expectation, actually be falling in love with the girl?

This required another glass of brandy. And then he'd better stop because his thoughts were becoming fuddled. He couldn't be in love with her because he didn't have the capacity to do so. To fall in love, that was. He'd reached almost thirty years of age and never loved anyone, except perhaps Dog. So how could he now be feeling this unsettling sensation in his stomach that had robbed him of all inclination to eat? Was that what being in love with another human being was? He'd rather expected it to be like the love he'd had for Dog. And it appeared it wasn't. If he was in love, that was. And he doubted he could be with a fierce determination. Because if he was, this marriage was going to prove more than awkward. For he was not the sort of man young ladies fell in love with. Indeed, no one could love him. Especially not a young lady of Serafina's intelligence.

He had to push these thoughts out of his head. Julian was what mattered right now. And little Freddie's succession rights. That was why they were both here.

Depression settling over him, he downed yet another glass of brandy, and on none too steady legs, wound his way upstairs to the room he'd taken for himself.

CHAPTER TWENTY-EIGHT

THE FOLLOWING MORNING, Max managed to rise at the intended time and was pleased to find he wasn't suffering from a significant hangover, although he was very thirsty. Having attended to his morning ablutions, he descended The Star's twisting staircase and headed to the same parlor as last night. There, he took breakfast with a decidedly quiet Serafina while, in the innyard, Badger, who had probably risen much earlier than his master, prepared their horses.

Little was said between him and Serafina as they ate, and she seemed quite relieved when the little serving girl arrived to inform them their carriage awaited outside the front door of the inn.

Max settled up with the landlord and handed Serafina into the landau. As a fine drizzle was falling, Elsie came to sit inside as well, leaving only Badger, in his voluminous great coat and cocked hat, to suffer the inclement weather. Which rendered private conversation impossible. Not that he suspected Elsie of being a gossip, but because she presented that risk and there was no way in which the reason for their trip should be allowed to become common knowledge. At least, not yet. If it all turned out to be true, which he was increasingly afraid it would, that would be a different matter. One he didn't even want to contemplate. Bloody Julian. Why couldn't he have slaked his lust with some bawd who didn't want a ring on her finger in order to give away something that probably wasn't even untouched? She must have seen Julian coming from a mile off. So much for their father having considered Julian the more trustworthy and dependable of the two brothers.

To do her credit, it wasn't long into the journey before Serafina came up with the ideal excuse for extending their journey down into Marlborough. "Are there any dressmakers shops in Marlborough?" she asked, eyes wide and innocent of all guile, as they left Oxford's gleaming spires behind them.

Max, impressed at her ingenuity, could answer that with ease. He smiled. "I believe the Misses Sedgewick have a most reputable establishment in that town. My mother and Maria frequent it for a lot of their clothing. The two ladies who run it should be able to meet whatever requirements you have for clothing." He cast a sideways glance at Elsie, who was staring out of the window at the passing countryside, mouth slightly open. "If we call there today, they can take your measurements and show you some pictures of gowns you might like. I'm not familiar with the process, but I think that's what Maria does. You'll need a new gown for the wedding. My mother would like you to order more than one gown, though, so if the dressmakers take your measurements, she can go down there tomorrow and place some orders. She has impeccable taste, you'll find." Was this the right way to go about equipping a young lady for marriage? Did it even matter if it wasn't?

Serafina nodded in satisfaction, despite the implication that she should have her gowns chosen for her. Maybe he shouldn't have suggested that. She returned his smile. "Precisely. Although, to be honest, I'm not sure I will need more than one or two new gowns. I'm very good at making ends meet and would not like to be the cause of too much expense."

Elsie took a sideways glance at her new mistress before reverting her gaze to the passing countryside.

Max cleared his throat as a warm hand clutched his heart at the thought of her having to patch old gowns and keep them useable, and how lovely she would look in some new ones. He had to clear his throat a second time before he could speak, and even then his voice came out throaty and gruff. "That was in your past. Your future lies with me, and I don't intend my wife to be criticized for her lack of decent gowns. You will have a generous allowance to spend on yourself which will include gowns and anything else you might need in that direction. And pin money, of course." He had a vague idea that women required all sorts of things that were beyond his ken, and that he didn't feel he should enquire about. Women's things about which he'd rather stay ignorant.

She bestowed a smile on him that he couldn't read. "Thank you. That will be most satisfactory." Her eyes twinkled for a moment before she returned to gazing out of the window at the wet landscape. Between the clouds a touch of blue gave hope of better weather to come before they arrived in Marlborough.

And that, due to Elsie's presence, was the extent of their conversation for some time to come, apart from a few niceties as Max pointed out things of interest along their journey. Things that were few and far between as the road traversed an abundance of open downland. Really, when you couldn't say what you wanted to say, long journeys by carriage could be very boring.

At last, Max was disturbed from the fitful sleep he'd fallen into by the wheels of the landau rattling over Marlborough's cobbled main street. He'd taken the opportunity to snatch this much needed slumber as last night he'd not slept well, due in the main to the influence of the alcohol he'd imbibed earlier and also to the fact that he couldn't stop himself from thinking about Serafina. She could be said to have haunted his dreams. And she'd kept on doing it as he dozed inside the landau. Drat the woman. What was it about her that was putting her constantly at the forefront of his thoughts? No other woman had ever had the power to do that to him, and he'd met plenty of much prettier girls than Serafina Gilbert during his time at Oxford and in the Dragoons.

He glanced across at her. She was sitting primly upright and looking out of the window with interest as the wide main shopping street of Marlborough came into view. At least from here they could return to Bratton this evening without having to undertake too long a journey.

The carriage rattled to a halt. Max didn't wait for Badger to climb down from his driving seat but opened the door himself and stepped out onto the pavement. He held out his hand to Serafina, who placed hers in his and descended, a little stiffly, it had to be said. She turned back to Elsie. "You may stay here with Badger. I shall be quite all right with Captain Aubrey. I can come to no harm at all in the middle of a town."

A good idea. Their investigations could not be carried out with a curious maid in tow. Far too delicate a matter. Max closed the door and nodded to Badger. The horses could have a well-deserved rest.

Serafina, meanwhile, was staring about herself in some confusion. "I had no idea Marlborough would be as big as this. How many possible inns are there? I mean, ones that an actress might stay in?"

Max pulled a rueful face. "Quite a few. It's a major coaching town. I suggest we eat in one and see if she's arrived yet. Someone once told me that more than forty coaches a day stop in Marlborough, so it's entirely possible we're too early. So, sustenance first." Not that he was feeling hungry, but she might be. His own stomach was doing some sort of ridiculous knotting he didn't understand. It must be worry about meeting this claimant to Julian's estate. For that was what the son would be.

"So long as we're not too late." Serafina shot him a radiant smile that lit up her entire face and Max's errant heart did a leap in his chest. What was going on? He couldn't recall ever having felt like this before and it was most unsettling.

On inspection of the inns on offer, Max immediately discounted *The Castle Inn* at the end of the street as being well outside of an actress's pocket, so they selected *The Angel* for their repast, an inn which was clearly a coaching stop as it possessed a wide archway leading through to a busy stableyard behind. The landlord, a cheery, ruddy-faced fellow, was apologetic that he couldn't provide such highborn guests with a private parlor as they were already taken by arrivals on the previous coach. He could, however, furnish them with an excellent dinner which he assured them was talked about the entirety of the Great Bath Road. "Like no other dinner you'll ever taste, sir. You'll eat in my hostelry and never want to go anywhere else again."

They took a table near the blazing log fire, and found the food, when it arrived, was similar to that which they'd been presented with the day before at *The Star*. However, yet again, neither of them could do justice to it. At last, having sat in a somewhat uncomfortable silence while each of them pushed their food about their plates, rearranging it rather than eating it, Serafina pushed her plate away. "I've had enough of this," she said as though issuing an ultimatum, but keeping her voice low as there were other customers in the taproom. "It's a mystery even my skills as an investigator can't work out."

Max raised his eyebrows.

She sighed. "I don't know what's going on, but I don't think either of us is sickening for anything, so we can't be off our food because we're ill. And now suddenly we can't talk to one another." Her face had flushed a becoming pink. "And I think this all stems from when we checked each other for fevers."

Max, a little taken aback by her pronouncement, could only nod. "I think you might be right." Heat had suffused his own face, sufficient to match hers. Why was he blushing like a girl? This wasn't like him at all.

"I am right," Serafina said. She'd clearly decided to seize the proverbial bull by the horns. "And although I'm sure I'm not ill, I have to admit to having been feeling quite odd in the stomach department." She met his eyes, her own challenging. "And I need to know if you are suffering in that direction as well."

One thing about her was that she certainly knew how to

speak her mind. Which was surprising, given her upbringing.

Max swallowed. "I am." He couldn't very well shirk this answer. Her own honesty forced him to be as honest back. "And I'm unused to such a feeling."

She was regarding him out of her candid gray eyes as though she was willing him to say something. Hope burned there, and determination, along with something else.

Max swallowed. It was now or never, and something was shouting inside his head telling him it had better be now. "Serafina." He reached out and took her hand, shocked by how much he'd wanted to do this. He had to swallow again. "I-I'm not sure what to say to you. I've never been any good at saying what I feel."

Her brow furrowed, but she was smiling a little, as if in encouragement. "Then just say what you can."

He glanced about himself at the other patrons, but none appeared to be looking their way. Was this the place to make any sort of declaration to a young lady? In public, amongst tradesmen and workers, and in the common taproom of a small inn? But the moment had presented itself and he couldn't go back now or he'd never have the courage to say anything. It would be past and over, never to come again. Every sense in his body was encouraging him to keep going.

He tightened his hold on her hand but she made no move to escape his grasp. Encouraging. "I-I am finding your company in this investigation both helpful and extremely pleasant." Oh no. That was not the way he wanted to go. Far too formal. This situation didn't need formal.

Her eyes widened in expectation. Clearly she didn't think he'd finished.

He cleared his throat. "I asked you to marry me because I liked you." That was a little better. "I like you a lot."

She nodded, that air of expectation shining out of her. "And I said yes because I liked you. And like you still."

"I think you're the cleverest young lady I've ever met." He

paused. "Perhaps the cleverest person, and with a brother as clever as Julian, that's a compliment. I knew it from the moment I met you in that blasted summerhouse in the cold. And when I made you an offer, it was because I knew you would always be a good companion to me. We would never be bored together." This still wasn't quite what he wanted to say.

She was staring at him so earnestly he could barely breathe. How had he ever thought her plain? Tendrils of her rich chestnut hair had escaped their confines to frame her face. Her skin possessed an inner glow. Her lips, slightly apart, were suddenly the most kissable lips he'd ever seen. A wild impulse seized him. Actions might well speak louder than the words that wouldn't cobble together for him into coherent sentences. On an impulse, he half rose and leaning across the table, pressed his lips to hers.

For a moment, he felt her flinch, and then her lips parted a little under his as though in acquiescence. She couldn't be angry.

The kiss, such as it was, was over in a moment. He sat back down again, a little breathless and aware that even more heat had flooded his face. "I'm sorry. I could think of no other way to show you how I've been feeling. How I feel about you all of the time." And indeed, that twisting in his stomach had renewed itself with a vengeance. "I must beg your pardon for my impetuosity." This time when he glanced over his shoulder one or two of the customers raised their tankards of beer to him as if in salute, and two men gave him a thumbs up. It seemed his actions had been approved of by more than just Serafina.

As for her, her lips were still parted and her bosom rose up and down as though she'd been running hard. "You have no need to apologize, Max, for I did not mind at all." A little smile flickered across her face. "In fact, I find I quite liked it." She frowned. "No one has ever kissed me before, and I have always wondered what it would be like."

Confidence welled. "I am glad, then, that I was the first."

She chuckled. "And I am too." Her pretty blush deepened, no doubt a lot more attractive than the way he must look. "And you are the only one who will ever do so, I hope." Her hand turned over in his and she slipped her slender fingers between his own. "I think we have discovered the cause of our lack of appetite… don't you? Perhaps the cause of a lack of appetite that has been going on for several days."

He nodded. "You are the cause."

She chuckled. "And so are you."

Max's heart soared as though it might break free of his chest and go careering out through the window of the Angel Inn never to be seen again. His cheeks almost ached from smiling. How could he not have realized that what he'd been feeling was love? How was it, indeed, that love felt like this? So different from his usual way of being. He gripped Serafina's hand. "Do you think we might forget the rather foolish notion I had of our marriage being a business arrangement?"

More blushing. She lowered her eyes for a moment to their clasped hands. "I think we might. I should like that very much."

Their nearest observer, an elderly, unshaven old countryman, gave a shout of delight. "Give the lass a kiss, why don't you? Any fool can see she loves you."

So Max kissed Serafina again, to the rousing cheers of the company in the Angel that afternoon.

CHAPTER TWENTY-NINE

IT WAS A very different two people who emerged from the taproom an hour later. Not much more food had been eaten, but a great deal of gazing had gone on. Eventually, though, reality had forced its rude and unwanted way back into their freshly discovered rapture in the form of the urgency of their investigation. Max, while paying for their barely touched food, elicited from the landlord a list of potential places where a presumably impecunious actress might have taken lodgings for the night.

Serafina, who had paid little attention to any of this, was walking on air, every footstep buoyed up by the wonderful sensation that Max was actually, unexpectedly and as far as she could tell, deeply, in love with her. She'd suspected for some time that she might have been in love with him, but that he could have been with her had come as such a glorious surprise she kept having to replay that kiss over and over again inside her head. He'd kissed her. He hadn't said the word 'love' yet, and neither had she, but that was surely what the kiss had meant. The world was the right way up again.

Only it wasn't.

"We'll start with The King's Head," Max said, bringing her back to their present predicament. "From what the landlord of The Angel said to me, that sounds like the sort of place an actress might stay." And, offering his arm, he set off down the street with her having to skip along to keep up with his long strides. Not that she minded one bit having to do so.

Glancing up at his handsome and determined profile, Serafina gave herself a little metaphorical hug of delight. But for the moment, thoughts of what had just gone on between them needed pushing aside. They had a strange woman and her son to locate and interrogate. "She may well be going under an assumed name," she said, as determined as Max to concentrate on the matter in hand. "We have only her appearance to go on. About five feet six inches tall, my height, with hair that was once blonde but is probably now gray, and noticeably blue eyes. I think the eyes might be the means by which we will recognize her."

Max nodded without looking at her, for they were now arriving at The King's Head. He held the door open for her and they entered the tap room. An elderly man behind the bar nodded a greeting to them. "Good afternoon to you, sir and madam. And how might I be of service to you?" His wispy gray hair stood out around his head like a halo, and indeed, with his white shirt, this gave him the appearance of an angelic being.

Max set out their mission in as cautious a way as possible, leaving out any details that might betray who this pertained to. Instead, he told the man they were searching for an attractive lady of perhaps nearly fifty years of age traveling with a young man some twenty years her junior who would have arrived by stagecoach either that day or the one before.

The angelic landlord shook his head sadly as though it pained him to be unable to help them. "I'm right sorry, sir, but there're no ladies residing in any of my rooms here. A few gentlemen only, and them not of the sort someone like you would be friendly with." He shrugged his shoulders. "But you could try The Sun. People what come in on the stagecoaches from London often choose to stay there. Tis a bit smarter than my humble hostelry, you'll see."

That hardly mattered, but Max said nothing so Serafina stayed silent. She'd reached the point where just listening to Max speak and watching him was taking over her entire being. Their mutual discovery had brought on the feelings she'd been fighting to control in a great leap of satisfaction which she could now no longer fully control. She really must concentrate. A lot depended on her keeping her head and not allowing herself to become distracted. But oh, how much she wanted Max to kiss her again…

Having thanked the angelic landlord for his help, they repaired to The Sun Inn, an altogether larger establishment but also lacking in producing anyone who might resemble the couple they were looking for. So on they went.

The next hostelry was called The Royal Oak. It had about it a rather splendid appearance with the rooftop hidden behind an elaborate façade, as was the current architectural custom. Sadly, yet again, this produced no possible suspects, as the only lady staying there turned out to be the wife of a prosperous farmer who happened to make her appearance while they were consulting the landlord. She turned out to be both at least seventy years old and possessed of none of the attributes one would have expected a once beautiful young actress to have laid claim to. Especially not the blue eyes.

At this point, Serafina confessed herself surprised by how many inns one small town could produce.

"Well, it *is* on the Great West Road," Max said, by way of explanation. "Every coach heading west, or nearly every one, stops here to change horses and to pick up or drop off passengers. And the inns need to cater for a wide range of different types of customers. As well as those that have nothing to do with the stagecoaches but perhaps come in just for the market."

Serafina nodded as though this meant something to her, although, in truth, it didn't. Having led such a sheltered life, the idea of people traveling in such numbers up and down the breadth of England was alien to her. Information to be explored at a later date. There were some places in England she'd read about in her father's old library that she'd love to visit. Why not? If she could persuade Max then she would do it. And travel the length and breadth of England in some of these coaches. Another little shiver of pleasure ran through her. Yes, she and her husband would travel. They would explore the mysterious reaches of her native land. Her husband. That this now meant a lot more than it had a few short hours ago had her succumbing to yet another metaphorical hug of her torso. She really must concentrate on the matter in hand. She and Max had the rest of their lives to be together.

As if her thoughts had caused it to appear, a stagecoach came rumbling up the street from the east at that very moment. Recognizable by its red livery and the six matching gray horses drawing it, the equipage came to rest right outside the very establishment where they'd taken their meal. The Angel.

As they were right now opposite The Angel and about to enter the next inn on their list, Max's attention was fixed on their next destination. Serafina paused for a moment to watch it as the guard jumped down from his seat at the rear.

The rooftop passengers, who numbered five and were all men, well-wrapped up against the cold, scrambled down in a hurry, and the driver, having to duck to do so, guided his horses with consummate skill through the low archway towards the stables at the back of The Angel.

Four of the rooftop passengers hastened into the tap room but the fifth, a short, sturdy young man with a mop of unruly sandy hair, lingered on the pavement as though waiting for someone. After a couple of minutes, a woman emerged from the archway. She must have been traveling inside the coach while her partner had been forced to take a seat on the roof in the cold.

Serafina stared at her. She wore a plain brown pelisse over what looked to be a matching dull brown gown, and a straw bonnet covered her gray hair. She was clearly some years older than the man awaiting her.

Serafina tugged Max's arm. "There. Look."

He turned his head.

The man and woman were talking, and as they talked, an

untidily dressed fellow, who might have been one of the inn's ostlers, arrived carrying two bags which he dropped on the floor in front of them, then stood there, waiting to be tipped.

The younger traveler picked up the two bags and turned his back on the man. There would be no tipping going on there. Together, the two travelers began to cross Marlborough's wide main street, heading for the same establishment as Max and Serafina. The disgruntled ostler, unseen by the couple, raised a single finger at them in a gesture Serafina knew to be rude and disrespectful. Then he turned on his heel and stomped back through the archway to the stableyard.

"Well spotted," Max said. "It could be them."

"Wait," Serafina whispered. "Let them go in first, and then follow them."

He gave her a brief nod, and for a moment they stood pretending to look in the window of a milliners shop, admiring the array of hats on sale.

The two travelers disappeared inside the doors of The White Hart Inn and Max and Serafina followed hot on their heels.

The White Hart appeared to be of the same sort as The King's Head, but without the cheery and angelic landlord. Instead, a thin, sharp-faced woman with her hair scraped back in so tight a bun the skin on her face looked stretched, inhabited the space behind the bar. The taproom was empty but for her.

The travelers had already approached her.

Serafina pulled Max close enough to hear what was being said.

"We require two rooms for the night, possibly for two nights," the woman said. She had a faint trace of an accent, but was trying hard to disguise it, which made her voice sound forced and overly refined.

Behind her, the man hung back a little, as though accustomed to her being in control.

"Names?" The sharp-faced woman said, as though no one who entered her inn could possibly be trustworthy. Perhaps she was correct on that.

"Mrs. Aubrey," the woman said, a note of satisfaction in her tone. "Mrs. Abigail Aubrey."

They'd found her. Serafina's heart skipped a beat, not, this time, from nearness to Max.

"And him?"

This caused the woman to hesitate. Might she be considering gracing her son with a title? What would it be if she did? Viscount something or other that Serafina couldn't remember. Julian's son's title. Would she dare?

"Mr. Quentin Aubrey. My son."

Beside hcr, she felt Max's body stiffen. That the woman and her son were using his family's name must hurt. But it seemed likely the woman had a right to do so. As far as they knew, they were watching the true countess booking herself into the inn.

The sharp-faced landlady nodded her head. "Rooms one and two. Top of the stairs."

Max released Serafina's arm and stepped forward. "Mrs. Aubrey? Mrs. Abigail Aubrey?"

The woman swung around and Serafina obtained her first proper view of her. A trifle shorter than George Paynter had described her, and now in possession of a stout and matronly body, it was her face that struck Serafina the most. She must be approaching fifty, but the lines on her face suggested she was older. They deeply incised her cheeks to either side of her nose, and beneath her jaw, badly concealed by a scarf, a crepey neck hung like chicken skin. Thin lips, thin eyebrows, a nose that jutted from her face. No hint of any beauty remained to her.

She frowned, already suspicious. "What's that to you?"

Serafina stepped closer and peered more closely.

Her eyes were not blue. Not even pale blue or gray. They were an unmistakable muddy brown. As was what remained of the color of her hair.

"It's not her," she said, before she could stop herself, looking up at Max.

"What?" He seemed to have been struck almost insensible by this meeting with the woman his brother had married and scorned. "What do you mean?"

"Her eyes. Look at her eyes."

The woman, Mrs. Aubrey as she claimed, narrowed those same eyes at them both, but particularly at Serafina. "What d'you mean? What's wrong with my eyes? And who're you to say I'm not who I've said I am?" Behind her, the young man hung back, his own eyes, also brown, wide with what had to be fear, his mouth hanging open. Guilt was written across every part of him.

After a long moment, Max nodded. "They're not blue," he said, addressing both Serafina and the woman before them. "You can't be Abigail Lewis. And you're certainly not Abigail Aubrey."

"I told you—" began the son, but the woman shot him a ferocious glare that shut him up. He hung his head, well and truly cowed.

"I've never had blue eyes," the false Mrs. Aubrey snapped. "And what's it to you, anyway?"

"My name is Aubrey. Max Aubrey, and the Earl of Westbury happens to be my brother," Max retorted. "And as for your eyes, you may not have blue ones, but the woman who married my brother twenty seven years ago did. So much so the men who witnessed the wedding have never forgotten them."

"Then they're mistaken," she almost snarled. "If they're still alive now, then they're old and addled and have made that up to please you. They couldn't possibly remember the color of my eyes after all these years."

Max shook his head. "I think you'll find you're wrong there. But even if their memories could be faulty, my brothers' won't be. He'll be able to recognize if you're Abigail or not. He won't have forgotten the color of her eyes."

"He's on his deathbed," the woman snapped. "I have reliable information that he's about to die."

"He might be dying, but he's far from dead yet," Max said. "And he's very much looking forward to meeting you."

Her mouth hung open and she gulped air in. It didn't look as though she'd expected to be brought face to face with the man she was claiming as her husband. Might that be why she'd delayed until now? When she'd heard the Earl of Westbury was on his last legs? When she'd thought she could stake her claim without anyone being able to recognize her as an imposter?

Behind the bogus Mrs. Aubrey, her son, if he was indeed even that, took another step backwards. "I'm sorry," he muttered. "I couldn't stop her…"

She swung round on him and dealt him a resounding slap across the face that made him reel. "Shut up, you bloody fool." Her accent had slipped.

Max nodded to the sharp-faced landlady who'd been listening in open fascination. "Send for the Constable. I want these two clapped in irons for fraud."

She needed no second telling.

The young man began to cry.

The woman, however, was made of sterner stuff. Serafina had to give her that. "You can't prove nothing," she managed, although she was supporting herself on the countertop of the bar now. The threat of the Constable and prosecution must have hit home.

"On the contrary, I can," Max said. "My brother has the fraudulent letter you sent him. I have the witness testimony from George Paynter in Oxford. You have tried to lie your way into a fortune." He paused.

Outside, Serafina caught a glimpse of the town constable running along the road in pursuit of the sharp-faced landlady. He must have been very close for her to have found him so swiftly.

She looked back at the woman. "If you're not Abigail Aubrey, then who are you?" She glanced up at Max. "She's certainly someone who knows about Abigail's and your brother's marriage."

The town constable staggered in through the inn doors, puffing and red-faced. "What's going on here, then?"

Max turned to him. "These two are attempting to blackmail my brother, the Earl of Westbury, out of his fortune. They have arrived here solely for this purpose. I need you to apprehend them and confine them to the town lockup."

"Fraud means deportation to the Colonies, all right," the constable said, between attempts to catch his breath. "Not been much crime going on lately so they'll go before the magistrates this week."

This was too much for the son. Tears running down his cheeks, he dropped to his knees in front of them all. "Oh no. Please don't do this to me. It wasn't my fault. She made me do it. I'll tell you everything."

His mother, if that was what she was, aimed a kick at him but was restrained by the constable and the landlady, against whom she could not fight. Even her fiercest glare couldn't keep the young man silent, though.

"The Abigail my ma's pretending to be was my aunt," he stammered, in between sobs. "She was married to your brother, your lordship, like we said, but when he up and left her, she came back home to my ma and grandma. Ma says she soon found out she was expecting his child. Ma said as she had the baby and died. The baby a bit later."

He sniffed and wiped his eyes on the sleeve of his coat. "This all happened before I was born. I'm only twenty-one, and my name isn't Quentin. That was the baby's name. Mine's Tom. Tom Trafford." He threw a terrified glance at his mother, who was scowling furiously at him as though she wished him dead. "She said as Aunt Abbie's husband was an earl now, and he was old and ill and going to die any day soon, and if we said we was my aunt and her baby, all grown up, he'd not be well enough to see us and know her for a fraud, and we'd get what we wanted. All his money and a big house. Just for me. She made me do it."

"Honor amongst thieves is clearly not a real thing," Max said, a trifle wryly. "Constable, you may take these two away. What you do with them is entirely up to you, but I don't wish to have to see them ever again. And neither does my brother, the earl. He will be very grateful to you."

His face flushed with self-importance at having arrested two such ruffians, the constable escorted the two fraudsters out of the inn.

The sharp-faced lady retreated back behind the bar and fished out a bottle of brandy. "Well I never," she said with a considerable thawing of her attitude. "When I got up this morning I didn't think the day would end like this. That I didn't." She produced three glasses. "Will you join me? It's Captain Aubrey, isn't it? You look just like your brother the earl used to when he came to town as a young man. I should've recognized you sooner, only he's not graced us with his presence for a good few years now."

She poured generous measures of the brandy and Max and Serafina both took a glass.

Serafina, feeling much in need of sustenance, didn't sip hers but gulped it down in a way Araminta would have condemned as being most unladylike, and heaved a sigh of relief. "And now," she said with a shaky smile for Max, and still feeling a little shocked after the confrontation, "I think we'd best go and get me measured by the Misses Sedgewick, or Elsie will wonder what we've been up to, and I won't have a gown to wear for the wedding."

CHAPTER THIRTY

WITH THE DEPARTURE of the prisoners with the somewhat self-satisfied constable, and the downing of the brandy, an unexpected quiet momentarily fell over the interior of The Royal Oak. Max also heaved a heart-felt sigh of relief to match the one Serafina had just made.

Turning to their hostess, who was already pouring herself a second and even more generous measure of brandy, he reached a hand into the interior pocket of his coat for his wallet. "Madam, I won't see you out of pocket for the loss of the custom of those two reprobates." He jangled a few coins together, but didn't yet hand them over.

The woman's avaricious eyes fixed on them, her brandy glass arrested in its progress to her lips. She did have about her the appearance of someone fond of her tipple.

Max rubbed the coins together as though considering his offer. "I trust that if I compensate you well for their absence from your establishment, I can rely upon your discretion both now and in the future? My brother is not at all well, and I wouldn't like it to come to his ears that our private business was the talk of the town."

He held out a handful of coins, that glinted even in the subdued light of the taproom. Guineas, by the look of them, and far more than the landlady would have garnered from the letting of two rooms for a night or two. Enough, it was to be hoped, to keep her silent.

The woman held out her hand and Max dropped the coins into her palm. In an instant she had them secreted about her person. "You may rely upon me, Captain Aubrey, and so may his lordship your brother. He's always been good to us here in Marlborough. I can keep my mouth as tightly closed as a knot in a bootlace. You mark my words. If anything of this gets out it won't be from me. It'll be that constable. I've always thought him a tattle-tale."

Max nodded. "Thank you, Mrs....?"

"Browne," she said. "Margaret Browne, Captain."

He nodded. "Thank you, Mrs. Browne. Much appreciated. I feel I will now sleep easy with the knowledge that this matter is sealed and will never be spoken of again."

The incident seemed to have loosened Mrs. Browne's previously frozen face muscles and she even managed a smile. Or it might have been the brandy, of course. Whatever the cause, having the local gentry in her establishment no doubt pleased her no end.

Max glanced across at Serafina, who was looking very pleased with herself and her detective work, and a little pink cheeked from the glass of brandy. Thank the lord she'd been with him. If it had been left to him, he probably would never have recalled that the woman they were looking for should have had blue eyes, and even if he had, he might not have noticed the discrepancy. Eye color wasn't something he noticed very often, although not in Serafina's case. How could he not notice those wide gray orbs?

A smile that was a peculiar mixture of relief and love spread across his face. "And I'll never forget that I've you to thank for working out that woman was a base imposter. I'd never have done it alone."

She broke into a wide smile, her eyes shining with the excitement of having succeeded. "It was an elementary conclusion, my dear Max. Mr. Paynter had given us such an excellent description, as soon as I laid my eyes on the woman, I knew her for a fraud. Besides which, did you not take a look at her face? Her dead sister might have been able to capture your brother's heart, but not that woman, even if she'd shared her sister's eye color." She paused. "And right from the start, I've been certain there was something decidedly fishy about her making this claim now, with your brother so ill. I was straightaway looking for reasons not to believe her, and there one was, staring me in the face. Literally."

Max couldn't resist her infectious enthusiasm. On an impulse, he reached out and pulled her into his arms. "And now that's done and my family is safe, we'd best do as you say and repair to the Misses Sedgewick's shop and let them measure you for your wedding gown." And he bent and kissed her on the lips. Her soft mouth yielded and her body seemed to melt into his. But they had to part. This was not the place for declarations of love.

Mrs. Browne's eyes must have lit up at the mention of the wedding dress. There was even a proprietary look about her as though she thought herself partly responsible for their coming matrimony. "May I be the first to offer my congratulations to you both." She bobbed a little curtsey. "And wish you many years of happiness together."

Serafina's face, so close to Max's now, broke into an even wider smile, as she turned in his arms to regard their hostess, who now had a much more mellow air to her, as the second brandy had vanished. "Thank you, Mrs. Browne. And yes, if we don't visit the dressmakers, I think my maid is going to think us a poor couple to work for who don't ever do as we say." And with that, she took Max's arm, tucking her hand into its crook, the smile now all for him.

An enormous longing to be able to cover that small hand with his own useless right one swept over Max, to have as much contact as he could. Impossible. Resigning himself to that frustrating fact, with a final nod of thanks to Mrs. Browne, he escorted Serafina out of the inn, and headed her towards the Sedgewicks' shop.

AS IT HAD stopped raining some time ago, after Serafina had now been measured and exclaimed over by the two Misses Sedgewick, she and Max returned to *The Angel* where Badger was patiently waiting beside the coach with Elsie.

With no intention of sharing the interior of the landau with her maid again, Serafina suggested Elsie should travel on the driving seat with Badger, a fact that seemed to please the girl. So, alone at last and deprived of further worry about claims on Julian's estate, Serafina and Max mounted into their carriage, and Badger set it rumbling on its way towards Bratton once more.

As the buildings of the town vanished behind them, Serafina turned towards Max where he sat close beside her to find him staring at her with an intensity that made water of her bones. Oh, how often she'd longed to have him look at her in just this way, never expecting it to come true. Within the confines of her stays, her heart gathered pace, and warmth climbed from her breasts, up her neck to her cheeks.

She couldn't miss the matching flush in his cheeks, nor the smoldering heat in his dark eyes. Yes, this must be what love was. This mysterious and uncontrollable longing to be with the one you loved, to give yourself to him freely, to melt into his arms. How awful it would have been to have lived her life without ever having known this. Or worse, to have had to control it forever because it wasn't reciprocated. How lucky they both were to have met one another. The thought that if she hadn't come to London with Letty, he would have met and married someone else in order to secure his inheritance, chilled her blood for a moment. How awful would it have been if they'd met next year, and still fallen in love, when it would have been too late then for this. She found her breathing coming fast and furious as though she'd been running and her mouth uncommonly dry. She licked her lips.

Max lifted his good left arm and cupped her chin in his hand. His skin felt warm against hers, as his thumb gently massaged her cheek. "You are so beautiful, my Serafina."

Yes, she was his, and he was hers. The realization of this drenched her in heat and the urge to deny his words melted away. If he was saying she was beautiful, then she must be in his eyes, even if not in the eyes of anyone else. Nor even her own. "No one's ever said that to me." Her voice was hoarse.

"Then they're fools."

She managed a smile. If her heart beat any faster it was going to come leaping out of her mouth and land in his lap.

"I love you, my Serafina; my fiery angel."

She blinked. He'd said the words. Words she'd never thought to hear anyone say to her. The only other person who'd loved her unconditionally until now had been her father. For the last eighteen years she'd lived without the love of any other person, starved of it, deprived. Letty and her brothers and sisters didn't count. No one but her papa had ever loved her for who she was, rather than what she could do for them.

She swallowed. "I love you too, Max." The words tumbled out, and every one of them seared into her heart. She was in love. She was loved in return. What more could she ever want?

He leaned closer, his face only inches from hers. "I'm very glad chance caused us to meet in that summerhouse, and I was forced to find myself a bride I thought I could tolerate living with. If neither of those things had happened, I'd never have met you." His eyes bored into hers. "I liked you from the moment I met you, and if I hadn't been such a fool, I'd have known it was love I was feeling much sooner than I did. I was an idiot. I didn't think myself capable of love, nor of being loved. How wrong I was. Such a fool."

His breath was warm on her cheek. She inhaled it, making it part of herself, gazing into his brown eyes. "I'm very glad too. And glad for having lived in my brother's house, for if I hadn't, I'd never have met you. It took so many things to bring us together. I think it was always meant." She licked her lips which were unaccountably dry. "I never knew love could feel like this. Like you, I didn't think I could love or be loved." She shivered. "My heart wants to soar up to the sky, and I want to shout to everyone that I love you."

He chuckled. "That might shock Badger and Elsie. Not to mention the horses."

His face moved closer.

She swallowed. Anticipation coursed through her, making water of her bones.

His lips touched hers. Different now, to the kiss in The Angel Inn, and the one in The Royal Oak in front of the delighted Mrs. Browne. They had been sudden and impulsive, whereas this was anticipated, longed for, a culmination of the past days of dancing around one another, each unsure how the other felt, and unsure, as well, of how they felt themselves. Made all the more poignant because theirs was a joining of two people who had always seen themselves as unlovable and never expected to feel like this.

Serafina allowed her lips to part under the pressure of Max's kiss, feeling his good arm draw her close against his chest. Was that his heart beating in time with her own hasty rhythm? Joining in so they beat as one. Her bonnet slid awry as his tongue slipped between her lips and touched her own.

No wonder people liked kissing. A sudden vivid image of the moment when she'd caught Letty with that stable boy leapt into her head, the naughty hussy pink-cheeked and flustered. How could she have blamed Letty for what she'd been doing when the doing of it gave so much pleasure?

She lifted her own arms and put them around Max, reveling in the feel of his strong body so close to hers and running her fingers through his dark hair. How often had she looked at him and wanted this without knowing it was what she wanted? And now she had it, and their marriage would no longer be a cold and formal business arrangement. She would have everything she'd ever wanted.

His kiss deepened and her tongue tangled with his in return, as passion coursed through her body, burning a fiery trail and causing every nerve within her to spring to vivid life. She knew only that she needed more than this but couldn't put a name to it, as desire pulsed through her to her very core. She wanted his hands all over her, she wanted his body as close as she could get it. Closer. A part of her. Bonded forever.

The one thought foremost in her mind was that their wedding day could not come quickly enough.

THE JOURNEY BACK to Bratton Park was a little less than five miles and, with their well-rested horses, took a bare three-quarters of an hour. Long enough to render Max extremely aroused and uncomfortable and the object of his affections more than a little disarrayed in appearance.

As they passed between the twin gatehouses, Max disentangled himself from Serafina with reluctance. "Nearly home. You'd best try and tidy yourself. We don't want to give the servants cause to gossip or my mother cause to reprimand us." But he was almost laughing. Her bonnet was lying discarded on the floor, her hair was tousled and somehow her pelisse had come off and the top buttons of her gown were undone.

A shiver of desire ran through Max, despite his efforts to regain control. His kisses had run down her throat towards her breasts, and with tentative fingers he'd loosened her gown and she'd not objected. For one delirious moment, he'd slipped his fingers inside and felt the rounded softness of a breast and her sigh of pleasure had almost undone him.

She giggled, a glorious sound. "As do you. If you could see yourself..."

He glanced down. Apart from the obvious uncomfortable bulge in his breeches, his waistcoat was undone, his cravat loosened and his shirt untucked at the front where she'd slid a hand inside and let it run over the taut and all too sensitive skin of his belly and chest. Another thing that had almost undone him. Her touch. Dwelling on this was not doing his predicament any good. He could hardly get out of the landau with such arousal so evident. He had to think of calming thoughts not associated with

Serafina's opulent mouth and soft breasts and… Damnit. He groaned.

She was patting her hair back into some semblance of normality. That was going to be difficult. To distract himself from the throbbing in his groin, he bent and picked up her bonnet. "Here. Best to cover up that bird's nest of hair."

She giggled again. "I don't think we can hide this, you know."

He retied his cravat with one hand. Badly. A dead giveaway. "You may be right."

She'd retied her bonnet now, which went a long way to rendering her respectable. "Let me do your hair for you."

Bad idea. Having her run her fingers through his hair did nothing for his condition. As if anything other than heading straight for the marriage bed right now was ever going to do that. "I think I'd better do it myself."

Another giggle. Far more merriment than he'd ever heard her produce. He gave a huff, but it was not out of annoyance and only made her giggle again. "I'm glad you find this funny."

She did up her top buttons. "And so it is. I think you're worrying too much. No one will mind in the least that we have decided we are more than just friends."

The landau swung into the main driveway in front of the house. Damnit. What did he care? He leaned forward and kissed her quickly on the lips. "I know for one that my mother will be delighted. And so will Julian. For more than one reason. And now, for a short while, we need to behave decorously and go upstairs to tell my brother the good news. You'd better come with me."

And as he said this, the carriage ground to a halt in front of the doors.

He smiled. "Shall we go inside?"

CHAPTER THIRTY-ONE

THE COMMON LICENSE from the Bishop of Salisbury was waiting for them on the table in the entrance hall, so, having tucked it away in the inside pocket of his coat. Max escorted Serafina upstairs to Julian's study with the intention of revealing the outcome of their investigation.

They found Julian seated at his desk, surrounded by piles of papers and open textbooks, a tray of untouched food by his side. He looked up as Max ushered Serafina through the door, raising anxious, bloodshot eyes and tossing down his pen. It left a string of inky blots across the page he'd been writing on. "Well? Do you have news?" There was an unmistakable tremor in his voice. The last few days of what must have been terrible worry had wrought changes upon him, and not for the better.

Better put his mind at rest straightaway. "You may rest easy," Max began with. As a soldier he'd learnt that hedging around a subject never helped. You had to get to the nub of the matter straightaway. "She wasn't the woman you married, and she's gone. Crisis averted." He pulled out the one chair for Serafina, who sat in it, a thoughtful expression on her face.

"She wasn't?" Julian asked, relief flooding his face. "She wasn't Abigail?"

Max nodded. "I'm sorry, or perhaps glad, to have to tell you that Abigail Aubrey died not long after you two parted, in giving birth to her... your... child. Who also died. The woman we met in Marlborough today, who was fully intending to hoodwink our entire family, was her sister, to whom she must have confided the whole sordid story before she died. The young man she was going to pass off as your son is that woman's own son. They are both now in the custody of the constable. For fraud. I had the impression he's delighted to have made such an arrest."

Julian's mouth had fallen open and his chest was heaving for his scanty breath. "She's dead? You're sure?"

Max grit his teeth and nodded. This was not the brother he'd looked up to all his life. This was a man who'd lied to the young actress he'd married in order to bed her, then left her, and married a second wife in the full knowledge that the first was probably still alive but thinking herself not legally wed. A glance at Serafina's face told him she shared his opinion. Would he ever look at Julian the same way again?

"I can't believe it," Julian said. "She's dead? And the child? I just can't believe it." He hung his head. Were those tears? "She was so vital, so alive. I would not wish death on her or her child. I would not."

He rose a fraction in Max's estimation at these words.

"Nevertheless, whatever you would not wish on her," Max said, determined to rub in the wrongdoing, "if she were living, you would be in a monumental mess. A scandal that would ruin this family and any prospects your children might have had. And nothing about this result detracts from what you did to that girl, and then went on to do to Maria."

"I'm sorry for what I did," Julian said, shaking his head. "Sorry I married her, sorry I lied to her and left her, sorry for what I could have been doing to Maria and our children." He looked up, his eyes brimming with anguish. "And without you, Max, the scandal would have become real."

Max dropped a hand onto Serafina's shoulder. "It's not me you have to thank, but my betrothed. It was her astuteness which brought about the denouement of the fraudsters. She has a bent for investigation like no other I've ever met." He let his fingers caress her shoulder and she tipped her head to settle her cheek against his hand. This did not go unnoticed.

Julian coughed into his handkerchief, but his eyes appeared to be taking in the rather bedraggled appearance of his two investigators. "Thank you, Miss Gilbert—Serafina—with all my heart. You are undoubtedly the savior of this family's... no, of *my* honor." A faint smile ghosted across his face. "And even I can see that the pursuit of these vagabonds has brought you two closer together than I could have hoped for."

Max couldn't help the smile. "It has indeed."

As it was late in the day, Max put off visiting the vicar in the village to arrange the wedding until the next morning. Their luck held, and the day dawned bright and clear, as only the earliest of spring mornings can, with dew sparkling on every blade of grass and only a few clouds left in the sky when the morning mist had cleared.

Arm in arm, Max and Serafina strolled down to the village, having shunned the idea of taking the landau. As Max said, they'd both had enough of being cooped up in a carriage over the last few days. Fresh air would be much nicer. They passed the busy Home Farm and the estate manager's house, crossed the wide, tree-dotted parkland, and followed the gravel driveway where it wound through the woods with just the glint of the ornamental lake in the distance.

At the vicarage, a square built house beside the church in the center of the village, they found the vicar, Reverend Bentley, at home. His housekeeper brought them tea in his study, and Max explained the circumstances at Bratton pertaining to Julian's condition and therefore to the carrying out of the marriage. He brought out the Common License from his coat pocket, and Mr. Bentley, the same bewigged incumbent Max had known since boyhood, happily agreed to perform the marriage service in the estate chapel on the following Saturday. The elderly vicar shook hands with Max and kissed Serafina's hand, obviously delighted to be able to marry one of the Aubrey family. "It won't be the first marriage I've conducted in that little chapel, as so many of his lordship's tenants choose to marry there. But I think it will be the first for one of you Aubreys."

With that sorted, Max and Serafina wandered back through the village and into the park together, neither of them in much of a hurry to return to the castle. This was ground Max had roamed over as a boy and very young man, and he somehow felt more at home out here than he did within the confines of the castle. In the same way he'd felt at home while on campaign in foreign lands.

He unhooked his arm from Serafina's and instead took her hand in his. "I could walk here with you forever on this idyllic spring morning. It's as if nature knows of our love and has sent this day as a special gift just for us."

For a moment, she pulled away, but only to remove her gloves. Once she'd done that, she took his hand again, skin on skin, warm and comforting. "I could too." The throaty quaver in her voice had the immediate effect of rendering Max's breeches once more most uncomfortable. Damnit—how did she succeed in doing this to him just with two words?

He stopped, where a chestnut tree overhung the road, and turning, pulled her into his embrace, his one arm holding her close. "It's no use. I have to do this." And he bent and kissed her. Her response was immediate. Her mouth opened beneath his, and her body melted into his as though made of putty. If only he had two arms with which to hold her.

Eventually, they had to come up for air, though, both of them gasping. She laughed, the sound music in Max's ears. So much so that he had to kiss her again. For longer.

When they finally parted this time, somehow, Serafina's demure bonnet had come undone and fallen to the ground, and Max was thinking longingly of their wedding night in just four days' time.

She picked up her bonnet, dangling it by its ribbons. "I think we'd better keep walking before someone comes along and catches us like this." There was no reprimand in her words though. She was not a coy miss out to tease him.

Max seized her hand again, and, not hurrying their steps, they continued. All around, the hint of bluebells to come showed, where their pointy leaves were pushing up out of the ground. No sign of the flowers as yet, of course, but a solemn promise of the color to come. Max lifted his chin and looked upwards at the sweep of the greening branches overhead. "Spring is coming."

She nodded. "I think it's already here."

"When I was a boy, I used to roam all over this estate. I know every corner of it. Sometimes with some of the boys whose fathers worked for mine. Often alone. I wasn't a boy who had to be part of a group, either here at home or at school."

"And yet you became part of a group when you joined the army." Her breasts were rising and falling as if she'd been running. He couldn't take his eyes off the shape of them beneath her gown. So tantalizing. Did she feel as aroused as he did? The color in her cheeks told him yes. What would it be like to...? No. He mustn't think of that... not yet, anyway. Time enough in four days' time. Four days. God, that was a lifetime.

With difficulty, he gathered his wits. "I know. But it didn't feel the same. The army is one large group of which everyone is a member, yet within that group there's scope for individuality. I hung onto mine. And it taught me to rely on the friends I had." He paused, remembering the shades of the men he'd known and lost. "But it inures you to loss, I think."

Any other person might have pushed him to say more. Not Serafina. She just tightened the grip she had on his hand as though in comfort. And it was comforting. More comforting than any words could have been. Unfortunately it did nothing for his state of arousal.

She stared ahead of herself, continuing with their conversation as though she hadn't noticed the prominent bulge in his breeches. A bulge he couldn't hide. "Did you have any favorite places on the estate? I did, as a child. A place I would go to when I was sad and missing my father, and Araminta had been nasty to me." She shrugged. "Which I have to admit was quite often, especially at first. After a while, I learned to keep out of her way and avoid things that would anger her. And to make myself useful so she might appreciate me." She paused, as if reflecting. "Not that she ever did. Or not much at any rate."

"Where did you go?"

"When my brother took over the estate after my father's death, he decided to take back some of the farms from our tenants. Not that we had many. He said he wanted to make the estate more efficient, and they weren't paying enough money. I found this out when I was older. At the time, I was too young to recognize what was happening. But I did wonder why the farmhouses were empty where before there'd been families and children I'd played with."

She stopped and shaded her eyes as a shaft of sunlight slanted through the branches. It brought out the gold in her hair, making it shimmer.

"And did it make your brother richer? Taking away those people's livelihoods?"

She frowned. "I have no idea. The way he and Araminta scrimp and save you'd think they were paupers. My one hope is that when Ogden dies, little Teddy will become a spendthrift and run through all his father's hoarded money. I believe children raised in such a parsimonious fashion often do." She gave a guilty chuckle. "Am I wicked to think like that?"

"No. But where did you go? You haven't said."

"I went to one of the farmhouses. I knew where the key was kept, under a plant pot at the back door. The farmer's wife had shown me when she still lived there, and my father and I would visit, and she'd give me cakes hot from her oven. With her gone, I would let myself in and pretend it was my house and that I lived there with my papa..." Her voice trailed off.

"You pretended he was alive, still?"

"Yes. It helped me. I would have long conversations with

him. He was my support."

"Good to have a support. And a place to go where you could be alone."

Her smile was radiant. "Oh, I was never truly alone. I had my father."

His heart could have burst with love for that lost and lonely little girl who'd conjured back her father's ghost for a companion because she'd had no other. Well, now she had him and she'd never be alone again. Nor unloved.

She tugged at his hand. "But what about you? You haven't told me if you had anywhere special you went to?"

He halted, turning towards her. "I did. Would you like to see it? It's not far from here."

Those wide gray eyes gazed back up at him so full of love he could hardly breathe. So this was what true love was, this breath-snatching, heart-hammering, limb-melting cauldron of longing to protect her forever mixed with an almost crippling desire for her physical body to be his.

She nodded. "I would. Very much so."

The longing to take her in his arms again and kiss her all over had to be controlled. Instead, he turned off the driveway and into the woodland to their left, heading down towards the ornamental lake some long-gone ancestor of his had caused to be dug. Hidden from the main house, open parkland ran down to it on three sides, and on the fourth a white limestone folly stood, close by the water's edge. It was to this that he led Serafina.

The folly itself, constructed in the style of a small Greek temple, complete with a pillared portico, nestled in its woodland setting as though it had always been there. As Serafina surveyed it, Max slipped his arm about her shoulders. "My grandfather had it built for my grandmother, nearly a century ago. They used to come here when they wanted to escape the pressures created by being an earl and a countess and having a huge estate to run. Julian showed it to me when I was very small. And when he was gone to Oxford and London, and I was lonely, I used to come here by myself."

They crossed the grass, mown short by deer and sheep, of which there was no sign, and approached the folly. Four Doric pillars on a small terrace supported an overhanging, sloping, tiled roof. Beyond, a doorway opened into the inner sanctum. Max pushed the door open and led Serafina inside.

It was much as he remembered it from the last time he'd been here. Dusty, a few cobwebs, but he could have left it yesterday instead of more than ten years since.

"It's beautiful," Serafina said, on a breath of admiration. "I think your hideaway is far superior to mine."

A dusty chaise longue stood away from the back wall; a rug covered the marble floor, a few dead leaves had found their way inside; sunlight slanted in through the cobwebby windows to left and right.

Max brushed the dust off the chaise longue and coughed. "In need of a clean, I fear."

She'd followed him and was standing very close. "Not at all. This is just as it should be. If anyone had cleaned it, we'd know someone else was using it. Like this, it's ours and ours alone. It's meant to be a secret and now it's ours."

"I like that." He bent his head and kissed her, and as he did, she put her arms around him, hugging him close, pressing her body against his so hard she must have been able to feel the suddenly springing arousal that had accompanied the kiss.

Her fingers were in his hair, pulling his head closer to hers. Her lips were as hungry as his. He pulled her harder against him as they sank down onto the chaise longue together. Drat that bloody arm for getting in the way.

As SOON AS they stepped into the folly, Serafina had known what would happen there. Heat had flooded through her body in a tidal wave of pure desire as unexpected as it was alien to her. As he'd kissed her, she'd felt her knees buckle, and together they'd half-fallen, half-sat on the chaise longue. His tongue was on hers, his hand touching her breast through the stout covering of gown and stays, and all she knew was that she wanted more. And she wanted it now. Saturday was too far away.

As though driven by something far from common sense, as Max leaned over her, she wrapped her legs around his body, drawing him in ever closer, feeling that glorious throbbing object he had in his trousers that was thrilling her to her core as it pressed against her through the thin cotton of her gown and making her almost squirm with desire.

Nothing else mattered. They were here, in this moment, and it was the right moment. He was leaning his weight on his arm, unable to do anything more than kiss her. What did four days matter? She was ready to give herself to him right now in this secret hiding place he'd shown her. To make it theirs forever by the consummation of their love. She pulled her skirts up and out of his way as he pressed himself against her.

His lips sent fiery trails through her body as his kisses descended from her lips to her neck to her breasts. The buttons of her bodice flew undone and a deep groan of pleasure exploded from her lungs. She wanted him with all her being. With her body and her soul.

But reason and conscience must have seized him. He pulled back, pushing himself upright, hair tousled and eyes uncertain yet still smoldering with passion. "We shouldn't." He didn't sound all that convinced.

She shook her head. "We should."

His eyes widened. She could see the longing in them, but also the doubt and the guilt. "You want this? I would not force myself on you."

"I can assure you that you're not. I want this as much as you do."

"You're sure?"

Lying on the chaise longue, her skirts around her waist, she nodded. "I am. Now is the right time. I know it. I can't wait four days for this. I want you now."

"Then stand up. I'm not making love to you in a hurry as though we were yokels in a hedge."

She got to her feet, a tiny part of her wishing they were indeed yokels in a hedge, free to rut as and when the fancy took them.

"Turn around."

She did as he said. Breathing heavily, he stood behind her, his fingers fumbling with the fastenings of her gown, but he had them undone at last and the gown pooled at her feet on the rug. He moved on to the petticoat and stays. He seemed to know how they worked and was surprisingly good at it with one hand. She'd ask him about that later. They came off, leaving her in just her slip and stockings, still with her back to him.

She heard the rustle as he removed his own clothing, but stood resolute, nervous anticipation crackling through her body, unquenchable desire burning in her core.

"Sit down."

She turned. He was wearing just his shirt. Dark hair curled below his throat and across the part of his chest she could see. His eyes were hot with desire. The nervous anticipation turned to liquid fire at her core, and she sat, her hands automatically going to cover her breasts under the almost transparent fabric of her chemise.

He knelt before her, his hand on her left ankle. "These need to come off too."

"My legs?" She couldn't resist a giggle. Perhaps a nervous one. Definitely a nervous one. She'd seen enough on the farms of Milford to know what must be coming next, and it frightened her a little, despite the longing for it to happen.

"Your stockings. Let me."

He ran his hand up her calf, over her knee to where her garter secured her left stocking. The touch of his fingers sent shivers through her body, starting in her toes and cascading up to the top of her head, where it felt as though her scalp had tightened. He undid the garter and slid the stocking down her leg, his touch firm and confident. Lifting her foot to his mouth, he gently sucked first one toe, then each in turn. Good heavens. The sensation that cascaded through her had her panting with something that had to be lust. That touching such a simple, useful thing as a toe, but in this way, with his lips and tongue, could do this to her…

Then he reached up to do the same to the other stocking.

This was almost too much for Serafina. As his hand slid over her thigh, she leaned forward and kissed him on the mouth. His fingers froze on her leg as the garter came undone and he kissed her back. Then his hand slid up her thigh towards the center of her longing. Upwards, his fingers exploring until she could bear it no longer. With a gasp of pleasure she released his mouth and fell back on the chaise longue, eyes closed, her body and his hand the only things that existed. Those fingers. That touch.

How had she never known this sort of pleasure could exist? As if by themselves, her legs parted as he continued his exploration, touching, teasing, goading her body into responses she'd never known it possessed. She arched her back and as she did so, she felt him enter her at last. A strangled cry escaped her lips, partly from shock and partly from pleasure, as for the first time in her life she discovered carnal love.

His lips were on hers again, his body on top of hers, her legs wrapped around his torso as though she never wanted him to stop. Pleasure shivered through her, throbbing, pulsating, driven into her until she could almost bear it no longer. The pleasure was painful, sharp, tender. Everything she might have dreamed of, had she known it existed. She never wanted it to stop, but as she felt his body tense, it did. It was over. She was his and he was hers. Forever. More so than any marriage ceremony could ever have made them.

After a few moments, Max rolled to one side. "Now you'll *have* to make an honest man of me."

She chuckled. "I'm glad our first time was here."

He nodded, his cheek against hers. "I am too. This is my

special place. I feel it won't be the first time we do this here."

"I think you might be right."

He turned her head to face his. "I always am." And he kissed her again.

THE END

About the Author

After a varied life that's included working with horses where Downton Abbey is filmed, riding racehorses, running her own riding school, owning a sheep farm and running a holiday business in France, Fil now lives on a widebeam canal boat on the Kennet and Avon Canal in Southern England.

She has a long-suffering husband, a rescue dog from Romania called Bella, a cat she found as a kitten abandoned in a gorse bush, five children and six grandchildren.

She once saw a ghost in a churchyard, and when she lived in Wales there was a panther living near her farm that ate some of her sheep. In England there are no indigenous big cats.

She has Asperger's Syndrome and her obsessions include horses and King Arthur. Her historical romantic fiction and children's fantasy adventures centre around Arthurian legends, and her pony stories about her other love. She speaks fluent French after living there for ten years, and in her spare time looks after her allotment, makes clothes and dolls for her granddaughters, embroiders and knits. In between visiting the settings for her books.

Social Media links:
Website – filreid.com
Facebook – facebook.com/Fil-Reid-Author-101905545548054
Twitter – @FJReidauthor